UNDYING LOVE

"Did our months together mean anything to you, Tazia?" Kirk asked.

"I no longer trust *anyone*. Maybe if you leave, I can try to pick up the pieces of my life and rebuild it."

Suddenly, he reached down and grabbed her by the shoulders, his mouth pressing against hers. Her sounds of protest were quieted as she was overcome with raw desire and hunger. It was a flame that seared her body and soul — and she could not resist or deny her strong emotions.

Slowly and reluctantly, Kirk lifted his lips from hers and said: "One day I will make you forget everything that happened; I will teach you how to trust and love again."

With these words she ran to the door and fled. Overcome with tears, she realized that it was too painful to be with him now — now that she knew he had murdered her brother. Somehow, someday, she would force him to forget her — and all traces of the love they had once shared . . .

Tazia's Torment

BY SYLVIE F. SOMMERFIELD

ZEBRA BOOKS

KENSINGTON PUBLISHING CORP

ZEBRA BOOKS

are published by

KENSINGTON PUBLISHING CORP.
475 Park Avenue South
New York, N.Y. 10016

Fifth printing: October 1985

Printed in the United States of America

SOUTHERN CALIFORNIA

LOS ANGELES

SAN GORGONIO MTS.

X CASA DEL SOL - TAZIA'S HOME

PAUMA VALLEY

SAN LOIS REY R.

ENCINITAS

ESCONDIDO

PURAKA

TIJUANA

1

A cool breeze blowing off the Gulf scented the predawn air. Most of New Orleans slept. Most, but not all. In a dimly lit cabaret on Canal Street, four men sat at a table. The room was unusually crowded and filled with an air of expectancy, as one of the men sat back in his chair looking coolly at one of the other men.

"Well, Louis, what's the surprise you wanted me to see so badly?" the man asked arrogantly. The speaker was Garrett Flye. A man of about thirty, tall and slender, he had the hawk-faced look of a predator. His eyes were pale-blue and cold. The man to whom he spoke was somewhat younger, clean-faced, with golden-brown eyes. He was tall and he could have been strong, but the paunchiness of dissipation was evident. He bore the soft look of the self-indulgent wealthy.

"You'll see soon. Be patient, Garrett. This beauty is worth waiting for. I've never seen anything like her in my life."

Garrett gave a brittle half-laugh. "Louis, you find . . . ah . . . beauty in the strangest places."

This remark brought a chuckle from one of the other two men at the table. It was obvious that they were related to one another. There were only subtle differences in their appearances. Delmond LaCroix was a tall, slender man, but his looks were deceiving, for he had a wiry strength. His square-jawed face bore widely spaced blue eyes and a long, straight nose. His mouth was wide, and there were fine lines at the corners of his eyes that revealed his sense of humor. He smiled often. Streaks of pale blond swept through hair the color of molten gold. He watched the other two men, a soft smile flickering over his lips.

Across from him sat Cameron LaCroix, his brother, younger by only one year. At twenty-eight, Cameron was an inch or two taller than his brother's six feet. He had a heavier, more muscular build, but he was graceful in spite of his size. The familial square facial structure held eyes that were a smoky gray-blue that changed hue with his clothing and his moods. White, even teeth were revealed by his wide smile. His hair missed being brown by the pale blond that streaked it and the short beard and moustache that he wore. Cameron had been called "Kirk" by his brother as long as he could remember, simply because Delmond, as a child, found "Cameron" to be too difficult to handle. "Kirk" it had become, and "Kirk" it remained.

Their eyes met across the table.

"Kirk, you think Louis has really found something this time?"

"If he has, it will be the first time. I tend to agree with Garrett. Louis does seem to see beauty in the strangest places."

Louis gave an exasperated cluck of his tongue. "You're all in for a surprise this time. Just remember, I found her first."

They were just about to answer him when the lights

8

were extinguished, except for several that surrounded a small, empty square of floor in the middle of the room. The soft strum of a guitar silenced everyone, and they waited in hushed expectancy. No matter what they expected, the three men were taken completely by surprise by the vision of loveliness that stepped onto the floor. Louis leaned back in the chair with a chuckle as he recognized the sound of the softly hissed intake of breath from Kirk and saw the gleam in Garrett's eyes as he leaned forward in surprise.

She was tall and willowy, yet her body had a voluptuous look. Her arms were raised above her head, and her fingers clicked castanets gently. Her closed eyes and upturned chin made her appear to be in a trance. Long black hair, swept back from a high, smooth forehead, fell in an abundant cascade to her hips. Behind one ear she had pinned a red flower that heightened the blue-black color of her hair. Her skin was as pure as ivory, enhanced by the dark brows over her lowered eyes and the moist redness of her sensuous lips.

Slowly her body began to sway, and the guitar picked up the beat, following her moving hips. Her feet began to gently tap the rhythm, accompanied by the castanets.

Louis closely watched the effect this beauty was having on his friends. Garrett's eyes were unblinking. He sat slightly forward in his chair, intent only on the woman who swayed before him. Del looked as though he had been struck a blow and could not catch his breath.

As for Kirk, he had the most incredulous look on his face, as though he were seeing something beyond his imagination. Yet, somewhere deep in his mind, a faint memory stirred. Had he seen her somewhere before? No! If he had seen this vision, he would never have forgotten her. Still, there was something so familiar. He watched, completely spellbound, as the tempo of the flamenco picked up. Neither feet nor castanets missed a beat as her body throbbed to the wild strum of the guitar. Faster, faster, until the rapid tattoo of her feet and the castanets drowned out in the mind of each man in the room every thought but of this magnificent, pulsing woman.

Then, as suddenly as she had appeared, she was gone . . . and the guitar was silent. A gentle sigh seemed to escape everyone's lips. The four men at the table were speechless. They were trying to pull together their emotions.

"Well?" said Louis, with a laugh. "She will dance again, one more time, and then she will simply vanish. I've tried every way I know to find out her name or where she stays, even how she disappears so fast, but . . . ." He shrugged his shoulders and sighed.

Garrett opened his mouth to speak, but he shut it immediately, for his attention was drawn back to the floor. As fiery as she had been the first time—her dress blazing red, to match the flower in her hair —now she was cool and regal. Her flowing white dress had a high neckline and long sleeves and revealed none of her skin, yet it hugged her body from the shoulder to below her hips as though it were part of her. Her hair had been coiled tightly on top of her head, and pinned behind her left ear was a white flower.

Her body swayed slowly to the music. A violin had added its plaintive voice to that of the guitar, while she had put aside the castanets. She moved as one with the music and held her audience in captive silence. She came closer to the table where the four men sat. Within two feet of it, she lifted her eyes to the men, and a slow smile formed on her lips. Motionless, Kirk felt as though he had reached out and touched a live flame.

She had eyes of midnight blue so deep they were almost purple—and they met his directly.

He was stunned and he felt himself holding his breath for the few seconds that their eyes held.

When her eyes finally dropped away from his, she moved away, and he felt a sudden sense of loss, as if part of him were suddenly missing. This was a new emotion for Kirk LaCroix. With his charm and exceptional good looks, he had never had any difficulty finding his way to the beds of many beautiful women. Unaffected, he had gone his way loving, never committing himself. Now he felt like a schoolboy, anxious for the first encounter. The feeling left him shaken.

He was not alone. Garrett and Delmond were suffering the same plight. And Louis was thoroughly enjoying their discomfort. After all, why should they not suffer as he? he thought. These three, who could have almost any woman in New Orleans at the snap of a finger, should learn how it feels to yearn for something out of their reach.

Again the music stopped abruptly, but this time she did not disappear: she stood in the center of the floor and bowed deeply. The applause was deafening. All of the men were standing, including Louis and his friends, and they thundered their pleasure.

Reaching up to her hair, she withdrew the flower. She inhaled the delicate scent for a moment, then threw it directly at Kirk. He caught it automatically, much to the displeasure of the others. Once more her eyes met his across the room. In them he saw . . . what? Challenge? Or laughter? The thought stirred him beyond anything he had ever felt, and he lifted the flower to his face, his gaze still intent on her. Then she was gone. There was a flurry of activity as waiters were called to different tables to carry messages to her.

"We'd best be going. There's nothing else here of any interest," Louis said quietly.

"Damn! I've got to see her. I've got to find out who she is," Garrett replied angrily.

"I've a feeling, Garrett, that she'll be found only if she wants to be found," Louis said resignedly. "We'll wait, if you care to try, but I'll tell you now what you'll find. If you go backstage, you'll find an old Spanish lady who speaks no English. She will shrug her shoulders and say nothing. You see, I've tried and tried."

Delmond was watching Kirk, who stood silently holding the white flower in his hand.

The four of them left the club together and rode home in the LaCroix carriage. When Louis had been left at his home and Garrett had been dropped off, the two brothers rode in silence for a long time.

"I wonder who she is," mused Del. Kirk didn't answer, engrossed in the flower he still held in his hand.

At any other time, Del would have been amused and would have happily stepped aside and let his brother take over. But this was one time he felt the urgent desire for a woman, and he was going to wait for no one, not even Kirk.

12

2

For several nights afterward, the four of them returned to the club to watch Fantasia dance. To them, as well as to the other men who came, each night was a miracle of beauty. As before, she danced only twice. After the second dance, she again disappeared. All of their cards were returned, including Garrett's, much to his surprise and frustration.

This time, Del and Kirk both went back to her dressing room with Louis and Garrett. Exactly as Louis had said, they found an old Spanish lady who spoke no English—or so she implied. Kirk looked deeply into her intelligent brown eyes and immediately felt that she understood every word they were saying.

She was a very tiny woman, her head barely reaching the buttons on Kirk's vest. She looked up at him with a polite smile on her face.

"Fantasia?" he questioned.

"Sí, Fantasia," she answered, nodding her head.

"Where has she gone?"

The woman continued to look at him as though she did not understand. He had a strong urge to grab her and shake her until she spoke.

"Where has she gone?" he repeated deliberately.

"No comprendo, señor," she said quietly, with a small shrug of her shoulders. But her eyes glittered with amusement.

"See, I told you," Louis said in exasperation. "I've tried before, but I always get the same 'No comprendo, señor.' "

"Well," Kirk said softly, watching the woman's eyes, "I think she understands every word we say. She's an ugly old hag, but I hope she's not as stupid as she looks."

The Spanish eyes snapped from guarded amusement to fiery anger before she dropped them from his face, but in that moment he knew he was right.

They knew they would get nothing more from her, so they turned to leave. At the door, Kirk turned back and spoke to her so softly that the others could not hear.

"I know you understand. You tell your mistress that I'm not a man who gives up easily. If I want something badly enough, I generally get it."

Her expression was under control now, and she looked up at him with simple innocence. He chuckled, then whispered, "And I didn't mean the insult. I'm sure you're quite a lady." The glitter returned to her eyes as she closed the door behind him. She bolted it and turned away, going to a small door at the side of the room that had been concealed by a huge folding screen. She gave two light taps on the door and heard the bolt slide on the other side. The door opened and Tazia stepped into the room, pulling it shut behind her.

From across the dance floor Tazia was beautiful. Closer, she was amazingly lovely. Her skin had a faint ivory glow. Her dark purple eyes, shaded by long black lashes, were stormy. She spoke to the old woman in Spanish.

14

"He is arrogant," she said coldly.

"I think you would have trouble with this one. Come, let us go home and forget these men," the old woman pleaded.

"Manolo's death cries out to me, Old One. Would you have me leave before I have avenged him?"

"Revenge can sometimes find its place at the wrong door, Little One. These men are strong, especially the last one. Would it not be wiser to let Manolo rest in peace?"

"He can never rest in peace while Kirk LaCroix and his three friends breathe the breath of life," she replied vehemently. "I swore on oath when they brought me news of how he died that one of them would pay, and pay he shall."

The old woman looked at her, a deep sadness filling her eyes. "Tazia, did you love Manolo?"

Tazia's dark eyes were clouded with pain. "I will not listen to any more from you. If you want to leave, go home. But I will not leave until I have avenged Manolo's death."

"You know I would never leave you, my child," the old woman replied.

Tazia threw her arms around the old woman's frail body. "I'm sorry," she said gently, "I know you have been faithful to me. It is only my sharp tongue. Forgive me."

The woman patted her shoulder, but the sadness in her eyes remained. She watched the girl change her clothes and pick up a dark cloak in preparation for leaving.

It is not love for Manolo that goads you, she thought. It is guilt that you did not love him that sets you on this path. She sighed deeply and picked up her own wrap. Instead of leaving by the front door, they left by the door through which Tazia had entered and crossed a small room. Opening the outer door, they stepped out onto a narrow, dark street. A huge man stood there holding the reins of three horses. Tazia smiled at him, and he grinned a silent reply as he helped them mount by lifting them effortlessly to the saddles.

"We have succeeded in getting all four of them here, Juan, and I'm sure they will be back soon. We will start with the small blond one, this . . . Louis Plummer."

The big man nodded his head as he watched her with eyes that glowed with admiration and respect.

"Tomorrow night, Juan, after I have finished my dance, send a note to him. You know what to say in it. Bring him to me. I think he is the weakest of the four, so we eliminate him first—after we have the information we need about the others."

The next night, Tazia danced as she had never danced before. When she removed the flower from her hair, she threw it to Louis, who caught it to his breast as though it were alive. She smiled at him, as he gazed at her beauty with open-mouthed wonder.

The men sat back in their seats after she had gone. Garrett stared at Louis with an angry glare that did not daunt Louis's rapturous feelings.

Del laughed shakily as he watched Louis's good fortune with unbelieving eyes.

Kirk silently twirled the stem of his wineglass and gazed moodily into it. After several moments of complete silence, a waiter stopped at Louis's side. He looked up questioningly.

"I have a note from the lady, sir."

Louis gaped in amazement. "For me?"

"For Louis Plummer, sir."

Louis gulped convulsively and reached out with a shaking hand to take the note from the waiter. He was quivering so much that he could hardly open it. When he did finally manage it, his face turned completely white.

"What does it say, Louis?" asked Kirk quietly. But Louis continued to stare at the note, disbelief written clearly on his face.

"Louis?" growled Garrett.

"Wha . . . what?"

"What does it say?"

Slowly Louis regained his composure. He folded the note and slipped it into his jacket pocket. Then he rose from his chair and looked at this three companions, who watched him closely. "You gentlemen must excuse me. I've been invited to join a lady for late supper and I don't want her to have to wait for me." He gave a small bow and, with a delighted grin, left the table.

Garrett and Del exchanged looks of complete bewilderment, while Kirk continued to twirl his wineglass between his fingers, a slight frown drawing lines on his brow. Something familiar kept gnawing at the outer edge of his memory and, try as he might, he could not put a name to it.

Louis moved through the crowd as rapidly as he could. The blood rushed through his veins, making him almost giddy with excitement. He arrived at Tazia's dressing room door and knocked hesitantly. It was opened by the same old woman they had encountered the night before.

"Señor, entrada, por favor," she said politely, motioning him inside.

He stepped into the room, and Tazia rose from her seat with a warm smile, her hand extended to him.

"It was good of you to come, señor," she said softly, her accent making her voice even more alluring to him. He took her hand in his and looked down into

17

the beauty of her smiling face. He could feel his heart throb painfully against his ribs.

"It was very good of you to invite me. I am very honored, señorita," he managed to stammer. She gave a small laugh.

"My carriage is just outside, señor, if you would care to join me at my home."

Louis felt as though he were the luckiest man alive as he nodded his head. She lifted her cloak from the chair and handed it to him. With hands barely under control, he draped it around her shoulders and followed her to the door. When they had gone, the old woman called in the waiter and then sent him back to the table with a note informing Louis's companions that he would not be joining them again that evening. Then she gathered her things and left.

Louis and Tazia rode in silence through the darkened streets. He was amazed at the size of the man who drove the carriage. He could see why Tazia would feel completely safe.

They left the outskirts of the city, and Louis began to look around him. "Is your home far?"

"No, just a few more minutes and we will be there."

They turned up a lane and stopped at a small house that sat well-hidden from the road. Light shone from one room. Louis took her hand to help her from the carriage and escorted her to the door. She opened it and they went inside.

The room was lit by several candles, and a table with a white cloth cover stood in front of a lighted fireplace. There was a double setting on the table.

Tazia dropped her cloak on a chair and walked to a small table that sat against a wall.

"Would you care for a drink before dinner, señor?"

"Thank you." He smiled as she handed him a glass

of wine. She turned back to the table and poured one for herself. He did not see that she poured it from a different bottle.

She moved to his side and lifted her glass with a smile. "Let us drink a toast, señor, to a very lovely and rewarding evening."

Louis looked down into her promising eyes and believed her. He raised his glass to touch hers. He drank half the wine before lowering the glass again. She moved away from him to stand beside the fire. The glow outlined her body, and he gazed at her loveliness until an overwhelming desire enveloped him. Slowly he walked to her side and slid his arm around her waist. He was surprised at his own courage—and even more surprised that she did not pull away from him. He lowered his head and touched his lips to the softness of her cheek.

"Señor," she said gently, "you are too quick. Let us eat first."

First, he throught delightedly. He watched her as she took both wineglasses back to the table. Then she turned and looked at him.

Her face seemed to waver strangely in front of him. He felt a warm lethargy creep though his limbs until he could barely move. She continued to watch him intently.

Too late the truth struck him, as her shape began to fade before his eyes and the room began to grow dark.

"Why?" he mumbled as he collapsed. "Why?"

Tazia walked to his side and looked down at his crumpled form, the look of amazement still on his face. Her eyes were cold and filled with anger.

"Juan!" she called.

The big man entered the room.

"Take him and tie him well. When he awakens, we have many questions to ask Señor Plummer."

3

The city came to life early with the calls of vendors pushing their carts through the freshly washed cobbled streets. They did not awaken Kirk, however, who lay with his hands behind his head and the same lines between his brows as he chased an errant memory about in his mind. He had been awake off and on most of the night. Each time he drifted into sleep, violet eyes would smile at him. Soft, white arms would enclose him, and he would taste those sensuous, red lips . . . almost. He cursed himself for a million kinds of fool as he punched his pillow and struggled again for elusive sleep.

What was it about her that called to him? he wondered. He had shared the affections of many beautiful women. But it was *she* who haunted his thoughts, awake or sleeping, and he knew he would never rid himself of her until he had solved this mystery.

A knock sounded lightly on the door. It was pushed open slowly by his brother.

"Awake, Kirk?"

"Yes."

"We've got to go over the designs for La Fleur today. I thought we might get an early start." Both

Kirk and his brother were successful architects. Even though their parents were very wealthy, they would have done quite well without their money. Things had always come easy for both the brothers. They were rich, handsome, and intelligent. Doors had always opened for them effortlessly, including the doors of bedrooms. Maybe that was the reason they found Fantasia so difficult to believe. She was a woman who offered herself, then vanished, only to return and make the same offer to someone who had never had the ability or means to enjoy the same pleasures they had enjoyed.

"So you can't sleep, either," Kirk grinned.

"No," his brother laughed. "I just don't believe Plummer's luck."

"Yes, and I'm sure Plummer would do his best to accommodate the lady's . . . reason."

"No, I don't mean that. I think there's something she wants from Plummer. I wish I could remember. Somewhere I think I've seen her before, but I just can't place it. I have a feeling that when I do I'll solve the mystery of why she's so elusive and why she picked on poor old Plummer."

"How the hell would you forget someone who looks like her?"

Kirk shook his head. He could not answer, but he was convinced that they had not seen the last of Fantasia. He hoped they hadn't, for he could not keep his mind on anything else while she hovered constantly on the edge of his memory.

He rose from the bed and gathered up his clothes.

"Del, let's get those La Fleur plans out of the way and take a ride over to see old Louis. I'm sure he'll have a lot to talk about. You know his loose tongue. Maybe we can find out from him just where they went last night."

"Good idea," said Del, lifting his tall frame from the bed. "I'll see you downstairs. We'll get to the plans right after breakfast. By noon we should be free to go over to Louis's."

They ate breakfast rapidly and went to the study, where they worked for three hours on the plans for the new La Fleur mansion. Kirk finally rose from behind the desk and stretched.

"We've accomplished enough for today. Let's get going. I'm stiff as a board, and a good ride would make me feel a hell of a sight better."

Del nodded in agreement. They left the house, had their carriage made ready, and rode to Louis Plummer's house. When they arrived, they had themselves announced and waited patiently for Louis to present himself. They were both surprised when Louis's sister entered the room. It was obvious she had been crying.

"Jeanette, what's wrong?" Del asked.

"Oh, Del . . . Kirk . . . I received a note early this morning. It said Louis was taking a short journey and would not be home for a few days."

The brothers exchanged glances. "What makes you think something's wrong, Jeanette?" Kirk asked softly.

She held out the note to him with trembling fingers. "You know my brother well, Kirk. Read this. You'll see that it is not like him at all. Oh, the handwriting is his, but . . . well, read it."

Kirk took the note from her hand and read it: "My Dear Sister, I find it imperative that I take a sudden journey. I shall be gone for several days, possibly a few weeks. Do not be alarmed. It is important business. See you soon. Affectionately, Louis."

Kirk looked up from the paper. "If Louis wrote this, someone was standing over him at the time."

"Let me see it." Del reached out, took the paper from Kirk, and read it quickly. "What important

22

business could Louis have to take a trip for?" he asked Jeanette.

She gave a little half-smile. She loved her brother dearly, but she also understood him perfectly. Their parents had left them a great deal of money upon their deaths. The plantation on which they lived was extremely productive under the care of their father's overseer. Louis had never done a day's constructive work in his life.

"There's no reason for him to go anywhere. Kirk, I'm terribly worried. Something's very wrong. Please help me."

Kirk laughed and patted her hand, which clung to his arm. "Don't worry, Jeanette, we'll find out where he's gone for you."

He looked across at his brother. "And I think we know exactly where to start." Del nodded.

They soothed Jeanette's fears and left the house. They rode slowly toward their own home.

"We'll go back to the club tonight." Kirk said firmly. "This time we won't take 'No comprendo' for an answer. We have a lot of questions to ask a certain lady."

They worked on and off all afternoon, but neither of them could concentrate. The day dragged slowly into early evening. Finally, they left the house and went to the club, where they waited patiently for Fantasia to dance. Time ticked away slowly, and they had several drinks before it occurred to either of them that the time for her to appear was past. Kirk called the waiter to their table.

"What time does Fantasia appear?"

"She is not here, monsieur. She had to go away for a few days. But she will return soon."

Kirk felt a frustrated anger. "Where did she go?"

The waiter shrugged his shoulders. "I do not know,

23

monsieur. She merely told the owner she would be gone a few days. With her beauty and talent, he does not question her whims. He is just grateful she dances at all. I am afraid business will be slow until she returns."

"Bring us another drink."

"Yes, monsieur." The waiter left the table.

"Do you think she really will come back?" Del asked quietly.

"Yes. I think she'll come back. I think there's more going on than we can guess right now. I think she's after all four of us. I just wish I could figure out why—and where the hell I've seen her before."

Both of them spent another sleepless night wondering about the connection between Fantasia, Louis Plummer, and themselves.

Louis stirred to consciousness. His eyes opened and he shook his head a little to clear the fuzziness from his brain. Suddenly everything flooded back to him: He was seated in a chair with his arms tied firmly behind it. His legs were also tied, and there was a gag in his mouth. He gave a little whimper of fear as the door opened and the huge man who had driven the carriage came in. He looked at Louis and, without a word, turned and went back out. Within five minutes, the door reopened and the huge man came back, accompanied by Fantasia. But it was a different person who looked at him now. She wore a white long-sleeved man's shirt, open at the throat. Dark pants hugged her hips like a second skin, and high black boots and a black, flat-crowned, wide-brimmed hat that tied under her chin completed the outfit.

"Ah, you are awake, señor. We thought you were going to sleep all day," she said pleasantly. But her eyes were frosty pools of deep purple. She slowly withdrew a slender stiletto from the sheath at her waist and walked toward him. His eyes widened with fear, and perspiration beaded his brow and ran down his face.

But she simply reached behind him and cut the ropes that bound him. As the blood began to recirculate in his hands, he winced with pain. One slice of the sharp stiletto loosened his feet, and she removed the gag from his mouth.

"What do you want with me?" he gasped. "What are you going to do?" He watched both of them, but for a few moments neither of them spoke, and he began to shake with terror.

"You, señor, are going to write a note to your sister explaining your absence for a few weeks. Then you and I are going to talk," she added softly. "You know many things about which I'm very curious."

"What can I tell you? I don't even know who you are," he almost sobbed.

She smiled, but the smile did little to ease the fear in Louis, for it was as frozen as ice.

"You do not know me, señor?"

"No," he gasped. "You have the wrong man. I've never seen you before."

She walked over to him and knelt in front of the chair. Her face, only inches from his, was filled with angry passion. "You pig. Look closely at me, and remember. Before you taste my revenge, remember. Look back two years: a gambling table . . . five men sit at cards . . . you are one of them and a young Spanish boy is another. Someone cheats. The boy becomes angry. A gun is fired, and the boy lies dead. Of course, it is a matter of honor, so the four men agree that the boy should be accused of cheating, no matter what it does to his name or to his family. This is done. A great name is dishonored, and an only son is dead. Do you remember now?"

While she spoke, Louis's eyes grew wider and wider and filled with terror. "De Montega!" he gasped. "Manolo de Montega."

"Sí, señor, Manolo de Montega . . . my brother."

Tears began to well up in Louis's eyes as he looked into the cold, merciless eyes before him.

4

The huge, silent man who accompanied Tazia came to stand beside her as she rose from Louis's side.

"Get up and come with me," she said, "and quickly."

"Where are we going?" Louis asked with renewed fear, as he gazed up at Tazia's companion.

"To a very safe place, where you and I and a friend of mine will have some time to talk."

Louis knew there was absolutely no sense in trying to oppose a man who was more than twice his size—or the very sharp weapon in the hand of a woman whose eyes told him very clearly she would use it if necessary. Without another word of protest, he got to his feet shakily, and, with one of them on either side of him, they left the room. Outside the house, two horses waited. Tazia mounted one, her companion the other. Then he motioned Louis to mount behind him. They were taking no chance on him getting away on a horse of his own. They rode rapidly and in silence, and they soon arrived at the waterfront. Juan arranged for the horses, and they walked to the end of one of the docks, where a small boat waited. Once in the boat, Juan swung the oars out, and within minutes they were skimming rapidly over the water. After almost half an hour, Louis felt Tazia move up beside him. Suddenly a piece of black cloth was tied over his eyes.

"Sit still. You will not be harmed. We just don't want you to see where you're going from here." Louis sat very still, too frightened to do anything else. It seemed to him that many hours passed before he felt the boat bump against land, but it had been less than two hours.

Tazia removed the mask and Louis looked around. It appeared that they were on the edge of a marsh. They left the boat and Tazia urged Louis along a path through the dense foliage. Suddenly they came to a clearing, in the middle of which stood a magnificent house. Louis gaped at the house and turned to Tazia. "Please, where are we?"

"Barataria," she said shortly.

"Oh, God!" Louis moaned. "Barataria! The house had to belong to . . . Lafitte . . . the pirate! He turned his frightened eyes toward Tazia, who laughed and urged him forward again. They climbed the steps to the long, shadowed porch.

The two-storied house was huge, with white pillars guarding the front entrance. When they opened the door and stepped inside, Louis was amazed. It was the most beautiful place he had ever seen, outside of the governor's mansion. The entrance alone was half as big as Louis's home. A large crystal chandelier hung over the black-tile floor. A spiral stairway extended from the center of the floor upward past oversized windows. The carpet was gold, in contrast to the white of everything else in the room.

At that moment, a tall, slender man came down the stairway. He was smiling, and both his hands were extended to Tazia. "Ah, ma petite chérie, as beautiful as ever. To what do I owe the pleasure of this visit?" he laughed.

Tazia smiled in genuine fondness and let him kiss her hands tenderly. "Jean, I have need of a very great favor."

"But of course, chérie, anything you wish is my command."

"I must speak to you alone, Jean. Can you keep this gentleman . . . safe for a few weeks?"

Lafitte turned and looked closer at Louis, who gazed back into the intelligent eyes of one of the most notorious pirates of the age. Lafitte was a very handsome man, with a sparkling sense of humor — and a pirate of great courage.

"Take him to the back bedroom upstairs, Juan, and leave him there." He spoke quietly to Louis, "If you should try to leave the house, let me warn you that the jungle around Barataria swarms with poisonous snakes and alligators. It has kept me safe here for years. One who comes in very seldom gets out unless Lafitte shows him the way. Do you understand?"

Louis nodded and Juan led him away. Jean turned back to Tazia. "Come, share a glass of wine with me and tell me why you have sought me out at this hour. I am in the mood for a good adventure."

Tazia laughed, a soft, warm laugh of friendship. "When are you not in the mood for adventure of one kind or another, Jean?"

"Ah, Tazia, you crush my feelings. You know you are the woman dearest to my heart. Why don't you come to Barataria and stay with me? We would be wonderful together."

Now Tazia laughed with real delight. "It would last about a week, Juan. You are a man who must share his heart with many women."

He turned to look at her, his eyes unfathomable.

29

"And you are a woman who can share her heart with only one man. I only wish I were he." Then he shrugged and laughed and put his arm about her shoulders. "Come, talk to me. Tell me what you have been doing since I last saw you and that wicked brother of yours."

He felt her stiffen slightly in his arms. Her eyes had gone dark with sadness.

"Manolo?" he questioned quietly. She nodded. "Dead?" Again she nodded. "Come chérie, I think we both need a drink." He led her into the library and closed the door behind them. She talked quietly while he listened in silence. When she finally came to the end of her story, her eyes were moist with tears. He wanted to go to her, to tell her things about her brother she should have known, but he cared too deeply for her to add more pain to what she already felt. Right or wrong, he would help her in whatever she decided to do.

"What is it I can do for you, chérie?"

She smiled at him in gratitude. As he always did when he was near her, he wished that he could stir another emotion in her as easily.

She briefly outlined the plans she had made and what help she needed from him. He nodded as she spoke, and when she finished, he rose to his feet and reached out to her. "You go and get yourself some sleep. I will discuss these things with our friend. Believe me when I tell you that when you leave in the morning you will have any information you desire from Louis Plummer. We will keep him here as long as necessary for you to complete your plans."

"I shall be eternally grateful, Jean. If there is anything I can do for you, you need only ask."

"Don't tempt me, Tazia. I would ask for the one thing I know you cannot give."

She looked up at him, sorrow written plainly on her face.

"And don't look at me like a broken little bird. You don't feel the least bit of pity for my plight." They laughed together, her laugh genuine, his with just a hint of unhappiness.

She went upstairs to a room she had used many times. Jean Lafitte, pirate or not, had been a good friend of her family since she was only ten and he a dashing twenty-five. She prepared herself for bed, but she could not sleep. Her mind drifted from her brother to the men involved in his death. She had to prove that one of *them* cheated and not her brother. She had a fierce pride in her family and her name. She could not let them be tarnished by anyone. Finally she dozed, and when she did, she dreamed. In her dreams, a pair of smoky-gray eyes met hers across a table, and she felt again, as she had the first time, the warmth stirring deep within her. Against her will, Kirk LaCroix entered her dreams again and again.

Meanwhile, Jean made his way to Louis's room. There were many things he wanted to know, and not all of them were the things Tazia sought to learn. He searched for another truth that she would never know of.

When Jean walked in, Louis rose from his chair. "How long do you think you can hold me here?" he demanded. "People are probably looking for me at this moment."

"Of course, monsieur, but let us not bandy words. I could hold you here forever, and no one would ever find you."

"What do you people want from me?" Louis asked. "What—" Jean held up one hand placatingly.

"Be silent for a few minutes, monsieur. I will explain to you exactly what I want, and I assure you

31

nothing will happen to you if you tell me what I need to know." The doubtful look on Louis's face caused Jean to laugh heartily. "You need not be afraid of Tazia, either—if you give me the information I need."

"She appeared to me to have my imminent demise in mind," Louis said.

"Tazia will listen to reason when she finds out the truth," Jean replied confidently.

"You have much more faith in that than I. I feel that if I tell her everything she wants to know my body will end up floating somewhere in the marshes, never to be found. The thought leaves me rather hesitant. I'm sure you understand my sentiments," Louis said dryly.

Jean smiled and gave a slight nod of his head. "But I'm sure you will understand mine when I tell you that I have many ways to acquire the information I need. I am merely choosing the easiest way. But I assure you, monsieur," he added, his eyes turning cold despite the smile, "you are expendable either way. Why not seek my protection from Tazia, for at this point she is the one who would rather see you dead."

Louis sighed and sat back on the bed. He acknowledged that Jean was right. "What is it you want to know?"

"Well, to begin with, who were all the players in the card game?"

"Garrett Flye, Kirk LaCroix, his brother, Delmond, and I. And, of course, Manolo de Montega."

"Tell me exactly what started the argument and what transpired afterward."

Louis cast another doubtful look at Jean. "You are not going to believe me."

"You may be surprised, monsieur," Jean replied

softly.

"Well, the game had been going on for quite some time, the winning being about even all night. I imagine it was about three or four in the morning. Along with me, two others had suspected that cheating was going on, but we couldn't spot it. The pot was large. Flye and Kirk had put everything they had into it. Montega didn't have enough on the table to call, so he wagered his half of his hacienda. It was Flye who finally detected the cheater, and he called attention to it. That's when it happened. In five minutes Montega was dead. That's exactly what happened."

"And Montega was cheating, was he not?" asked Jean, his voice low and controlled.

"I told you you wouldn't believe me."

"On the contrary, monsieur, I do believe you. I have also known Manolo de Montega since he was a child. I know him, I think, better than anyone else in the world."

"Then you *do* believe me? You understand what happened? The one who shot Manolo did so in defense of an unarmed man. We decided not to say anything more about it."

Jean nodded. "But one more thing I must know."

"Yes?"

"Who shot him?"

"LaCroix."

"Which one?"

"Kirk."

"Well, monsieur, relax and make yourself comfortable. I must have time to think this out. I will find some way to get you home. But first I shall try to find some way of easing Tazia's grief and stopping her vendetta."

Louis nodded, and Jean rose from his chair. He extended his hand to Louis, who took it gratefully. "Be of good faith, monsieur. Jean Lafitte has never failed to do what he says he will do."

Louis, much relieved, watched Lafitte leave the room, closing the door quietly behind him.

5

Kirk cursed for the tenth time that morning and threw his pencil across the room. It had been three days since Louis had disappeared. They had exhausted every means they knew to find him. It was as though the earth had opened up and swallowed both Louis and Tazia. He found it impossible to do any work, and he was becoming aggravated with himself.

He looked up with a black scowl when the door opened. Del came in and moved to the chair opposite his desk. He sat down and stretched his legs out in front of him, all the while grinning at his brother's expression. "May as well put the work away. Until we get this mystery settled, neither of us is going to be able to concentrate."

"Well, I wish you'd come up with a constructive idea instead of stating the obvious," Kirk snapped.

Del chuckled. "I think the obvious thing to do is just sit back and wait patiently until she decides to find us."

Kirk's frown deepened. "I'm really worried about Louis now, Del. He's been gone three days."

"I know, I'm worried, too, but what is there left that we haven't done to try to find him? We've covered every means of leaving New Orleans. No one with their descriptions has been seen."

"I know," Kirk said with exasperation, "but I feel we should be doing *something*." His brother laughed again, but he quickly smothered it as Kirk glared at him.

"Is it good old Louis you're hungry for information about? Or a certain elusive black-haired beauty?"

Kirk grinned wryly. "Well, if we find her, I'm sure we'll find out about Louis, too."

"There's no way she could have left this city without our knowing about it, so obviously she's still here somewhere. The question is where. And who is helping her keep Louis incommunicado?"

"We know every important family in this state. Not one of them would do anything like this," Kirk replied thoughtfully. "And she strikes me as a lady of means, who would be very careful choosing her friends."

"A lady of means," Del murmured to himself. "Kirk, what if she's visiting the city for just this purpose? Surely she would not involve friends in this type of affair."

"We've been looking in the wrong places," Kirk answered quickly. "She must have found a place to live quietly alone until she did whatever it was she came to do."

"I think we'd better check the rental agents. See if anyone of her description or nationality has rented accommodations in the past few weeks."

Kirk rose from the desk, his eyes aglitter with the first real hope since Louis had disappeared.

"I'm going down and check all of the rental agents. I've finished the plans, so it's your job to go over them with La Fleur."

"My job!" said Del sharply.

"Yes," laughed Kirk. "It's your turn, remember?"

"Lady Luck must sit on your shoulder," Del grumbled. "All right, but let me know if you find anything."

"I will."

Del rose, rolled up the plans that were spread on Kirk's desk, and, with one last baleful look at him, left the room, closing the door firmly while Kirk chuckled.

Kirk retied his cravat, buttoned the sleeves on his shirt, and slipped into his jacket. He left his office and sent for his carriage.

Two hours later, he was again losing hope. He had gone to four agents, and each one gave a negative answer to his description. He then entered the firm of Chevell and Sons without much hope of success. When he was told that a Spanish woman had rented a house two months ago, he was taken by surprise. He quickly asked, "What did she look like?"

"She was an old woman," the man answered, "but a . . . how shall I say . . . an aristocrat."

"A small woman, about this size?" he asked excitedly, as he held his hand up level with his chest.

"Yes, monsieur, a very little woman, but a lady."

"Was no one else with her?"

"Yes, monsieur. A huge fellow. I shouldn't want to tangle with that one."

"Where is this house?"

Chevell described it and provided instructions on how to get there.

"In what name was the house rented?"

"Ah, let me see," he said, fiddling with some papers while Kirk waited impatiently. "A Señora María Sebastian and Señor Juan Sebastian. I imagine they are mother and son," he said helpfully.

"Or housekeeper and bodyguard," murmured Kirk.

"Monsieur?"

"Nothing," Kirk smiled. "Thank you for your help, Monsieur Chevell."

"You're most welcome, Monsieur LaCroix. I hope you find your friends to be well."

"I hope I find *all* of my friends," Kirk replied solemnly.

Chevell watched Kirk's broad back as he left the office, and he shook his head.

Kirk stood outside the establishment for a few minutes debating whether to go home and get Del or to go on to the house by himself. He finally chose the latter and climbed into his carriage. He gave directions to the driver and sat back against the cushioned seat.

It was a longer drive than he thought it would be, and it was quite dark before they arrived at their destination.

He stepped down from the carriage and stood contemplating the small, darkened house. Then he walked slowly up the steps and onto the front porch. He found the door locked, so he circled the house —only to discover that the back door was locked securely, too. Checking all around, he found a small side door that, to his amazement, had been left unbolted. He opened the door cautiously, stepped inside, and shut it behind him. He had to stand still for a few moments to allow his eyes to adjust to the darkness before he could make out the shapes of furniture in the room.

He had stepped into a small sitting room, where he found a couch and two chairs opposite each other in front of a small fireplace. There was nothing on any of the tables or the mantle that suggested occupancy. He worked his way slowly around the furniture to the first open doorway. Here he found a small dining room and off it a tiny kitchen. Checking further, he found three bedrooms, none of which seemed to have been lived in. It was then that he noticed what appeared to be bundles beside the front door, and he walked over to investigate.

Kirk never saw Juan nor heard him move quietly toward him in the dark. Suddenly the world seemed to explode with a cascade of brilliant stars inside his head. A black void came rapidly up to meet him, and he sagged into it. Juan caught him as he fell and lifted his large body as though he were a child, laying him gently on one of the couches.

Juan stepped back from him while a lamp was lighted. Lafitte's face peered at him from above the light. "Well, Juan, I guess we don't have to go to Monsieur LaCroix after all. He has come to us."

"Sí." Juan chuckled deeply in his throat. "Señorita Tazia will be pleased."

"Well, Juan, I don't think we'll take him to Tazia just now," he said. Juan looked at him, not quite comprehending, since his loyalty and affection for Tazia were unlimited. "But she said . . . ."

"I know what she said, Juan," Jean interrupted patiently, "but we do not want any harm to come to Tazia, do we?"

Juan shook his head no, but he still eyed Lafitte doubtfully.

"Then," Jean explained slowly, "I must question the gentleman first myself, to see just how much he knows. After I am sure he can cause Tazia no harm, I shall bring him along."

Juan was still hesitant and cast his eyes from Kirk to Jean.

"I shall take care of everything, Juan. You know I would do whatever is necessary to help Tazia, don't you?" Juan nodded. "Then take Tazia's and Maria's belongings to my house. Tell Tazia I shall be along

39

soon." He looked at Kirk. "When he awakens, I will discuss a few things with him. Then, if I feel it is necessary, I will bring him to Barataria. If not, I will send him home, and we will make our plans accordingly."

Juan moved away slowly, as if he were still not quite sure he shouldn't take Kirk along with the rest of the bundles. When he had finally gone, Jean locked the door, picked up a bottle of wine and two glasses, and seated himself comfortably in a chair opposite Kirk's inert form to sip a drink and wait.

He was well into his second drink when Kirk groaned and stirred on the couch. When he opened his eyes, he glared at Jean, who lifted his glass to him with a delighted smile.

"Ah, welcome back to the world, Monsieur LaCroix," he said. "I was beginning to wonder if you were ever going to wake up."

Kirk reached up and touched the back of his head gently, but even that brought a wince of pain. "Did you hit me?"

"No, I'm afraid that was Juan. He sometimes does not know his strength."

"Juan, the big man, eh?"

This brought a surprised look from Jean and a short, painful laugh from Kirk.

"I have looked very deeply into your background in the last few days, Monsieur LaCroix. May I call you Kirk, as the rest of your friends do? I have a feeling we are destined to become good friends. We have something in common."

"Of course. And what do we have in common . . . and who the hell are you, anyway?"

"Oh, allow me to introduce myself, monsieur," Jean said. He rose with a light laugh and, making an exaggerated bow, he said softly, "Jean Lafitte at your service, sir."

"Jean La . . . Lafitte, the pirate?"

"Oh, monsieur, that is a harsh word. I would rather say 'privateer.' "

Kirk groaned as he sat up. He put both feet on the floor and held his head in his hands for a moment. Then he looked up at Lafitte. "The more I find out, the more mysterious this whole thing becomes. Where are Louis Plummer and Fantasia, and what is her connection to us?"

"Relax, monsieur," said Jean as he extended a glass of wine to Kirk. "You and I are going to have a long talk, and if you agree, we will soon bring all the pieces of your puzzle together."

Kirk took a sip of the wine, leaned back comfortably on the couch and smiled at Jean. "All right, talk away. I've spent a bad three days, and I'm anxious to find out just what this is all about."

6

Jean refilled his glass and sat down opposite Kirk. "Well, monsieur," he began, "I will start this tale about ten years ago. I ran across a merchant ship and was about to relieve her of some of her unnecessarily heavy ballast . . . for navigational purposes only, you understand." He laughed, and Kirk responded with a nod and a smile.

"When we boarded her, the captain, Señor Ramón De Montega, was brought to my presence."

"De Montega?" Kirk said slowly. "That name sounds familiar."

Jean raised a hand. "Have patience, monsieur. It will all be clear to you soon." He took another sip of wine and continued. "The captain had a request. It seems the doctor on board his ship had died, and his son, whom he had with him, had contracted the same illness. He wanted to have our doctor look at the child, for he was afraid the boy was dying. I brought my doctor on board, and, while he took care of the boy, his father and I came to a mutually beneficial agreement. The child lived, and I acquired a business friend in his father. I went to his home for the first time about a year later, and there I met Tazia, Señor de Montega's daughter. She was about ten at the

42

time—and probably the most beautiful child I'd ever seen. Her brother was five years older, and it was obvious that she and her parents worshipped the boy." Jean lowered his eyes to his glass and spoke softly, "I think, monsieur, that I am the only one who saw the boy as he really was: a heartless, conceited, arrogant, and evil little monster, who would take anything he wanted. Oh, he was beautiful around his family simply because they adored him. But I knew the other side of his nature.

"Tazia was content to stand in her brother's shadow. He was the heir, he was the carrier of the name, he was the holder of the pride of the de Montegas. If they had only realized, as I had, that Tazia had more pride than her brother would ever have. Well, that is beside the point. . . . As the boy grew older, he had one problem after another, and, because of his family, I helped him out. Then, one night about two years ago, he got into trouble—trouble I could do nothing about." He watched Kirk's face and saw the light of understanding grow in his eyes.

"Manolo de Montega," Kirk said softly.

"Oui, monsieur, Manolo de Montega," Jean answered.

"What is Tazia's real name?"

Jean chuckled. "Señorita Elena María Constancia Fantasia de Montega. You can see why I soon shortened that to Tazia."

"Does she know who shot her brother?"

"She does not . . . but I do. She is trying to find out. Her pride and her blind love for her brother will not let her rest until she does."

"And when she does?"

"She intends to kill him," Jean replied.

"She is questioning Louis?" asked Kirk.

"I have already talked to Louis. He will tell her

nothing for the time being."

"What are you going to do?"

"I have a half-formulated plan that, if you agree to it, may help."

"Why are you doing this for me?"

Jean laughed as he stood up. He walked to the window and pushed aside the curtain. He looked out, without seeing, his mind transported to another time, another place.

"I do nothing for you, monsieur. Manolo got what he had long deserved, and you mean nothing at all to me. But I will not let Tazia be hurt any more by either her brother's hand or her own."

Kirk was silent for some time. When Jean turned from the window, their eyes met, and Kirk read the truth in them. "You love her." He stated it as a fact, not a question.

"Since she was ten, monsieur," Jean replied. "I will do everything in my power to protect her, even from herself."

Kirk stood up and faced Jean across the room. "What do you want me to do? I shot Manolo because he was about to kill an unarmed man who had caught him cheating at cards. There was nothing else I could have done at the time."

"I know that, monsieur. The urge to kill Manolo has been so deep in me sometimes that I could barely hold myself back. But we must stop Tazia before she destroys herself. She is a woman of fierce loves and loyalties, monsieur."

"How can you possibly stop her? She knows all the players in the game. Soon she will know who fired the gun that killed her brother."

"By that time, monsieur, I hope she knows him too well to be able to kill him."

"You intend for us to meet?"

"I intend for you to do more than that. I want you to become friends."

"But she knows I was part of that card game."

"She will think she is fooling you, monsieur. By the time she finds out the truth, I hope that you will have become such friends that it will keep her from killing, for I think it would kill her, too."

"You're taking a big chance with my life," Kirk said dryly. "How are you going to get us together?"

Jean's eyes crinkled with amusement. "Just leave the details to me. But if you receive an invitation in the next few weeks, please accept."

"And my brother? I don't want anything to happen to him in the meantime."

"Your brother will also receive an invitation."

"Is this to be a competition?"

"You are competing for your lives, monsieur," Jean said, his voice becoming low and cool. "I suggest you put forth every effort, for Tazia will not hesitate to eliminate you."

Kirk felt a swift throb of excitement surge through him. The thought of meeting Tazia again under any circumstances was pleasing to him, but the thought of becoming closer was even more electrifying. He walked across to Jean and extended his hand. "I'll do everything in my power to keep her from killing me," he said, laughing. "For her own good, of course."

Jean gripped his hand firmly and returned the laugh. "Of course. Now you'd best be on your way, monsieur. I must go home and explain, if I can, why I did not bring you to Tazia, and you must go and do the same with your brother."

Kirk nodded and Jean extinguished the lamp. He took a key from his pocket and unlocked the front door.

"Was the side door left unlocked on purpose?" Kirk

asked.

"We saw you coming, monsieur. You would have been very suspicious had we left the front door open, would you not?"

"Yes, I guess I would have."

Jean was still absorbed in thought while he closed the door behind Kirk. He stood motionless for a few minutes, gathering his thoughts. Then he left the house and bolted the door.

When he arrived at his house, he was faced with a cold-eyed, furious Tazia.

"Jean," she said with deceptive softness. "Juan tells me you captured Kirk LaCroix. Why didn't you bring him here?"

"Come into the study, Tazia. I want to talk to you. I think we have a better plan than just killing someone."

"Did he tell you which one of them shot my brother?"

"No, he did not. Will you listen to my plan?"

"Why should I change my plans?" she asked angrily.

"Because mine will make them suffer just a bit while you find the guilty one," he said. He walked to her side and put his arm around her shoulders. He could feel her body trembling. "Tazia, you came to me for help," he said gently. "Let me help you. You know I am your friend, and you know I would never betray you."

He could feel her relax as she replied in a faint voice, "All right, Jean, I know. It is just that I find this waiting so difficult. Louis Plummer will tell me nothing. I must find out which one killed him . . . I *must*."

"Come, sit down and listen to me," urged Jean. They went into the study, where she sat stiffly in a chair. He poured her a little wine while he studied her face. She was tired, and her nerves were as taut as bowstrings.

"Here, drink this," he said as he handed her the glass.

After she had sipped a little wine, she said, "What is your plan, Jean?"

Mentally he crossed his fingers and began to speak. He followed her eyes as he outlined his plan. She listened to every word intently, and he could see her gradually beginning to accept what he was saying.

"You are a lovely woman, Tazia. It would not be hard for you to drive a wedge between two brothers who are so close. To make them hate one another enough to point a finger at the guilty party would cause them considerable pain. Make *them* pay the price for Manolo's death before you get the one who fired the shot."

She agreed. "How are you going to bring about our meeting?"

"Oh, that is quite simple. I intend to throw a ball, to which I will invite the eminent LaCroix brothers and a friend of theirs, Monsieur Garrett Flye. These three men are close friends. It will be amusing to watch you slowly tear that friendship apart. You can play each one against the others until they fall all over themselves to tell you who is responsible for Manolo's death."

She nodded her head slowly, while her mind assessed the plan. Jean watched her formulating what she would do, and he felt a deep pang of envy. He wished she were planning to turn her charms on him. She was so lovely that he wanted to call a halt to the whole thing, tell her how he felt about her, and beg her to stay with him. But he knew it would be of no use. He gave a deep sigh, which she understood.

"Your plan is excellent, Jean. When do we have this ball?"

"I thought, perhaps, in two weeks. I am going to arrange for Monsieur Plummer to take a small voyage. Then I will make all the preparations."

"Good!" she replied as she rose to her feet. "I think I shall be able to sleep better tonight knowing everything is in good hands. Good night, Jean." She kissed him lightly on the cheek and left the room.

Jean could barely control the urge to follow her. He silently cursed Manolo de Montega and Kirk LaCroix. He was convinced that because of one man he was going to lose her to the other—and he was helpless to do anything about it.

7

Del tapped the white envelope against his fingertips and looked at it thoughtfully before he handed it across the table to Kirk.

"Well," Kirk said quietly as he began to read its contents. "Our long-awaited invitation."

"Kirk, are you and Lafitte sure this is going to work?"

"Lafitte has known her for a long time, Del. I'm sure he would not have suggested it if he didn't think it would work."

"Hmm . . . But it's not *his* life he's playing with."

"All we have to do is let her believe we don't know who she is. Lafitte thinks she will not be able to kill someone she has become friends with. Just remember," laughed Kirk, "she's trying to make us jealous of one another, so don't let it get to you."

Del grinned. "I could say the same to you. I expect to do quite well myself."

"Care to make a small wager?" Kirk said, amused.

"Name it."

"If I can get her to admit she cares more for me, you'll step aside without any questions."

"Done."

"Well, the ball is next Tuesday evening." Kirk

smiled across the table. "From then on, it's every man for himself."

They laughed together and shared an enjoyable breakfast. Neither of them thought, in his masculine pride, that this would be anything but another challenge to his ability to make a conquest. It was to become a conversation they would both remember well . . . and regret.

The evening of the ball was warm and beautiful. A soft breeze blew in from the Gulf of Mexico, and stars lit the sky like millions of glowing candles.

Kirk was retying his tie for the fifth time. He wore dove-gray trousers and a jacket that hovered between blue and silver, which emphasized the deep color of his eyes. White lace frothed on his shirt front beneath a silver-blue brocaded vest. The clothes looked like they were molded to his tall, broad-shouldered frame. He looked magnificent.

Del came in as Kirk finally finished tying his tie. He turned to look at Del and gave a low whistle.

"You do look fine, but I'm afraid it just won't be enough. I intend to sweep the lady off her feet tonight."

Del wore bone-colored trousers and a deep-green jacket. With his blond hair, the clothes gave him a dashing look, sure to stir the heart of any young lady. He chuckled as he watched his brother.

"Why don't you just give up now? I've heard that all dark-haired señoritas fall for blond men. It sort of balances out in the children."

Kirk laughed aloud. "You'll never get *that* far!"

"Don't count your packages before you've opened them."

They left the room together, trading quips. Outside, their carriage was waiting and drove them to Lafitte's town house.

"How does a pirate like Lafitte get away with what he does . . . and then have the nerve to own a house right in the middle of the city?" Del wondered.

"The governor is in Lafitte's pocket. Jean has delivered a considerable amount of goods to New Orleans, some of which has found its way to the governor's mansion. Under those circumstances, he tends to ignore the demands of countries that call for Lafitte's head. Also, Lafitte can't be gotten to at Barataria, where he usually stays when he's not sailing."

"Clever man."

"Under the circumstances, I hope he's at his cleverest tonight."

Music could be heard drifting through the open windows as they descended from the carriage. The house was aglow with light. Slowly they mounted the four steps to the front door, which opened like magic as they reached it. Lafitte's major-domo was an alert man, and he did his job extremely well. He had been told to watch specifically for the two men who had just arrived.

"Good evening, Messieurs LaCroix."

"Good evening, ah . . . ?"

"Philippe, sir," he answered pleasantly.

"Well, Philippe, it's a lovely evening."

Philippe took their coats, and they walked together to the doorway of the ballroom. The room was huge, holding almost two hundred people. Brilliant jewels glittered as lovely ladies in bright-colored gowns whirled around the floor. Kirk searched for Tazia in the crowd, and it was not long before he found her. Her back was toward him, and she was speaking to Jean, who was listening intently. Then Jean caught sight of them over Tazia's shoulder, and he murmured something to her. Kirk could see her back stiffen as she turned slowly to face them.

Her hair had been gathered into a cluster of curls atop her head, pulling the hair back severely from her face, but the back fell in long, thick waves to below her waist. She wore a gown that was deep rose, bordering on red. It was off her shoulders, caught daringly just above the creamy rise of her breasts. A band of silver ribbon cupped her breasts, its strands hanging down to her waist. The dress then fell in soft folds to the floor, but they did absolutely nothing to hide the curves beneath.

Del and Kirk gazed silently at the beauty working her way toward them.

When they were three steps away, Jean spoke, "Ah, good evening, my friends. I'm glad you both could accept my invitation."

"Who in his right mind would not accept an invitation from the famous Jean Lafitte, a chance to see inside his home—a lovely one, indeed," Kirk said, his eyes drifting from Jean to Tazia. The severity of her hair made her eyes appear like two deep-blue pools of innocence. He could read nothing in them, but he knew she must be controlling her feelings as carefully as he was.

"Allow me to present one of my dearest friends: Señorita Elena Sebastian. This is Señor Kirk LaCroix. And this is his brother, Señor Delmond LaCroix."

"Señorita," murmured Del, with a slight bow. "It is a pleasure to meet you."

Kirk stepped to her side, and, lifting her hand, he gently kissed her fingers. The mere touch of her hand sent a warm current through him, and he could tell by the startled look in her eyes that she felt it, too.

"Have we not seen you before, Señorita Sebastian? Beauty such as yours cannot be forgotten easily."

She smiled at Kirk. "Gracias, señor. Sí, you have

seen me before, but I shall leave it to you to remember where."

"How could I possibly forget? I still have the flower you threw to me. Maybe you would let me send you a flower in return for the one I keep."

"You are too kind, señor."

"Señorita Sebastian," interrupted Del, "would you do me the honor of dancing with me?"

"Of course, Señor LaCroix."

"Please call me Del. And may I call you Elena? It is such a lovely name." He took her hand and led her to the floor. As he passed Kirk, he winked at him. Kirk responded with a light chuckle.

Kirk could not take his eyes off Tazia as his brother slid his arm around her waist and they moved together about the floor. He had almost forgotten Lafitte was there until he heard him say, "Be careful, monsieur. She will spring her trap very soon if you continue to look as you do."

"She's the most beautiful woman I've ever seen in my life," Kirk whispered. A sudden anxiety filled him as he watched the couple dance. This was going to be more difficult than he thought. Already he felt a stir of desire for her deep within him, and he realized what his brother must be feeling, holding her in his arms. It was the first time in Kirk's life that he could remember wishing his brother were somewhere else.

"Come, monsieur, let us have a drink. There will be many dances this evening." He watched Kirk reluctantly turn his eyes away from the two. "I know how you feel, monsieur. Can you imagine having her living in the same house with you? It is not easy, believe me, it is not easy. Were I not a man of honor, and if I did not care so deeply for her . . . .well . . . " He shrugged his shoulders, noting the dark look that crossed Kirk's face.

As they were about to turn away, Garrett Flye came into the room. He spotted Kirk almost immediately and came toward him.

"Garrett," Kirk said, "did Del explain everything to you?"

"Yes."

"This is Monsieur Jean Lafitte . . . Mr. Garrett Flye."

"Ah, yes, the fifth member of our little game of chance. A pleasure to meet you, monsieur."

Each of the men took a drink from a tray offered by one of the maids and sipped it in silence. Garrett's eyes had found Tazia, and he watched her without realizing the other two men were watching him. A look of naked hunger had come into his eyes, causing Jean to frown and Kirk to realize that Garrett, and not his brother, was the real danger to him.

When Del and Tazia rejoined them, she was laughing at something he had said, which irritated both Garrett and Kirk.

As the ball continued, Tazia danced several times each with Del, Garrett, and Jean. It was late in the evening before Kirk finally asked her to dance with him.

He held her lightly as they moved silently about the floor.

"You dance very well, Señor LaCroix," she said. Her accent was faint, but alluring.

"I'm surprised," he said.

"Surprised?"

"With someone as lovely as you, it's very difficult to concentrate on one's feet."

She gave a pleased response to his compliment, but her eyes were unreadable as she assessed him. They did not speak again, and he took the opportunity to simply enjoy holding her. She moved gracefully, her body swaying with the rhythm of a born dancer. She awakened every sense in his body. He was aware of the scent and feel of her as he had never been with any other woman before.

He looked down into her upturned face and realized that she had been studying him intently. Her eyes continued to hold his steadily, which caused the blood in his veins to tingle and his body to become warm. His feelings must have shown in his eyes, for her lips parted slightly and her cheeks grew rose-colored. He had never felt this way before. He could only think of one thing: his urgent desire to pull her into his arms and feel her body against his, to taste her soft lips.

The low murmur that escaped from her made him realize that his arm had tightened involuntarily and he was pulling her closer. He was very grateful that the music stopped at that moment, for he was afraid of what was happening.

Kirk did not know that his emotions were echoed in her. She had felt the same warmth that night when their eyes had met across the table in the cabaret. The sound she had made was one of fear—the fear that she was losing control, that she was responding to a man who might have shot her brother, the man she had sworn to kill.

8

Tazia, engrossed in thought, paced slowly back and forth in the library of Lafitte's house on Barataria. She stopped and poured herself a small glass of wine and curled up in a huge chair to sip the wine slowly. Her thoughts drifted back to the ball and Kirk LaCroix. For some reason, she suddenly felt alone and afraid. She had been deeply attracted to him, there was no doubt, and he had been just as drawn to her. She could see it in his eyes every time he looked at her. She felt again the warm stirring deep within her, a feeling she had never experienced before with any man.

At that moment, she desperately wanted to talk to someone. She thought of her parents, who had sanctioned her mission. The bitter thought came to her mind that they should never have let her go. They should have protected her: a beloved daughter and the last of the de Montegas. But, of course, Manolo had really been the last of them. The last male. The last to carry the proud name. Then what was she? Where did she belong? Her eyes suddenly filled with hot tears of self-pity.

She had not heard the door open and close, nor did she now see Jean leaning against it watching her. His heart twisted when he saw the tears in her eyes. She is so young and vulnerable, he thought. He muttered a curse on the soul of Manolo de Montega, only this time he included the parents whose blind love for their son had allowed a sensitive child to go through this with no one to defend her.

"Tazia," he said softly.

She lifted her eyes to his, and, before she could mask them, he saw the pain and fear deep inside. The pain of an unloved child and the fear that she would fail in her obligation, or what she mistakenly believed was her obligation to Manolo. She quickly covered her emotions with a smile. "Would you like some wine before bed?"

"What kind of an invitation is that?" he laughed.

"Just for a glass of wine," she said lightly.

"Oh, well," he sighed, and he accepted the glass she had poured for him. He watched her closely, but her face was calm now, her eyes clear and unreadable.

"What do you think of Garrett Flye?" he asked.

"I do not like him. He gave me the distinct impression he would have liked to strip me and attack me there in the ballroom."

"He was not alone in his feelings. There were at least a hundred men there with the same thoughts —and as many women who would have liked to eliminate you completely."

She laughed a little, but then her eyes became serious. She looked into her wineglass and swirled the contents around before she spoke. "Which one of them killed my brother, Jean?"

He did not reply, for he knew the question was directed as much at herself as at him.

"Are you still sure you're doing the right thing now that you've met the men involved? Maybe you should

57

investigate the situation more closely."

"What is there to investigate? One of those three men shot and killed my brother."

"Flye?" he asked. "Del LaCroix? Kirk LaCroix?" he thought he saw a slight flicker of alarm in her eyes when he mentioned Kirk's name.

"I don't know. No matter how much I studied them tonight, I could not picture any of them committing such a crime."

"Listen to me, Tazia. Get to know them better, while they still don't know who you are. Given time, you may find out a great deal."

"You are right, Jean. Eventually I will find out what I need to know."

He fell silent again, wondering whether she would survive the truth.

"I have invited some guests to spend a few days here at Barataria next week. If you like, I will include the three among them."

Her attention seemed to be centered on the wine she swirled in her glass. Finally she answered very softly. "Yes, I think that would be a good idea."

Tazia remained deep in thought while Jean watched her, wondering where her mind had drifted. If he had known the battle she was fighting, he would have been amazed. She was recalling the warm glow of Kirk's eyes and his strong arms around her as they danced. Against that raged the thought that it might have been Kirk who killed Manolo.

"I think I will retire now, Jean, if you don't mind," she said.

"Of course, chérie, get some sleep. We can talk tomorrow." After she had left, he sat for some time deep in thought, for a new idea had occurred to him and he wanted to examine it thoroughly. It would be almost two hours before he finally left the room and went to bed.

Tazia climbed the stairs and entered her room, which was dimly lit by two small candles on the night stands. María was placing her nightgown across the bottom of the bed when she came in.

"How was your party this evening?" she asked.

"Quite interesting, María. We've now met the three men who concern us."

"Tell me about them."

"Well, Mr. Garrett Flye—he is about thirty, tall and rather good-looking. But, María, he is cold, very cold. I'm sure he has a great deal of money, and he acts as though it can purchase anything or anyone he wants. I think he's used to have anything that pleases him."

"And you pleased him?"

"I believe so," Tazia laughed.

"And the others?"

"The LaCroix brothers are quite handsome. Del is tall, friendly, and very, very charming."

"And his brother?"

Tazia was silent for a moment. "He's quite attractive, too, María. His eyes are warm; they smile a lot. I hope . . . ."

"Hope what?"

"Oh, nothing. I'm very tired. I'm going to bed. Good night, María."

"Good night, child," María said softly as she slipped out of the room.

Tazia removed her dress and put on the nightgown. She pulled her hair over her shoulder and braided it and then climbed into the big bed. She knew sleep was not going to come easily, so she tried to keep her thoughts from wandering uncontrolled.

"I hope he did not kill Manolo," she whispered aloud.

María had gone back downstairs to speak to Juan about some inconsequential matter. As she was returning from her errand, the library door opened and Jean came out. They walked up the stairs together.

"Is she sleeping?"

"I think not. She has not slept well for many nights, but tonight I think she is more restless than usual. Tell me of this Señor LaCroix, the one named Kirk."

"He is a fine man, María. He would be good for her, if we could get this violence out of her head."

"Is he the one?"

Jean stopped and turned to assess the old woman. He saw immediately the intelligence in her eyes. "Yes, he shot Manolo."

"She has no idea?"

He shook his head no.

"Don't you think Tazia should be told the truth about her brother?"

"Do you think she would believe it?" Now it was María's turn to shake her head.

"What are we going to do, Señor Lafitte?" she asked desperately. "She does not deserve the hurt she is going to receive."

"Either way she's going to be hurt. If she learns the truth about Manolo—or the truth about Kirk. I hope time will give us the ability to replace the hurt with something else."

"What?"

Jean hesitated for a moment, then decided to tell her everything.

"Tazia is deeply drawn to Kirk. If I throw them together as much as possible, maybe we will find the alternative to hate."

"What about his feelings?"

Jean laughed. "I watched the young man tonight, and I know a great deal about him. He is a man of honor, and he is as much in love with Tazia as a man can possibly be. I just don't know if he realizes it yet. Did she mention him tonight by chance?"

"Not by chance. I asked about them. She told me of the other two, and I could read her eyes when she spoke of this man. I repeat, Señor Lafitte, what are we going to do?"

"Leave it to me, María. There are going to be some surprises in the next few months."

Neither Kirk nor Del was surprised when he received the invitation to stay at Barataria. There was no question about whether they would accept.

"We'll just wind up the La Fleur plans," Kirk said. "You told me he was satisfied with them. After that, we'll be free for a while. I'm certainly looking forward to being a houseguest at Barataria. I've heard Lafitte's hideaway palace is beautiful."

"Well, it's not the beauty of Lafitte's hideaway palace that interests me, it's the beauty of one young lady who will also be there," laughed his brother. Kirk found it very difficult to control the surge of jealousy that shook him. He was amazed at the violent emotion he suddenly felt.

"Does that upset you?" Del asked quietly.

"The lady has the right to her own choices," Kirk said with a slight shrug of his shoulders. But deep inside he was wishing away the hours so he could see her again. He wanted to wipe every other man out of her thoughts forever.

They wound up their business within a week and packed to leave for Barataria. When Lafitte's men came for them, Kirk was amused to see Juan's rather closed face.

"Can you handle all these things, Juan?" Del asked.

"Del, Juan is a very strong man. I can attest to that. I don't imagine there is anything he can't do."

Juan grinned. "Sí, señor. I can handle anything Señorita Sebastian or Señor Lafitte tells me to do."

Kirk chuckled. "Quite loyal, aren't you? Does that mean *anything*?"

Juan's face became very still. "Anything, señor," he answered softly. The glimmer of warning in his eyes was not missed by Kirk, who realized that Juan would not hesitate to kill him or his brother if Tazia or Jean thought it necessary.

9

The front approach to Jean's mansion on Barataria was not the route by which Tazia and Juan had brought Louis, nor that by which they had smuggled him out to board one of Jean's ships. The captain of the ship had been given explicit orders concerning Louis: he was not to be harmed in any way, and he was to be treated as a guest once they had cleared land. Jean intended Louis no harm. He only wanted him to be kept under control until Tazia and he had solved their problems with Kirk, Del, and Garrett. This plan was carried out just minutes before Kirk's and Del's carriage arrived, followed by Garrett and Jean's other guests.

Jean had invited the most amazing assortment of characters Kirk and his brother had ever seen. The first carriage that stopped discharged from its plush interior the most fantastic creature they had ever laid eyes on.

Molly Thatch was the name she used. What her real name was and what was hidden in her past were known only by Molly and Jean. She weighed almost two hundred pounds and she glittered with jewels in every place it was possible to put them. Her face was extremely beautiful. Her large almond-shaped brown eyes and even features were—before they became surrounded by layers of fat—a sight to behold.

She climbed down slowly from her carriage and adjusted her clothes, waiting for each person's undivided attention. When everyone had finally turned toward her, she shouted, "Jean! Come over here and greet me properly!"

He was quick to meet her outstretched arms, laughing heartily. "Molly, lovely Molly! I'm glad you could come." He took her hands in his and kissed her vigorously. Molly gave a deep, rumbling laugh that shook her entire body like jelly.

"Have you been faithful to me?" she teased.

"Always, Molly, always," Jean answered.

"You are such a liar, my dear Jean, but I love you in spite of your one and only fault." She turned to face Tazia, who had been watching with amusement. "And who is this gorgeous creature? What have you been keeping from me?"

"Molly, this is Elena Sebastian, the daughter of a very old friend. Elena . . . Molly Thatch, probably the dearest friend I've ever had."

"Pleased to meet you, Mrs. Thatch," Tazia said softly.

"M'name's Molly, child, not *Mrs*. anything."

Tazia smiled. "Molly."

Molly chortled, "We'll get along famously. You tell me all the things about Jean I don't know, and I'll tell you all the things you should know."

"Molly," Jean said in mock severity, "you behave yourself."

Their conversation was interrupted by the arrival of another carriage.

Kirk and Del were even more amazed by the passengers who disembarked from this carriage: three prominent citizens of New Orleans, men that the brothers would never have believed had even heard of the pirate Lafitte. That was not all. Each man was accompanied by a lady who was not his wife. Jean urged them all inside for cool drinks and the comfort of his home.

They were hardly settled with their drinks when Garrett Flye's arrival was announced. He was followed by a carriage that held Madame Annabella Forge and her three daughters. Before long, at Jean's urgings, they were all chatting and drinking together like old friends. It was Jean's policy not to question the background or morals of the friends he had invited, although he knew much more about them than they did about him.

Molly and Tazia became immediate friends. Molly took her under her protective wing, and, drawing her away from the group, they sat together and talked. Soon they were laughing together like old friends. It did not take Molly long to notice the occasional drifting of Tazia's eyes toward Kirk's tall figure, as he stood in deep conversation with Jean and some of his friends.

"He's quite a handsome boy, that LaCroix, is he not?" Molly said softly, watching Tazia's face closely. Tazia flushed a little but held herself under tight control.

"Which one, Molly?"

Molly chuckled, "The one you've been watching for the last half hour."

Tazia's chin came up, and her eyes were haughty as she looked coolly at Molly. "I don't know what you're talking about, Molly. I'm sure I haven't given any particular notice to either of the gentlemen in question."

Aha, thought Molly. There's more here than meets the eye. This child is angry at someone or something.

65

I wonder. . . . At that moment her eyes met Jean's across the room. He grinned and lifted his glass in a silent promise. She nodded her head slightly and turned back to Tazia. She quickly changed the subject, and soon things were back to normal. Molly promised herself that she would soon corner Jean and find out what was going on.

But it was not until the wee hours of the morning, when all of the guests were settled in their rooms, that Jean heard the light knock on his door. He laughed to himself, for he knew who it was. Molly's curiosity would never have allowed her to sleep until she found out what was happening. He had invited her especially for that reason. She loved excitement, romance, and mystery. They were her main interests—after herself, of course.

He opened the door and smiled at her. "I wondered how long it would take you, Molly. According to my calculations you're about an hour late."

Molly guffawed. "If I were ten years younger and a hundred pounds lighter, I might have been here an hour ago, my love," she said as she sat on the edge of his bed and patted it suggestively. Jean threw back his head and laughed, but he walked over to sit beside her on the bed.

"Tell me exactly what's going on. There seems to be quite an attraction between LaCroix and Tazia. Are you playing matchmaker, Jean? That doesn't sound like you. You would be more likely to tumble the girl into bed yourself than to help someone else do so."

Jean's eyes became still and serious. Molly had known him many years, and he had helped her through a severe crisis in her life. In fact, he had once been the only person to stand between her and destruction. She loved him dearly and she understood

66

him completely. Now, as she watched his eyes darken, she realized that she had hit closer to home than he would ever admit.

Slowly Jean began to recount the situation to her, leaving out only his feelings for Tazia. She listened carefully, without interruption, until he was finished.

"So," she said, "that is the way of it? The girl is a fool. Maybe I should tell her the things I know of her brother."

"No, Molly, I don't want her hurt any more than necessary. I just want this violence out of her head. It would be best if we replaced it with something better."

Molly regarded him, narrowing her eyes shrewdly. "Why don't you make her forget, Jean? You're quite a man, you have everything in the world to offer a girl, and," she grinned, "you've quite a bit of experience." She was surprised when this remark brought not a chuckle but a deeper frown.

"She sees me only as a friend, and she trusts and depends on me completely. I won't jeopardize that faith, Molly. She has no idea how I feel, and neither of us will ever tell her." He looked directly at her as he said the last words slowly and firmly.

"All right," sighed Molly. "But I wonder who's the bigger fool here." Jean's annoyed glare made her hold up her hand. "I'll say no more. What is it you want me to do, Jean?"

He rose from the bed and began to pace as he spoke. "Get close to her, Molly. Become friends —friends enough for you to tell her about Baptiste and Paul and yourself." He stopped pacing and looked at Molly, whose face had paled, her eyes now distant and filled with pain. "I'm sorry, Molly. I don't mean to hurt you. But it is necessary just this one time to help another who might be doing the very thing you did. Do you understand?"

Molly's voice trembled slightly. "I do understand, Jean. I would never want that beautiful child to be in my place. I'll do everything in my power to stop her."

"Thank you, Molly. I knew I could depend on you."

"She's very attracted to this LaCroix boy. How does he feel about her?"

Jean grinned. "I don't think he knows it yet himself, but he's as in love with her as . . . ."

". . . as you are?" Molly added.

Jean nodded. "Our job is to bring them together before she finds out who killed her brother or, if possible, keep her from finding out at all."

"You're playing with fire, Jean. She's bound to find out, and she'll hate you."

"I'd rather have her hate me, Molly, than have to live with murder. I don't think she could survive it."

"Hmm, I know. It is a very difficult thing to live with."

"Suppose she had enough . . . hate or . . . courage to kill Kirk, and then found out about her brother. What do you think would happen to her then?"

"You're right. I'll do my part, you can rest assured. We can only hope and have faith that Le Bon Dieu will help with the outcome."

"Thank you, Molly. I'll be eternally grateful."

Molly's eyes twinkled. "Maybe I'll take advantage of your gratitude, chéri."

Jean gave an answering laugh. "You're a wicked woman, Molly, and I love you dearly. Go to bed before you lead me astray."

Molly gave a delighted chuckle at this remark and kissed him on the cheek. "Good night, Jean."

After he had closed the door behind her, his smile faded. He extinguished the lamp and walked to the window, drawing aside the curtain. He stood for a long time looking out into the dark, star-filled night, praying fearfully that he was doing the right thing for Tazia. Sacrificing her love for him, because her survival was the only way he could see out of the problem.

Molly's thoughts were as dark and deep as Jean's. He had opened a door in her mind that she had closed and tried to forget a long time ago.

"Baptiste," she murmured softly to herself as her eyes blurred with tears. Then she caught hold of herself. It was impossible to let herself go on this way without it destroying her. Instead, she turned her mind to Jean, Tazia, and Kirk. She promised herself that at the first opportunity that presented itself she would tell Tazia her story. Maybe she could do something to stop her from making the same mistake.

Jean had planned several activities for his guests. Their first desire, of course, was to tour Barataria and see firsthand the stronghold of one of the most notorious men of the day. Tazia, having spent much time there, was completely familiar with all the grounds. She was unprepared for Jean's request that she help him guide the guests around, but she had no reason to refuse. Molly chortled into her drink when she heard Jean blandly request that he wanted her to take Molly and Kirk and show them about. Behind everyone's back, Molly raised her glass in a toast to Jean, whose impassive face showed no sign of recognizing her salute to his cleverness.

His plan worked well, and, with Molly's cooperation, Kirk and Tazia were together every day. The results were plain to see on Kirk's face. He had eyes only for Tazia when he was in her presence. And he was restless and edgy when she was with anyone else or out of his sight. Jean detected the effects on Tazia through the subtle changes in her attitude toward Kirk.

For the sixth time in as many days, Molly excused herself when Tazia suggested a picnic lunch and a day out. Since Molly had decided not to go, Tazia and Kirk decided to ride instead of using the buggy. They left shortly after lunch, planning to picnic in late afternoon and to be back before dark. Jean stood at the stable door and watched them ride away. It was good that Tazia could not see his face, for his smile turned into a decidedly wicked grin, which would definitely have upset Tazia.

They rode in silence for a long time, absorbing all the beauty of the countryside. The air was warm and a breeze blew in from the Gulf, carrying the scent of flowers.

Tazia slowed her horse to wait for Kirk to ride beside her. Then they dismounted and walked the animals for a short time, side by side.

"Jean has found heaven on earth here at Barataria," Kirk said.

"Yes, it *is* lovely. But I prefer home," she replied.

"Casa del Sol," she said softly, her eyes seeing inward to the place where her heart lay, "is serenity, gentleness, and life—all in one. It is not just the house which is built of white stone and is long and cool with large airy rooms. Nor is it the stone patios with fountains of cool water. It is not the lovely gardens of my mother's or just the high green grass meadows in which my father raises the most beautiful horses. It is feeling, a feeling of being close to God as if it were made in heaven and given to us mortals as a precious gift.

"The mountains are not too high, just high enough to bring us the cool water we drink. The valley is fertile, giving life to everything planted there. When I am there, I feel as though I am one with it and when I am away I feel the emptiness of great loss. In the day we have the bright warmth of the life-giving sun, and at night," she sighed, "the nights are magic, the sky seems to be made of black velvet and the stars are so close you can reach out and pluck them from heaven."

"I'd love to see it sometime."

Tazia choked back the words of invitation she desired to speak instead replying softly, "It is. I love it very much." Then, to cover her thoughts, she said with a laugh, "I'll race you to that stand of trees!"

"You're on," he said, and they both urged their horses forward. She was pulling to a stop just inches ahead of him when the girth of her saddle snapped and she began to slip sideways. Seeing her predicament, Kirk came up alongside, grasped her about the waist, and pulled her free just as the saddle fell to the ground. In her fear, she flung her arm about his neck and clung to him as he brought his horse to a stop. He held her tightly against him, reluctant to set her free.

"Tazia, darling, are you all right?"

She didn't answer for a moment. Then she slowly lifted her eyes to his. Their gazes clung to one another for several long moments. Then, without words, he lowered his head and captured her lips with his.

10

Taken by surprise, Tazia's lips were soft and yielding under his for a few moments. Then she stiffened in his arms and drew back from him. The look in her eyes was unreadable. It was a good thing, for if Kirk had known the confusion his kiss had caused, he might have continued. And if he had continued, she thought for one panic-filled moment, she would have surrendered completely.

He looked down into her face and smiled.

"I'm not going to say I'm sorry, because I'm not."

"Please, put me down, Kirk," she said softly.

He held her against him for a few more seconds. Then he sighed and released her gently to the ground. He dismounted his horse and stood beside her.

"We're too far for me to walk back," she said.

"My horse can carry double," he suggested.

Tazia wanted nothing more than to spend an hour in Kirk's arms on the ride back.

"That's not necessary. I'm sure when my horse returns riderless someone will be sent to find out what the problem is."

Kirk was suddenly elated. She's afraid of me, he thought. Or she's afraid of *herself*.

"There's some cool shade over there under those trees. Shall we wait there for our rescuers?" She nodded, and they walked over into the shade without speaking. She sat down and leaned against a tree trunk while he tied his horse nearby. She watched Kirk as he walked toward her. Dressed in riding clothes, he was an extremely handsome figure. Sunlight drifting down between the trees picked up the golden highlights of his hair. His tanned face made his light-colored eyes more pronounced. His white teeth flashed in a smile as he sat down beside her, his shoulder touching hers. Now she was not so sure that riding back on one horse would not have been a better idea.

"Tazia, there's something I must say."

"Please, Kirk," she whispered, "I'd rather you didn't . . . not now, not here."

"There couldn't be a better time or place. Back at Lafitte's, it's impossible to get you alone for a minute."

Tazia started to rise, but Kirk held out his arm and stopped her. She looked directly into his eyes. This is what I wanted, she thought. So why am I afraid? Her mind whirled in confusion. Just the night before, Del had told her he cared deeply for her, but his kiss left her still in complete control of her feelings. Why, then, this sudden panic at Kirk's kiss? He gazed into her upturned face, her eyes wide and frightened. Her lips were parted, and he could feel the slight trembling of her body. He lowered his head slowly and sought again the sweet taste of her lips. Her head began to swim dizzily, and she was unprepared for the fiery glow that spread through her body. She only knew that she was losing herself in his kiss—and welcoming the loss. His lips parted hers and his tongue lightly touched the soft inner flesh of her mouth.

Her mind screamed urgently at her to stop, but her body knew only the awakening of her senses. She was aware of everything about him. Every nerve tingled in response to his touch. Her mouth parted willingly to accept him, and she put her arms around his neck, feeling the thick, silky hair that curled against the back of his neck. He whispered her name as his lips moved from her mouth down the soft skin to the tiny hollow of her throat, where he felt her pulse throbbing in response, down further to where the parting of her blouse created a valley between her breasts. Now his arms circled her tightly and pulled her against him. Slowly he worked the blouse loose from her riding skirt and slid his hand underneath it against her soft, velvet back, caressing it gently with the tips of his fingers and sending delightful tremors through her body. She felt as though she were on fire. It wasn't until she felt the touch of his hand against her breast that she realized he had deftly loosened the buttons of her blouse. Finally her mind began to awaken to what she was letting happen. He was smoothly turning the tables on her, and she was enjoying it.

He felt the sudden change in her, the slight stiffening of her body. He sought again to reclaim her lips with his.

Her mind fought fiercely for control of her wayward body. Think of Manolo, it raged. You are giving yourself like any common slut to the man who may have killed him. The thought helped her gain control of her careening world. She put her hands against Kirk's chest to push him away.

"Please . . . please, Kirk . . . stop."

"Tazia," he whispered, "I love you." He tried again to bring her closer to him, but now she was regaining her control. With a firm twist of her body, she moved away and stood up. She turned her back and began rearranging her clothes. She was reluctant to face him again. Hearing him move, she still did not turn. He came up behind her but did not touch her. She closed her eyes for a moment and could sense him with every nerve in her body. There was nothing she desired more than to turn and throw herself into his arms.

"Tazia?" he said softly.

She still did not turn around. Then he gently took her shoulder and turned her toward him. He put his hand under her chin and lifted her face.

"Look at me, Tazia," he said gently but firmly. She looked into his eyes, and what she saw there turned her legs weak. The warm affection stirred her beyond anything she had ever felt before.

"Kirk—"

"No, don't say anything. Just listen to me for one moment. I love you. I never thought I'd ever say that to someone and mean it as sincerely as I do. I know this is not the right time or place, and I'm sorry, but only because of that, not for wanting you. I love you, Tazia, I think I've loved you from the moment our eyes met. I'm a very stubborn man. I'm trying to warn you that when I want something as badly as I want you, I'll do everything in my power to have you. I won't step aside for anything or anyone." He cupped his hands on each side of her face. Then very gently he kissed her eyes, her cheeks, and finally her mouth. She could feel the desire deep inside him and his efforts to control it. A deep sadness suddenly filled her so painfully that she almost cried. Then his hands left her, and he stepped back.

"We'd better ride double. I think it's safer than staying here any longer," he said hoarsely. She nodded her head, not trusting herself to speak. They walked silently to where his horse was tied. He mounted, then reached down and effortlessly lifted her into the saddle. He held her around the waist, her back firmly against him. They did not speak again, but still she was aware of the steady beat of his heart and the feel of his hard-muscled arm around her.

They had almost reached the house when they met Jean and a stable boy coming toward them.

"Your horse came back without you and his saddle. We were worried you might be injured. Are you all right, Tazia?"

"Yes, I'm fine. My saddle girth broke and, luckily, Kirk caught me before I fell."

Jean pretended not to notice the flush in her cheeks and the tremor of her hands. "That was fortunate. You could have been badly hurt. Come, let's get you back to the house, where you can rest awhile before dinner."

"I'm perfectly all right, Jean."

"Nevertheless, I'll feel better if you get some rest." He pulled his horse around and started back the way he had come. The stable boy followed silently, wondering why, if Monsieur Lafitte was so worried about Mademoiselle de Montega, he had taken his time saddling his horse and then walked it all the way to where they met Kirk and Tazia. He shook his head and gave up wondering about all the strange things grown people did.

When they arrived, Kirk lifted Tazia down from his horse. He tried to catch her eye, but she kept her face averted.

"Thank you, Kirk," she said softly. Then she ran lightly up the stairs to her room, where she quickly closed the door behind her. She leaned against the door, her eyes shut, trying to erase from her mind the warmth of Kirk's mouth against hers and the strength of his arms around her.

At that moment, Jean was knocking on the door of Molly's room. He was mentally congratulating himself on the success of his plans when Molly opened the door.

"Jean, you look like the proverbial cat—you're actually licking the cream from your whiskers. Come in and tell me about it."

He explained as rapidly as he could what he had done and the result it had brought.

"You mean you deliberately cut that saddle girth? Jean, she could have been hurt!"

"No, Tazia is too good a horsewoman to get hurt. And I counted on Kirk to come to the rescue," he chuckled. Then, more seriously, he said, "I want you to go to her while she is still shaken, talk to her. Now is the right time. If we're going to change her mind about revenge, this may be the only chance we have to do it."

Molly sighed deeply. The agony of remembering was going to be hard on her, but she was willing to do anything to help Tazia, whom she had grown to like immensely since they had met.

"All right, Jean, I'll do my very best."

"I know it will work, Molly," he said quietly. "I want you to know I would never ask you if I didn't think the need was so great. I don't want to see another life ruined."

She patted his arm. "I know, Jean, I know."

He opened the door, letting Molly precede him into the hall. They walked together to Tazia's door, where he gave Molly a swift kiss on the cheek. "Good luck, Molly."

She watched him walk away from her, then raised

her hand and knocked on the door. A pale-faced Tazia opened it. Molly pointedly paid no attention to her color, or to the fact that she had been crying.

"Tazia, Jean just told me what happened. Are you all right, child?"

Bereft of anyone to confide in for so long, Tazia suddenly felt her courage crumble. "Oh, Molly," she said with a small, choked sob. Molly opened her arms and Tazia collapsed against her, crying.

"What am I to do, Molly? I'm so confused."

"Why don't you tell me what's wrong? Maybe I can help." She led Tazia to the bed and sat down beside her. She listened without interrupting while Tazia poured out the whole story, including her feelings for Kirk. When she had finished, she looked at Molly with wide, fear-filled eyes. "What should I do, Molly?" she whispered. "I cannot forget my brother."

"Tazia, I can't tell you what to do, but I can tell you something that may help you make up your mind."

Tazia looked at her questioningly.

"It's been fifteen years now," Molly began. "Fifteen long, lonely, miserable years. You may not believe it, but once I was as slender and pretty as you are. I met and fell in love with Baptiste Mireau. I was happy, carefree, and gay, and I thought the world was a beautiful place. Then Baptiste was called away to some business for his father. He sailed for France. I was very lonely, and when he sent for me, I was so excited I made passage on the first ship leaving for France. The captain of the ship was Paul LaFere. He frightened me, but I didn't hesitate to sail, because I could not wait to be with Baptiste."

Her voice became quiet, and she sat for a moment remembering. Then, slowly, she continued.

"Halfway through the trip, Paul began to make advances toward me. No matter what I said, he would accost me anywhere, anytime. I became very frightened and stayed in my cabin. Then one night, even that wasn't enough. He came to my cabin. I was not strong enough to defend myself." Tazia could hear the pain in her voice. "He took me that night and laughed at my tears and my fear. I could only beg him to leave me alone, but he paid no heed to my words. He returned night after night. I said I would tell the authorities, but he only laughed and said that many people died at sea. Then I really became terrified. I knew he did not plan for me to ever see Baptiste again. I knew I had to do something.

"When we were two days from France, I bribed the cabin boy with my jewelry to cut loose a lifeboat. Then I went over the side and collapsed into it. It took me four days to reach shore . . . four days without food or water. Hate kept me alive. Revenge was all I could think of. When I finally washed ashore, I was more dead than alive.

"The people who found me listened to my story and sent for Baptiste. Dear, sweet Baptiste. He tried so hard to help me, but I could only think of revenge. I ranted and raved—I even called him a coward for not avenging me. Then, when he could stand it no longer, he turned from me and went to find Paul to kill him . . . to make me smile again. Oh, God! How many times I have regretted my need for vengeance. How many nights I have cried.

"At last they met, and Baptiste accused him of abusing me. They fought, and Baptiste killed Paul, but not before he received a mortal wound himself. I sat by his side and nursed him, but it was no use. The fever claimed him . . . and he died. He died in my arms, begging me to be happy and to smile at him again.

"There was no life for me after Baptiste died. I met a man named Jasper Thatch. After a few weeks, we were married. I didn't care about anything at the time, so the fact that Jasper owned a house of prostitution meant nothing to me. Even the fact that he expected to use me in it did not touch me. Then Jean came along. How he knew my story I don't know. But he picked me up and took me aboard his ship. I was prepared for anything, but he never touched me. Slowly he put the pieces back together and gave me a new life. So you see, chérie, where revenge took me. It is a two-edged sword, Tazia. It kills the wielder as well as the victim. Don't let it kill you. Don't let it rob you of a man like Kirk and the love he has to offer."

11

Louis Plummer sat cross-legged on the deck of *La Mouette,* deftly constructing a rope from thin strands of fiber. He was a completely different man from the one who had been smuggled out of Lafitte's house onto the ship. His face was tan and he had slimmed down to hard muscles.

When Louis first came aboard, he was belligerent and antagonistic to everyone. He had thought the captain a barbarian when he was told he was expected to pull his own weight. His objection to physical labor had been very strong and very verbal. Then, slowly, as he began to work with the crew, he discovered he had a natural affinity for the sea. He had never felt more pleased with any accomplishment in his life than when the crew began to accept him as one of them. Eventually he and the crew established a kind of camaraderie, and he began to feel a contentment he had never felt before. Despite this, there was never a doubt about the fact that he was a prisoner. When they arrived at a port, he was locked in the captain's cabin. Still he enjoyed the friends he had made and the work he was doing. The only regret he had was not being able to get word to his sister, who he knew must be worried to distraction about him.

And he wondered what the situation was now between Tazia and his friends. Taking everything into
consideration, he was more contented with his life
now than he had ever been.

"Mornin' Plummer."

Louis looked up from his work. "Mornin' Jack."

"We gonna be in port in another two days. Maybe
if you gave the cap'n your word of honor you'd not
try to escape, you could go ashore with us for a while.
You must be damn tired of this ship."

"Now Jack, you know until he gets word from
Lafitte, he isn't going to let me out of his sight."

"Sure would like to take you ashore and show you
around. Bet you need a little somethin', eh?" Jack
grinned and nudged him in the ribs.

Louis chuckled. "I wouldn't mind, Jack."

"Well, the cap'n's takin' a likin' to you. I think he's
beginnin' to think you're a gentleman. Maybe he'd
take your word for one night out. Why don't you ask
him? You got nothin' to lose."

Louis considered this. He had a letter he had
managed to write to his sister in his pocket. All he
needed was someone to post it for him without the
captain's knowledge. If he could get on land, even for
one night, he was sure he could find someone to do it
for him. "Maybe I'll ask him. You're right, I've got
nothing to lose."

Jack grinned again. He was pleased with his idea.
He liked Louis, and he was impressed with Louis's
consideration for his friends and his special kindness
to him.

Jack was a small man, with arms so long he looked
a little like a monkey. Watching him swing about in
the rigging had shaken Louis at first, but then he
realized Jack was completely safe and quite at home
there. Jack's face could only be described as ugly. His

nose had been broken and had healed crookedly. He had lost several teeth in many fights and had had them replaced with gold, so his smile looked like a glittering patchwork quilt.

The only redeeming physical feature Jack had were twinkling blue eyes that continually found life an amusing adventure. It was Jack's sense of humor that had put Louis on an even keel after he was brought a board, and it led to their becoming good friends.

Louis put aside the rope he was working on and went below to the captain's cabin. He knocked on the door and, at the captain's request, stated his name.

"Come in, Mr. Plummer."

Captain Touseau was a tall, slender man of indeterminate age. His hair was dark and his skin tan and unlined, but his gray eyes had a knowledgable look that comes only with years of hard living. He and Louis had found that they shared a passion for chess, and they had spent many quiet evenings together at the chessboard, deep in concentration. Only once had Louis broached the subject of Captain Touseau's past and his friendship with Jean Lafitte. He never did it again, because the captain had simply closed him out and had not called him to his cabin for several days. Louis missed his intelligent company, so he apologized and never raised the subject again.

"Ah, come in, Louis. I was just about to go on deck. Was there something you wished to discuss with me?"

"Yes . . . uh . . . Captain Touseau, do you think it would be possible for me to go ashore with the men, just for one evening? I am thoroughly bored with being cooped up on this ship."

"Louis," the captain answered, with genuine sympathy in his voice, "you know I would if I could, but I fear it is impossible."

"If I stayed with Jack and the others and gave my word of honor not to try to escape, would you at least consider it?"

The captain's gray eyes met his across the room. They seemed to be looking into the depths of his soul. Louis desperately wondered what was he seeing. And he wondered why he wanted this man to trust him, for he had never given a thought to putting his honor on the line for such a person before. Why did it mean so much to him now? He waited, never letting his eyes leave the captain's. At that moment, he knew he would return to the ship if he had to crawl on his hands and knees.

"Louis, I must tell you one thing. My men and I know these parts like the backs of our hands. If you did manage to elude us, we would find you, and I would clap you in irons for as long as Jean wants you kept. It would not be pleasant. Do you understand?"

Louis's heart leaped. He was going to let him go. "Thank you. You'll never regret it. I'll return with the others just as I promised."

"I hope so, Louis. It will go quite hard on you if you don't."

Louis nodded and left the cabin. He was elated. He could hardly wait to tell Jack the news. He found he was as excited about going ashore as Jack was. He hadn't realized how long it had been since he had shared a comradely drink — or had a woman, for that matter. The two days before they sighted land were the longest Louis had ever spent. He was very impatient to be adventuring in this new place. Although Louis had traveled a great deal in his lifetime, it had never been under such circumstances but on well-organized trips that contained nothing of the adventure Louis longed for. He dressed in rough sailor's clothes and went up on deck to stand at the rail and watch their approach to the harbor. Inside his shirt, next to his body, was the letter he had written to his sister explaining his abduction. He had promised Captain Touseau that he would not try to escape, and he would not, but he had not promised not to write a letter. When they had docked and all the work details were done, the men were given permission to go ashore until dawn of the following day. Admonished once again by the captain, Louis was finally permitted to leave the ship.

Although they were now friends, Louis knew that Jack and the other men were watching his every move. Then, suddenly, he was absorbed in the sights and smells around him. The small town was a beehive of colorful activity. Vendors of every sort peddled their wares to the visitors disembarking from the ships, each calling loudly the value of what he was trying to sell. Women, old and young, plied a trade older than time, and Louis was offered promises of glorious nights at unbelievably small cost.

"Don't pay no attention to these whores. Most of 'em probably got the pox, anyway. Send you home with a nice dose of somethin' you have a hard time gettin' rid of," Jack said.

Louis laughed. "Some of them look pretty good to me."

"You been on ship too long, boy," chortled Jack. "You come with me and I'll show you where there's some real classy stuff."

Louis grinned and followed Jack as he elbowed his way through the crowd, pushing aside the women who tried to stop them. They made their way to a small, dimly lit cafe. Several men stood against the bar, and most of the tables were filled with men drinking, playing cards, or talking to women in bright-colored gowns.

"This here is Madam Keyo's place." Jack said quietly. "Behave yourself and there ain't nothin' you can't get here."

"And if you don't behave yourself?" Louis asked with amusement.

"You could find yourself floatin' in the ocean —very, very dead."

Louis looked closely at Jack, for he thought at first he was joking, but he could see that Jack was very serious. He was about to speak again when Jack broke in. "Let's have a drink, and I'll show you around."

Louis nodded, and they walked toward the bar. Jack paused several times to introduce Louis to friends of his. When they reached the bar, they ordered whiskey, and they had consumed several drinks before they began to look around for a free woman. The room they were in was large, one side taken up completely by the bar, behind which hung the largest picture of a naked woman Louis had ever seen. It must have been nearly twelve feet long. Directly across the room, a flight of red-carpeted stairs went up to several rooms on the second floor. There was no doubt in Louis's mind what these rooms were for. In the shadows at the end of the hall, another flight of stairs ascended to the third floor. Louis wondered if they were divided by the degree of cost or the degree of woman.

Louis sipped his drink and listened absently to Jack's conversation while his eyes drifted about. He was about to turn back to the bar when a woman started to come down the second flight of stairs. He watched her intently as she moved slowly down the stairs, as though she were reluctant to enter the room. Something in her manner, the erect carriage of her head, perhaps, gave Louis the impression she did not belong in this place. She was very slender, yet her body was curvaceous and feminine. Her hair was golden, the color of newly minted coins, and her skin was a soft, glowing pink. Louis thought she was very delicate and lovely. She went to the end of the bar and quietly said something to the bartender, who nodded his head. Then she turned and faced the room and let her eyes sweep over the crowd. When she reached Louis, her gaze rested for a moment on him, taking note of a new face, and then moved on.

"Now, *there's* a woman I'd like to meet," he said quietly to Jack, who turned to follow his gaze and almost choked on his drink. Louis, surprised, had to pound on his back to bring him under control.

"What's the matter, Jack, you look like you've seen a ghost."

"Louis, don't even think of layin' a hand on her. She's way out of your reach."

"Who is she?"

"Madam Keyo, that's who. And if you have any ideas in your head, forget them."

Louis looked at her with even more interest than before. Somehow, the idea of an untouchable woman in a place like this intrigued him.

Jack knew what he was thinking and gave a groan of despair. "You crazy bastard, don't try it, I'm tellin' you. She's had bigger than you chewed up and thrown away. She's *not* one of the girls around here," he added emphatically.

"Tell me about her," Louis said, ignoring Jack's vehement words.

"I don't know nothin' to tell. I don't think anyone else does either. All *we* know is her girls are clean, her liquor is good, and her tables are honest. Beyond that, no one knows a thing about her past, and no one can get close enough to find out."

"Just what keeps everyone from finding out about

her?"

Jack pointed over Louis's shoulder. "There's what keeps people from gettin' too nosy and causin' her any trouble."

Coming down the stairs was a huge black man. His glittering eyes took in every man in the room. He stood well over six feet tall, and Louis estimated that he must have weighed over two hundred and fifty pounds. From what he could observe, there was not an ounce of fat on him. His shoulders were broad and muscular, but it was his hands that Louis noticed most of all. They were huge, and they looked as though they could wring a man's head from his shoulders with a minimum of effort.

Louis turned his eyes again toward the blond vision at the other end of the bar, only to find her looking at him with amusement. He raised his glass to her and gave a slight bow before he drank its contents. He never took his eyes off her.

If she was surprised, she did not show it. To Jack's amazement, she raised her glass in return. The huge black was standing beside her now, watching Louis closely. She touched him gently on the arm, and when he turned to her, she said a few soft words to him. He glanced toward Louis and nodded his head, then made his way slowly to Louis's side.

"Miz Keyo wan' talk wif yo', suh," he said softly. There was no subservience in his voice. It told Louis very clearly that this was a royal summons, and he would go if he had to be carried.

Louis grinned. Causing a problem was not in his mind, for he wanted to talk to her even more than she wanted to talk to him. He walked slowly at the big man's side until he stood beside her.

"You wanted to talk to me ma'am?" he said with a slight bow.

12

Without turning around, Louis sensed that the black man had not left them, that he was watching every move.

"You're new here," she stated, rather than questioned. "Did you come in on *La Mouette* with Jack?"

"Yes, we arrived today."

She continued to study him. "You're not an ordinary seaman, despite your clothes, and I know all the men from *La Mouette*. I would say from your accent you're from . . . New Orleans?"

He chuckled. "Correct. And I would say from yours, you're from . . . Mississippi? Georgia?" He felt the man behind him give a startled exclamation, and he did not miss the warning look that leaped into her eyes and then vanished as quickly as it came.

"You're close," she laughed. "Actually, Virginia. You've made me curious Mister . . . ?"

"Plummer, Louis Plummer at your service ma'am." He gave another slight bow. "How have I made you curious?"

"Because, Mr. Plummer, despite your attire, you very obviously do not belong here, and that arouses my curiosity. Just where do you belong, Louis Plummer?"

He smiled again. "I might ask the same of you. If I

have ever seen the proverbial fish out of water, it's you. What's a lovely Southern lady like yourself doing not only *in* a place like this but *owning* it, as well? You must admit it's enough to rouse the curiosity of any gentleman."

" 'Gentleman.' I think you have put your finger on the problem, Mr. Plummer. You're a *gentleman* from New Orleans, traveling on one of Jean's ships, dressed as an ordinary seaman, and watched, I would say, rather closely by your shipmates."

"Jean's ship!" Louis said quickly. "I take it you know Lafitte."

A low, guttural sound came from the man behind him, and the woman's eyes suddenly became blank and cool.

"Do not ask so many questions Mr. Plummer," she said softly. "It is not conducive to your continued good health. Suffice it to say, I have many friends in many places. Keep your curiosity under control while you are here, or you may remain here longer than you choose."

Louis was stunned by her unveiled threat, and she turned and started to move away from him before he regained his wits.

"Wait!" he said, as he started to move toward her retreating form. An arm blocked his way, and he looked up into the cold, dark gaze of her bodyguard.

"Mind yo'self, suh," he said quietly. "Don' try to follow the lady. If she wan' talk to yo' some more, she send for you. If not, best yo' keep yo' mouth shut and move on."

Louis did not doubt for a moment the man would drop him where he stood if he tried anything. "All right, nemesis." Louis laughed and shrugged his shoulders and moved away from that deathly gaze.

When he returned to Jack's side, he was met with a

reproving chuckle. "I warned you, Louis. What happened, did you get your fingers burned?"

"I think there's more than my fingers burning," he answered, and they laughed together. But Louis continued to think about the beauty that had just touched him.

The rest of the evening was a delight for Louis, who had been away too long away from such amusements. He thoroughly enjoyed everything, most of all the girl who had somehow found her way to his side. Although she was young, her eyes were old and wary. She said her name was Theresa, but he doubted very much if it was her real name. He didn't want to get her alone too soon, for it might arouse Jack's suspicion. But he intended to see if a few extra coins would buy him the added service of posting his letter.

After much laughter and talk—and a little more drinking than he really wanted—he finally began to make it obvious that he wanted to get the girl alone. Pretending to be more drunk than he really was, he began to kiss and fondle her, while she tried half-heartedly and with much laughter to push his hands away. This prompted Jack to further explorations. Finally Theresa stood up and pulled him to his feet.

"Come with me," she laughed.

"Theresa, are there any windows in your room?"

"No, why?"

"Go along with her, Louis, I know you'll enjoy yourself. Theresa's a great girl to spend a long night with."

Jack's remark was greeted with renewed laughter from his shipmates. Theresa drew an unhesitant Louis away from the crowd and up to her room.

The room was practical for its use: bare of everything except a bed. It would have been obvious to anyone that it was only her place of employment. To Louis, at that moment, it could just as well have been a dark cave. All that was in his mind at the moment was the softness of the willing woman in his arms and her moist, warm lips, which he kissed again and again. He felt the ache in his groin caused by long abstinence from such luxuries. He pulled away her clothes and caressed her soft, warm body. She helped him undress, laughing at his urgency, and they fell together on the bed. She was filled with fire as her body answered his.

Theresa was one of the best at her trade. Her hands, mouth, and body drove him to a frenzy of desire.

When he finally rolled away from her, they lay quietly for a while. If Theresa had known his thoughts at that moment, she would probably have been furious. Even though he had just had a very willing woman, an untouched desire boiled deep inside him. Her blond beauty hovered in the back of his mind.

Damn! he thought, I don't even know her first name, and I want her as I've never wanted a woman before in my life. The soft scent of her perfume lingered with him, and he wished it were somehow possible to see her again. He knew as soon as he left the room Jack would have to get him back to the ship. His mind scrambled desperately to formulate some plans.

He turned to Theresa, who smiled at him. Slowly he lifted her hand to his lips and kissed her fingers gently. She said nothing, but her eyes registered surprise at his gentleness. She had had many men, but no one had ever treated her with such consideration after he had possessed her. She had expected from this sailor a few coins thrown on the bed and a hasty departure to rejoin his friends. Instead, he wooed her slowly and gently, kissing her cheeks, then her throat, caressing her until she felt the warmth of desire flow through her. Then he took her again, as tenderly as one takes a beloved, and Theresa's hard inner core melted like snow in the summer sun. Louis knew then that he had just bought more than possession of her body for one night.

They were met with a great deal of laughter and bawdy remarks when they finally did come out of her room, but for the first time in many years Theresa did not feel like a whore. Louis smiled at her as they prepared to leave.

"Take care, Theresa. I hope to see you again one day," he said quietly.

"Thank you, Louis . . . for many things. You are mucho hombre, and I shall never forget you. *Vaya con Dios.*"

She watched them leave and then walked to the bar and ordered a drink. This time she paid for it herself with the money Louis had given her. For the rest of the night, she would belong only to herself, to no man. For this she was grateful to Louis. Grateful enough that she would post the letter Louis had given her, without question and without telling a soul about it.

Jack wondered at Louis's silence on the ride back to the ship, but he laughingly dismissed it as exhaustion.

"Christ, boy, over two-and-half hours in there with Theresa. Couldn't you get it ready, or was it too ready?"

"Mind your own business, Jack," he answered with a grin. "That's something you'll never know."

Jack chuckled, but he kept quiet for the rest of the

trip back to the ship.

It must be near dawn, Louis thought as they staggered up the gangplank. Something was wrong, and for a time he could not put his finger on what it was. Then it came to him. There were no preparations being made for leaving, and they were supposed to sail with the morning tide. He made his way to the bridge, where the first mate stood watching their arrival.

"Mr. Gunner, sir."

"Yes, Mr. Plummer?"

"I thought we were sailing with the morning tide?"

"As you see, Mr. Plummer, we are not."

"Yes, I see, but why?"

"That's not your affair—or mine, Mr. Plummer. We just follow orders. By the way, Captain Touseau would like to see you in his quarters."

"Now?"

"He said as soon as you came aboard. I imagine that means now."

Louis said nothing more. Instead he went directly below to Captain Touseau's cabin. A tingling along his spine gave him the premonition that the change of plans had something to do with him, but he couldn't figure out just what the connection could be. A light rap on the door brought an immediate answer from within, and Louis wondered if the captain were up early or if he had been up all night. He stepped inside the cabin and closed the door behind him.

"You wanted to see me, sir?"

The captain looked intently at Louis for some time before he spoke. Then he broke the tension with a slight smile. "I see you're a man of your word, Louis. I'm glad."

"Begging your pardon, Captain." Louis said dryly.

"But the bodyguard I had, it would have been impossible for a mouse to have escaped."

"Still, you did not try, and I'm pleased."

"Is that what you wanted to see me about?" Louis asked rather stiffly.

Captain Touseau chuckled. "Don't get your hackles up, you know that what I'm doing is by orders, not by choice."

"I'm sorry, sir. But I'm very tired, and I'm not thinking clearly."

"Well, you'll have plenty of time to rest. We'll be here for a while. There's a problem with the ship, and we have some repairs to be done."

The words did not ring true to Louis. He did not know the ship very well yet, but he knew there had been no problems on their arrival. How did they suddenly develop? Louis took a deep breath to ask a question when it hit him: perfume in the captain's cabin! Not just perfume but *familiar* perfume—and it had only been a matter of hours since he had first smelled it. She'd been here, and not too long ago. She knew Lafitte, and she'd been responsible for the change of plans. A million questions tumbled about in his mind, but he did not voice any of them. No, if she wanted him to remain here, it was because she wanted to see him again, and that fit in with his desires completely. What he really wanted to know were her connections with Lafitte and how she was able to get Captain Touseau to change plans Lafitte had given him. He knew it was only a matter of time before he found the answers to his questions. For now, he did not intend to say anything to make the captain suspicious, lest he change his plans again.

"Well, I hope there's nothing seriously wrong with the ship, sir."

"No, nothing serious. Just enough to keep us in

port for a few days."

"That's good, sir. May I go now, sir? I'm really tired."

"Of course. Good night."

"Good night, sir."

Louis left the captain's cabin but did not go below to bed. Instead, he went on deck and leaned against the rail, watching the town begin to stir in the first light of dawn.

The first move had to be hers, and he prayed she did not wait too long to make it. He felt elated. His letter was on its way, and now that he was sure his sister would know of his safety, he didn't care if they stayed in port forever.

Too keyed up to sleep, Louis threw himself into work that day and fell into an exhausted sleep that night. After three days of the same routine, he began to wonder if he had been imagining it all. Then, on the fourth day, he looked over the rail and saw the huge black man standing on the dock at the foot of the gangplank. It was one of the greatest sights Louis had ever seen. He wanted to shout with delight. Instead, he walked to the head of the gangplank, looked down at him, and said coolly, "Can I do something for you?"

The huge man grinned. He knew people, and he knew Louis was anxious to learn why he was there. "Miz Keyo wan' talk wif yo', you come wif me," he stated firmly.

"I'll have to ask the captain's permission to leave the ship," replied Louis.

The man gave a short nod of his head. "You ask, I'll wait." He leaned against the rope-rail of the gangplank and folded his arms across his barrel chest.

Louis spoke to the captain and was not at all surprised when he got no argument from him. Everything had obviously been well-planned.

"Give me your word you won't try to escape, Louis. That will be sufficient."

"You have it, Captain. I will return as soon as possible."

"I'm sure you will," the captain replied with a grin.

They both knew that the man waiting for Louis would see to it that he did not alter his plans. He rejoined the black and was led silently to a waiting carriage. They sat opposite each other during the ride, and although Louis tried conversing with him, he was answered with guttural grunts. He finally gave up. Whatever was in store for him, he was not going to know about it from this man. He sat back in the carriage seat and waited patiently for whatever was to come.

13

The guests gathered for Jean's last dinner party before leaving Barataria. Kirk waited impatiently for the last few people to join them before going in to dinner. Tazia had not come down yet, and Kirk's eyes kept straying toward the stairway. For over a week, she had managed to never be alone with him. Despite his maneuvering, she always seemed able to evade him. He had also noticed a subtle difference in her: she was quieter, more contemplative. Often he would see her close into herself as though she were caught up in deep thoughts that demanded all her being.

Kirk's eyes were not the only ones that watched Tazia closely. Jean and Molly were both observing the change in her, too. After what Molly had told Tazia, they had become even closer friends. Molly understood the mental battle Tazia was fighting, and she prayed she would make the right decision and discontinue seeking revenge. She also hoped nothing would happen to disclose her and Jean's parts in the situation.

When Tazia finally arrived amid laughing chatter, they all went in to eat. Jean sat at the head of the table, with Tazia at his right. Del sat across from her, and Kirk sat on her right. Conversation flowed brightly. Tazia seemed to have a new magnetic sparkle. After watching her animated conversation for some time, Jean suddenly realized that she had fought the battle with herself and had successfully reached a decision. It was obvious from the way she leaned toward Kirk, listening intently to every word he was saying, that she had decided in his favor. Jean wanted to shout with pure delight.

Kirk himself did not realize what was happening for a few minutes. Then suddenly it burst into his consciousness. He felt exuberant. He wanted to gather Tazia up in his arms and carry her out of the room to where he could kiss her at his leisure.

Del realized the truth at almost the same time. Although he hated to do it, he knew he had to accept defeat, for the look in Tazia's eyes was not to be ignored. He raised his wineglass to his brother and smiled. "I always pay my debts, Kirk. I guess I owe you one now."

Kirk smiled broadly and raised his glass in response.

During dinner Kirk hardly knew what he was eating, for all his senses were filled with the lovely woman at his side. He couldn't wait for dinner to end, but it was almost an hour and a half later before they rose from their seats to have drinks and dance in the ballroom. As they entered, Kirk took Tazia's hand and led her out through the large French doors into the garden, where he tucked her hand under his arm and they walked through the flower-scented garden in relaxed silence.

At the opposite end of the garden he turned toward her. They didn't speak, for words were not necessary. Slowly he drew her toward him until they were almost touching. There was a current flowing between them that would have been impossible at that moment for either of them to break. He reached up and touched her smooth cheek with his fingertips, tracing the line of her jaw to her lips. Inhaling the soft perfume she wore, he could feel a throbbing desire for her course through him. She never took her eyes from his, and they spoke volumes to him that he instinctively understood.

Putting both hands around her slender waist, he drew her against him, absorbing the warm softness of her body. They seemed to flow together and join as one. He murmured her name against the silken softness of her hair. Still she did not speak, but held him as tightly and lay her head against his shoulder. A deep sigh escaped her as she surrendered completely to the joy of the moment and the feeling of contentment and belonging that his arms gave her.

After they had stood together quietly for a time, Kirk put his hands on her shoulders and held her slightly away from him. Then he lifted her face with the tips of his fingers under her chin, asking without words . . . . She answered with her eyes.

Slowly he bent his head and kissed her lips gently. They were warm and soft under his. Time stood still for them as he pulled her tighter into his embrace. Slowly her lips parted under his, and he felt her body begin to tremble in response. He knew that if he possessed her forever he would still never have enough of her. He wanted her now, as he had never wanted another woman before in his life.

With this knowledge came the realization that a lie stood between them. What if she found out the truth? What would she do, turn from him in hatred? He could not bear the thought of her looking at him with hatred or turning away from him. He decided then that he must take her away to a place where they could live together in peace, without the past hanging over their heads, threatening to destroy their new-found happiness.

"Tazia?" he said softly.

She tipped her head up to look at him. Her eyes were aglow with the joy of loving.

A lump formed in his throat, and for a few minutes he was speechless at the wonder of what was happening. "I love you," he said quietly. "Deeply and with my whole heart. I feel I've loved you since the beginning of time, and I shall love you 'til the end."

"Kirk, *mi amore,* there is something I must tell you."

His heart skipped a beat. He did not want her to confess to him, for that would only make his part in the conspiracy harder to bear. He pulled her back tightly into his arms, as he spoke softly. "Just tell me that you love me as I love you, Tazia. That is all that matters from this moment on. Anything that is past is past. Let's forget everything that came before us. We'll live for tomorrow and all the tomorrows after."

"But—"

He put a finger to her lips.

"Tell me, Tazia! Tell me what I want to hear."

"I love you, Kirk."

"Then that's enough. Nothing else has any importance. Believe in my love for you, no matter what. I told you that I'm a very stubborn man. I'm also very selfish. I want you for myself for as long as we live, and I will never give you up for any reason."

Tazia, who had never had the love of her parents, who had been used ruthlessly by her brother, suddenly found herself responding completely to the warmth of Kirk's love. She put her arms around his neck and drew his face down to hers. Their lips blended in a kiss that shattered all her stony walls and flooded her with the warm love she needed so badly.

Kirk felt as though he were holding a live flame in his arms. He drew her tightly to him, as if he could never hold her close enough. It was not enough; it would never be enough. They separated. Both of them realized this was not the time or the place, that they could not continue to touch as they were without being lost. He put his arm around her waist, and they walked slowly back through the garden to the ballroom. Once there, he was still reluctant to let her go, so he swung her out onto the ballroom floor, where they swayed together to the music.

Caught in the magic of their love, they did not notice the reactions of the people around them. Jean was happy for them, yet he felt a deep wrench of painful desire for something that he wanted but knew could never be. And Del knew that no matter how he felt about her, Tazia could never have the same feelings for him. Unable to love his brother less for loving Tazia, he wisely put his emotions in their proper perspective and loved them both.

Only one pair of eyes watched them coldly, calculatingly, and with an emotion closer to hatred. Garrett watched them dance together, his desire for Tazia unchanged, a feeling of hot lust roaring through him, mingled with a malevolent hatred for Kirk.

"They make a beautiful couple," came a mild voice at his side. Masking his feelings, which Garrett was expert at doing, he turned to face the speaker. It was Del speaking as he watched the dancers.

"Yes," Garrett said softly. "Let us hope they both get everything they deserve."

Something stirred in Del when he heard Garrett's answer, and he turned to look at him. Garrett's face was empty of emotion. There was no hint of the inner turmoil he was experiencing, yet an alarm rang in

Del's mind, and he promised himself to warn Kirk as soon as possible.

Later that night, when all the other guests were asleep, Kirk and Jean sat together in the library, sipping wine and talking.

"I've got to get her away from here, away from anyone who might tell her about what happened."

"One can not run away from one's fate, Kirk. It is impossible. Whatever will be, will be."

Kirk was silent for a few minutes. Then he replied thoughtfully. "Maybe you're right, Jean, and maybe you're not. I intend to do my best to see that she never finds out what really happened, to make her forget everything but our future."

"Kirk, don't delude yourself. The first thing she will want to do is talk to her parents. Once back in their grasp, she will be lost."

"Not if I'm there to stop it."

"There! Don't be ridiculous. You can't go back there with her. Her parents are clever, and they worshipped Manolo. Neither of them knew what he was. You would suffer an . . . unfortunate accident if they ever found out you were even a *participant* in that game."

"How could I refuse to go home with her without her finding out the truth? She would have to tell them a lie: that I was not even connected with Manolo's death. Would she do that?"

Jean sighed in frustration. "Not if she were back in their power. Kirk, take her somewhere miles away. Make a new life. Don't ever return to Casa del Sol."

"We're going back to the city tomorrow. The longer we stay there, the more dangerous it will become. I'm going to do my best to get her to marry me right away instead of going home. I have some friends in Virginia. I'll take her there. After we've

103

been married for a while, then we can take a trip to her home. Maybe then they will not be so suspicious of me."

"That's an excellent idea. I wish you good luck in convincing her and—" A knock on the door silenced both men.

"Come in," Jean called.

Del opened the door and stepped inside, closing it behind him only after he had checked carefully to see if anyone else was around.

"Del, come in. Have a glass of wine," Jean said.

"Thank you." Del turned to Kirk after he had taken the wineglass from Jean. "Kirk, I have to tell you something. I'm not sure I'm even right about it. It's mostly intuition."

"What?"

"Well, tonight when you and Tazia came in from the garden . . . well . . . ah . . . the situation was pretty obvious to everyone."

Kirk chuckled but did not say anything, and Del proceeded to tell him what Garrett had said and to describe how he felt about it.

"You're imagining things, Del. Why would Garrett have anything against me?"

"Christ, it's obvious. He wants Tazia."

Kirk stiffened, and the smile disappeared from his face. "Tazia!"

"You've been so busy you haven't noticed the way he's reacted to the situation. He's a dangerous man to have at your back, Kirk."

"I thought you three were friends?" Jean said.

"More drinking friends than real friends," answered Kirk absently. "Del, do you really think this is serious?"

"I think you should watch yourself—and him. The way he was looking at Tazia tonight . . . yes, I think

104

it's serious. I think he wants her badly, and I think he wouldn't stop at too many things to get her."

"Then all the more reason for me to get her away from New Orleans. Jean, before we leave tomorrow, I'm going to ask her. While I go back to New Orleans to wind up my affairs, will you keep an eye on her for me?"

Jean laughed. "I've been keeping an eye on her for years. I guess a few more days won't make a big difference."

The three men discussed their plans for a while longer and then retired for the night. They were so sure of what they intended to do that they did not take into consideration the malicious hand of fate, which often upsets the best-laid plans of ordinary mortals. She was about to make her presence known in a way that would stun all three men and change the course of each of their lives.

14

Jeanette Plummer held the letter in her hand and continued to stare at it long after she had read the contents. Louis had tried to explain everything to her without causing her to panic. He told her at the end of the letter that he was content, he would write to her again as soon as possible, and she was to do nothing more to find him. In due time he would be home.

Louis had been a completely changed man when he had written the letter, but this was something Jeanette did not know. She only remembered the boy who had disappeared: spoiled, selfish, and, she thought, completely unable to take care of himself. What must he be going through, she thought. Poor Louis! She must do something to get him back to the safety of his home, to restore his shattered life. Jeanette read things into the letter that had not been intended. She saw her baby brother brutalized and beaten, unable to get help from anyone. In the unaccountable way of a woman, she blamed Kirk and his friends, and she was determined to find some way to do something about it.

Her first move was to call at the LaCroix home, only to find that they were both guests of Jean

Lafitte. Putting two and two together and coming up with five, she prepared to go to Barataria to discover what they were up to and to demand the immediate release of her brother. She sent for her carriage. When it arrived, she told the driver to take her down to the dock, where she had no trouble hiring a boat to carry her to Barataria.

Jean and Tazia stood at the dock and said their farewells to Kirk, Garrett, and Del. Then, as fate would have it, one of Jean's captains sent for him, and he left Tazia for a short time to settle a minor dispute.

Tazia was happier than she had been for a long, long time. She had a horse saddled and rode it over the path she and Kirk had previously followed. Then she sat under the tree where she and Kirk had sat. Closing her eyes, she could still feel the strength of his arms and the pressure of his mouth against hers. She had followed Molly's advice and put aside everything except Kirk. Now she tried to put things in perspective. She could not believe that Kirk had anything to do with killing her brother. Kirk would come home with her to Casa del Sol, and she would convince her parents. They would have to find another way to track down the man who had shot her brother. Deep inside she felt it was Garrett Flye, and she was going to tell her parents so. Firmly setting things in her mind, she mounted her horse and rode slowly back to the house. For the first time in a very long while, she was completely at ease.

Tazia dismounted at the stable and flashed a bright smile at the stable boy who handled the horse. She walked to the house, wearing the same black riding skirt and white blouse she had worn the day she rode with Kirk for the first time. Her hair was parted in the center and drawn back tightly to a chignon at the nape of her neck. Her dark blue eyes glowed with happiness. In fact, she even hummed a little to herself as she opened the front door and stepped inside. Philippe was there to meet her.

"Did you have a nice ride, miss?" He smiled pleasantly at her.

"Oh yes, Philippe. It's a lovely day."

"You have a visitor, miss."

"A visitor? Who?"

"A Miss Plummer."

"Oh dear, Miss Plummer. Are you sure she asked for me, not Jean?"

"Oh no, miss. She asked for you."

Tazia chewed thoughtfully on her lip while she contemplated this turn of events. Then she shrugged her shoulders. She would simply tell her the truth. She was sure that as a woman she would understand. Then she would tell her that they would release Louis safely as soon as possible.

"Where is she, Philippe?"

"In the library, miss. Shall I serve tea?"

"Yes, Philippe, that would be fine, thank you."

Tazia walked to the library and stepped inside, closing the door quietly behind her.

Jeanette stood up and turned toward the door when she heard it open. The two women faced each other across the room. Jeanette was an attractive young woman. She resembled her brother in that she was fair-haired and blue-eyed. Her hair was parted in the middle, drawn back behind her ears, and gathered in a mass of soft curls. She was slender and small-boned giving her a somewhat fragile appearance that belied the real strength of the woman.

"You are Tazia," she stated softly. Her blue eyes were observant of everything about Tazia, who looked at her in mild surprise at her knowledge.

"Yes, and you are Louis Plummer's sister."

"Where is my brother?" Jeanette said coldly.

"At this moment, Miss Plummer, he is safe aboard a ship named La Mouette, and he will be brought home to you as soon as possible."

"I knew it. I knew he had been kidnapped. But you are wrong. He is not on a ship now. I just received a letter from him that I think he was forced to write."

"A letter . . . forced . . . how did he . . . ?" Tazia was taken by surprise, but she quickly gathered herself together. "Miss Plummer, I assure you your brother has come to no harm. You have nothing to worry about. If you will sit down, I will explain everything to you. I am sure you will understand."

Jeanette sat down slowly on the edge of the chair. "I should like to hear this," she said quietly.

Philippe came in with the tea tray, and both women were silent until he left the room again. Tazia poured a cup of tea for each of them and then sat back in her chair and studied Jeanette for a moment. She was an intelligent-looking woman. Tazia began the story with the abduction of Louis, but she left uncertain the reasons for her desiring to meet Kirk and the others. Hoping that Jeanette would not ask too many questions, Tazia fabricated a story she hoped would satisfy her.

"That is an interesting story," Jeanette said softly, although she believed none of it. She did not want to antagonize Tazia until she was sure of her brother's safety. "I have your word my brother will be returned soon, unharmed?"

"You not only have *my* word, but Jean's, as well."

"A pirate!"

"Jean is a man whose word means a great deal. He is, if you must call him a pirate, an honorable pirate."

Jeanette said nothing more. She rose and looked at Tazia for a long time. Tazia's eyes never left hers.

"Do not think I will be silent, Tazia," she said quietly. "If my brother is not returned to me in a reasonable time, I shall shout from the rooftops. We are not without influence. Our name means a great deal to the governor and others of importance. Believe me, I shall not keep silent."

"Nor would I expect you to," replied Tazia. "If it were *my* brother I would feel the same. I assure you again: he will be returned soon, completely unharmed."

Jeanette took out Louis's letter and handed it to Tazia. "When you have time, read this. I think you, too, will be quite surprised."

Tazia took the letter, folded it, and put it in the pocket of her riding skirt. She walked Jeanette to the door and stood for a long time watching the carriage as it disappeared. She intended to read the letter as soon as she went back inside, but Jean's arrival caused her to forget it. After she and Jean had talked awhile and made plans for their trip to New Orleans in a few days, she went upstairs, where her bath had been prepared. Being both mentally and physically exhausted, she discarded her riding clothes without remembering the letter.

Later, when she had gone back downstairs for dinner, her maid came to clean up the room. As she was picking up Tazia's discarded clothing, she heard the rustle of paper and withdrew the letter from the skirt pocket. She then put the letter inside her mistress's jewelbox for safekeeping. By the time Tazia had retired for the night, she had completely forgotten about the letter.

*   *   *

110

Tazia hummed to herself as she prepared the things she would take away with her. It had been a long time since she had been truly happy, she thought. In fact, she could not remember a time when she had felt this way, for she had never known anyone who loved her as Kirk said he did. He had asked her to marry him before he left Barataria, and she had accepted. She wanted to take him home to her parents and be married there, for deep inside she still desired the love and acceptance of her parents. They would love Kirk as much as she did, she thought, and somehow they would put together the pieces of their lives, and Kirk would help fill the void left by her brother's death.

The days passed slowly, as she waited impatiently for Kirk's return. He also chafed at the slowness of time while he made wedding preparations. It was something he had not told Tazia about yet. He still had to convince her that they should marry and take a honeymoon before going home. He intended to prolong the honeymoon as long as possible.

Jean wanted them to be married at his home in New Orleans. After some persuasion on Kirk's part, Tazia finally accepted. Jean gave Kirk the key to his home and a letter to his caretaker. Kirk was to make all the preparations and then come to Barataria to get them. Meanwhile, Tazia had hired a dressmaker to make a wedding gown for her from her own design.

A few evenings later, Tazia and Jean were just finishing dinner when the sound of an arriving carriage broke the night silence.

"Kirk," Tazia said softly as she rose from her seat.

Jean smiled. This was the way he wanted to see her, face aglow and softened by love, not filled with anger and hardened by pain.

As soon as Kirk walked into the room and their eyes met, all others were forgotten. He put out his arms to her, and she stepped inside them. He enfolded her in his embrace and held her close to him.

"God," he whispered, "it's been so long since I've held you."

She closed her eyes and enjoyed the security and peace his embrace gave her.

Jean chuckled and said, "I have to get you two married as soon as possible."

"Not soon enough for me," Kirk answered. "Everything is ready." He turned a warm gaze on Tazia. "All I need is my bride."

"I'm ready, and so is Jean. I'm all packed. Do we leave tonight?"

"Right now. The wedding's first thing in the morning."

Tazia turned to Jean. "You will give me away, won't you, since my father cannot be here?"

"I would have been crushed had you asked anyone else. After all, I feel I'm responsible for bringing you two together."

Tazia missed the surprised look Kirk threw Jean at the blatant reference to his interference in their affairs.

Tazia was bubbling with happiness and laughed and chattered freely on the ride to New Orleans, where they were greeted by Del and a houseful of friends who had been invited for the wedding the next day. Nothing could dim Tazia's gaiety on this beautiful evening as she moved gracefully from person to person, causing them to smile at her joy. Kirk's eyes followed her everywhere she went. He reveled in her beauty and in her acceptance by his friends. His look of adoration was remarked upon often and rather wickedly by his brother and some of his friends, who offered several reasons for Kirk's enraptured gaze.

The next day Tazia awoke with the dawn. She lay still for a long time. The house was quiet and she was alone with her dreams . . . and her memories. Manolo. Was she betraying him by loving Kirk? She fervently prayed she was not. Both Molly and Jean had assured her over and over again that she had a right to search for happiness for herself. And she was happy, happier than she had ever been before. So happy, in fact, that she was afraid something would happen to spoil it.

She was about to get up when she heard a light rap on the door. Her young maid came in to tell her with a shy smile that some of the guests were arriving and it was time for her to dress. She bathed slowly, luxuriating in the warm, scented water. She wanted to be perfect for this day of all days. She regretted that her parents were not here, but Kirk assured her that they would go to her home after the honeymoon. Her maid coiled her hair on top of her head, drawing it back from her face. Then came the gown: soft, shimmering folds of satin, caressing her body from under her bodice to the floor. The top was made entirely of lace, with its neckline high about her throat. The sleeves were long and fitted, the lace showing glimpses of her ivory skin. Then an ivory-colored comb, over which was draped a white lace mantilla that hung to the floor. A drop of perfume, and she was ready. She surveyed herself in the full-length mirror. Happiness made her eyes shine and turned her cheeks a bright pink. Satisfied, she turned toward the door.

Kirk stood by his brother and watched Tazia and Jean come slowly down the staircase. There was a half smile on her face, and her eyes glowed like two brightly lit candles.

I'd like to keep her as happy as she is now, he thought. As God is my witness, I'll not let anything hurt her again.

She stopped beside him, and as Jean stepped away, she looked up into his eyes. He could feel the current spring between them, and he had to fight the desire to reach out and hold her.

The vows were said, first by Kirk, then repeated very softly by Tazia. "'Til death do us part," she finished, as the pressure of Kirk's hand emphasized what he was telling her in words.

The priest intoned the last of the ceremony and then smiled at Kirk. "You may kiss the bride."

Kirk pulled Tazia into his arms and softly whispered, "I love you," as his lips claimed hers.

The rest of the day was spent laughing, eating, and drinking with well-wishing friends. When the music started for the evening's festivities, Kirk swung Tazia onto the floor for the first waltz. They were so engrossed in one another and so deeply in love that the guests became hushed for a few moments just to watch.

Del chuckled. "They make a beautiful couple. I hope you have room for another guest, Jean."

"Another guest?"

"Yes, I've turned the entire house over to them for tonight. I've arranged everything for when they arrive home."

"You are a welcome guest, *mon ami*. Let us toast the happy couple." He raised his glass. "May God bless their lives and make their future a happy one."

"Amen," responded Del softly. He sipped his drink, but his eyes were on a dark figure who stood in the shadow of a doorway across the room. "Amen," he muttered again.

—15

They were silent as they rode together in the carriage toward Kirk's home. Tazia sat with her head on Kirk's shoulder, his arm about her tightly. They were both contented.

"Kirk?"

"Ummm?"

"Kirk, I must speak to you about something."

He tilted her chin up, and in the semidark she could see the warm glow of his eyes. He kissed her gently, a light touch of his lips on hers.

"Speak to me of love tonight, Tazia, my beautiful wife. Let's not let anything of the world intrude on us now. For tonight there is only you and me. I love you, Tazia, beyond anything in the world. Nothing else matters at all."

"But—"

Her words were silenced by a kiss that stopped all rational thought. Sliding his arms down from her shoulders to her waist, he lifted her onto his lap. His hand found the opening to her cloak and slipped inside to caress her body lightly. He was unhappy when he found he couldn't maneuver the hooks at the back of her gown.

"Confounded women's clothes should be redesigned

so you could get out of them easier."

He was answered by a soft gurgle of laughter as Tazia buried her head against his shoulder. He grinned in response, but he did not stop his efforts. Slipping his hand under her skirt onto her soft, warm thigh brought a gentle sound of approval. Kirk became so engrossed in Tazia that neither of them realized that the carriage had stopped, until a discreet knock on the door gave them warning. By the time he opened the door, Kirk and Tazia had re-arranged themselves. With the exceptions of the blush on Tazia's face and the gleam in Kirk's eyes, nothing was amiss.

When they reached the door, Kirk unlocked it and Tazia prepared to enter.

"Just a moment Mrs. LaCroix, if you please."

She looked at him questioningly.

"I'll have no bad luck cross this doorway because I've forgotten something." With this, he swung her up in his arms and carried her across the threshold and then across the foyer into the drawing room. A fire had been lit in the fireplace, and in front of it sat a small table with a bottle of champagne and two glasses on it.

"Del thinks of everything." He let her feet slide to the floor, but held her against him, reluctant to let her go.

"Shall I pour you a glass, my husband?"

He nodded his head and watched her as she moved slowly to the fireplace. There was a burning ache in him that chafed at the emptiness he felt when she left his side. When she turned toward him with the two glasses of champagne in her hands and smiled seductively, he was drawn to her like a magnet. Instead of taking one of the glasses from her hand, he reached up and slowly began to pull the pins from her hair, loosening the heavy coil until it fell. Then he worked his hands through it until it drifted about her in a black cloud. His eyes never left hers for a moment. She could see the brilliant flames of the fire reflected in their depths. Then he took the glasses from her hands and placed them on the table.

"We don't need this tonight," he said quietly. He pulled her into his arms and kissed her tenderly. Her lips parted under his, and she could feel the glowing flame deep inside her burst and flood her whole being like molten lava. His hands slid down to her hips and held her tightly, letting her feel the hard demand of his passion.

Kirk loosened the hooks at the back of her gown and slid it from her shoulders to lie in a heap at her feet. The thin chemise she wore under the dress hid nothing of her body. He could see the rapid rise and fall of her breasts through the gauzelike material. He held her again and kissed her deeply, letting his kisses roam down her throat to the swell of her breasts. His seeking hands and mouth found the soft skin beneath her chemise.

Kirk then lifted her in his arms and carried her to the long couch that sat by the fireplace. He placed her against the cushions and stood above her. The slender whiteness of her body against the red velvet cushions sent sparks of desire through him. She watched him begin to remove his clothes. First his coat was thrown hastily onto a chair. Then his muscular brown arms appeared from beneath his white shirt. The rest of his clothes followed rapidly, and he stood before her in the glow of the fire—long brown limbs, taut and heavily muscled, broad shoulders and chest that tapered to strong, narrow hips. Tazia rose on one elbow and gazed at the muscular beauty of her husband. She wanted him as much as he obviously wanted her. She lay back on the pillows with a smile and lifted her arms to him.

"Kirk . . . *mi amore* . . . my husband," she whispered.

Never having been a hesitant man, Kirk needed no further invitation. He knelt beside her and slipped the chemise from her body. Then he gathered her into his arms and kissed her again. His tongue probed the soft moistness of her lips, which parted under his and answered, timidly at first, then more urgently, as her need for him filled her. He wanted to touch and know every inch of her. Moving his lips down her throat to a rose-tipped breast, he gathered it with his exploring mouth. She felt the fire flow from his lips to her, and she arched under him with a soft cry of passion. Then his lips escaped down to the gentle curve of her hips and across the plane of her stomach to the inner flesh of her thighs, which parted willingly. He brought a soft moan from her as his mouth discovered soft, intimate places. Then the hardness of his body was suddenly between her thighs, and with a cry of surrender matching his groan of pleasure, he entered her and filled her with his love, holding her fast to him. He was still for a moment as she trembled under him at the first breaking of her virginity. Then he began to move slowly, lifting her body with him to establish a rhythm. Soon she picked up the rhythm herself, and he now possessed her fully, moving deep and hard as she arched against him. She whispered soft words of love to him as she clung to the hard muscles of his back. Her hands drifted over his back and shoulders up to his hair, where she twined her fingers. She pulled his mouth down to hers. Never had he encountered this fiery passion in any woman. She enveloped him and held him deeply within her, taking the love he had to give and returning it more fully than he could have imagined in his wildest fantasies. He groaned her name as the world spun in a cataclysmic spiral and exploded. Nothing that had ever happened to either of them had prepared them for the wonder of this. They clung to one another, molded together as though they were one. Slowly he lifted himself and looked down into her glowing face. He brushed the hair back from her perspiring forehead, cupped her face in his hand, and kissed her very gently.

"You and I," he said softly, "are one person—one body, one soul. I love you now, and I shall love you as long as I live."

Her eyes filled with tears, and he pulled her head to his shoulder and held her. They lay for a long time, holding one another, content just to be together.

The fire died to glowing embers and the pale light of dawn slowly appeared through the curtained windows. During the night he had wakened her again with warm nuzzling of her shoulder and she had turned to him willingly to give again her love. He could never seem to get enough, for every time he touched her, it created the desire to touch her again.

He had pulled a coverlet over them, and they had slept, her head on his shoulder and his arms around her. Now he caressed her gently and she stirred, but did not waken.

"Tazia?"

"Ummm?"

"Let's go see what the world has to offer today."

She put her arm across his chest and buried her face in his neck. "Let's just stay here."

She could hear the rumble of laughter in his chest. "Come on, sleepyhead. Let's go out and have a big breakfast. Then we can go and explore New Orleans. There are a million things I would like to share with you." He watched her graceful, long-legged beauty as she rose from the couch, stretched, and yawned. "On second thought," he laughed, reaching for her, "you had the right idea. Let's just stay here."

But she moved just out of reach of his hands and grinned wickedly at him. "Too late, Frenchman. You should have taken my first offer. I never offer twice."

"I'll keep that in mind in the future, madam," he said as he sat up and swung his legs to the floor. He watched her intently until she took her eyes from him, and as quick as a cat he was beside her. She gave a squeal as he lifted her up and then buried his face between her breasts. She bent her head over him, and they were enclosed in the black mist of her hair.

"Animal," she laughed. "Put me down."

Slowly he let her slide the length of his body. By the time her feet touched the floor, her arms were around his neck and their lips were joined in a searing kiss. All plans for the day were forgotten as they lost themselves again in one another.

Later, when they were sitting at the breakfast table, they heard a persistent knock on the door. They looked at one another in surprise. The servants had been given the day off, and no one was expected to call. Kirk shrugged into a robe and went to the door, where he found Jean and Del, somewhat the worse for drink, swaying in the doorway. Tazia joined Kirk, and they stood and watched the two intruders with amusement.

"Del, what are you two doing here?" Kirk said gruffly, trying to hide his amusement.

Del put a finger to his lips and grinned evilly at his

brother. "Shhhhh," he said.

Tazia smiled at her new husband's brother. Then she turned to Kirk and said, "I'm going upstairs, my love. You can take care of our guests, can't you?"

Kirk chuckled. "I think what we'd better do is put them to bed." He kissed her lightly and watched her walk upstairs.

As the other two men watched her leave, they began to chuckle, then to laugh out loud. Soon they were convulsed with laughter and leaning against one another.

"What are you two bastards up to?" Kirk asked in mild alarm.

Unable to speak coherently, they continued laughing uncontrollably.

Kirk began to frown. "Del, Jean, what's going on?"

"Jus' wan' to collect a bet, Kirk ol' boy," mumbled Del, "jus' collect a bet."

"What bet? What have you two done?"

"Bet you two would never make it to the bedroom," Del gurgled, almost choking, "an' I won . . . you din' go in the bedroom." He waggled his finger at Kirk accusingly.

Kirk tried his best to keep a straight face, but he found it nearly impossible. Then, at the sound of returning footsteps, he turned to see Tazia coming back down the stairs.

"Kirk," she said almost too sweetly, "I think we should help them to bed, don't you?"

Noticing the twinkle in her eyes, he agreed, and they led Jean and Del upstairs to what was to have been the bridal chamber.

Tazia whispered to Kirk, "There is a powder on the bed that causes one to itch. Shall we put them to bed now?"

Kirk contained himself with some effort as he and

121

Tazia disrobed the almost unconscious pair and dumped them in the bed.

Several hours later, just as they were returning from a carriage ride, wild curses and splashing sounds could be heard coming from the house. They climbed the stairs and peeked in the bedroom door to find both Del and Jean soaking and scrubbing their bodies to remove the cause of the violent itching that plagued them.

Tazia stuck her head into the room and called in a soft, velvety voice, "When you gentlemen are through bathing, would you care to join us for some lunch?"

When the abashed pair finally came slowly down the stairs, Tazia, unable to contain herself any longer ran to them and kissed each one firmly. Realizing they were forgiven, they joined the happy couple for lunch. They all then spent a delightful afternoon together.

At dinner that night, Del raised his glass to Tazia. "Welcome to the family," he said with a warm smile.

The dinner was concluded amid happy chatter and laughter when Kirk finally got the point across that it was time for their uninvited guests to depart.

After the men had left, Kirk turned to Tazia and said, "Shall we check and make sure there are no more bed problems?" She nodded in agreement. A few hours later, they were absolutely certain that there were no more bed problems.

16

The carriage rolled to a stop in front of a large two-story brick house. The house was surrounded by a tall fence of iron posts topped by spikes that would discourage any intruders.

Either she was a very reserved person or she was very afraid of something, Louis thought as he was escorted through the gate by his huge bodyguard. When the door was opened, they were ushered into the foyer. It was a circular room with a stairway up the center and a set of double doors with huge brass knobs on the left. On his right was a series of three doors set about ten feet apart. All the doors were closed.

His attention was drawn away from the room by the sound of a door closing upstairs and then the tap of approaching footsteps. Then she came down the stairs slowly—exactly as he had seen her the first time: flawless porcelain complexion and golden hair braided atop her head like a coronet. She walked toward him with her hand outstretched. Without hesitation he took her cool, slender hand in his and raised it to his lips.

"Thank you for coming, Monsieur Plummer."

"It would indeed be ungrateful of me to say I had

no choice," he replied.

She smiled. "Would you rather not stay? It can be arranged for you to return to your ship."

"Madam," he said softly, his eyes twinkling with amusement as they caught hers, "it would take a team of horses plus your overgrown bodyguard there to drag me away from here."

She laughed and withdrew her hand from his. She was magically intoxicating to him, a combination of soft, lovely female and woman-of-mystery. It was a mystery he was determined to solve.

"Would you care to join me in some supper, Monsieur Plummer?"

"Thank you, I'd be delighted. Could you please call me by my given name?"

"Of course. It's Louis, is it not?"

"You remembered," he said softly.

She flushed a little, then motioned him toward the double doors, which she then proceeded to push open. It was a large room, and it looked very comfortable, as though it were used often. There was a fire in the fireplace, which took up almost an entire wall opposite the door. All the woodwork was a deep mahogany color and had been carefully polished to a brilliant shine. The furniture was large and slightly worn, reinforcing the impression that it was a frequently used room. The wall to his left encased a set of large double windows with heavy gold draperies. The opposite wall held shelves from floor to ceiling containing several hundred books. There was a table next to the fireplace that held a bottle of brandy and two glasses. She went to the table, poured the brandy, and handed a glass to him. He looked at it with a slight smile, to which she raised her eyebrows in question.

"The last time a lovely lady gave me a glass of

brandy I ended up on a ship miles from home. You will forgive me if I am a little hesitant?"

Without a word she walked over to him. The faint odor of her perfume assailed his nostrils and caused a warm stirring in his loins. She took the glass from his hand and, without taking her eyes from his, drank from it. Then she handed the glass back to him. Without doubt, she could see his desire for her in the warmth of his gaze. She raised her glass to him in a wordless toast, and he raised his in response.

"Now," he said quietly, "can you tell me why you changed your mind about me?"

"Changed my mind?"

"Well, at our last meeting you didn't seem exactly . . . uh . . . receptive to me."

"You were asking too many questions. Sometimes it is not wise to question too deeply, too soon."

He watched her closely. Did her hand tremble slightly? He tried to read her face, but it was impossible. He sighed deeply and came directly to the point. "What do you want of me?"

"What makes you think I want something from you? Maybe I'm just interested in you."

He became slightly angry. *She* had brought him here! She wanted something, and by God he wanted to know what it was. He was tired of being pushed around without knowing the reason why. He set his glass down firmly.

"You'll excuse me, Mrs. Keyo, if I leave now? It's obvious we are not getting anywhere." He turned and strode toward the door.

When his hand was on the doorknob, he heard her soft voice. "Wait, please."

The words were spoken so quietly he was not quite sure he heard them. He turned to see her blue eyes clouded with distress and one hand slightly raised toward him. He didn't move from the door. He wasn't about to play her game any longer.

"Well, are you going to tell me what's going on, or do I leave now?"

"You are an impatient man, Louis."

He made an angry sound and turned back to the door.

"Don't go," she said, this time with sincerity. "I need your help desperately, Louis. Sit down. I will tell you exactly why I sent for you."

He went back and sat in the large chair next to the fireplace. She walked over and sat in the chair opposite him. The chair was deep-blue velvet, which picked up the color of her eyes so vividly he could have drowned in them.

"I have asked Captain Touseau many questions about you," she began. "In your time with him you've told him many things about yourself. The rest he was told before you were put on board. So, you see, I know you quite well."

"Why?"

"I wanted to know what kind of man you are, Louis—whether you would be the kind to help me or not."

"And?"

She had been looking into her glass while she spoke, swirling the brandy around slowly. Now she raised her eyes directly to his. "I think you are an honorable man, and I think you would understand. Also, I think you are the only man I know who can help me."

He leaned back in the chair and smiled at her. "If there is anything I can to do help you, tell me. Although, in the position I am in now, I don't see what I can do."

"Let me tell you. Then we can see just what you

126

can do."

"Go on."

"My name is not 'Mrs. Keyo,' " she began.

He laughed. "I didn't think for a moment that it was."

"My name is Gabrielle Saint-Albin."

"Saint-Albin . . . I know the name from somewhere."

"Have you ever been to Virginia?"

"Of course. I have some friends there. So do the LaCroixs. We've gone there for holidays many times. But . . . Saint-Albin . . . ?"

"Maybe you remember the Five Points Plantation?"

"Five Points! Of course, I've heard of it. Who in Virginia has not? It is reputed to be one of the most beautiful in the state. *Now* the name is familiar. Five points is owned by Martin Saint-Albin. Are you his daughter?"

She didn't speak again for a few minutes, and he could see that she was fighting a memory. He waited patiently for her to continue. He was in no hurry, for it was a pleasure just to sit and look at her.

"I must tell you the story from the beginning," she said softly.

Again he waited in silence.

"My brother and I were cousins to Martin Saint-Albin, who was the original owner of Five Points. When he died, we were the only living heirs. We were located in France and asked to return and either take over or dispose of our inheritance. When Paul and I arrived, we immediately fell in love with the place and decided we would stay. For a while, life was beautiful. Then I began to notice a difference in Paul. He became nervous, and he would get angry very easily if I questioned him. Then one morning . . . ." She paused for a moment, as if the memory were too painful. "One morning they came to tell me Paul was dead."

The last words were almost whispered. Louis wanted to reach out and hold her hand, but he sat very still, controlling himself and waiting for the rest of her story. There were tears in her eyes, and she took a moment to compose herself.

"It seems he had been gambling quite heavily and had lost a great deal of money. Then, during a card game, he accused his opponent of cheating. There was an argument, and Paul was shot."

The story sounded so familiar to Louis that he was going to remark that a similar situation had brought him to her. But another question occurred to him. "What did that have to do with you leaving? Weren't you still heir to Five Points?"

"It seems that Paul lost his share of Five Points to the man over the gaming table."

"God, I'm sorry, Gabrielle," he said softly.

"I could have borne even that if that . . . monster had left me alone. But that was not to be. He came to me, the night after Paul was buried. He suggested that it was not necessary for me to leave, that I could stay at Five Points . . . as his mistress. I said never! Never would I let him touch me. Then he said there were many ways to deal with an obstinate woman. I knew fear then as I had never known it before. He did not intend for me ever to leave.

"Then . . . ." Her voice broke, and she was caught in the pain of the past.

"Then?" he said softly.

"Then he raped me." Her voice was so low he had to strain to hear it.

"The bastard!"

"He struck me and dragged me to the bedroom and . . . ." She shook her head, unable to continue.

"Later, Raf heard me crying because I knew I would never be able to escape. He came to my room, wrapped me in a blanket, and took me from the house."

"Raf is your bodyguard?"

She nodded. "He and his mother, Melissa, somehow got my jewelry from the house, and with their help I managed to get here. We bought this place and have been here ever since. I hate this life. I want to go home. I want Five Points back."

"What do you want me to do, Gabrielle? If I could get away from here, I would go back with you and kill that animal. But I cannot. I am a prisoner."

"I know," she answered. "I know the whole story. But if I could get you to swear on your honor you would not go back to New Orleans unless Jean sent word, Captain Touseau would leave you in my care."

Louis's heart leapt. "I will give my word. Captain Touseau already knows I never break it."

"I know. Captain Touseau has many good things to say about you."

"You've spoken much of me?" he asked.

Again a faint flush tinged her cheeks a rosy pink. He was fascinated. "After we get the captain's permission, then what?"

Her next words shook him more than anything she'd said so far, yet they were spoken very gently. "I want you to marry me, Louis."

He started to reply, but she held up her hand. "Just hear me out. I want to make a bargain with you for the temporary use of your name. Just for a few weeks. If I go back alone, I will fail and he will have me where he wants me. I could not bear that again. If I go back with my husband, then I can fight for my share of Five Points. If I can buy him out and get him to leave . . . you will be rewarded, believe me. I have a great deal of money now. I would ask nothing of you but to stand behind me. Then when he is gone, I will repay you and you will be free to seek a divorce."

"I agree," he stated firmly.

She looked at him in surprise. "Just like that?"

"Just like that. I would have agreed without any reward. What he has done deserves punishment. If the law does not do it for you, then maybe *I'll* find a way."

"Just marry me, Louis, and come back to Five Points with me. Together we can get him out of there."

"All right, when?"

"The day after tomorrow."

"Then we can leave for Five Points immediately?"

"Yes, it should take about three weeks to get there."

"Don't worry about anything. We'll get your home back for you."

"Louis . . . ."

"Yes?"

"I know you are a man of honor, and I do not mean to insult you after you have been so kind to me, but . . . ."

"Go on."

"This must be a marriage in name only . . . ."

"I understand. You don't want—"

"It's not that I *don't* want. You are an attractive man. It's that I can't. Since that night, I have not been able to . . . I can't bear . . . I—"

"Don't distress yourself any further, Gabrielle," Louis said gently. "I understand. It's one more thing he must pay for."

Her eyes shone in gratitude. "Then it is agreed?"

He nodded.

"Good, then let us have some supper together. We should get to know one another better."

He had never enjoyed anything more than the evening spent with her. She was vivacious and charming. When he finally rose to leave, Raf was waiting in the carriage. They did not speak all the way back to the ship, for Louis was lost in thought. He put Tazia and Kirk from his mind. They would have to settle their own problems. His mind was set on the man who had caused Gabrielle such misery. There were two things he vowed to do: one was to avenge the loss of her honor; the other was to help her forget the pain she had suffered. For he wanted her—as a woman and as a wife. He resolved to break the barrier she had built around herself and reach inside to touch the woman he knew existed there. In two days she would become his wife, and he intended to see that they stayed married for the rest of their lives.

17

Gabrielle stood beside Louis and softly spoke the words that made them man and wife. He did not have to look at her to know she was there. Every sense he had shouted her presence. The perfume she wore was the same and had the same effect on him. Her hair had been brushed until it shone, then braided and wrapped about her head. He had a strong desire to loosen it and thrust his hands deep into its silken strands. She wore a blue dress that accented her eyes. She was completely female, completely lovely, and damn it! he wanted her so badly he could almost feel the blood rush through his body.

They had spent two days together while the wedding arrangements were being made. Captain Touseau had given his permission immediately. And Louis had given him his word not to return to New Orleans. Two days had been enough for Louis to realize that keeping his side of the bargain was going to be difficult, since they would be traveling together for over two weeks. It would be difficult, but he was determined to try to make her want him as much as he wanted her. They would have over two weeks. In that time he intended to woo her in every possible way. He wanted to make her his wife in more than name.

The ceremony was over quickly. Louis didn't know whether he was to kiss the bride or not. He turned to face her, and for a fleeting moment her eyes registered fear. Then she smiled and lifted her face to him. He brushed a kiss lightly across her lips. No, he wasn't mistaken, he thought. When he touched her, he could feel a shiver of fear run through her body.

They immediately went back to her house, where they gathered her baggage and put it in the coach. He possessed very few things and took only a few minutes to collect them. Within an hour of the ceremony, they were prepared to leave. He put out his hand to help her board the coach. Then he climbed in beside her.

"Well," she sighed, "I am finally on my way back to Five Points, back home. Oh, Louis, I thought I would never see it again."

"You'll not only *see* it again, Gabrielle, it will be your home, as it should have been all this time."

"Thank you for you confidence, Louis. You don't know how grateful I am for it. Without your help, I would never be able to go back."

Raf stuck his head in the door. "You'all ready to go, Miss Gabrielle?"

"Yes, Raf, we're ready."

Raf took one last, long look at Louis, who chuckled to himself. If Raf were given his way, Louis would have been running alongside the coach instead of riding with his mistress. Someday, somehow, Louis had to convince Raf he had only Gabrielle's welfare at heart.

Raf climbed on top of the coach, slapped the reins against the horse's rump, and they were on their way.

There was no doubt that Gabrielle was nervous, so Louis chatted calmly with her, telling her about himself and asking questions about her until she was talking freely and not thinking about the reason for her trip.

He discovered that she had been raised about 40 miles from Paris in a small chateau. Her parents had not had a great deal of money, but they had enough to educate their daughter and ensure that she had every opportunity. She and her brother, Paul, had been very happy and very popular. Then, suddenly, her parents had been taken from them in an accident, and she and Paul were orphans. It had seemed like a miracle when they received the news about their inheritance from a distant uncle. Louis knew the rest of the story.

They fell silent, riding along with their own thoughts. Gabrielle leaned her head back against the cushioned seat and closed her eyes. After a while, she fell into a light sleep. Slowly Louis put his arm behind her and let her head drop to his shoulder. He was content to hold her while she slept and let his mind drift to how it could be for them when the ghosts of her past were exorcised.

They stopped for lunch at a small inn, but, except for resting their horses occasionally, they did not stop again until the sun began to disappear below the horizon. Finally they prepared to stop for the night. The inn where they stayed was small but clean. They were given a good supper and then escorted to their room. Once inside, both of them were silent. There was only one bed and no sign of a couch or a chair on which he could sleep.

She was looking at the bed. "Louis?"

"Don't worry, Gabrielle, I'll keep my word. I'll not lay a hand on you."

"Thank you," she said so quietly he barely heard her.

They began to make preparations for bed. He tried his best not to watch her, but it was almost more than he could stand when she sat in her nightgown and unbraided her hair to brush it. It flowed soft and golden to her waist.

"Damn," he muttered as he strode out the door and closed it roughly behind him. He went downstairs and sat in front of the fireplace and had several drinks, waiting until he was sure Gabrielle was asleep. Half an hour later he walked slowly up the steps and stood outside their door for a minute before he pushed it open and walked in. There was one candle burning on the dresser, and it cast shadows across the room. He stood above the bed and looked down at Gabrielle. "So beautiful," he murmured.

Louis sat down on the opposite side of the bed and removed his boots. He hung his coat over the edge of the bed, loosened his cravat, and lay back against the pillow. If he could just get through the first night, he thought, maybe he could get used to her sleeping next to him. But he doubted it. The minutes faded into hours, and he began to doze. He didn't know how long he had been asleep when he heard a soft murmur. Gabrielle stirred beside him, and he then realized the sound was coming from her.

Louis sat up and looked down at her. In the flickering light of the candle he could see tears glistening on her cheeks. She was moaning softly in her sleep. "No, no . . . don't, please don't," she whispered. "Please, dear God . . . don't touch me . . . no, no."

He knew what she was dreaming about, and he cursed the man who had caused her to suffer like this. She stirred restlessly and cried out again. Then she began to strike out at the menace in her sleep. She cried out loudly now, "Mama! Papa! Paul . . . somebody, please." He caught both her arms and pulled her against his chest. He wrapped both arms around her and held her close while he talked to her.

"Shhh, Gabrielle. It's all right, darling. No one's going to hurt you again. Gabrielle, don't cry. It's going to be all right. Hush . . . shh." He stroked her hair until she quieted.

He knew she was fully awake now, but he could not bring himself to let her go. Then she stirred and looked up at him. He smiled reassuringly. "It's all right, Gabrielle. It's just a bad dream."

"I know," she said weakly. "I dream the same dream every night. Oh God, will it never go away?"

He lay back on the pillow and pulled her to him. For a moment she lay stiff and trembling. "Gabrielle, relax, go to sleep. You'll be safe. Try to get some rest. Maybe the dream is gone for the night."

He could feel her trembling slowly cease and the stiffness relax. Then, after a short while, her regular breathing told him she was asleep. It was a long time before he closed his eyes.

When Louis wakened, he felt the warmth of Gabrielle's softness against him. During the night she had turned and thrown her leg over the lower part of his body and her right arm across his chest. He could feel the curves of her body against his side and the whisper of her breath on his neck.

Louis did not make any effort to move. He wanted to enjoy this moment as long as possible. Sunlight crept across the room and found the couple in the large bed. Gabrielle stirred and woke up slowly. Louis felt a slight quiver as she became aware of her position. He closed his eyes and breathed deeply, as though he were still asleep. Moving slowly, so as not to awaken him, she got out of bed. Louis secretly watched her move across the room, pour some water into a basin, and wash her face and hands. Then she slipped her nightgown down to her waist and washed again. She dressed and then brushed her hair and rebraided it. She stood in the sunlight with her arms upraised as she pinned the braid in a tight coil. Her slender body bathed in sunlight was a sight Louis knew he would never forget as long as he lived.

When Gabrielle had finished, she went to the side of the bed. Even with his eyes closed he could feel her presence. Then her cool hand touched his arm. "Louis, are you awake?"

He opened his eyes and grinned at her.

"Good morning, Gabrielle."

She sat down beside him. "Louis . . . I . . . I want to thank you."

"For what?"

"For last night."

"Gabrielle—"

"Louis, please," she said softly. "It meant a great deal to me. It is the first time in a long while that I've slept. I owe you a great deal, Louis. I shall never forget it."

She smiled and suddenly bent to kiss his cheek. "Come along, lazybones. I'm going down for some breakfast. Will you join me?"

He nodded yes and then watched her walk seductively to the door. When she had left, he rose and made rapid preparations to join her for breakfast.

They ate quickly and were soon on their way. They traveled in silence for a long time before she spoke. "Louis, I'm sorry about last night. When we say we're husband and wife, we're automatically given one room. If . . . if you don't think . . . I mean—"

"Gabrielle, I wish you'd stop worrying about me.

I'm fine. Don't you give me any credit for self-control? After all, I didn't attack you last night, did I?" He said the words before he realized what effect they might have on her.

She froze for a second. Then her eyes became angry. Tilting her chin in the air stubbornly, she turned her face away from him.

Louis wondered whether she was angry because of what he said or because of what he *didn't* try to do the night before. A small idea insinuated itself into his mind and began to grow. Finally he decided to make the situation work for him. By the time they had stopped for lunch on the second day, she was slightly puzzled. On the third day her eyes were filled with questions she was too stubborn to ask. They spent two more nights together, during which he completely ignored her and went immediately to sleep. He had to stop himself from holding her each time he heard her cry out in her sleep. He would sometimes awaken to her quiet footsteps as she walked around the room. The third night, just before dawn, he felt her standing beside the bed, looking at him.

The following night he began to see doubt and fear written in her eyes. She was beginning to wonder if there were something unattractive about her. She was also beginning to wonder if she could ever really put the fear of the past behind her. If he were to reach out and touch her, would her body recoil as it always did in the past? Or would she be able to kill the fear that rose in her?

Eight nights later, they were making preparations to stop for the night when she said, "Louis, would you help Raf put up the horses and unpack for the night?"

He looked at her with surprise, because until now,

Raf had been doing that himself. He shrugged and agreed. He and Raf spent over an hour together while they unharnessed and fed the horses. Then they rubbed them down and covered them for the night. Louis then picked up two of Gabrielle's cases and started off toward the inn.

"Mr. Plummer," Raf said quietly.

Louis put the cases down and turned toward him. "Yes, Raf?"

"Miz Gabrielle. She been hurt bad by that man. When me and Lissa took her from that house, she one twisted, pain-filled baby girl."

"What's that got to do with me, Raf?"

"I been taking care of Miz Gabrielle ever since we escaped. I seen a lot of men try to get close to her. She always freeze up."

"And I'm different?"

"Yessir, you're different. With you, Miss Gabrielle don't seem to be so afraid. Maybe she might even find out what a lovin' woman she really is."

"Why are you telling me all this, Raf?"

Raf chuckled as he looked directly into Louis's eyes. "I see the game you been playin' with that child. You got her wondering and worrying if she is really a woman. She's innocent. If she gives, it will be everything she's got. I don't want to ever see her hurt bad again. If you're playin' a game, and if you hurt her to prove a point, I . . . I'll rip your head off your shoulders."

Louis wanted Raf's friendship, and he wanted him to understand. "Raf, would you believe me if I tell you that I want what's best for Gabrielle? That I firmly believe someone or something has to pull her out of the shell she's been living in because she can never do it alone? I'm going to do whatever is in my power to put the pieces back together for her. I only hope it works and I don't hurt her worse."

Raf nodded after he studied Louis's face. "Yes, I believe you."

Louis smiled and turned again toward door.

"Mr. Plummer?"

Louis turned again to look at him.

"Do you love her?"

Louis smiled. "Yes . . . yes, Raf, I do."

Raf nodded his head with satisfaction and turned away to go to his own room.

Louis hoped he was doing the right thing, for he did not doubt for one moment that Raf would do exactly what he had threatened to do.

He walked upstairs with Gabrielle's luggage and kicked against the door for her to open it. There was no response, so he put one case down, lifted the latch of the door, and pushed it open. He reached down for the other case and entered the room, but he stopped short after two steps. Gabrielle had lighted several candles and prepared for bed. At the sound of his entrance, she had turned to face the door.

She had been brushing her hair, and it hung about her in a pale golden mass. It took every ounce of concentration Louis had not to put the cases down and take her in his arms. He had to look away from her to regain control. He dropped the cases on the floor and he walked to the bed, where he sat down and removed his boots. He could hear her moving about, but he deliberately kept his eyes away from her. Finally he felt her creep softly into bed and pull the covers over her. He lay down and concentrated all his efforts on self-control. After a while, he dozed off into a light sleep.

It must have been several hours later when he wakened. He found himself turned toward her side of the bed. Then he realized that she was no longer there. He searched the dark room until he finally could make her out, standing by the window with her back to him.

"Gabrielle?" he whispered. He saw her stiffen slightly, but she did not turn around. He rose from the bed and went to stand behind her. "Gabrielle, what's wrong?"

Still she did not turn around or answer. He took hold of her shoulder and turned her to face him. Even in the first pale light of dawn, he could see the tears glistening on her cheeks.

"Gabrielle," he whispered again softly as he pulled her gently into his arms. He held her and caressed her hair, rocking her gently in his arms until he felt her body relax against him. Then he lifted her face to his, and amid the salty taste of her tears, he captured her soft lips with his.

18

Louis knew that she trusted him now, so he held himself under the most rigid control he'd ever managed. He knew he'd taken a step in the right direction, but he didn't want to ruin everything by moving too soon. He smiled at her and put his arm around her waist.

"You're cold. Did you have the same dream again?"

She shook her head no.

"Then what are you doing up at this hour in the cold?"

"I . . . I just couldn't sleep. Louis?"

"Yes?"

"Would you kiss me again?" she asked softly.

"Not unless you really want me, Gabrielle. This is not a game. You can't play with *my* emotions either. I'm human. I won't deny I want you. You're the loveliest woman I've ever seen. But you have to want me, too." He watched her face intently for any sign of fear. There was none.

"Louis," she whispered.

"Yes?"

"Things haven't been the same for me since the night you held me. I want you to hold me again. I

142

want you to kiss me again . . . I want you," she added softly.

"Are you sure, Gabrielle?"

She nodded her head. Slowly he put his arms around her and drew her to him. He could feel the curves of her body beneath her nightgown. He just held her, enjoying the warmth and the fragrance of her. Then, twining his fingers in the silken strands of her hair, he kissed her deeply. Her lips parted under the demanding pressure of his lips, and she moaned softly as she surrendered completely to him. Her arms crept up around his neck as he ran his hands down the curve of her hips and pulled her against him.

When they separated, he searched her face again for any sign of fear, but there was none. Her eyes glowed and her lips parted in a half-smile.

"Come," he said softly, "let me love you."

Louis put his arm around her waist, and they walked back to the bed. The gray light of dawn made her a pale shadow. He pushed the nightgown from her shoulders and tried to absorb the loveliness of her as she stood before him. With gentle hands, he caressed the long line of her throat, letting his hands run down her shoulders to cup her breasts.

"You are lovely, Gabrielle, so very lovely, and I want you to love me as I love you. My wife," he added softly as he sat down on the edge of the bed and pulled her onto his lap. She unbuttoned Louis's shirt and he slipped it from his shoulders. Twisting sideways, he let her fall to the bed and claimed her lips again. This time the kiss was fierce, and filled with all the passion he had held in for so long. She gasped at the urgency of the hands that searched her body, seeking, discovering all the sensual places that sent sparks of flame through her. Gone were the memories and the fears. All she knew was the deep desire to hold him even closer, to consume him. Her body moved with a will of its own, and soon she opened her legs to receive him. There was no holding back for either of them. He took her deeply, and she murmured words of love as he lifted her to meet him, beginning the age-old rhythm of man and his mate.

Neither of them paid any attention to the sunlight as the dawn brightened into day. He held her close to him, and they talked in whispers, excluding the rest of the world from their lives for the moment.

"I never knew anything could be so beautiful, Louis," she said. "I thought I would never be able to love after what happened."

"From this minute on, you are to forget everything from the past," he said as he placed a gentle kiss on her shoulder. "When we get to Five Points, we will take care of your business. Then I would like you to come back to New Orleans with me for a while. I've got some friends I would like to have meet you, and I have a little affair I must get straightened out."

"Affair! You mean you . . . ?"

"No!" he laughed, delighted with the thought that this lovely creature was jealous of him. "There is no one but you, chérie, believe me. This is another type of affair entirely."

He proceeded to explain the situation that had brought him to her. He told her the whole story, from the card game to that moment.

She listened intently and then said, "Louis?"

"What is it?"

"I don't understand something you said. The men in this card game — would you describe them to me physically?"

"Why? Do you know any of them?"

"I don't know. Can you describe them?"

Louis spoke slowly as he tried to remember the

faces of the card players. First he described Del, then Kirk. Then he began to describe Garrett and Manolo. Gabrielle's eyes never left his face as he spoke. Her eyes widened and her lips became pinched as the color slowly drained from her face. As he watched her, his voice began to slow. Finally he broke off the story and said softly, "Gabrielle, you *do* know one of them, don't you?" When she did not answer, he gave her a slight shake. "Answer me, Gabrielle. You *do* know one of them?"

She nodded her head silently as tears rolled down her cheeks. He pulled her tightly against him. "Which one, Gabrielle?"

"Louis, the man who took our plantation worked together with another man. They cheated many people like me and Paul." Slowly she raised her eyes to his. "I'm sure one of them was your friend Garrett Flye."

"And the other?"

"The other," she whispered, "was Manolo de Montega, the man who . . . who . . ." Her voice choked and she fell silent.

He held her trembling body against his as the shock of what she had said engulfed him. He tried to sort things out in his mind. Then it all suddenly became clear to him. Garrett's unexplained wealth, his introducing Manolo into the game. "Good God!" exclaimed. "He not only set Kirk up, he set Manolo up, too. He needed to get rid of him. Manolo must have been putting some pressure on him. He must have led him to believe this would be the same type of confidence game. Then he somehow maneuvered the situation so that Manolo would die. He knew what kind of a shot Kirk was.

"Gabrielle, listen to me. Could you put off going back to your home? I have a feeling Garrett is not there. In fact, I'm sure I know where he is. Would you trust me and come with me? If we don't hurry, he may do to another woman what he's already done to you, and he may kill a very good friend of mine in the process."

She watched his face as he spoke, and she could sense the anger and fear he was feeling. "You know I trust you . . . even with my life, my darling."

He kissed her deeply and hungrily. "Thank you. You'll never regret it. Much as I hate to, we must get started. The sooner we get back to New Orleans, the more likely we are to stop whatever game it is Garrett's playing."

They began to make hasty preparations for the trip to New Orleans. No matter how hard they pushed themselves, Louis knew it would still take over a week to get home. He wondered what was going on at that moment and what would have happened if Lafitte had not intervened for Tazia. He knew, deep down, that somehow all this was aimed at either Kirk or Del—or maybe both of them.

During the day Louis fretted at their lack of speed. But during the long nights he put everything but Gabrielle out of his mind. They laughed and loved together until he could see and enjoy the change in her. She was happy with him, and he knew it. The only fear left in his mind now was that he would be too late to protect his friends.

The day started out overcast, threatening rain. At any other time, Louis would have suggested that they stay at an inn and wait out the storm, but he knew time was very important, so they decided to continue. Before they had gone far, the rain began to fall in a downpour that rapidly turned the road into a sea of mud. Several times Raf and Louis had to put their shoulders to the wheels of the carriage to free it from a muddy hole. It was obvious to both of them that they could not go on much further. Then, as they were grunting and heaving in one more muddy rut, a loud cracking sound could be heard. A wheel of the carriage had split completely away from the axle and the carriage tipped on its side. A scream from Gabrielle caused Louis to rush to the carriage. He climbed up onto its side, yanked open the door, and shouted, "Gabrielle! Gabrielle, are you all right?"

As he looked down into the carriage, he was rewarded with several sharp words from Gabrielle, which surprised him, and a flash of long white legs and petticoats as she untangled herself. Louis chuckled, but he quickly fell silent when he saw the glare he received from Gabrielle. He reached down and caught hold of her and lifted her up to the side of the carriage, where they sat in the heavy rain. They were soon completely soaked and bedraggled.

"Are you hurt, Miz Gabrielle?" Raf shouted above the sound of the downpour.

"Only my pride, Raf," she shouted back. She and Louis looked at each other for a few moments. Then she was caught up in the laughter she could see in Louis's face. She leaned against him and gave way to the humor of how they must look sitting wet and bedraggled on the side of a broken carriage in the middle of a violent rainstorm.

"What are we going to do, Louis?" she asked when she finally regained control of herself.

"We're going to ride the horses on to the nearest town and send someone back for the carriage. Have you ever ridden bareback, Mrs. Plummer?"

"No," she replied.

"Well, you're about to have your first experience." He jumped down and lifted her down beside him. Then he went to help Raf free the horses from the overturned carriage.

"I can't ride a horse with no reins, Louis. I'll never be able to control him."

Louis realized that this was true. He swung himself up on one of the horses. "Raf, put Gabrielle behind me," he shouted.

Raf lifted Gabrielle up behind Louis. She had never ridden astride a horse before. She had ridden only a gentle mare sidesaddle. Now she was frightened, and she clung desperately to Louis, her arms circling his waist and her head pressed against his back. She closed her eyes and hung on tightly as he kicked the horse into motion. Raf followed on another horse.

Gabrielle was miserable. She was thoroughly soaked and her straggly hair was pasted to her face. The insides of her legs were being chafed by the rocking of the horse. Worst of all, she was thoroughly afraid it was never going to end. What seemed to her like hours was only a matter of an hour and a half until the inn came in sight. Raf dismounted quickly in front of the inn and went inside to get help. Louis swung his leg over the horse's head and jumped down. Then he reached up for Gabrielle and pulled her down into the safety of his arms.

"Oh, Louis," she moaned as she lay her head on his shoulder. He pushed the door open with his foot and carried her in and across the room to a brightly glowing fireplace. He set her in a huge chair in front of the fire and wrapped around her a blanket that the inn-keeper's wife had brought him.

"Oh, the poor wee thing," she clucked. "She should never be out on this terrible night." She glared at Louis as though she were about to berate him for abusing Gabrielle.

"I'll take her upstairs and get her a warm bath and

help her get settled for the night."

"Thank you," Louis said humbly, trying to keep her from reading his eyes. "I would appreciate it very much if you would take care of her while Raf and I go get the rest of our things."

Louis and Raf turned to leave, while the inn-keeper's wife led Gabrielle upstairs, fussing over her the whole time.

It took two more trips back to the carriage, but Louis and Raf finally brought the last of their things back to the inn. When they went inside with the last of the cases they were both exhausted.

"Mrs . . . ?"

"Mrs. Thackeray," the inn-keeper's wife answered firmly. She was still not sure Louis was not an absolute beast to drag a sweet child like his wife out on a night like this.

"Mrs. Thackeray, how is my wife?"

"She's had a warm bath and a little to eat, and I've tucked her into a soft, warm bed. She'll be fine in the morning if she's not disturbed," she said pointedly.

"I'll go up and see her," he said quickly.

Mrs. Thackeray was quiet, but her entire body showed her disapproval.

"Mrs. Thackeray," Louis said quietly as he tried his best to appear shamefaced and worried. "You see, we're . . . we're on our honeymoon. I absolutely must see that she's all right."

"Oh, you poor things," she said sympathetically. "You poor, poor things. Of course, you must go right up and see her. It's the second door to the left."

Louis went up the stairs, grinning broadly, and entered the room. Gabrielle was sitting up in the middle of the bed, smiling brightly at him. He removed his clothes and rubbed himself dry with the towels Mrs. Thackeray had left for him. Then he slid under the covers and pulled Gabrielle down beside him.

"Do you realize Mrs. Thackeray thinks I'm an absolute animal, who's thoroughly abused his sweet little wife?"

"Well, I agree Louis," Gabrielle said quietly as her arms came up to circle his neck. "Do you realize, animal, you haven't made love to me or even kissed me for hours?"

"Give me half a chance and I'll remedy the situation," he murmured as his lips found hers.

"Mmmm, you *are* a beast."

"Yes, my love," he said as his lips moved along her throat and down the soft curve of her shoulders.

"An absolute animal," she whispered.

"Yes, my love," he said again. His lips found spots that sent wild fingers of fire flashing through her. Gabrielle spoke no more, for all her concentration was centered on the gentle hands that brought her to life.

Louis woke up suddenly just before dawn with the frightening feeling that something was terribly wrong. He slipped quietly from the bed and lit a candle. When he turned back to the bed, his heart froze.

Gabrielle lay on her back with beads of perspiration on her forehead. Her head rolled slowly back and forth, and a soft murmuring came from her. Louis moved quickly to her side and placed his hand on her forehead. She was ablaze with fever. Panic struck him. The possibility that he could lose the one thing he loved most in the world tore every other thought from his mind.

19

Louis pulled on his clothes as rapidly as he could and went immediately to Mrs. Thackeray's room. He pounded on the door while he called out her name. When the door was finally opened, Mrs. Thackeray peered out with a frightened look.

"What's the matter, young man? Why do you disturb me at this ungodly hour?"

"Mrs. Thackeray, please come as quickly as you can," he pleaded. "My wife has taken ill. Please hurry."

Without another word, she grabbed up her faded robe, pulled it on as she went, and ran with Louis to his room. Her eyes filled with pity, more, she thought, for the distressed husband than for the girl on the bed. She had nursed many people through the same type of illness. The girl would not die, but trying to convince Louis of that was going to be almost impossible. He was sitting now on the edge of the bed and holding Gabrielle's limp hand in his. He must love her very much, she thought. He's half out of his mind with the fear of losing her.

Louis turned to her. "Can you do something? Shall I ride for a doctor?"

"There's no need. First, there's no doctor within

fifty miles, and I don't trust them anyway. They're the devils breed. They kill more people than they cure. No, we'll make her better."

"What do you want me to do?"

"First, go into that chest and get me all the blankets you can find. Then go down and draw some water from the well. We'll need a lot of it. And boil it, too. We've got to break her fever."

Louis moved rapidly to follow her orders. After he deposited all the blankets he could find, he ran downstairs and out into the yard to the well. He started to draw up the water bucket.

The noise from the house and the well wakened Raf, who had been sleeping in the barn. When he went out to see who the intruders might be, he saw Louis at the well. One look at his face told him that something was seriously wrong. He ran to Louis's side.

"What is it, Louis? What's happened?"

Louis turned his sweating, worried face toward Raf.

"Gabrielle is sick, very sick. Mrs. Thackeray's with her now."

"I'll go for a doctor," Raf said quickly.

"There's no doctor to go for."

Raf looked at Louis steadily. "Is Miz Gabrielle going to die?"

Louis looked at him solemnly. He just couldn't connect that terrible word with Gabrielle. Not after he'd just found her. Not after his life had just begun with her. "Not while I've a breath in my body, Raf. I'll not let her die."

Raf nodded his head.

"Come, help me with this water. Mrs. Thackeray needs lots of boiling water. Get all the containers you can—and hurry up!"

With these words, he took the bucket of water and headed toward the house. Quickly Raf followed with another. Louis was in the kitchen rebuilding the fire and beginning to heat the water when Raf came in. They waited impatiently for the water to boil, and then they carried it upstairs to the bedroom. When they entered the bedroom, they could barely make out Gabrielle's slight form under a mound of blankets.

"Set the water close to the sides of the bed," commanded Mrs. Thackeray. They followed her orders and then slipped back to see what else she wanted them to do. She took several blankets and formed a tent over the bed. They immediately began to help her. Once the fourposter bed was covered, Gabrielle was enclosed in a steamy closet. Then Mrs. Thackeray threw something into the boiling water, the odor of which soon began to choke them. Mrs. Thackeray told them to leave, but Louis refused to budge. His eyes, glued to Gabrielle's white face, were filled with fear. He could barely breathe in the steamy heat, but still he sat on the edge of the bed and held her hand.

"The fever's got to break," Mrs. Thackeray told him. "When it does, she'll be all right."

Gabrielle began to moan and cough and then to fight the smothering blankets and steam.

"Keep her covered, Mr. Plummer," Mrs. Thackeray ordered. "Whatever you do, keep her covered until she begins to sweat. She must sweat a great deal to break the fever."

Louis sat by her through the night and into the next day. His eyes became red from the steam and lack of sleep. A stubble of beard on his face made him look even more exhausted, but he would let no one take his place. During the night, on Mrs. Thackeray's orders, they changed the water and kept the smelly steam contained within the blankets around the bed.

Dawn brought no change in her, and Louis again turned fear-filled eyes toward Mrs. Thackeray. "She's no better," he said in a ragged voice.

"It takes a long time sometimes, son," replied Mrs. Thackeray.

"But she *will* be all right?"

"I think so."

"Think so!"

"Calm down, Mr. Plummer. I've done everything possible. All these things are in the hands of God."

Hour followed agonizing hour until Louis could hardly stand it any longer. He watched Gabrielle's face for any sign of the fever breaking. Her eyes remained closed and occasionally she would moan softly, but she did not regain consciousness. If willpower alone would have made her well, then she should have been miraculously better, for Louis had enough will for both of them.

Nightfall. Another day. Another night, and still she showed no sign of recovery. Louis refused to despair, however, and he refused to let anyone else touch her. He bathed her tenderly, but after a while his movements became awkward from exhaustion.

Louis then sat beside her on the bed, for if he had sat anywhere more comfortable, he would have fallen asleep immediately. Hours later he saw the first beads of perspiration form on her brow, but it took him a few moments to realize the importance of this. He leaned forward, afraid to trust his eyes, and touched her forehead. It was still warm, but not as fiery as it had been. Best of all, it was wet! His eyes became moist with relief.

"It's broken," he muttered to himself. "Thank God, it's broken." He was so exhausted that the release of the tension he had been suffering was almost too much to bear. Enclosed in the obnoxious-smelling tent, tired, dirty, and emotionally drained, Louis lay beside her, pulled her head onto his shoulder, and fell asleep.

Once the fever had broken, Gabrielle fell into a normal sleep. When Mrs. Thackeray came in to check on her progress, she found the two of them asleep in each other's arms. She smiled to herself and left the room, closing the door quietly behind her.

Raf met her in the hallway with a questioning look in his eyes.

"The fever's broken. Mrs. Plummer is going to be all right. They're both asleep now."

Raf breathed a deep sigh of relief.

It was several hours before either of them stirred. Louis awakened first. He was disoriented at first, and it took him several minutes to put together the pieces of the past few days. He turned to Gabrielle and examined her closely. She was pale, but the blazing fire that had raged in her was gone. He touched her forehead and felt the coolness with profound relief.

Slowly he lifted himself from the bed. He washed and shaved and put on clean clothes, the first since Gabrielle had become ill. When he went back to the bed, Gabrielle's eyes were open, and he realized that she had been watching him for some time. She smiled weakly.

"Good morning. How do you feel?" he asked.

"What happened? I feel so weak . . . and thirsty."

"You've been very, very ill, my darling, but you're all right now. I'll get you something to drink."

He brought her a dipper of water and lifted her shoulders from the pillow to help her drink.

"What happened, Louis? I feel so terribly weak."

155

"You've been sick for almost a week."

"A week! The last thing I remember was kissing you good night after the storm."

"Well!" he laughed. "Don't try flattery on me, young lady. I know I'm a remarkable fellow, but I don't think one good-night kiss would render a girl unconscious for a week."

She laughed and put her arms around his neck. "Are you afraid to kiss me again to see if it was your fault or not?"

His eyes suddenly became serious. "Promise me you'll never scare me like that again, Gabrielle. You don't know what I've been through the last few days. I thought I was going to lose you."

"You'll never lose me," she murmured as their lips met.

Gabrielle was too weak to get out of bed for several days. She was upset because she believed her illness had stopped Louis from reaching his friends to tell them the truth about Tazia's brother and his connection with Garrett, Kirk, and Del.

Louis was helping Gabrielle eat some lunch. She watched his face for any sign of disappointment, but it was completely unreadable.

"Louis?"

"Eat," he commanded gently.

"Louis, please."

"Just eat. We'll talk when you're stronger."

"But we must talk now."

"No, darling, we must not. You must eat now or you'll never regain your strength."

"You are impossible."

"And you are impossibly beautiful."

"But—"

"No 'but's. You're getting nothing from me except

a lot of care until you're really well."

She knew she would get no further, so she ate obediently. A short time later, she was sound asleep again. Louis smiled as he looked down at her slight form curled up under the blankets. She slept for several hours, but much to her distress, Louis would still not allow her to get out of bed. He brought her another tray of food and sat beside her to make sure she ate everything on it.

This routine continued for two more days. On the third day, Gabrielle rebelled. Louis awakened in the morning to find her out of bed and dressed. No matter what he said, she adamantly refused to return to bed. She insisted that she was able to take a walk with him in the sunshine. Louis gave in reluctantly, and they left the room and went downstairs, where they were greeted by a delighted Mrs. Thackeray and a much happier Raf. They walked along a path that led from the back of the inn through the adjoining woods. Sunlight tangled its fingers through the leafy trees and escaped to touch the ground here and there. It was shaded, peaceful, and very beautiful.

"Louis," she said quietly. "I'm well enough to continue our journey."

He did not answer, but he continued to walk slowly, immersed in his own thoughts.

"Louis? Did you hear me?"

"Yes, Gabrielle, I heard you. I want you to have more time. I want to know you're completely well. I don't want you to go through that again. What if I drag you away again and you get sick in some God-forsaken place that doesn't have a Mrs. Thackeray?"

"Louis! I'm completely well, I assure you." They both stopped and faced each other. As he looked down at her, his eyes filled with the love and fear he felt for her. Then, slowly, she smiled. She lifted her arms, threw them around his neck, and put her mouth against his. For a moment, he was too surprised to respond. Then he embraced her tightly while his lips invaded hers. When they finally separated, he chuckled. "I guess you are well . . . very, very well."

She laughed. "We'll be on our way again tomorrow?" she asked.

"Yes, tomorrow," he said with resignation.

"Good."

"But I've got other plans for tonight," he teased.

She gave another happy laugh as he put his arm about her waist and they walked back to the inn.

Raf and Mrs. Thackeray were both delighted to see the young couple happy again. When the two of them had retired, Raf sat in front of the slowly dying fire and contemplated all that had happened in the last few weeks.

Several hours later, Raf was dozing in his chair, the fire almost out, when Louis came downstairs to find him. He stood by the chair and touched his arm. "Raf."

"Yes, what's the matter?"

"Nothing. I just wanted you to know we're leaving in the morning."

"Good. Is Miss Gabrielle all right?"

"She's fine." Louis smiled.

"Mr. Plummer—"

"Louis."

"Louis. What's going on? Can you tell me?"

Louis pulled up a chair, sat down beside Raf and began to explain the urgency of the situation.

20

Tazia stretched and yawned. Then she rolled on her side and curled up against Kirk for warmth. He did not waken and she lay contented for quite some time. She was relaxed and at peace with the world. She did not remember a time when she had felt this happy. In fact, she could not remember being happy at all until this moment.

Tazia lost herself in unwelcome memories. All her life she had known that her birth had been unwanted by her parents. They had conceived their heir, Manolo, and that was all either of them required, except their proud name, their money, and their position in society. She had been raised by her nurse, Marguerite, who had loved her as much as she had been allowed. Discipline for Tazia had been very strict. By the time she was fourteen, blind obedience to her parents and worship of her brother were so firmly ingrained in her that they were part of her nature. Her parents informed her then that she was expected to marry a man of their choice, a man of great wealth. She accepted this as her fate, and it did not occur to her to resist their will. She was amazed now that she had had the courage to marry Kirk without asking their permission. But she loved him so very much.

From where she lay, she could look across the broad expanse of Kirk's chest, which rose and fell with his even breathing. Her arm was across his waist, and his hand held it as though he needed to cling to her even in sleep. His hands were large, with long, slender fingers. There was a fine sprinkling of golden-brown hair across the knuckles and back of his hands. She grew warm with the memory of their touch. The night before, he had held and caressed her until she grew wild with desire for him.

Although Tazia had been obedient, for the most part, she was still a strong-willed woman. She remembered the pain of the news of Manolo's death and how her parents had almost lost their minds with grief. She had an urgent desire then to avenge his death. It did not occur to her that she felt this only to redeem herself in the eyes of her parents, to gain their acceptance of her existence, and to make up for the fact that she was alive and Manolo was dead. Well, she thought, soon we will be going home. No matter what it took, she wanted her parents' acceptance of Kirk, even if she had to lie to gain it. She began to contrive a story that would be acceptable to them. She believed that Garrett was the guilty one, and she intended to tell her parents this.

Since this was to be their last night in New Orleans, Tazia and Kirk planned to have their first big party since their marriage five months ago. Five months! Had it been that long? The months had flown. It had been a happy and exciting time. Kirk had shown her his city with great pride.

Tazia stirred again and sighed deeply. She closed her eyes and began to drift away into sleep. Kirk's left arm crept up and began to stroke the silky strands

160

of her hair.

"Tazia?"

"Umm?"

"Let's watch the sun come up."

"It's cold," she mumbled.

"Come on. I'll keep you warm." He rose from the bed and pulled her up with him.

She shivered in the early morning air. "You are terrible," she grumbled.

He chuckled as he flipped one of the blankets from the bed and wrapped it about her. They walked to the window, where there were several cushions on the window seat. He sat down, leaned against the cushions, and pulled her down onto his lap. Tucking the blanket firmly about her feet, he held her close to him, with her head resting on his shoulder. The soft, gray light cast shadows over the world. One line of pale gold bordered the horizon. Slowly the gray clouds whitened as the sun began to show its faint rim on the horizon. The beauty of the sunrise held them both spellbound. Then the huge orange globe lighted the early morning sky with a brilliant glow. An amazing blend of red, gold, orange, blue, and white dazzled their eyes.

"Oh," she murmured, "It's so beautiful, it almost hurts to watch."

He held her tighter in silent agreement. They did not speak for a long time as they watched the glory of God light up the world. The sun warmed them, and they sat quiet and contented.

"Do you know, my lovely? I can't decide which is more beautiful, watching the sunrise like this or making love to you."

She looked up at him. He seemed to be seriously contemplating the question. Then he grinned. "Yep, I've decided. Making love to you beats out the sunrise

161

every time."

She laughed.

"Are you happy, Tazia?" he asked, serious now.

"Very, very happy, Kirk. I consider myself one of the luckiest women in the world today. I'm so glad I found you."

"Tazia . . ." He hesitated and then lost the courage to tell her the truth.

"What, *querido*?"

"Don't let anything . . . anything spoil what we have. No matter what happens, will you remember that I love you very much?"

She was surprised at the sudden seriousness in Kirk's eyes, the grim lines between his eyes, as if everything in the world depended upon her answer.

"What is it, *mi amore*? Why should anything come between us? We have a whole lifetime to spend together. What could possibly happen?"

"Nothing, I guess," he answered slowly. He pulled her head down on his chest and held her tightly, so that she would not see the answer to her question in his eyes. For some unaccountable reason, she felt afraid. She shivered as a sudden chill came over her body, and a tight knot in her stomach left her dizzy from its intensity. She was about to ask him another question when there was a knock on the door. For the first time since their marriage, Kirk was glad for the interruption. He shifted Tazia to the window seat and rose to go to the door.

"Yes?" he called through the closed door.

"Mr. LaCroix, your brother and Monsieur Lafitte are downstairs. They would like to see you."

"Tell them I'll be down in a few minutes, as soon as I've dressed."

"Yes, sir."

He could hear the receding footsteps. Why could

he not shake this feeling of impending disaster? he thought as he turned from the door to look at Tazia, who was again contemplating the bright new day. They were happy, and after tonight's party they would be leaving. Only not for Casa del Sol. He was going to talk her into visiting his friends in Virginia. A few more weeks and he felt he would be emotionally and mentally prepared to meet her parents.

Tazia turned and looked at him. Then she smiled provocatively as she rose slowly from the window seat, letting the blanket drop away from her. With the bright morning sun behind her, she looked like a golden goddess.

He smiled. "You know we have company downstairs?"

She nodded her head with a half-smile on her lips as she moved slowly toward him. He reached out and gathered her against him, catching her upturned mouth with his. Then she slipped out of his arms, gathered up the robe that she had discarded the night before, and pulled it about her.

"That is to make sure you do not entertain too long," she laughed.

"I won't entertain at all," he said as he grabbed her up in his arms. "We can just send those two intruders away. They can see us at the party tonight." He kissed her soundly several times until she was clinging to him in helpless laughter. Then he let her feet slide to the floor.

"Go down and see what they want. I have to choose my gown for tonight, and I don't want you to see it."

He agreed reluctantly, and only after several more kisses did she push him away firmly. He closed the door on her laughter and went downstairs.

Kirk entered the library, where Del and Jean sat waiting for him. They both smiled broadly when he came inside, and they subjected him to a few ribald remarks about the lateness of the hour for him to still be abed. He laughed with them and accused them of an extreme case of jealousy. Then he ordered coffee sent in.

"Now," he said as he sat down in the chair opposite them, "what exactly do you two reprobates have as an excuse for calling here this morning?"

Meanwhile, Tazia hummed to herself as she pulled a huge white box out from under the bed. She opened it and looked at the lovely gown within. She had ordered it made especially for this night, and Kirk had never seen it. It was made of emerald-green silk with ivory-colored lace over it. The sleeves were long and fitted, and it had a daring décolletage. The dress was gathered just under her breasts and fell in long pleats to the floor. She had decided to wear the diamond necklace that Kirk had bought for her just after they were married.

Tazia was afraid Kirk would come in and see the dress, so she quickly put the lid on the box and pushed it back under the bed. She rose, washed, and dressed for the day. Then she became curious about why Jean and Del were there, so she decided to go down and investigate. She left her room and walked to the top of the stairs. She was about to go down when Kirk and his brother and Jean came out of the library. They were talking as the door opened.

"You should get her out of New Orleans as soon as possible," Jean was saying.

"I've made preparations. We're—" Jean interrupted him with a hand on his arm. Kirk followed his eyes up to Tazia at the top of the stairs. God! How much had she heard? Did she connect it with her? For a minute he stood motionless. Then he smiled.

"Tazia, come down and help me throw these two

out on their respective seats."

Her answering smile caused all three of them to breathe sighs of relief.

"Del, Jean, where have you both been? We haven't seen you for weeks."

"I haven't seen you or your new husband breaking any records to get to our door," laughed Jean. "In fact, we thought maybe you were never going to come out of this house again."

"Are you coming to our party tonight?" Tazia asked, ignoring Jean's remark.

"We wouldn't miss it for anything in the world," Del answered. "Kirk tells us you're going away tomorrow."

"Yes. It's time Kirk came with me to meet my parents. I know they must be anxious to meet him. I wrote them just before the wedding to tell them we would come home soon."

"But . . . I thought—" Jean stopped abruptly as he received a warning look from Kirk.

"Well, since you're going away tomorrow, I must claim several dances tonight," Del filled in immediately.

"But of course. How could I refuse my handsome brother?"

"Good! I look forward to tonight. Good-by for now." He grinned and then kissed Tazia's cheek. Jean kissed her, too, and they left.

"Kirk, who were you talking about getting out of New Orleans? Is someone in trouble?"

"Don't worry your pretty little head about it, darling," he said quickly. "Believe me, it's unimportant."

He kissed her and changed the subject. She chattered on while he tried to control the heavy pounding of his heart. He could feel a fine film of perspiration break out on his body.

Damn, he thought. I'm glad this will be our last night in New Orleans for a long time. That was just a little too close for comfort.

It was closer than he thought, for Tazia had not missed the reaction, no matter how hard he tried to hide it. There were some unanswered questions on her mind, and she was determined to find answers . . . and soon.

21

The house was aglitter with thousands of candles. It sat like a magnificent jewel against the black night sky. Soft strains of music floated out through the open windows and across the gardens. Tazia stood in front of the mirror in her small dressing room. She could hear Kirk moving about in the next room while he dressed. Arranging the folds of her dress for the last time, she smiled in satisfaction at her reflection and prepared to face her husband. She had not allowed him to watch her dress as he always liked to do. She had insisted that he wait to see her until just before they went downstairs. The dress was still not complete, because she wanted Kirk's opinion on whether she should wear the diamonds or something else. The diamonds still lay in her jewel box, where she had put them after Kirk gave them to her.

Satisfied with her appearance, she turned to her dressing table and lifted the lid of the jewel box. The first thing to catch her eye was the folded white envelope that lay inside. At first she could not understand what it was or why it was there. Then she remembered Jeanette Plummer's visit. She took the letter from the box and was about to open it when the adjoining door opened and Kirk came in. She did not know why she did it, but she quickly refolded the letter, put it back in the box, and closed the lid. She turned to Kirk with a smile. He stopped in the doorway to admire Tazia's gown. He gave a low whistle as he leaned against the door frame.

"I can see right now this night is going to be a disaster," he said.

"A disaster?" she asked in alarm, the smile fading from her face.

"Any man who looks at you is going to turn into my mortal enemy." He sighed. "I can see I'm going to make a lot of enemies tonight."

She laughed warmly. "Should I wear the diamond necklace you gave me or the gold?"

Pushing himself away from the door, he walked toward her with a small black box in his hand. He stopped beside her. "A new gown deserves a new jewel, although I still can't find anything to make you more beautiful than you already are."

He took her hand and walked to the mirror, where he stood behind her and took from the box a beautiful necklace of gold and emeralds. She gasped at its beauty as he hung it about her neck and fastened the clasp. Then he bent and kissed the back of her neck.

"Your maid would only tell me that your dress was green. This was the best I could do under the circumstances."

"Oh Kirk, it's so beautiful." She turned to him and put her arms around his neck. Very gently he touched her lips with his.

"I don't know what you said, but it sounds like you feel exactly the way I do. I'm going to have to learn your language. It's beautiful."

"I said, 'I love you, my darling.' "

"Keep that sentiment in mind until the party's

168

over. I'll remind you later. Maybe you can elaborate on it then." He grinned lasciviously at her.

"For now, let us attend to our guests," she said firmly.

They went down the stairs together. The guests watched them with affection. They were so much in love that everyone around them was caught up in the magic. Everybody, with one exception. He stood in the open French doors that led out to the stone patio and the gardens beyond. He had a smile on his lips, but his eyes were cold and hard as he watched his hosts dancing together, oblivious to everyone about them.

"Enjoy yourself, my friend," he muttered. "It will be the last time you shall enjoy her."

He made no attempt to approach either of them, for he knew that other eyes watched his every move and that Jean Lafitte was not a man to cross. No, he had made his plans, and they included patience. He moved a step backward and watched, as a spider watches the victim caught in its web. Tazia was radiantly beautiful, and he fought an almost irresistible urge to drag her from the dance floor, to ravage that sensual mouth, to touch the lovely ivory body that he imagined beneath the emerald gown.

The hours passed, and Tazia laughed and enjoyed herself as she never had before. All of Kirk's friends enjoyed her vivacious company. Kirk had a hard time keeping her to himself for an occasional dance. He would give her up reluctantly to some engaging young man, only to follow her with his eyes until he could reclaim her.

It was almost midnight before Tazia could escape for a few minutes alone. She felt warm, so she went out to the patio for some air. The night was warm, but a light breeze touched her lightly. She was floating on a cloud of happiness, and she smiled a little when she remembered Kirk's promise for the night together. She was about to go back into the ballroom when she suddenly sensed another presence nearby. Her eyes moved restlessly to the corners of the patio until she saw a man standing alone, watching her intently.

"Good evening, Mrs. LaCroix," he said quietly.

She nodded coolly to him.

"Monsieur Flye."

"It's a lovely evening, isn't it?"

"Yes," she agreed, "it is." She turned to leave.

"Don't go in yet. Please. I've something important to talk to you about."

She hesitated. "To me? What could you have to tell me?"

"Would you take a short stroll in the garden with me? I'm sure what I have to say will interest you more than you can imagine." She hesitated, and he chuckled softly. "Are you afraid of me? I assure you that you have nothing to fear from me."

Tazia's chin rose stubbornly, and her eyes became clouded with anger. "I am afraid of no one, señor," she stated proudly.

"Then . . ." He motioned toward the garden.

Slowly, with her head held high, she passed by him and walked down the stone steps into the garden. She could sense his presence behind her, and for the first time she felt a tingle of fear. She wondered what she was afraid of. He would certainly not hurt her physically, she thought, and what could he say that would cause her any problems?

They walked together slowly, and she waited patiently for him to speak. Finally she stopped and turned to him. "I must insist you speak now, Monsieur Flye. What is it you want to say that you think would interest me?"

"You amaze me, Mrs. LaCroix. May I call you 'Tazia'?"

She nodded. "Why do I amaze you?"

"You strike me as a woman of great pride, yet—"

"What are you talking about, Monsieur Flye? Please come to the point. I must return to the party or Kirk will be looking for me."

"You know they're using you, don't you?"

"Who, Monsieur Flye? Who is using me, and for what?" She spoke now in a sharp exasperated voice.

"They knew long ago the reason for your being in New Orleans. They knew about the kidnapping of Louis Plummer and the reason for it. They planned to bring you and Kirk together to protect him from your revenge." His angry voice became sharper. "Jean and Molly used you . . . used you to protect the LaCroix's."

"No . . . no," she whispered.

"I was a participant in that card game. Do you want to hear the truth, or do you want to continue to swallow the lies you are being fed?"

"Tell me," she said softly, her face frozen and expressionless.

"Kirk LaCroix shot your brother."

She stood perfectly still.

"He and Jean and Molly have planned everything that has happened since then. Kirk does not love you. But it was convenient to marry a wealthy, beautiful woman, especially since it kept her from killing him."

There was no sign on her face that she heard anything that he said to her.

"Tazia?"

"Leave me alone," she whispered. "Please, just leave me alone."

"I shall, but I want you to remember I'm your

171

friend. I've told you the truth because I thought you had the right to know. You should not be used any longer. Kirk does not love you. You were a convenient way out. If you need a place to go, I will help you leave New Orleans. I have a ship in the harbor that is at your disposal. I've told the captain you might use his services."

She did not answer. Garrett touched her arm lightly and then walked away from her. The smile on his face was one of deep satisfaction.

Tazia had no awareness of how long she stood alone in the garden while the world disintegrated about her. The words kept echoing in her head, "He does not love you . . . he does not love you . . . he does not love you." She faced the black abyss of life without Kirk. Tears appeared at the corners of her eyes and then fell unheeded down her cheeks. Her slender body trembled like a leaf in a gale. Her mind refused to accept the implications of what she had heard. She suddenly remembered the letter. It had to be a lie. What he had told her was vicious, and it had to be untrue. It had to! She must read the letter now. Very slowly, as if unsure of where to put her feet, she walked toward the house. She had to go upstairs without being seen. She went around to the front of the house and opened the door. Closing it very quietly behind her, she climbed the stairs like a sleepwalker. She was afraid to know the truth and afraid not to. She was more afraid than she had ever been in her life. Up to now she had been able to function in an unloving world, but after Kirk would she be able to do so again? The blackness engulfed her. No! It was an unbearable thought. Life without Kirk would be as dark as the darkest moonless night.

Tazia did not hear the voice that called to her. Del stood at the bottom of the steps and called out her name several times. Immediately he realized that something was dreadfully wrong. She walked as though in a dream. In some manner unknown to him, he realized what must have happened. He turned away and almost ran back into the ballroom in search of Kirk.

One step after another, Tazia climbed the stairs and crossed the hall until she reached the bedroom. The room was dark, but she knew it so well she did not need a light. She crossed the room, lifted the lid of the jewel box, and took out the letter. She then walked to the window and pulled aside the heavy drapes, for she did not have the time or the inclination to light a candle. She opened the letter. The bright moonlight made the words on the pages clear . . . much too clear. Louis had written everything to his sister. Everything he thought was true at the time. A soft moan came from Tazia, a sound like the last agony of someone dying. She wanted to cry out against this pain. Heavy footsteps could be heard running up the stairs. She knew immediately that it was Kirk. She moved to his dresser, and from his bottom drawer she took one of his pistols. Holding it at her side, she turned to face the door.

When he came through the door, the light from the hallway silhouetted him in the doorway. He could not see her for a few moments, since the room was shrouded in darkness. Then he made out the faint outline of her body against the pale light of the window.

"Tazia—"

"Don't come near me, Kirk." Her voice was filled with torment. "Just tell me the truth."

"Tazia, please. Let me talk to you. Let me explain," he begged.

Del, Jean, and Molly appeared behind Kirk. He

held out his hand to keep them from entering the room.

"Don't. Don't go in," he whispered. He had seen a glimmer of moonlight on the silver barrel of his pistol. "She has one of my gun."

"Oh God," Del whispered.

Jean cursed softly to himself, and Molly caught her breath.

"Tazia, darling. Put the gun down. Please let me talk to you. Let me explain. It's not what you believe."

"More lies, Kirk. With my *friends* to back up what you say. Oh Kirk," she cried softly, "I loved you so."

He was shaken to his very soul by the anguish he heard in her voice. Tazia, who had given everything to their love, felt used and betrayed. He knew there were no words that were going to reach her. He was deathly afraid she would use the gun on herself. It did not occur to him that she might shoot him.

"Tell me, Kirk. Tell me the truth for the first time."

"Tell you that I love you, Tazia? That is the only truth that exists between us. What we have is beautiful. Don't destroy it. Tazia, please, just let me talk to you."

"Don't speak to me of love, Kirk. I never want to hear that word from you or any other human being for as long as I live. Just tell me the truth about my brother."

"It's not as simple as that, Tazia. Yes . . . yes, I shot Manolo." He watched a quiver of shock run through her, and he heard her swift intake of breath. The gun wavered for a second, and he took a step toward her. But she steadied the gun and pointed directly at his heart. "There are circumstances you must understand."

"Did you arrange to meet me through Jean—my very dear friend?" she asked scathingly. Jean winced at the thrust.

"Yes, but it wasn't the way it sounds."

"And our marriage. That was something you all planned, too, wasn't it?"

"No! Tazia, you've got to believe me. I love you. I love you more than my life."

Tazia was losing control over the pain. It was a live, throbbing pain deep inside her, thundering for release. Her choking sob echoed through the room before she was again able to speak. "Back away from the door, all of you."

"What are you going to do? I'm not leaving you in this room alone," Kirk said. "Tazia, just put the gun down and let me explain everything to you." He was pleading, while at the same time he was edging slowly toward her.

"Kirk," she said very firmly, "if you come one step closer to me, I shall kill you."

"Tazia, don't do this. I love you. We all love you."

"My friends! My betrayers!" Her voice had risen to near hysteria. "Get out of this room."

"We'd better do as she says for the moment, Kirk," Del said. "She's hysterical."

He took Kirk's arm and pulled him slowly backward until they all stood against the wall on the opposite side of the hall. Tazia came to the door and stood in the light. It was a view of her Kirk was to remember for a long, long time. Her face was pale and tear-stained. Her body trembled with unrestrained grief, and her eyes . . . her eyes looked at him with a combination of pain and hatred that could almost be felt like a tangible thing. Then, suddenly, she stepped back into the room, slammed the door shut, and shot the bolt across the lock.

"Tazia!" Kirk shouted as he pounded on the locked door. It was made of solid oak and did not budge an inch. They could hear her moving about in the room.

"Help me!" Kirk shouted, and the three of them put their shoulders against the door. Even with their combined weight, it was some time before the lock gave and the door flew open. They were greeted with an empty room. In the middle of the floor lay Tazia's green gown, and on top of it lay the emerald necklace he had just given her. Kirk ran to the open window, but there was no sign of her. Without a word, he turned and ran from the room. The others followed him to the stable, but the giant Juan barred the door.

"She wants time to get away, and I will give it to her," he stated firmly.

"Juan, I must get to her before she does something she'll regret." Kirk pleaded with him, but Juan's face remained closed and he did not move.

"Juan, please. If she leaves now, without knowing the truth, she'll never come back."

Still Juan would not step aside.

"Let's take him," whispered Del. "He can't handle both of us."

"Yes, try it," said Juan harshly. "For what you have done, I would be glad to have the opportunity to break you both into small pieces."

Without doubt, Juan meant every word he said. And to make matters worse, they knew he could do exactly what he threatened.

With the greatest despair Kirk had ever felt, he stood and waited until Juan thought enough time had passed. Now he knew it was too late to follow her, and he didn't know what to do or where to start looking for her.

22

After Tazia slammed the door, she ripped the necklace from her neck furiously. "A bauble to buy her," she thought angrily. She tore off her dress and flung it in a heap on the floor with the necklace on top of it. With all the speed she could manage, she pulled on her riding skirt and a blouse. Kirk and the others were beating against the door while she flung open the window and ran across the balcony to the steps that led down to the garden. She fled across the garden to the stables, where she found Juan. She told Juan breathlessly that he was to stop anyone . . . *anyone* from following her, including Kirk. He merely nodded his head, but Tazia knew that no one would get past him.

Her horse was saddled and she was on his back in a matter of seconds. She heard several people running toward the stable as she rode out the back door.

She rode for some time, urging the horse to greater and greater speed, until he was lathered and straining to keep stride. Then she slowed down to a walk to let him cool off. It was then that everything that had happened began to crowd in on her. Black oblivion faced her—despair as she had never known before in her life. Even when she first realized her parents' love was only for Manolo, she still had an outlet for her emotions in her own love for her brother. After his death, she concentrated her emotions on revenge. But for the past four months, all her hopes, dreams, and love had been centered on Kirk alone. Now there was no place for them. She felt lost and bereft of all happiness. When she had fled from the house, it was to get away from the misery and hurt that was there. She was running away, but to where? She stopped the horse and sat very still for a while. Where could she go? If she did not find a place to go, Kirk would soon find her. She could not bear to see him again. She knew the numbness she felt now would not last. If she saw him soon, she felt she would surely kill him. Things he had told her in the past few months began to seep into her consciousness. She blocked them out quickly. She didn't want to think of his tenderness or the warmth of his love. It was deceit! All love was deceit. She would never allow it to touch her again. Never as long as she lived. She would never allow anything or anyone to get close enough again to hurt her as she was hurt now.

Again she nudged the horse into motion. Now her direction was toward the dock where the *Raven* was berthed. She remembered Garrett's offer. If she could reach the ship, they could leave on the morning tide. Tazia had decided to go home. There was no more love there for her than anywhere else in her cold world, but it was at least a familiar place, and right now she needed a familiar place.

Leaving her horse with a young boy she encountered, she told him he would be rewarded well if he took the horse back to the home of Kirk LaCroix and told Kirk a woman had sent it back. Then, walking along the dock, she examined each ship until she found the *Raven*. She stood at the bottom of the gangplank.

"Ahoy aboard the *Raven*," she called.

"Aye?" called a voice from the darkness.

"Can I come aboard?"

"Come ahead," called the voice.

Tazia climbed the gangplank, holding the rope handrail.

A man stood at the rail and watched her. When she stepped on deck, she smiled at him. From the looks of his uniform and hat, she knew he was not the captain.

"I have to speak to the captain."

"Ma'am, the captain's asleep, and he'd probably skin me if I waked him now. Can't it wait until morning?"

He smiled at her, letting his eyes drift over her. It was quite obvious where he would like her to spend the rest of the night. A bright glow of anger flashed in her eyes as she glared back at him. She had taken all the masculine abuse she could handle for one night. Through gritted teeth, she smiled at him.

"If you do not send word to the captain now, I shall begin to scream very, very loudly. Loud enough to wake the dead. Then I shall proceed to tell him how you tried to rape me."

"Rape? You . . . I . . . I never tried—"

"Yes, rape. I am Mrs. Kirk LaCroix. The name, in case you do not know, is very prominent here in New Orleans. I imagine you would be spending quite a lot of time locked away safely aboard this ship."

Their eyes met, and he realized immediately that she meant every word she said. He licked his lips nervously, for he knew his captain's temper. He was caught in the middle. If he did call the captain and what she had told him was a lie, the captain would keelhaul him. If he *didn't* call the captain and she was telling the truth, he would still be keelhauled. He watched the anger boil up in her eyes. As she opened her mouth to scream, he said quickly, "All right, all right. Wait right here. I'll call the captain. But if what you say isn't true, I'll see that you pay for it."

Tazia heard his footsteps disappear, and she turned to the rail. If everything was as Mr. Flye said, she would be on her way home within an hour or so, for it was nearing dawn and the tide was due to change.

Home, she thought. Was there a haven there for her? Would her parents understand what had happened? No, they would only know she had failed. She looked down at the bright gold band that circled her finger. A wave of agony swept over her so strongly that she almost cried aloud. With trembling fingers, she slipped the ring from her finger and dropped it into the murky water.

"Mrs. LaCroix?" The gentle voice came from behind her. She turned to face the captain. He was a tall, slender man, about fifty-five. His deep-brown eyes were kind and gentle. There were fine lines at the corners of his eyes and deeper lines at the sides of his lips. He had seen much of life and had learned to compromise with it, clinging to the good and allowing the bad to pass by.

"Captain. Did Señor Flye tell you I was coming?

"Yes, I've been expecting someone, but not someone as young and lovely as you, my dear." His smile brightened the harsh thinness of his face.

She brushed aside the compliment. "We must leave as soon as possible. I'm being followed, and I want to be gone before my pursuers know there was even a ship here." He could see the bitterness and pain on her face, and he felt a deep sympathy for her.

"Come, I'll show you to your cabin. We'll leave with the tide."

"How much longer will that be?"

"I'd say about half an hour. If you would like, I could arrange something to eat."

"If you'll show me to my cabin, Captain. I'm very tired."

"Of course. Come with me."

She followed him to the companionway, and he stepped aside so she could enter. When they reached the bottom of the steps, she waited for him to take the lead. He walked a short distance and stopped in front of a door.

"This is not a luxury cabin, Mrs. LaCroix, but it is the best that this ship has to offer. I hope it is comfortable enough. If there is anything else you need, please feel free to ask me. Mr. Flye left a good deal of money, in case there were things you might need to purchase along the way."

For the first time, Tazia came to the realization that all she had in the world were the clothes on her back—and no money at all.

"Will we make port soon again?"

"Any time you choose. We are at your disposal. Those were Mr. Flye's orders, and since he is the owner of this ship, we will do our best to make you as comfortable as possible."

"Thank you, Captain. If we could make just one stop so that I could purchase some clothes, I would be grateful."

"Of course. The first port we reach, we'll stop for a few hours."

His eyes observed the tired look about her eyes and the droop of her shoulders.

"You look exhausted. Why don't you sleep for a while? I'll call you before we make port."

"Thank you again, Captain. I am very grateful for your kindness and consideration. I shall never forget them."

He smiled again, and she returned the smile unconsciously. "Get some sleep," he said as he patted her shoulder gently. Then he turned and walked back the way he had come. As she stood and watched him leave, she was suddenly aware that she was being watched. Slowly she turned. Deep in the shadows at the far end of the hallway, a man stood silent. She could not make out his features, but she felt his eyes on her. It made her skin prickle with a chill of fear. She pushed the door open and closed it quickly behind her.

"Thank God," she murmured to herself as she realized there was a lock on the door. She shot home the bolt just as soft footsteps passed her door. She could hear a very soft chuckle in the darkness.

Tazia turned to look at the room. It was small, indeed. It contained a bunk, a huge chest, and one stand on which sat a bowl and pitcher for washing. There was a full bookcase against the far wall and a huge, comfortable chair in front of it. When she saw these, she realized that the captain must have given her his cabin.

Suddenly she was so tired she could barely move. She went to the bed and pulled back the covers. Slowly, as though each movement were painful, she removed her clothes. Then she climbed into the bed and pulled up the covers. Exhausted as she was, she could not sleep. Instead of sleep, the dreaded memories returned: warm arms enclosed her; a soft voice whispered words of love in her ear.

"Go away, Kirk," she moaned. "I hate you. Get out of my life. Get out of my dreams."

Hot tears flooded her eyes. The final realization of her betrayal was hitting her like a tidal wave. She turned her head and sobbed into the pillow. She cried until her eyes burned like fire and her worn body and emotions could stand no more. Finally she fell into an exhausted sleep.

The captain was standing at the wheel. His thoughts were on the young girl asleep below. He had not expected someone so beautiful—obviously a lady. He was used to the eccentricities of his ship's owner and the type of young woman that attracted him. This girl did not seem to be that type at all. He wondered whether the girl knew all about him or not. Well, he thought, he had not the right to interfere in Mr. Flye's or the young lady's business. His job was to take her where she wanted to go. Still, he wondered about her and felt an urge to protect her. He thought of his own daughter safe at home with his wife awaiting his return. He promised himself that if she needed his help and asked for it, he would do what he could to help her. The first mate came up beside the Captain.

"Everything well Stone?"

"Aye, sir. We'll make good time. The wind's behind us."

"Good. I want to stop at the first port. The young lady needs to shop for some clothes."

The first mate grinned, and for some reason that irritated the captain.

"What's amusing, Stone?"

"Nothin', sir. I was just wondering where Mr. Flye picked up a doxie that looks like this one."

"You don't know that's the story, Stone. I'd suggest you keep your thoughts to yourself until you do."

"Oh, come on, Captain Carothers. You know how many women Flye's shipped back and forth for all kinds of reasons. This is just another one. Though I'll admit this one has more class than the rest of them put together."

"Stone, you keep your mind and your hands off the lady. Do I make myself clear? Concentrate on your job for a change and not on the passengers."

"Yes, sir," Stone said mildly. But his eyes glowed as he watched the captain walk away. Stone hated the captain. It was the pure and simple hatred of an inferior man for a superior one. He stayed on the ship because he was a spy for Garrett and he did some of the things Flye knew the captain would not do. The captain had a sense of honor that would not have occurred to either Flye or Stone. He was something that was completely alien to them: an honorable, honest man.

Well, he had shared Flye's women before, and he certainly intended to share this one. He had stood at the end of the hall watching her talk to the captain. She was a luscious woman, with ivory skin and dark hair. He could even picture her without her clothes, moaning in passion beneath him. He licked his lips in anticipation. He would have her, and soon. He felt sure Flye would not care if he tasted their cargo before he delivered it to him. He had done so many times before.

The ship rose and fell gently with the waves as the morning sun crossed the horizon. Three people whose lives had suddenly become entangled were aboard. Tazia, asleep and dreaming her violent dreams. Stone, at the wheel, his mind on his future conquest. And Captain Carothers, who walked the deck of his ship, deep in thought. He was not unaware of Flye and his projects. Nor was he unaware of Stone's role aboard the ship. As long as what they did was not brought directly to his attention, he ignored it and did his job to the best of his ability. But his distaste for both of them and their ways was growing. He thought of Tazia, and he knew she was not Flye's woman, even though he had been told that she was. He also thought about Flye and Stone, and he made up his mind to protect her from both of them if it ever became necessary.

23

Kirk was frantic with worry. They had left no stone unturned, but it appeared that Tazia had just disappeared from the face of the earth. Jean was just as amazed at their failure to find her right away, for he knew just about everyone in New Orleans. He felt sure they would find her within hours. But when the hours turned into days and the days into weeks, he became alarmed. How did she get out of New Orleans? If she had not left the city, he would have known.

They were at Jean's home very late one night. Kirk was pacing the floor. His eyes were red from lack of sleep, and even his strong body was rapidly reaching the point of exhaustion. Added to this was the fact that he was not eating and he was consuming, to Jean and Del's alarm, entirely too much wine. He raked his fingers through his already disheveled hair.

"Somebody had to give her a means to get away," he groaned. "But who? And how, at such short notice?"

"You're right, Kirk. She had to have help getting out of the city, and I can't think of anyone she knows except Juan and María, and they are both still here under surveillance," Jean replied.

Del watched his brother. He had never seen anything unnerve him so. Del was so tired he could barely control the desire to just lean back against the chair and go to sleep. His mind was in such a deep fog he could not think straight. He held the glass of wine in his hand and kept turning it around and around. A thought in the back of his mind kept eluding him. He chased it through clouds of elusive memories, but he was incapable of grasping it. He took a sip of wine and leaned his head wearily against the back of the chair and closed his eyes. When he relaxed, it suddenly burst upon him. He opened his eyes with a snap. "Oh, God!" he exclaimed.

"What?" demanded Kirk.

"Who would gain anything by helping her?"

Kirk and Jean shook their heads.

"Think, damn it! Who wanted Tazia as badly as you did, Kirk? Who would have the means at his disposal to help her get away?"

Kirk's pale face became gray with alarm. His eyes sharpened to pinpoints of rage. "Garrett Flye," he replied slowly as he clenched his fists. "I shall kill that bastard." He moved rapidly toward the door.

"Wait, Kirk!" shouted Jean. He might as well have been talking to a hurricane for all the attention Kirk paid. Quickly Jean and Del scrambled to their feet and followed him. They were heading toward the stable when they heard his horse gallop away. They quickly saddled their own horses, hoping they would catch Kirk in time to keep him from killing Garrett or, worse yet, from being killed himself. They pushed their mounts, but when they arrived at Garrett's home, Kirk's horse was standing in front of it with the reins trailing on the ground. They dismounted and rushed up the steps to the door, but just then it was flung open and a wild-eyed and furious Kirk was standing in the doorway.

"He's gone. No one seems to know where. He's been gone for two weeks." He ground the words out between clenched teeth. "We've got to find out where and how he left town. There has to be someone who's seen him leave."

"Kirk, go on home and get some rest. Leave the rest to me," said Jean quietly. "I guarantee you, within a few hours I will have him run to ground."

Kirk's whole body was trembling with a combination of extreme anger, frustration, and exhaustion. Still, he was wise enough to see that he couldn't go on the way he was.

"You'll call on me by morning, Jean?"

"Absolutely."

"All right," he sighed. "I do need a few hours of rest."

Jean nodded to Del, who took Kirk by the arm. "Come on, Kirk. We'll get an early start."

They were silent as they rode home together. They went into the house, and Kirk walked slowly up the stairs to his room. He threw his jacket on a chair, removed his boots, and lay back against the pillows. It was the biggest mistake he'd made in the past few days. Tazia's perfume lingered on the pillow and surrounded him with memories. With a groan, he heaved himself from the bed. He could not sleep with that scent around him. He moved to a chair, leaned his head back against it, and closed his eyes. Almost immediately he was asleep.

Del was shaking his arm. "Kirk . . . Kirk, wake up."

He was so disoriented that he could only stare at Del for a moment. Then it all came back to him in a rush. "Del? Has Jean heard anything?"

"Yes. Garrett packed up and took the coach. He's on his way to southern California. Need I tell you where?

"No! He's going to Tazia's home. Then he must expect her to be there, too. But how did she—?"

"Garrett had a ship in port. He obviously had this all well-planned. He must have told her the truth at the party and offered her the use of his ship. I'm only glad that he didn't try to sail with her. He must have known she wouldn't put up with that, so he took the coach, but they're both headed in the same direction."

Kirk stood up and began to swiftly gather his clothes. He washed quickly and got dressed. By the time they were coming downstairs, Jean was already there waiting for them.

"What's the fastest way to get there, Jean?" Kirk asked grimly.

"The same way she's going. By ship first, then to California by coach. The way Garrett's going, even with a two-week head start, we should get there at almost the same time. Kirk—"

"Don't bother to warn me about anything, Jean. One way or another, I'm going to kill Garrett Flye." He said it with cold, clipped words.

"Kirk, you can't do that. I've got nothing against you taking some kind of payment from his hide, but if you kill him, Tazia will never learn the real truth. Then where will you be?" Jean asked logically.

Kirk stopped, his eyes two pieces of frozen blue ice. "If Tazia were *your* wife, Jean, what would you do to Garrett?"

Jean sighed. "I'd want to do the same thing you're thinking of doing. But use your head. If you want Tazia back, you've got to fight for her. The truth has

189

to come out, and you've got to get Garrett and Tazia and her family together. You've got to make them understand what really happened. The whole thing depends on you, so you've got to control that temper." He paused and watched Kirk closely. He was on the edge of explosion. "Kirk, do you hear me?"

"Yes, I hear you. I know you're right, Jean. I'll get myself under control." He turned to face Jean, and his eyes were filled with death. "But I guarantee you, if Garrett lays a hand on her, just touches her . . . I will kill him!" His voice was so quietly violent that Jean could only nod.

There was silence in the room as Del and Jean exchanged fear-filled glances. Then a knock sounded at the door. A caller at this early hour was a complete surprise to all of them. Jean tore his eyes from Kirk and walked to the door. When he pulled it open, he was completely stunned to find Louis Plummer, accompanied by one of the most beautiful women he'd ever seen. He stood in shocked silence, unable for a moment to comprehend the fact of their presence at his door. Louis grinned broadly. Looking forward to Jean Lafitte's shock was one of the things that made the journey a joy.

"Monsieur Lafitte?"

Jean had gotten complete control of himself now, and he grinned in return. "I must say, the sea air has been beneficial to you, Monsieur Plummer." He looked closely at the slender, tan, handsome young man before him. He was a completely different person from the one he had put on board his ship.

"I would say it's been very rewarding, also." He looked at Gabrielle with deep appreciation, which brought to her face a provocative smile and a blush.

"Monsieur Lafitte, may I present my wife,

Gabrielle Saint-Albin Plummer."

"Saint-Albin? Any relation to the Saint-Albins in Virginia?" asked Del.

"He was my uncle," replied Gabrielle. "I own Five Points Plantation," she said proudly.

"Louis!" A shocked Kirk looked at him from the doorway.

"Kirk, old friend. I'm glad I got to you in time. I've a story to tell you about Tazia and our old friend Garrett."

"I'm afraid we have a story to tell you, too, Louis," Del said. Kirk's face became black with suppressed anger.

Louis looked from one to the other, and then he noticed evidence of their imminent departure. "Maybe I wasn't in time after all," he said quietly. "Can someone explain just what's been going on?"

"We can't right now, Louis," Kirk replied. "We're wasting valuable time. Every minute we spend talking, he gets closer to Tazia."

"Well you've got to take a few minutes to listen to me. I think I've got the answers to why all this came about in the first place."

"Louis—" Kirk began.

"Wait a moment, all of you," Jean interrupted.

He turned to Gabrielle and smiled. "Lovely lady, would you consider being our honored guest for a few weeks? And would you also consider letting us borrow your husband for a short time if I promise faithfully to bring him back in good health?"

"Now wait a minute," said a surprised Louis.

"We are wasting time, Louis." Jean spoke gently but firmly, "If we exchange stories on the way, it would be best for all concerned."

"But—" Louis began.

"Louis." Gabrielle put her hand on his arm and

191

smiled up at him. "I would not mind at all being a guest of Jean Lafitte, since it is he who brought us together. It would only be for a short while, and if you can help your friends, you should. After all you've told me about Monsieur Flye, I think you would be helping me also."

"The lady is not only beautiful, she is very intelligent. You are a very lucky man, Louis." Jean bowed slightly toward Gabrielle, who acknowledged his compliment with a bright smile.

"Gabrielle." Louis took her hand in his. "Do you mind staying here for a while. I could take you home to my sister, but that would mean another long drive."

"Nonsense, darling," she replied. "I'm sure I will be quite comfortable here, and I pray you make great speed, for we both know what kind of man pursues your friend's wife, do we not? You would not want him to reach her before you and your friends, would you?"

"I love you, Gabrielle," he whispered in her ear. He kissed her cheek. "All right, gentlemen, I'm ready."

Jean called Philippe and had him take Gabrielle to a room and make her comfortable. Then the four of them left for the dock. Jean's ship, the *Raven* was the fastest he could find. Within an hour, they were pulling away from the harbor and filling her sails, heading toward California and whatever they would find there.

It was late the next night. They had kept up a steady speed with the wind in their favor. Kirk stood against the rail and looked off toward the horizon. His mind was so deep in his own dark thoughts that he didn't hear his brother until he stood beside him. They did not need to speak. Del knew what Kirk was going through, and he sympathized silently.

They had exchanged stories, as Jean had suggested, each one of them amazed at the other's side of the tale. The realization of how well Garrett had planned the robbery of Gabrielle, the set-up of the card game, and finally the death of Manolo de Montega shook them all.

"God only knows what other things he's been involved in, how many other women he's taken advantage of," Louis had said coldly. "Garrett has much to account for."

All was quiet now on the ship. Kirk had thought all the others were asleep. He had found it almost impossible to sleep, even with the aid of the wine he had been drinking. He'd come on deck to try to gather together his thoughts and to get his violent emotions under control. Even if they did get to Garrett, he thought, would Tazia believe the truth about her brother? He was afraid. Deep inside, he was afraid she would never be able to forgive him. How was he to face the rest of his life without her? It was an impossibility. He did not want to even think about it. He closed his eyes for a moment. He could see her as clearly as if she actually stood before him—the first time he'd seen her dancing, again at Lafitte's house as they rode together, and finally when they were married. Then her face came to him again, tear-stained and filled with rage, but more than that with unbelievable pain in her dark-blue eyes. He would never be able to forget as long as he lived the way she had looked at him as she stood in their bedroom doorway. It was etched on his mind along with the hatred he felt for the man who caused all their grief. Visions of Garrett with Tazia tortured him.

Del watched the play of emotions across his brother's face. He felt deep pity for Kirk and frustration that nothing he could say or do at the moment would help. He put his hand on his brother's shoulder. "It'll all work out, Kirk. We'll find them in time."

"Even if we do find them in time, Del, is Tazia going to believe what we have to say about her brother? I don't think so. We have no proof except Garrett and Gabrielle. Gabrielle isn't here, and we might not be able to get Garrett to tell the truth."

"Kirk, you've got to stop punishing yourself this way."

"Did you see her face, Del? When she stood in that doorway, did you see her face? She'll never be able to forgive me for what I've done, much less live with me again as my wife." He uttered a small laugh that was so filled with pain it hurt Del to hear it. Then he added in a soft voice, "What do I do, wander through the rest of my life without her? At this moment, I find *that* the most impossible thought of all."

Del turned away. He could not bear the pain his brother was suffering, and he could do nothing about it.

Slowly the days and nights dragged by. It was with great relief that they watched the approaching shoreline. In a few more days they would be in California. They made the trip mostly in silence. All three of them watched Kirk closely. He was like a coiled snake, ready to strike. No one knew just how or when he would, or how deadly it would be when he did.

They arrived in Escondido in the early afternoon and hired horses to ride out to the hacienda. Kirk's agitation became more pronounced as they crested the last hill and looked down on Casa del Sol. "Valley of the sun," Kirk said softly. "She loved this place. I can see why. It's beautiful."

They looked down on a lush, green valley. The house was long, low, and brilliantly white against the green. It had a red-tile roof and walks alongside the house, shaded by a roof supported by arched columns. The house had the look of cool, quiet splendor.

The four men wondered what they would find there when they arrived. Slowly they urged their horses forward, up the drive to the front of the house. They were about to dismount when the door opened and Tazia walked out, carrying a rifle in her hand.

"Do not bother to dismount. You are not welcome here. Please leave immediately, or I shall be forced to shoot you," she said icily. Her eyes refused to meet Kirk's. It was as if she had willed him not to exist.

"Tazia," he said quietly, "listen to us please, for both our sakes. At least listen to what Louis has to say."

Tazia's face was pale, and her eyes were large and expressionless. "I do not want to hear what anyone has to say. The past is gone. We cannot resurrect my brother." Her eyes rose to Kirk. They were filled with such hatred that he was chilled. "We also cannot resurrect my father, who died of grief over the loss of his son. Go away, leave me in peace. Have you not done enough harm to my family? Go away . . . or I will kill you now."

They knew she spoke the truth, and they turned away. When they were out of sight of the house, they stopped. Kirk said nothing, for he was lost in his own grief. It was Jean who said slowly, "I wonder where Garrett Flye is?"

24

Tazia walked around the deck slowly. The late evening breeze was cool on her flushed face. Her cabin had been so warm she could not sleep, so she had dressed and wrapped a shawl about her shoulders and had gone up to get some air. They had stopped for a few hours in a small seaport town, where Tazia had purchased a few necessities. She felt uncomfortable taking any of Garrett's money, and she swore to the captain that she would repay it as soon as she was safely home. He admired the pride and courage she showed. He knew deep in his heart that this woman did not belong to Garrett Flye.

Tazia's hair hung down her back in a thick silken mass. She pulled her fingers through it to allow the breeze to cool her. She refused to allow her thoughts to go backward in time. If she allowed Kirk entrance into her mind and heart for one minute, she would not be able to survive. Never again was she going to allow anyone to reach her as he had. With grim determination, she fed the hatred in her until it blazed like a fire. Each time in her short lifetime that she had dared to love, it had been destroyed brutally and painfully. She vowed it would never happen again. Once she was home, Kirk could not reach her again. When she told her parents the truth, it would be impossible for Kirk to get to her without her father killing him. She would be safe . . . safe.

Tazia leaned against the rail and closed her eyes for a moment. They burned with the tears she refused to shed. In the past three weeks, she had grown thinner, and dark shadows lay under her eyes. It served only to make them look larger and deeper.

She was so lost in thought that she did not hear the footsteps behind her until it was too late. She turned around quickly. Stone was standing directly behind her, so close they were almost touching. He was without a doubt a handsome man, but the cold lust that burned in his eyes roused a feeling of fear in her.

"What do you want, Mr. Stone? I would like some privacy, if possible."

"My cabin is very private," he said suggestively. His eyes dropped from her face to her body, hidden beneath the folds of her shawl. She pulled it tighter. She could feel her skin crawl with aversion.

"Would you care to share a cool drink with me on such a warm night?"

"No, thank you. I'm going to my own cabin to sleep. Good night, Mr. Stone."

She tried to move past him, but he blocked her way. He took hold of her arm in a tight grip. "If you don't want to share my cabin, I don't mind sharing yours." He laughed ominously.

She jerked away from him and gave him a look of pure fury. "Let me alone, Mr. Stone. Let me alone."

Suddenly he reached out and grasped both her arms and jerked her toward him. He pulled her against his hard chest so suddenly and brutally that it left her breathless. She opened her mouth to scream, but it never escaped. Instead, his mouth covered hers in a savage kiss that bruised her lips. She writhed in his arms, but that only inflamed him more. He forced her mouth open, and his tongue invaded her. She tried to cry out, but only soft moans could be heard. Not enough to carry far. When he released her mouth, she was gasping and choking with anger.

"You're a good enough bedmate for Flye; what makes you think you're too good for me?" he snarled at her.

"You pig," she said coldly. "I am nobody's bedmate. Not Flye's, not yours, not anyone's."

"Now, that's not what Mr. Flye tells me. We're supposed to deliver you to him at Brownsville, and you'll travel the rest of the way to California together. I know he expects you to go most the way on your back."

"That's a lie. I'm going to California alone. Mr. Flye promised me safe passage all the way."

"Sure, safe passage. He didn't say anything about being *alone* all the way, did he? When you reach the coast, he'll be there to meet you."

She almost strangled in her fury. Again she had been foolish enough to trust a man. God help her. Would she ever learn they were all deceitful animals, not be to loved or trusted . . . ever?

"Let me go, Stone," she ground out between her clenched teeth.

"Not until I've tasted a little of the honey Flye's trying to reserve for himself." He had a tight hold on her and was pushing her into a dark corner, where they would not be seen. Again she opened her mouth to scream, when he struck a blow on the side of her face. For a moment, she was limp, as brilliant flashes exploded in her head. It was all the time he needed. He fumbled with her dress and then tore the bodice apart. Grasping her hair, he pulled her head back until she arched against him. His mouth covered hers

198

again as his hands fondled her roughly. She fought with every ounce of strength she possessed, but he was much larger and stronger than she. Suddenly he released her, and she fell away from him, gasping and sobbing. When she looked up, dazed, she saw Captain Carothers glaring at Stone.

"I warned you, Stone, to keep your hands off her. She is not the type of woman you and Flye are used to." His voice was cold and hard. "We're putting you off this ship at the next port, and I never want to see your face again—or I shall kill you. Do you understand?"

"Flye isn't going to like that. He's got her all lined up for himself, or for one of his houses. He'll be at Brownsville to meet the ship and pick her up. He's not going to like you interfering in his private business. Besides, what's the difference whether I enjoy her a little now or later? I'll get her either way."

Captain Carothers raised his hand and struck Stone open-handed across the face. It was a direct insult, for he did not bother to close his fist, as he ordinarily would have against a man. He struck him as a woman would. The blow sounded sharply in the night silence.

"I should have gotten rid of you a long time ago," he said quietly, "but thank God it's not too late to rectify my mistake. And as for Flye, I'll be leaving his service after this trip. I don't like him, and I don't like you. You are both the same kind of animal."

Stone glared at him for another moment. Then he looked down at Tazia, who was panting and trying to hold together the torn front of her dress.

"I'll see you again," he growled. "And the next time, it will be different."

"Stone!"

With one last look of hatred at both of them, Stone

turned and walked away.

Captain Carothers helped Tazia to her feet. She was trembling violently with fear and rage. "Did you hear what he said? If I go to Brownsville, Flye will be there. I must find another way home."

"You are right, but we must not let Stone know how you are traveling or he will find a way to get word to Flye."

"I have an idea. Come down and change your dress. Then we'll talk."

She nodded her head and preceded him to her cabin. He waited outside while she changed. Then she opened the door and he came in. She left the door standing open, which he observed in silence. She no longer trusted anyone, not even him.

He sat down on a chair and sighed deeply. He watched her sit down on the bunk opposite him. She had put herself close to the door.

"Child, there's no need to be afraid of me," he said softly, his eyes now gentle. "You remind me very much of my daughter. I would hope in such circumstances someone would help her as I would like to help you now."

"You will forgive me, Captain Carothers, but I have found that it is unwise to trust anyone. You said you had a plan?"

"My home is Matagardo Bay. My wife and daughter are there. I meant to go there on my return trip, but we could stop there now. They could arrange passage for you on a coach to your home. Neither Stone nor Flye need know where or how you've gone."

She considered this and then nodded her head slowly. He rose to go. From the door, he looked back at her. Despite her feelings, she looked very vulnerable and pathetically alone.

"Tazia," he said softly, "all men are not the same as these two. Some day you will learn the difference."

Her eyes flashed. "There is no difference. Whether they come mouthing words of love or in lust, it is all the same. I shall never let myself be fool enough to trust another man."

The captain's eyes were sad as he watched her.

"Don't be a fool, child, one has to have love in this world to exist. The fire of any other emotion burns away to ashes. It is only love that endures and grows stronger."

"Love?" She gave a harsh laugh. "Don't say that word to me. Love does not exist except in the sodden minds of poets. It is a beautiful word. Too bad it is used so to disguise such disagreeable things. Better to use such words as betrayal or lust. They are words that describe men more accurately."

"You've been badly hurt. But the world does not end with that. You go on, and someday things may change. You may find that you can love again."

"Please, Captain, I am very tired. It is no use for us to argue about such an unimportant thing. I am grateful for the help you have offered me. If I can get safely home, then . . ." She stopped as she realized something.

"Then . . . what?" he asked gently.

For a few moments she sat very still, looking inward. "I don't know," she whispered, almost to herself. She looked up again quickly to find his eyes filled with kindness. She could not bear to look at him.

"Good night, Captain."

He looked at her for another second, wanting to comfort her in some way, but knowing he was unable to reach her. Then, with a sad look, he closed the door behind him.

Tazia sat quietly on the bed. The shock of everything she had been through in the past month washed over her in a wave of black despair. Hot tears fell on her cheeks, but she did not brush them away. Instead, she put her arms around herself, bent her head forward, and gave in to the misery that engulfed her. She cried until exhaustion overtook her. Then she lay back on the bunk and fell into a deep sleep.

Captain Carothers was true to his word. Stone was put ashore at the next port. Tazia stood at the rail and watched him leave. The look of burning hatred in his eyes was almost a physical blow.

"You haven't seen the last of me," he said as he passed her.

She felt the cold chill of his hatred. When they cast off again, she was relieved that he was no longer aboard.

They traveled only two days more before they reached Captain Carothers's home. He introduced her to his wife and daughter. In private, he told them of her situation. They treated her with kindness and made all the arrangements for the continuation of her trip. Soon she was in a coach on her way toward Casa del Sol—home. When familiar country began to appear, she could barely wait to get home. Although she knew she would be greeted formally and with no show of emotion, it was still home. She desperately needed a sanctuary, a place where she could feel safe for the first time in a long while.

When they reached the town, Tazia acquired a horse from the stableman, who recognized her immediately.

"Señorita de Montega. It has been a long time since we've seen your pretty face around here. You have been away?"

"Yes, Miguel, for quite some time. But now I'm home to stay. How are my parents, Miguel? Have you seen them? Do they come to town often?"

"Señorita, I have not seen Don Ramón for weeks, and Señora de Montega has not been away from Casa del Sol for almost as long."

"Can I have one of your best horses, Miguel? I want to get home as soon as possible."

"*Sí*, of course. You shall have nothing but the best," he said with a smile.

The horse was ready within minutes. As she turned the horse to leave, she heard Miguel call after her.

"Welcome home, Señorita de Montega."

They were the first words of welcome she had heard since her arrival, and they made her feel elated. She turned her horse toward Casa del Sol. Home, she thought, I shall soon be home.

When she rode up the last hill, overlooking her home, she stopped the horse and drank in the beauty of the scene before her. Then she put her heels to the horse and rode down the hill to the front of the house. It was strangely quiet. Usually the servants and their children could be seen moving about. Now there was complete quiet. She dismounted, walked across the stone patio, and pushed open the huge front door. She stepped inside the cool house. Everything was just as she remembered, but there were no signs of anyone being home. She called out to her mother and father. For several minutes, it remained quiet. Then the sound of swiftly moving footsteps could be heard upstairs. She turned toward the stairs with a smile of expectancy.

Marguerite, her closest friend, came down the stairs. Her eyes were large with surprise. "Tazia," she said in a shocked whisper. "We didn't expect . . . I mean, we thought . . . oh, Madre de Dios," she whimpered.

Tazia's smile faded. "What's the matter,

Marguerite? Where are my parents?"

Marguerite's face grew white. Tazia ran to her, grasped her shoulders, and gave her a hard shake.

"Where is Mama? Where is Papa? Marguerite, tell me or I shall throttle you."

Marguerite began to cry, and Tazia realized she was frightened almost out of her wits. She dropped her arms and stared at Marguerite. With a feeling of dread growing in her, she asked softly, "Marguerite, where is my father?"

"Dead," Marguerite moaned.

Tazia gulped to keep from screaming.

"And my mother?"

"She is upstairs, but she is . . . is . . . oh, Dios Mio, she is like an empty shell. She does not see or hear. Since your father—"

Marguerite did not finish her words, for Tazia's world went suddenly black, and she slowly crumpled in a heap at Marguerite's feet.

25

Tazia came up from a deep, dark cave. She did not want to come back to this world filled with hatred and pain. Someone carried her upstairs and lay her on a bed. Someone was whispering somewhere in the room, but she did not have the strength to open her eyes and see who it was. If she opened her eyes, she would have to face the world again. Someone lifted her hand patted it gently. Finally, whoever was holding her hand must have become alarmed at her continued unconsciousness for she began to pat her hand more firmly.

"Tazia, Tazia, please wake up."

She opened her eyes and looked up into Marguerite's frightened face. Marguerite gave a small smile of relief. "Thank God. You had me so frightened. I am so glad to see you awake and well."

Tazia turned her face away and lay quietly for a few minutes. Then she said in a low, strained voice, "Tell me, Marguerite. Tell me what happened."

"Oh, can't we wait until you are rested and stronger?"

"No! Tell me now. I want to know how and why

my father died. And I want to know why my mother is in the condition she is. Tell me now, Marguerite. I want to know." Her voice died to a cracked whisper, but her eyes were tearless now.

"Well," Marguerite began, "it happened not too long after you left. One morning when your father was in his study, two gentlemen and a young woman arrived in a carriage. They were shown into your father's study. After a while, your father sent for your mother. Tazia, never in my life have I heard such shouting and anger from your father. It was a terrible, terrible fight. Suddenly someone screamed, and we all rushed into the study, afraid that one of them might have done some harm to your father or mother."

She stopped talking and sat remembering what she had seen.

"Go on, Marguerite."

"When we entered the room, your father was slumped over his desk, dead of a heart attack. Your mother was standing staring at him like a statue. The three people who had come to see them did not say anything to us. They simply left the house."

"Do you know who they were or what they could have told my father to upset him so?"

"We know who they were. We do not know what they could have said to upset Don Ramón, and they would not tell us . . . then, or now."

"Now? You mean . . . ?"

"It was Don Federico and his brother, Don Manuel. The woman was Don Federico's daughter, Cristina."

"They were friends of our family! Don Federico is a good man. What would he have told my father to make him so angry?"

"Tazia, it was not our place to question such a man as Don Federico. We buried your father, and I have taken care of your mother as I can. We did not know when you would return, but I have prayed to the blessed Mother every day to make it soon."

"Oh Marguerite, the whole world is a place of destruction and pain. I can't bear it." She began to cry, softly at first, but when Marguerite drew her into her arms to comfort her, it was almost too much for Tazia. She cried until there were no more tears left in her. Then, in a very hoarse voice, she told Marguerite all that had happened since she had left Casa del Sol.

"My poor child," Marguerite crooned softly to her. "My poor, poor little *chiquita*. Do not worry now. You are home with us. No one will hurt you again. We must care for you, dear one, as best as we can and try to make a new beginning for you."

For several days, Tazia moved in a dream world. She had gone to her father's grave the first day. Then she had gone to her mother's room. She could not believe what her mother had become. Most of the time her mother sat motionless. Then she would have lucid moments, when she would talk away to her husband or her son in Spanish. It hurt Tazia very deeply when she realized that none of her mother's conversation was ever centered on her.

No matter how gently they questioned her, she would say nothing more. She would simply step back into her fantasy world and cease to talk for days.

Tazia wakened early one morning several days later. Marguerite tapped on her door, and at a call from Tazia she came in bearing a breakfast tray. When Tazia swung her legs over the edge of the bed and stood up, a wave of nausea suddenly struck her and she had to grab the bedpost to keep from falling. She clung to it until her dizzy world stopped spinning. Marguerite rushed to Tazia's side and helped her sit back down on the bed. Slowly Tazia lifted her eyes to meet Marguerite's. A wordless question from Tazia's eyes was answered by Marguerite's eyes.

"No," Tazia whispered as her face filled with anger. "No, I won't have his child. I won't, I *won't!*"

"Tazia, that is a terrible thing to say," Marguerite said sharply. "The child is not to blame for the father."

Tazia did not seem to be listening to her at all.

"Why? Why did I not kill him when I had the chance?"

"That would have changed nothing, *querida*."

"What will I do? I do not want his child," she cried.

"*Querida*, listen to me. Do not say these things. You do not want something to happen to this child. Remember, although it is his seed, it is still you who possesses the child. He need never know. The child will be yours," Marguerite added with wisdom beyond Tazia's grasp. "Yours to love and care for always. No one can take that away from you."

Finally, what Marguerite was saying seemed to reach the dark corners of her mind.

"*Her* child . . . *her* child. Yes. Kirk need never know."

She nodded her head slowly, then stood erect. Marguerite was pained to see the expression on Tazia's face. This was the child she had raised since birth. She had always been a sweet, gently affectionate girl. Now, suddenly, she was a woman. Not a woman with love and gentleness, but a hard woman. It was as if the inner core of Tazia was afraid. Afraid for herself and afraid for the child. This was no longer a woman who would give love and warmth. This was a woman who would take everything people had to give and give nothing in return. Marguerite knew it was wrong, just as she knew there were no words she could say to change what had been done.

Marguerite's mind reached out to the man who had caused all this grief for her beloved child. She was a simple woman, to whom love and giving were second nature. But she wondered about Kirk LaCroix and what kind of a man he was. She wondered if he would ever come here to Casa del Sol. She prayed he would not, for if Tazia were left alone to bear her child and to learn to love again, perhaps she would be healed of the evil that now lived deep in her. It was a prayer that was not to be answered.

Tazia had begun to dress. She wore a white blouse and the full, flowered skirt of a peasant woman. She quickly fixed her hair in one long braid and let it hang down her back. Slipping her feet into a pair of soft, black sandals, she turned to Marguerite. She was about to speak when she heard the sound of approaching horses. Tazia ran to the window and pulled aside the curtain. Her face drained of its color, and cold, hard fury filled her eyes. Quickly she turned and ran from the room. Marguerite, taken by surprise, went to the window and looked down. Four men were sitting on their horses in front of the house. With a sinking heart, she realized that one of these men must be Kirk LaCroix. She turned from the window and left the room. As she went down the stairs, she could see Tazia standing on the porch with a gun in her hand aimed at Kirk's heart.

Marguerite stood just inside the door and listened. She heard him plead with Tazia to let them explain. She knew before she heard Tazia speak that nothing they said was penetrating her dark world. Watching Kirk's face, Marguerite knew two things for certain. He was suffering as much as Tazia was, and he loved Tazia deeply. Suddenly the feeling came to her that it was unfair that he did not know about his child. But there was no way for her to reach him without Tazia knowing. Marguerite would not let anything hurt Tazia again. She would not go to Kirk herself, for betraying Tazia was beyond her comprehension. But she would light candles at the church and pray that the Lord would help Tazia through this time and bring them together again.

Tazia stood and watched the riders until they were out of sight. From where she stood Marguerite could see that her whole body was trembling. Her face was very pale, and dark shadows under her eyes were prominent. She moved with a slow weariness.

"I want you to give orders to the men, Marguerite. None of those men are to be allowed on this property again. Do you understand?"

"*Sñ*, Tazia, I understand," she replied softly. This was an order she would take her time about giving. Maybe something would happen to change it.

Marguerite watched as Tazia stood the rifle in the corner and walked into the large living room. The room's ceilings had large oak beams, pale ivory-colored walls, and oak woodwork, polished to a deep glow. In the center of the wall facing the doorway, was a fireplace that Tazia could have stood inside. In fact, she often had as a little girl. The furniture was large and heavy. Bright-red cushions with threads of black and silver gave the room a feeling of warmth. The drapes were drawn back from the windows, which rose from the ceiling to the floor. It was a room that echoed times of beauty and laughter. Tazia stood in the center remembering those times.

"The man on the sorrel horse was Kirk LaCroix, was it not?" Marguerite asked as Tazia nodded.

"I watched his face as he spoke to you, little one."

Marguerite tentatively added, "He loves you, Tazia."

Tazia did not raise her voice. She did not even turn to face Marguerite. Her voice was cold and merciless.

"Marguerite, if you mention Kirk LaCroix's name in this house again, you will leave it and never return."

Marguerite was stunned. This was a completely different person from the one she had known. She felt hurt, but the pain was more for Tazia than for herself. Now Tazia turned to face her.

"Do you understand, Marguerite?"

"Oh yes, Tazia," she answered softly as she watched Tazia walk away to go to her room.

"I understand, my child, that you loved him then, you love him now, and you will love him until you die. And if something or someone does not help you, you shall surely die."

The days of the next two weeks were uneventful. Tazia was ill several mornings, but it did not last long. She was an active and healthy woman. She had accepted the child now as something that was part of her. She would not even consider it as part of Kirk, too. Every day was a struggle, but she was putting him out of her life completely.

Marguerite prayed and watched and waited, for she felt something would happen to enable her to get some word to Kirk, at least about the baby.

They were working together in the kitchen late one afternoon. Tazia wanted to prepare her mother's tray for dinner, hoping that there would be some sign of recognition for her. They were conversing erratically, neither of them really wanting to talk. Suddenly a shadow fell over the table. Both of them looked up at the same time. "Juan!" Tazia cried, she leapt to her feet and ran to Juan. She threw herself into his arms.

"Juan, how did you get here? Is Maria with you?"

"*Sí*, María is with me." the huge man grinned broadly. "It took us some time to get away, but I knew you would come home. As soon as Kirk and his friends left New Orleans, María and I started for home."

Juan knew Tazia was delighted to see him, but he could not understand what it was about her that had changed so. His eyes caught Marguerite's and she gave a slight negative shake of her head. Although puzzled by all this, he let Tazia draw him to the table. She asked him questions about his journey and about María. They talked until it was time for her mother's dinner. Tazia left bearing the tray, and Juan and Marguerite sat together in comfortable silence.

"Juan, Kirk LaCroix and his brother are in California. They were here at the hacienda just a few days ago."

"Marguerite, I still do not know what happened that night."

Marguerite quietly told him everything Tazia had told her. Then she told him about Tazia's parents.

"She has had so much trouble lately. It is best that she is home and away from that man and all the problems he brings her," Juan said.

"I do not agree," Marguerite replied.

"Why?"

"Because, although she will never admit it, she still loves him."

"After what he has done!"

"We only know one side of the story, Juan. What about his side? Tazia will not talk to him. She will not even let him on the property."

"Then there is nothing more to be done."

"Oh, I think there may be."

Juan grinned again. "What do you have planned,

old meddler?"

"I swore to Tazia I would not tell Kirk LaCroix a thing. But I did not promise not to tell you."

"Tell me what?"

"Tazia is carrying Kirk's child."

Juan said nothing more for some time. He studied Marguerite closely. "What would you have me do?"

"Go to him. Question him. Find out the truth. If you think he is just and honest and he truly loves her . . . tell him."

"And if he's guilty?"

"Use your judgment, Juan. If you think he's guilty, don't tell him anything."

"Tazia would never forgive you if she knew," he said gently.

Marguerite's eyes were frightened but steady. "Juan, if I can move her from the path she is on and make her happy, I can live with her anger. I cannot live with her dying inside day by day. Do what you must do. Let God be judge of the outcome."

26

Jared Stone eased his horse slowly forward. They moved at a methodical, plodding gait. He was not looking forward to meeting with Garrett Flye. In fact, he was a little afraid. Jared was not blessed with an overabundance of courage under any circumstances, and being aware of the character of Garrett Flye, he was hesitant to tell him how he had let Tazia slip through his fingers. Under no circumstances was he going to tell him how he had tried to rape her. He would, of course, blame Captain Carothers for interfering and helping Tazia escape. There was no love lost between Flye and Carothers, so he believed the story might be accepted without too many questions.

He rode along slowly, a deep scowl on his handsome face. Damn her, she'll pay . . . she'll pay, and so will Carothers. Garrett will find a way for me to get my hands on her again, and when I do, she'll beg me to take her before I'm done with her. Beg me! His mind dwelt pleasurably on the things he would do to her when he got her. He never doubted for a moment that their paths would cross again. Garrett was not a man to give up on anything he wanted. One way or another, he would win, no matter what he had to do. Why he was so determined to get at this LaCroix, Stone didn't know. Nor did he care. He just knew that if he helped Garrett get LaCroix, he would get his hands on Tazia again.

He was drifting into the outskirts of the town now. A collection of low adobe houses, one cantina, and a church encircled a small plaza. In the center there was a stone fountain that had long since ceased producing any water. It was filled with dust and debris. The town, if it could be called that, lay just three-hours ride across the Mexican border. It was only a two-day ride from there to Escondido, and less than a day to Casa del Sol.

He dismounted in front of the cantina and stepped inside the dimly lit room. When his eyes had adjusted to the light, he looked around the room. The bartender was a short, slender man with cold, squinty eyes. He leaned against the bar and watched Stone approach. At the other end of the bar stood a woman, who could have been sixteen or thirty. The type of life she led had worn her down until there was nothing attractive about her. That made Stone's mind drift back to Tazia again. Two young men sat at the far table, but they paid no attention to Stone.

"Tequila," Stone said to the bartender as he continued to let his eyes drift around the room. Flye was nowhere in sight. The bartender put a dirty glass down on the bar and poured a drink.

"Leave the bottle."

"*Sí Señor.*" The bartender thumped the bottle down and moved away.

"Wait a minute," Stone said. "Has there been a man in here looking for me? Name's Stone."

"*Sí Señor.* A man came in a few hours ago and

215

asked for you."

"Where is he now?"

The bartender pointed to a far wall. Now that he looked closely, Stone could see a ragged, dirty blanket covering a doorway. He nodded his thanks to the bartender, picked up his bottle and glass, and walked slowly across the room and drew the blanket aside. He entered a small, square room that contained only four things: a table, two chairs, and Garrett Flye. Garrett sat facing the doorway, across the table from Stone. He was smoking a cigar that was clenched between his teeth. His eyes gazed coldly at Stone through the wreath of white smoke. Stone felt the sudden tightening of his nerves he always felt when he looked into Garrett's expressionless eyes.

Christ, he thought, it's like looking a snake in the eye.

"Garrett." He smiled as he pulled out the other chair and sat down, putting the glass and bottle on the table.

"I hope you have a very good reason for coming here alone, Stone. I believe you were to have brought me something."

"Give me a minute and let me explain what happened," Stone began quickly. His hands began to perspire, and he could feel a choking fear in his throat.

"Where is she, Stone?" Garrett asked softly.

"Well, I guess by now she's got to Casa del Sol."

"And just how did you manage to let her slip through your fingers? She was alone on a ship. What did she do, walk away?"

"She got help from Captain Carothers, damn him to hell."

"How did Carothers know she needed help?"

"I don't know. For some reason he had sympathy

216

for her, and he just offered to help her, I guess."

Suddenly Garrett's hand flashed out. It struck Stone first on one side of his face and then on the other, rocking him back in his chair. Stone would have liked to kill Flye at that moment, but he lacked the courage to face a man and kill him.

"Now, let me tell *you* what happened, you stupid jackass," Garrett said furiously. "You thought you'd have a little tidbit to nibble on over the long journey, didn't you? I warned you about touching her before you brought her to me, didn't I? I told you I had plans to use her to get to LaCroix. You just couldn't wait. Captain Carothers would have followed my orders and not done a thing to stop you if, just for once, you had had enough sense to keep your greedy hands to yourself for just a few more days."

"Garrett—"

"Shut up!" Garrett was so angry he flung back his chair and stood up. Stone could feel his breath constrict in his throat as Garrett came around the table and stood over him. "You've put a big crimp in my plans. You've caused me no end of trouble and possibly spoiled any chance we have of getting her away from Casa del Sol. I really ought to kill you, Stone," he added softly, his eyes narrowing to fine, hard pinpoints.

"Garrett, please," he gasped hoarsely. "There must be a way to get her away from there. She's alone there. I heard tell her pa's dead, and her mother's gone crazy or something. She's alone there, I tell you."

"Alone? Are you sure of that?"

"Real sure. I told you, her pa's dead and her mother ain't no good for nothing. That leaves one old lady and that bodyguard of hers. Most of the vaqueros and their families don't live close enough to the main house to be any help. If we do it quiet, we could get in and get her out of there real easy."

Garrett contemplated this silently for a few minutes, causing Stone to sweat in an agony of fear.

"Maybe . . . maybe," Garrett said softly.

"Sure, I could get her out of there. I swear . . . "

"Shut up, Stone. I wouldn't trust you to do a job like that again. No, this time *I'll* get her out of there, and when I do, you'll take the message back to LaCroix that I've got her."

"And after you get LaCroix where you want him, what then?"

"Then you can have her for all I care," Garrett said.

If Stone could have read Garrett's thoughts at that moment, he would have been terrified. Garrett had no intention of giving Tazia up once he'd gotten his hands on her. Instead, he would eliminate Stone as just so much excess baggage. Then he would have the two things he wanted: Kirk LaCroix would be dead, and Tazia would belong to him.

He thought of her the last time he had seen her in the garden at Kirk's house in New Orleans. She had been so beautiful it had taken all he had to walk away and leave her there. But he was satisfied with the effect of what he had told her. He knew she would accept his offer of the ship as a way to leave New Orleans. He wondered what Kirk had gone through when he found her gone, and he gloated over the fact that it must have hurt him a great deal. Not as much as you're going to get, Kirk, my boy, he thought, but it's a start, it's a start.

"What do you have against LaCroix anyway?" Stone asked, immediately sorry. Garrett's face flushed with uncontained anger. It took a while for Stone to realize it was not aimed at him, but at Kirk.

"Kirk LaCroix has interfered in my business just one time too often. Besides, there's something he knows—he doesn't even know that he does—and I want to eliminate him before he stumbles on the truth by accident. If he should get together with his wife again, that just might happen. No, Kirk La-Croix's got to die, and his beautiful wife is going to be the means of getting rid of him."

"What do you want me to do?"

"You get yourself across the border to Escondido and round up three or four men to help us. Wait there until I give you the word. And Stone . . . "

"Yeah?"

"If LaCroix or Tazia sees one sign of you before I'm ready, and if you spoil my plans this time . . . you're a dead man. Do I make myself perfectly clear?"

"Yeah," Stone muttered.

"Good. Now get out of here."

Stone rose and left the room. Garrett sat at the table and made plans. The look on his face was one of malicious joy. He would kill LaCroix, maybe even Del too, if he had the chance. Then he would take Tazia with him. He contemplated the delight they would share. Like the conceited, arrogant man he was, he underestimated Tazia. His mind dwelling on his plans, he rose and left the cantina. Outside the back door, he climbed into his buggy, slapped the reins against the horses' rumps and rode out of town.

Stone did as Garrett had ordered. Crossing the border, he headed for the town of Escondido. When he arrived, he left his horse at the stable and found a room at the hotel. After purchasing a bottle of whiskey, he went to his room, where he sat on a chair in front of the window and watched the street.

It was a small town. It had one main street, with

four or five shops, a milliner and a hardware store on one side of the street and two grocery stores, a hotel, a bank and two saloons on the other side. On the north side of the street at the far end, sat a church. At the other end was the cemetery. Only three streets crossed the main one. Along these streets were the homes of the local businessmen.

For several days Stone spent his time closed up in his hotel room. He ordered whiskey and food from the restaurant that was attached to hotel. He only slept, ate, and drank, and very soon his nerves began to fray. After four days and nights, he was becoming irritable. He sat on the chair as he had for days, a bottle in his hand, watching the activities along the street.

Suddenly he sat up, alert, his eyes riveted on one of the stores across the street from the hotel. The person standing in the doorway was still in the shadow of the store, but he did not think he was mistaken about who it was. He watched closely. Kirk stepped out of the door's shadow, adjusted the hat on his head to shade him from the bright sun, and walked across the street toward the hotel.

Good God! He's right here in the same hotel with me. I wonder if his brother is with him. I'll bet he is. Damn, I'll bet Garrett will be glad to hear this. Now he has them all right where he wants them.

He leaned back in his chair and laughed. Then he took a long drink from the whiskey bottle and waited much more patiently for Garrett to get in touch with him. He knew he would not be able to go to the saloons to recruit help without risking running into one of them, so he decided to just stay put until Garrett sent for him.

Kirk crossed the street and entered the hotel. After climbing the stairs, he stopped at the second door along the hallway, knocked once on it, and went inside. His brother was standing in front of the mirror. He had just finished shaving and was toweling his face. His eyes caught Kirk's entrance in the mirror. God, he looks awful, he thought miserably. I just wish there were something I could say or do that would help.

They had stayed overnight in the hotel after leaving Casa del Sol. Kirk had been completely uncommunicative. But Del was sure he was intending to go home with them.

"Have you talked to Jean and Louis?" he asked.

Kirk nodded his head. He lay down on the bed, put his hands behind his head, and watched his brother finish dressing.

"When do we leave for home?"

"We don't," Kirk answered slowly, "or rather . . . *I* don't."

"Kirk, there's no way of reaching her. We've tried. If you go back there, she'll kill you. Isn't it what she planned to do in the first place?"

"I'm not going home, Del," he replied with quiet stubbornness.

"What are you going to do?"

"Del, you remember the card game?"

"God, as if I could ever forget it. It's what started all this. I wish to hell I'd never let Garrett talk us into letting Manolo in the game in the first place."

"Well, do you remember the last pot? Just before the shooting?"

"Yeah," Del said, his eyes filled with questions.

"What was in the pot?"

Del thought for a while. "Well, I had about twenty thousand in it, and you had more than that. Garrett had folded, and Louis had too, and Manolo had . . . " His eyes opened wide, and he stared at his brother's face. "Manolo had Casa del Sol," he added quietly.

"And *I* won," Kirk said very softly. "I own half of Casa del Sol from Manolo and the other half because I am Tazia's husband. In fact of law, Del, I *own* Casa del Sol."

"Kirk, you're crazy. If you go back out there and say that, for sure she'll kill you. You don't have much of a chance of staying alive if you try to take it away from her."

"Who said anything about taking it away from her?"

Del looked at his brother in amazement. "You don't think she'd let you stay there!"

"What choice does she have?"

"I'll tell you what choice! She'll kill you, sure as hell."

"There's a law against murdering your husband, Del, even way out here." Kirk gave a dry half-laugh.

"She'll shoot and ask questions later."

"Not if I inform the law first."

"Kirk, you're crazy. I'm telling you, you're crazy." Del's voice was filled with desperate alarm.

"Louis and Jean said the same thing." He swung his feet to the floor and stood up. "Del, I love her. I shall always love her. But aside from that, remember that Garrett Flye has disappeared. We both know him too well. He's somewhere waiting for an opportunity. With no one to protect her now that her father's dead, what's to stop him from moving against her. I'll tell you what: Me. She will need me, and if I'm any judge, it will be soon. I intend to be there with or without your help."

Del stared at him for a few minutes. Then he grinned.

"Who said it would be without my help? I'll help

all I can. But I still think you're crazy."

A knock on the door ended their conversation.

"Who is it?" Del called.

"Señors LaCroix. It is me, Juan. I have to speak to Señor Kirk."

Kirk and Del looked at each other in surprise. Then Del walked to the door and opened it.

Juan loomed in the doorway. "I must speak to you, Señor."

Kirk smiled for the first time in weeks.

"Come in, Juan, come in."

27

Juan watched Kirk with penetrating eyes. He had come here at Marguerite's suggestion to talk with the man who had caused his beloved mistress so much grief. It had taken Marguerite considerable persuasion to make Juan come, for he was fiercely loyal to Tazia. Now that he was here, he was determined to listen to all of Kirk's side of the story before he decided whether to tell him about the baby. Going behind Tazia's back to tell Kirk she was pregnant seemed to Juan to be wrong. But not telling a man she was carrying his child was also wrong. Juan was very confused, but he intended to remedy that as soon as possible.

"Do you want me to go, Kirk?" Del asked, one eye judging Juan for any sign of danger.

"Go on, Del, it's all right. Juan is just here to talk. Isn't that right, Juan?"

"*Sí*, just to talk," Juan agreed.

Del looked at Juan for a few seconds longer. Then he stepped around him and left the room. Juan stood for several moments in silence, not sure where to start.

It was Kirk who spoke first. "How is she, Juan?" he asked gently. "Is she well? Does she need any help? I heard about her parents. I'm sorry, truly sorry."

Now Juan was really in a state of confusion. This gentle consideration on Kirk's part was against everything he had been told. "She is . . . well . . . or at least as well as possible for someone who has gone through the things she has in the past two years."

"What did you want to see me about, Juan?"

"Señor Kirk, I must know the truth about what happened in New Orleans. About her brother and about her. I am not asking for myself, but if Marguerite and I are to help her, we must know the truth."

"Who is Marguerite?"

Juan explained Marguerite's unique position in Tazia's life and that it was she who sent him. Kirk vowed to thank Marguerite at the first opportunity.

"Sit down, Juan. I will explain everything to you." Juan sat. Kirk began to speak slowly so that Juan would understand completely, not only everything that had happened, but exactly the way he felt about Tazia.

Juan watched Kirk's face closely as he spoke. Instinctively he knew that what Kirk was saying was the truth. There were many things that Juan knew about Manolo that Tazia did not know, and like the others close to her, he would never hurt her by telling them to her. He also let her go on living in the shade of her brother, for he honestly believed at the time that it was better that way. Now, for the first time, he realized that they were all wrong. They should have told her what her brother was in the first place. Then maybe the shock of his death would not have set her on the path of revenge, for she would have known that he deserved what he got.

When Kirk had finished explaining what had happened in New Orleans, both men sat silent for some time.

"Juan, there is something else I have to tell you, now that I've made my decision." He went on to explain the circumstances of his ownership of Casa del Sol and what he intended to do.

"I'm not asking you to help me, Juan. I appreciate your loyalty to my wife. All I'm asking is that for a while you don't get in my way—at least until I've had a reasonable chance to prove to her that I love her and would never hurt her on purpose."

For several minutes Juan did not answer. Then he held out his hand to Kirk. "I will not help you," he said as they shook hands, "and if I see that you are hurting her, I will probably break you in two. But, for a few months, I will not stand in your way."

"Thank you, Juan. That's all I need. A few months should tell the tale."

Juan grinned in wicked amusement. "Oh *Sí Señor*. A few months should tell us many things. When will you come to *la casa?*"

"As soon as I get copies of our marriage license and Manolo's deed to me of the hacienda. Probably about two weeks, I would say."

Juan nodded and rose to leave.

"*Adíos, Señor*. I shall see you in two weeks, and if Tazia does not blow your head off or stab you to death some dark night, it may all work out. Good luck," he added softly.

When he had left the room, he wondered why he had not told him Tazia was expecting his child. It was not the right time, he thought. Maybe the time would come when Tazia could tell him herself.

He rode back to the hacienda. Before he could even dismount from his horse, Marguerite was at his side. "Did you speak to him, Juan? Did you tell him about the baby?"

Juan took his time dismounting which irritated Marguerite.

"You big ox," she said angrily. "Tell me what happened or I shall beat you."

Juan chuckled at this and said calmly, "Patience, Marguerite, patience. I shall tell you what happened. But first I need something to eat and drink."

Marguerite's face became pink with the anger she was trying to hold in check. She usually made no effort to control her anger, and being forced to do so now only made her angrier. She walked ahead of him to the kitchen, muttering threats in Spanish under her breath. Juan followed, enjoying her discomfort. He ate slowly and enjoyed thoroughly everything she put before him. When he was finished, she sat down at the table opposite him.

"If you don't tell me now, I shall poison you at your very next meal."

He laughed and began to tell her all that had transpired in his visit with Kirk.

"I was right," she said softly. "I could tell how he felt about her. Well, Juan, what's going to happen when he comes out here?"

"Well, I can imagine what's going to happen, and I intend to be away from this house when it does."

"She'll kill him," Marguerite muttered.

"He's bringing the law with him. I don't think she will kill him."

"No, but he will probably wish many times over that he'd never seen this place."

"Oh I don't doubt that one bit. But, I think Tazia for the first time in her life has met her match. This man is like iron, yet he feels a great love for her. I don't think she'll get him to leave. It is going to be interesting to watch."

"You didn't tell him about the baby?"

"No."

"Why?"

"Let us see what happens first. Maybe he can get her to tell him herself."

"I doubt it. The way she feels now, it is the last thing she would want him to know."

"Don't let them start off putting the baby between them. For now, it is best kept a secret. It won't be too much time before he finds out for himself anyway."

"*Sí*, I guess you are right. Still . . ."

"Marguerite, we will keep silent and let everything take its course. She cannot fight him about Casa del Sol. As far as the law is concerned, he is the legal owner. Let us wait and see if he is man enough to hold it when he has it. If he can do that and get Tazia, too, he deserves to keep it." He added as an afterthought, "But we will watch. If what he does is not for Tazia's good, as he claims . . . I shall make Señor Kirk wish he had never lived."

Marguerite nodded her agreement. For the time being, Tazia and Kirk would be more closely watched than they ever had been before in their lives.

Marguerite watched Tazia daily. She seemed quieter but more content than she had when she first arrived. Under the impression that Kirk and the others were out of her life for good, she seemed to be content to sit back and drift for a while.

Each morning she woke at the first sign of dawn. She would dress each day in the same type of loose-fitting peasant blouse and flowered skirt. Her bare feet in sandals and her hair in a braid down her back, she looked nothing like a wealthy Spanish lady. She rode over the lands of Casa del Sol as if she could not absorb enough of it. Casa del Sol was nestled in the

Pauma Valley, about sixty miles north of the Mexican border. It was bordered on the north by the San Gorgonio Mountains and on the south by the San Luis Rey River. It ws a lush, green valley of rolling hills and grass-covered plains, covering about thirty thousand acres. Casa del Sol had been deeded to her grandfather by the King of Spain as a reward for his bravery and loyalty to the crown. She knew every inch of it as well as she knew herself. It was the place where her heart dwelt, and she knew she could never be happy living anywhere else. It is mine, she thought with a surge of pride. Mine, and I shall hold it for my son.

Each morning Tazia would return from her early ride rejuvenated and content. She would then prepare for her mother a breakfast tray which she would carry to her room. She would get her mother out of bed and wash and dress her. No words were ever spoken, for her mother's eyes remained blank. Tazia would handle her gently, as though she were a child. After dressing her, she would seat her in a chair by the window, where she could bask in the early-morning sun. Then she would coax her into eating breakfast. This was a task she refused to let anyone help her with. Even Marguerite, whom she loved as a second mother, could not talk Tazia into letting her help. It would hurt Marguerite to hear Tazia's gentle voice pleading with her mother to eat. She knew Tazia was praying that one day her mother would look at her with recognition, maybe even with love. Often she would see Tazia leave her mother's room and go silently to the small chapel that had been built at the far end of the house. There she would quietly light a candle at the feet of the Blessed Mother and kneel to pray that her mother would be made well again.

Today Tazia was dressed in a manner that befitted her station, for she had decided to ride to the neighboring hacienda of Don Federico Reyes. There were many questions she wanted to ask him. What happened in the study the day of her father's death was known by only three people: Don Federico, Don Manuel, his brother, and Cristina, his daughter.

Her black riding habit hugged her breasts, now fuller, which gave her a voluptuous look. The skirt was full, and no sign of pregnancy could be seen. She wore a white scarf about her neck and a flat-crowned, wide-brimmed black hat, tied under her chin and tipped over her right eye. Her hair was drawn back severely in a chignon at the nape of her neck. She looked cool and regal. None of the worries that flitted through her mind could be seen on her face or in her deep-blue eyes.

She rode slowly on one of her father's most beautiful palominos. Don Ramón de Montega had been famous throughout California for the beautiful horses he bred.

Having ridden since she was a child, Tazia was at ease on the huge stallion. The day was bright, the sky blue and almost cloudless. Behind her rose the beautiful mountains, and the scent of trees drifted about on the slight breeze. Crossing the border between her property and the Reyes's she let her horse slow to a walk while she prepared in her mind the question she would ask Don Federico.

She remembered him with a feeling of kindness. He had shown her a great deal of affection when, as a child, she played with his daughters Cristina and Juanita. He was a tall, distinguished man — very handsome in Tazia's memory, with dark hair and deep golden-brown eyes that had smiled a lot. His skin was deeply tanned, and he had the proud bearing of a man whose ancestors could be traced back to the conquistadores.

The Reyes home, built somewhat on the order of Casa del Sol, was slightly larger and shaped like a box with one end open. In the center was a large stone patio with a huge fountain, where the sound of cool running water could be heard.

She dismounted at the front of the house. Two wide stone steps led up to the shaded flagstone patio that ran the length of the house. A huge black oak door stood out against the beauty of the white stucco walls. The brass knocker was composed of a square plate and a huge circle of metal with which she sounded her arrival. Within a few minutes, the door swung open and Serafina, the housekeeper, stood in the open doorway.

Serafina had also known Tazia from childhood. She had given her cookies and other treats in the huge Reyes kitchen many times. Now her face went white, and her eyes grew large with surprise.

"Señorita Tazia, what . . . I mean, it is good to see you again."

"Thank you, Serafina. Is the family at home? I know I should have sent word I was coming, but I was out riding when I remembered I hadn't seen my old friends since I arrived home. I just decided to come over."

"Sí Señorita Tazia. They are all home. Won't you come in?" She held the huge door open, and Tazia walked past her, aware that Serafina was trembling, but it was with an emotion completely different from what she had expected. If she could have seen a reason for it, she would have sworn it was fear.

"If you will wait a moment, Señorita Tazia, I will tell Don Federico and Señorita Cristina that you are here."

"Thank you, Serafina."

"Señorita Tazia?"

"Yes, Serafina."

"It really is good to see you again. You are even prettier than before."

"Thank you again, Serafina. It is good to be home again."

"You are home to stay then?"

"Of course," Tazia laughed. "After living at Casa del Sol all my life could I ever be happy anywhere else in the world?"

"No, of course not. Excuse me. I will tell Don Federico you are here."

Tazia nodded and watched Serafina walk slowly away.

She turned and looked around the room. Oh, the happy days she had spent in this house. She and Cristina and her younger sister, Juanita, had been the very closest of friends. She walked about the room, touching an object now and then. At a sound from the doorway, she turned around with a smile on her face. Her eyes widened a little in surprise, and the smile slowly faded from her face as she looked into the deep-brown eyes of Don Federico Reyes.

28

Her first thought was that he was very ill. But upon looking closer, she could see that something had aged Don Federico. His black hair was streaked with silver at the temples. The once-olive skin was sallow, as though he had not been in the sun for a long time. But more than that, it was his eyes. They looked dead. She smiled her brightest smile and held out both her hands as she walked rapidly toward him.

"Don Federico."

He smiled in return, but it did not reach his eyes. "Tazia, my child. It is so good to see your lovely face again. You have been away too long."

"Well, I am home to stay. I have missed my home and my friends, most of all Cristina and Juanita and you, Don Federico."

At this, Don Federico fell silent. Then, with a smile, he put his arm about her shoulder. "I am sure Serafina is at this moment telling Cristina that you are here," he chuckled. "In fact, I expect her to come dashing into the room in a very unladylike manner in a few minutes."

Almost before the words had left his lips, they

heard the sound of someone running down the stairs. Then a young woman burst into the room. Cristina Reyes had probably been closer to Tazia than a sister. She had been the one to whom Tazia had confided her loneliness, frustrations, and dreams. She was a tiny, slender woman. Her hair was the color of spun gold, and her eyes were sea-blue. To see her as the daughter of the dark Don Federico had always surprised people, until they saw her mother. Don Federico, on a trip to England, had taken as a bride a fair-haired English girl. Her daughter looked almost exactly like her.

"Tazia!" she shouted in delight. The two girls embraced and began to chatter at once. Don Federico stood by and watched. It was fortunate Tazia did not see his face, for it did not reflect his daughter's happiness to see her.

"Oh, Papa! Is it not wonderful Tazia is home again?"

"*Sí*, it is good you two are reunited. Tazia, she has missed you dreadfully."

"We must have a party to celebrate your homecoming, Tazia," Cristina said quickly.

Tazia laughed. "Soon, Cristina. First, I would like to get accustomed to being home again. Tell me," she added softly, "all that has happened since I've been gone."

Both of them were silent for a moment. Then Don Federico replied. "First tell us about your trip to New Orleans. I hear that it is a very beautiful city. Your trip was sudden, was it not, Tazia?"

"It may be a beautiful city, Don Federico, but it holds nothing but bad memories for me. You know we received word that my brother Manolo was killed there. I went to New Orleans to find out why . . . and how."

"And did you find out?"

"Yes."

"And?"

"It is finished. It is all finished," she replied softly. "Then I came home to find my father dead and my mother . . ." She left the last sentence unfinished. It ws not necessary to finish it, for they both knew how her mother was.

"It is a terrible thing about your father, Tazia," Don Federico said gently. "You know I was there when he had his attack. It was a severe heart atack and he died suddenly. No one seems to know why this kind of thing happens. Please believe me when I tell you no one is sorrier for all that has happened than I and my family."

Tazia felt that Don Federico meant every word he said, just as she felt he was not going to tell her anything about the argument he was having with her father when he died. They would not tell her anything *now*, she thought, but someday, somehow, she would find out what went on in that room.

"Come, Tazia," Cristina said, taking her by the hand and leading her to a seat. "Tell me all about New Orleans. Did you see the whole city? Is it beautiful? And tell me," she grinned wickedly, "did you find many handsome gentlemen there?"

Tazia's mind instinctively flashed to Kirk. Should she tell them she was married? She knew that they would hear this news sometime. She could not hide the fact that she was pregnant much longer.

"Yes, Cristina, there are any number of handsome caballeros there. In fact, I married one of them."

"Married! You married, and I did not get to be maid of honor at your wedding? Oh, Tazia, how could you?" Cristina wailed.

Tazia laughed.

"It was really a very sudden decision. You see, I didn't even get to send word to my parents. We were married over seven months ago."

"Where is your husband now? Why didn't he come with you? I should like to meet the man who captured you, Tazia. He will be the envy of every other man in California."

"He . . . he had business that kept him in New Orleans. I doubt if he will be able to come here for quite some time."

Tazia had been talking to Cristina while not realizing that Don Federico was watching her closely. His piercing eyes took in every detail of her appearance and her story. He had realized in an instant after they first met that Tazia had changed a great deal in the past year. Two things were very obvious to his experienced eye: she was lying about her husband, and she was carrying a child. He went to a side table and poured three glasses of wine. He carried them over on a small tray and handed one to Tazia and one to his daughter.

"Let us drink a toast to Tazia's return to us," he said. They drank together. Then Don Federico turned to his daughter and unspoken words passed between them. "I shall leave you two to talk over old times and old flames," he said with a smile. "You may even plan to have a party to welcome Tazia home. Now, if you will excuse me, I have much to do before the day is over. Come to visit us again soon, Tazia."

"I will, Don Federico, and thank you."

"For what, my dear?"

"For making this such a beautiful place to come to."

She watched him bow slightly to her, turn, and walk away.

Again she was struck with the feeling hat Don Federico was somehow much older.

She turned back to Cristina and sat down again.

"Tell me Tazia, are you happy?"

"As happy as I ever expect to be," Tazia replied.

"Tell me about your husband."

Tazia described Kirk, his brother, and New Orleans. She also told her about their house in New Orleans and the good times they had shared. Then she described their wedding at Lafitte's home.

Many people had made the mistake about Cristina that Tazia was making now. They thought of her as a delightful child, rather scatter-brained and unworldly. Tazia, who should have known better, was reacting without thinking. Her mind was so hurt and confused by the things that had happened to her in the past that she had slipped into thinking of Cristina as being exactly as she looked. That was why she was so surprised when Cristina asked gently, "Tazia, what is wrong? What has happened to hurt you so very badly?"

"Wrong? what makes you think . . . " But she did not finish the sentence. Instead, she remembered. No matter how Cristina looked, she was a perceptive, intelligent woman and her dearest friend. "Oh Cristina . . . everything is wrong."

"Do you want to tell me about it?" Cristina asked gently as she reached out and took Tazia's hand.

"Yes. I need someone to talk to. Someone I can trust. The world seems to be made up of people who deceive and use you."

"It will do you good to talk. It will be like old times, before you went away. Tazia, you are like a sister to me. If I can help you in any way, please let me."

Tazia began by telling her about how they had

received word of Manolo's death and about her parents' reaction. Cristina did not interrupt, but she held her own thoughts about Tazia's parents. Tazia continued the story of how she had planned to avenge her brother. Then she filled in the remainder of the story: her marriage, her discovery that Kirk was the guilty one, her escape, the truth about Garrett Flye, and her aid from Captain Carothers. Finally she told Cristina about the child she was carrying.

When she had finished speaking, both women were silent for a time. Then Cristina said quietly, "Poor Tazia. You have been through so much. It is good you are here at home among your friends and the people who love you."

"Thank you, Cristina. I knew I could count on you as a friend. I always could, even when we were children and I got into trouble."

"And you were always getting into trouble," laughed Cristina.

"And you were always getting me out," replied Tazia, echoing her laughter. "You and Juanita. By the way, where is Juanita?"

"She . . . she is in Los Angeles. I don't think she will be coming home for some time," replied Cristina. She did not look directly at Tazia as she spoke, and her fingers plucked nervously at the folds of her skirt.

"But why? Is she married? Does she live there? Tell me about her, Cristina."

"Tazia, Juanita has some problems that have to be worked out. She is at the convent of the Sisters of Mercy outside Los Angeles. She plans to stay there for a while until her problems are solved. Then I hope . . . I mean, I imagine she will come home."

Alarms rang in Tazia's mind. There was something more to this than Cristina was telling her. "Cristina—"

"Tazia, please. This is a subject I cannot discuss at the moment. I am not free to tell you everything. When Juanita gets things sorted out in her mind and makes her decisions, then she will probably tell you herself. Until then . . . you understand, I am not free to tell you." Her eyes pleaded for Tazia's understanding. There was nothing for Tazia to do but accept her words and ask no more questions. She agreed, and they changed the subject. For the rest of the afternoon they laughed and talked together as they had done when they were children.

Don Federico came back to the hacienda accompanied by Don Manuel. He was as tall and slender as his brother. His hair was thick and black, in deep contrast to the silver streaks in Don Federico's hair, yet he was six years older. He greeted Tazia with a warm smile and a kiss on her cheek.

"You will stay for supper, will you not, Tazia?" Cristina said. "We have just begun to talk. I must learn about the fashions in New Orleans and about their entertainments."

Tazia laughed. "Not tonight. I did not inform Juan or Marguerite that I would be gone so long. They are probably beginning to worry about me at this moment. I'd best get home before they send out a search party for me. You known how Marguerite is."

"Yes," replied Cristina. "Marguerite always fussed over you as though you were her own daughter."

Tazia did not miss Don Federico's deepening frown toward his daughter, nor her abrupt silence.

"Well, I shall go home now, but I shall be back soon, Cristina. Then we can talk as long as you like."

They walked to the door and watched her mount her horse and ride away.

"Cristina, you must be more careful . . . what you say. This child has had enough to bear. The past is dead and buried. It must remain so. Since Manolo and his father are both dead, there is no reason that old wounds should be re-opened."

"*Sí*, I know my foolish tongue almost slipped. It will never happen again, Papa. I will be more careful. I love Tazia as a sister. You know I would never do anything to hurt her."

Don Federico sighed deeply and put his arm around his daughter's shoulder. Then he kissed the top of her fair hair. The three of them walked slowly back into the house.

Tazia rode toward home very slowly, her thoughts on the Reyes family. First, where was Cristina's mother, Catherine? Was she with Juanita? Why was Juanita at a convent? What problems could be so severe as to take her away from her home and family? All the Reyes family were changed somehow . . . and why would Don Federico keep secret what happened to cause her father's death? She was even sure that Marguerite knew much more than she was saying. Deep down inside, Tazia was hoping that loving care would bring her mother out of her trance-like state so she could finally learn the truth.

As she rode along, she was suddenly conscious of feeling that she was being watched. The setting sun still gave off enough light for her to see a great distance around her. There was no one in sight. Still, she could not overcome the feeling that someone was watching her from somewhere. She urged her horse forward in a quick trot, which ate up the distance home quickly. She arrived at the stable just as the sun disappeared below the horizon. Dismounting, she handed the horse's reins to a young stableboy.

"Where is Juan?" she asked.

"He went to town for something, *patrona,*" the boy replied. "He left a few minutes after your company arrived."

"Company? I expected no company. Who is it?"

"I do not know, *patrona.* The gentlemen is a stranger to me. He came to see you a short time ago. We told him you were away, but he said he would wait."

"Where is he now?"

"Waiting in the house. He insisted on coming inside. It was a strange thing to say, *patrona,* but he said he would feel much safer there. Do you know what he meant?"

Tazia walked quickly from the stable to the house. She pushed open the front door and walked rapidly across the foyer to the living room, where she stopped in her tracks. Leaning against the fireplace with his arms crossed in front of him was Kirk LaCroix.

29

Their eyes met across the room in silence. She was aware of the quietness in the house. It was as though they stood in a world of their own. The dull throb of her heart almost made her cry out. Her face whitened, and small ridges appeared at the corners of her clenched mouth.

"What are you doing here?" She demanded coldly. "I thought I told you you were not welcome in this house. Have you not caused enough grief?" Must you forever return to haunt me and cause more pain? Her voice cracked with the intensity of her anger.

"Do you think anything you said could drive me out of California before I could talk to you, to tell you—"

"I don't want to hear anything you have to say, Kirk. What was between us before was a lie. All I want is for you to leave me in peace so that I can forget everything that has happened."

"Would you have peace, Tazia? Can you really ever forget what was between us?"

She was desperate to get him out of the house before anything she said or did might make him notice her condition. Kirk had always been very observant of every detail about her. He knew every curve and plane of her body intimately. She also knew him too well not to believe the truth would come out if he stayed any length of time. She turned from him and walked to the wide windows. The dark shadows of early evening filled the room with a gray half-light. She stood collecting her thoughts, well aware that his eyes had never left her.

"Leave me alone, Kirk. Leave me alone with my grief and pain. Let me find my own way. I do not need you, nor do I want you. I can put the pieces of my life back together if you just stay away. I know that the church does not allow a divorce, but I will not let that stand in the way of your freedom. Find another woman who will believe your fine lies. I do not want to see you again . . . ever."

"I'm afraid it's too late for that," he replied, gently.

She was so startled that she whirled about to face him. Did he know about the child? No! How could he? Only she, Marguerite, and Cristina knew. Then what did he mean by "too late?"

"Too late?"

"Yes, much too late. I could go a million miles away and I would never forget for one minute anything about you. The way you walk, talk, smile . . . everything about you is burned so deeply into my soul, I shall never forget. I love you Tazia, and . . . you are my wife."

She stood in the half-light and stared at him. His words echoed in the silent room.

"No! I shall never be your wife again. I would die before I would ever let you use me again. I was a fool for your lies once, Kirk. I shall never be fooled by words of love again. Take your precious *love* and give it to some woman who wants it. I want only for you to leave my life, leave my home, leave my valley. Leave

California!"

"As I said before, Tazia, it is too late for that."
"You see, this is now my home also."

"Get out!" she shouted. "This is not your home.
Casa del Sol is mine . . . mine alone, now that you
have killed my brother and my father. It's mine, and
you can never share it with me!"

She stood trembling in rage. Kirk could almost feel
the hatred burning in her from where he stood.
Would he ever reach her, ever make her understand
what he was about to do? For a single moment he
thought of leaving, but he knew it would always be
impossible to get her out of his mind or his heart.
With a deep sigh, he moved toward her until they
stood only inches apart. Slowly he pulled from his
pocket the papers that were proof of his ownership of
Casa del Sol and held them out to her. She refused to
touch them. Instead, she continued staring at him.

"These papers consist of two things, Tazia," he said
as gently as he could. "One is the deed for Manolo's
share of Casa del Sol, made out to me. He lost it to
me in the card game. The other is our marriage cer-
tificate. You see, my love, *you* do not own Casa del
Sol . . . I do."

She swayed on her feet as though someone had
struck her violently. He put out one hand, for he
thought she was going to faint. Suddenly she took a
step away from him, raised her hand, and struck him
as hard as she could. She trembled so violently that
he was afraid for her.

"Tazia—"

"You have taken everything in my world away from
me, Kirk LaCroix," she said vehemently. "but you
can never reach me. This was my home. You say it is
yours. My father and brother died because of you.
Let me give you warning now. I will never leave Casa

del Sol, and you will regret to the day you die that you ever saw me. I will make you pay, Kirk," she cried. Her voice softened to almost a whisper. "I will make you pay for every moment you spend here. One way or another, you will pay in full for all you have taken from me." She turned and walked out of the room. If she could have seen his face at that moment, then she would have known that he had already begun payment.

Tazia went to her room and sat on her bed, too stunned and hurt to cry. She knew Kirk too well. He would never have told her these things unless he had proof. She desperately needed someone to talk to, someone whose strength she could rely on, but there was no one. She would have to stand up to Kirk and defend herself. Somehow, Casa del Sol would be hers again. He said he loved her. She wondered if she really believed he did. Maybe there was a way through his so-called love to get back at him. Grimly she made her plans. No matter what she had to do, she would do it. She was going to drive Kirk LaCroix out of her home and out of her life, and she had to do it soon. If he ever found out she was carrying his child, it would be too late. He would never leave then. No, it had to be soon. She stood in the darkened room and allowed her mind to wander down every conceivable pathway. She did not see a way out. She was his wife in the eyes of God and in the eyes of the law. As such, he had every right to all her possessions. But he will live to regret it, she thought. If he continued to live—

A knock sounded on the door, lifting her from her dark thoughts. "Tazia? It is I, Marguerite. May I come in?"

"Yes."

Marguerite opened the door and found the room completely dark. Then she made out Tazia's still form sitting on the bed.

If only she would scream or throw something, Marguerite thought. *That* she could handle, but this deathly stillness made her very much afraid, both for Tazia and for Kirk. "Are you all right?"

"Do you know what has happened, Marguerite?"

"Sí, he told me when he first came tonight. He is now the owner of Casa del Sol . . . *el patrón*."

"Never! He may own it temporarily, but he will never be *el patrón* here . . . not as long as there is a breath in my body."

"What can you do, little one," she asked, her voice deep with sympathy. "You are really his wife?"

"Yes," Tazia answered softly. "Yes, I am really his wife, for all the good it will do him."

"Does he know yet he's to be a father?"

"No, and no one will tell him."

"Tazia, it is impossible to keep this kind of thing a secret for long. Soon he will need only to look at you to be able to see."

"By that time, Marguerite, he will be gone from Casa del Sol."

"But—"

"Marguerite, I want you to swear you will never tell him. Swear!"

"All right. I will never tell him, but I think it is wrong. I think he loves you more than you will ever know."

"I don't want to hear what you think. There is a way somehow, and I will find it. I will get him away from here and out of my life forever."

"What are you going to do?"

"For now, nothing. We will go about our business as usual. When the time is ripe, I will know what to do."

Marguerite nodded. "I shall prepare dinner. Will you be down?"

"No, I will have a tray in my room. If he wants to enjoy the hacienda, he will do so without any help from me."

Marguerite nodded and left the room slowly, closing the door quietly behind her. As she started down the stairs, Kirk appeared at the bottom of the steps and looked up at her. "Is she all right?"

"*Sí, Señor.* Except for her anger, she is well."

"Marguerite, I want to talk to you."

"There is nothing you need say to me Señor Kirk."

"I want you to know the truth. I want you to understand. Will you let me explain?"

She studied his face for a long time. His eyes never left hers. They did not beg or plead; they merely tried to tell her of his sincerity. Then she nodded her head, and she led him into the living room.

He talked to her for over an hour. When he had explained everything that had happened, she began to feel sorry for him.

"Maybe if you left and let her get herself back together, things would be different. Maybe she would begin to realize, as I do, that she truly does love you."

"I can't do that, Marguerite. I can't take that chance. Don't you think I would if I could? I am tied to her with my love, and there is nothing I can do about it. I will stay and fight for her if it takes the rest of my life."

"It will be a difficult thing, Señor. Tazia's loves and hates are very strong. Your stay here will not be pleasant."

"Marguerite, staying here with Tazia hating me is by far better than trying to get along without her somewhere else."

"You are a determined man, Señor."

"I love her, Marguerite. I do not love easily, but there is no changing it. I want her as my wife, and I will stay here until that is an accomplished fact or—" he paused to chuckle—"until she eliminates me completely."

"Don't underestimate her, Señor. That could be most dangerous."

Kirk narrowed his eyes and watched her closely. "Do you really think she is capable of killing me, Marguerite?"

Marguerite contemplated the question seriously before she answered. "There are many kinds of killing, Señor Kirk. No, I do not think she is the kind of person who can physically kill. But to kill the spirit, to kill the soul—yes, I think she is hurt enough and angry enough to do that, even if it means her soul dies a little in the process."

"I will be very careful . . . but I will not leave," he said softly as he rose and left the room.

Marguerite sat thinking for a long time before she rose and went to the kitchen to prepare Kirk's dinner. Later, after Kirk had eaten, she was in the kitchen cleaning when Juan came in.

"Marguerite. Has Tazia found out about Señor Kirk owning Casa del Sol?"

"*Sí*, she has."

"How is she taking the news?"

"As you would expect, Juan. She is very angry. She wants him to leave before he finds out about the baby. They had an argument, and she has not come out of her room since. She is sitting up there planning revenge, and I am afraid."

"For Señor Kirk? I think he can take care of himself."

"Not for him. I am afraid for her. It is not good for anyone to carry hatred inside. It eats the soul like a disease. But to feel such emotions when one is carrying a child . . . well, it is not good."

"What can we do to help her?"

"I don't know. I have sworn not to tell him of her condition, even though I think he has the right to know."

"*You* have sworn," Juan replied. "I have not."

"No, wait for just a little while. If the time comes that there is no other way, then you can tell him."

"Ah, Marguerite, the things that have happened to this family in the past two years have almost destroyed it. All of it because of one person. It does not seem fair that all the others are paying for his evil ways."

"What way does anyone have to prove to her that the things that are known about her brother are true? Who could tell her in a way she would believe? Even Don Federico and his family, after what they have suffered at his hands, could never make her believe."

"I know one who could."

"Who?"

"Her mother."

"Her mother was incapable of seeing the truth about her son before she was in this condition."

"You and I both know what has made her like this. Someone has made her face the truth, and she could not bear it."

"Who could have the proof?"

"I believe Don Federico could, if he wanted to. I imagine he cannot bear any more misery for his own family, and that keeps him from bringing everything out into the open."

"Is there any way you could find out, Juan? It would be of great benefit if someone besides Señor Kirk were to prove to her the truth about Manolo. Maybe then her pride would allow her to come to him."

"I will do my best," he replied.

"Good, now for a while we will do nothing except

stay out of their way as much as possible. I don't think being in their company is going to be very pleasant for the next few weeks."

"Why only a few weeks?"

Marguerite laughed. "Tazia does not have much time before it is obvious she is pregnant. Believe me, if he finds out, there will be no thought of his leaving. He would not want to leave her under normal circumstances, but if he thought she was carrying his child. . . ." She shrugged.

While they talked in the kitchen, Tazia lay on the bed in her darkened bedroom. She was aware of memories Kirk's presence in her house had brought, and her disobedient body was responding to her thoughts. She placed her hand on her belly, where Kirk's child grew. If only things had been different, she thought. Then she took hold of herself severely. She refused to let herself think of anything except a way of getting Kirk LaCroix out of her life forever.

Kirk also lay sleepless, in the room Marguerite had given him, deep in thoughts about Tazia as she had been after their marriage, when they were together in New Orleans. He could still feel the soft surrender of her warm lips against his, the silken feel of her body as he'd held her tightly against him. He did not try to shake the memories away as he usually did. Instead, he opened the doors of his mind and allowed himself the dubious luxury of enjoying them. He was aware that Tazia lay only two doors away from him. What could she do if he decided to break the door down and take her, as he desired? He contemplated the thought seriously for a moment. After seeing her again, he wanted her as badly as he ever had before, but he finally discarded the idea. He wanted her, but he wanted her warm and willing, as she was before. Tazia had been his once, and she would be his again.

250

30

Tazia could not place the sounds that had awakened her. Bright sunlight created patterns across her bedroom floor, and she could hear morning sounds. Birds called to one another from the treetops. Within the house, there were small sounds from the kitchen, where Marguerite was working. These were not the sounds for which she listened, however. They came again, the deep voices of men in conversation. She rose from the bed and looked down into the courtyard. Don Federico Reyes and his brother, Manuel, set on their horses. They were deep in conversation with another man, who stood within the porch's arched pillars. She knew instinctively that the man she could not see was Kirk. She heard Don Federico laugh at something. Then she turned from the window and quickly began to wash and dress. Within minutes she was closing her bedroom door behind her and starting down the steps to the front door.

Kirk had risen early, primarily because he had not slept most of the night. Dreams of Tazia had wakened him several times, and when the first streaks of morning light touched the sky, he rose, dressed, and went downstairs. There was no one else awake in the house yet. He walked outside and strolled down the colonnaded porch. It was no wonder Tazia loved this place so very much, he thought. There was a deep, peaceful beauty that touched the soul here. They could be happy here if only she would let them. It was not going to be an easy task, but someday he would break through her resistance and reach her heart again. Until that day came, he would content himself with just being in her presence and try his best to learn the management of a large hacienda. He had absolutely no intention of ever leaving Tazia again unless it was to take her on the honeymoon they had never had. He chuckled a little to himself. If she had known his thoughts at that moment, she would have been furious.

The sound of approaching horses drew Kirk's attention to the large gate at the opposite end of the courtyard. He watched two men ride in on two of the most beautiful horses he had ever seen. They clattered into the courtyard and stopped. When they noticed Kirk standing there, they looked at one another for a moment and then slowly walked their horses toward him.

"*Buenos días, Señor,*" Don Federico said softly.

"Good morning," Kirk answered, watching them closely.

"I am Don Federico Reyes," he stated proudly. He had a feeling he knew to whom he was talking, and he wondered why Tazia had told them Kirk would not be there.

"I'm Kirk LaCroix."

"Ah! Tazia's husband." Don Federico smiled. "It is a pleasure to meet you, Señor. We are your neighbors and friends of the de Montega family for many, many years. This is my brother, Don Manuel."

"Good morning, Don Manuel, Don Federico. It is a pleasure, I assure you. Won't you come in and have some breakfast with . . . us?"

"Gracias, Señor LaCroix."

"Kirk, please."

"Kirk, has Tazia come down yet?"

Don Federico watched Kirk closely. He saw the shuttered look of his eyes when Tazia's name was mentioned. There was something amiss here, and he would wait and watch.

Kirk was about to answer when Tazia's voice came softly from the doorway.

"Good morning, Don Federico, Don Manuel."

"Now the day has achieved full brilliance. Good morning, Tazia. You are beautiful as always this morning."

Don Manuel bowed over Tazia's hand and smiled at her.

"It is good to see you again, Tazia, my child. Just to look at you takes years off these old shoulders." Kirk watched Tazia's face soften and smile at these two older gentlemen. His eyes devoured her hungrily. He wanted to see that look on her face again for him. Without realizing he was being observed, Kirk continued to watch Tazia as she spoke in soft, flowing Spanish to Don Manuel.

Then Kirk suddenly realized that Don Federico's warm brown eyes were observing him closely. He pulled his face into a blank mask, but not soon enough for a wise man like Don Federico not to see the hunger and misery that lurked behind his eyes. He must talk to this husband of Tazia, find out what kind of man he was and, if possible, what great thing stood between them. Don Federico also noticed very quickly that although she looked at him and his brother with affection, her eyes never turned toward her husband at all. It was as if . . . as if she did not want to recognize his existence, he thought in surprise.

"We have just met your husband, Tazia" he said slowly. "Let me again congratulate you both and wish you a long and happy life together and . . . may all your children be healthy and happy." He stretched out his hand to Kirk, who took it in a strong grip.

"Thank you, Don Federico."

"*Sí*," Tazia answered coolly. "I appreciate your good wishes, but all these things are in the hands of God, are they not, Don Federico?"

"Yes," he answered softly. "That should always be remembered. Everything is in the hands of God."

Tazia's eyes would not meet his, for she understood exactly what he meant. Instead, she turned to Don Manuel and, tucking her hand into his arm, smiled warmly at him.

"Come, join us for breakfast. Tell me stories, as you did when I was a child. I want to hear how everything has been going since . . . since I've been gone."

With the two of them leading the way, Don Federico and Kirk followed behind, just out of hearing distance. They could hear only Tazia's tinkling laughter at something Don Manuel had told her.

"Your wife is a very lovely woman, Señor Kirk. I hope you appreciate her rare qualities."

Kirk chuckled. 'Señor Reyes, I don't think there is another person in the world who so much appreciates her . . . rare qualities."

"You have known each other long?"

"Not really. I met her just after she arrived in New Orleans. You might say ours was a whirlwind courtship. We've been married now for just a little over seven months."

"Seven months," Don Federico repeated softly. "Maybe you knew her brother also, Manolo de Montega? He also was in New Orleans."

Only the faintest shadow flickered across Kirk's face, but his muscles tightened, and a small nerve quivered in his tightened cheek.

"Yes, I met her brother once," he answered.

"Ummm, it was a shame that he had to die so young. I hear he was involved in a game of chance and someone shot him. Tragic, tragic. She needs protection now that her father is dead."

Kirk turned to face Don Federico.

"She has all the protection she needs. I know that Tazia has seen a great deal of grief. But that is all behind her. Given enough time, I will change these things. Given enough time, I will make her life happy again."

Don Federico smiled at him, his eyes warm and friendly. He liked this husband of Tazia. He was a strong, determined man, just what a girl with Tazia's pride needed to make her happy.

"Señor Kirk, one day soon we must ride over our lands together." His eyes held Kirk's. "I think there are many things we need to tell each other."

Kirk nodded. He didn't know exactly what had transpired, but he realized he had just made a very valuable friend.

Although a stream of inconsequential conversation was kept up during breakfast, Don Federico was well aware of the strained tension between Tazia and Kirk. She did not look at him often, and when she did, it was a quick glance that shifted away again, as if she were a little afraid of holding his eyes any length of time. Kirk, on the other hand, was all attention to everything that was said at the table. He seemed to be searching for some word, some sign that would give him a key to that solitary room that was Tazia's heart.

"Cristina said something about your having a party

soon, Tazia. I think it is an excellent idea to introduce your husband to our friends," Don Manuel said.

Tazia did not get time to answer.

"Yes, We're going to have a party. It's planned for two weeks from tonight. I hope you both can attend." Kirk said the words authoritatively, but he watched Tazia closely. Two bright spots of color on her cheeks and the momentary trembling of her hands were the only signs of the furious anger she felt.

"Marvelous!" Don Manuel smiled. "Of course, we will both attend. I would not miss the excitement for the world."

"Excitement, Don Manuel?" Kirk asked, puzzled by the word.

Don Manuel chuckled at what he considered a very good joke. "Señor Kirk, you have stolen the loveliest lady in the valley from under the noses of her many suitors. It will be a great deal of pleasure to watch you defend your prize."

Kirk laughed. "Don't worry, Don Manuel. What is mine is mine. Nobody takes it away from me."

"Ah! *Caballero*, when I was your age, it was the same with me." Don Federico smiled in reminiscence. "What a battle I had for my lovely Catherine. Before I married her and during our marriage, it was always the same. What is of real value in this world is worth the fight, is it not?"

"Always," Kirk answered softly. His eyes were on Tazia, who did not smile in return. Her mind was elsewhere. What's his is his, she thought furiously. Well, he shall soon find I am not his. A party he wants, a party he shall have. But I think he will regret it.

"If you gentlemen will excuse me, I have much to do if we are going to have a party so soon," Tazia said as she rose from the table.

"Of course, *querida*," Don Federico said. All three men rose as she left the table and watched her walk away.

They sat back down, and Don Federico leaned forward and spoke again to Kirk. "Señor Kirk, it was not only for the purpose of seeing Tazia again or meeting you that my brother and I rode over here this morning."

"Really, Don Federico? And what were your other reasons?"

"Great problems have developed in this area during the past few days. As you know, Don Ramon, Tazia's father, my brother, and I successfully joined our two *ranchos* in a mutual effort to perfect our palominos."

"No, I didn't know. But I am certainly interested in anything that affects this *rancho*. What is this problem that has arisen?"

"Don Ramon has here one of the most beautifully perfect palomino mares in existence. I, on the other hand, have ownership of my marvelous 'El Furio,' without doubt the most perfect stallion of his breed."

"Go on."

"Don Ramon and I have consented by handshake to breed these two beauties and share the rewards of their production."

"I don't see where this presents a problem, Don Federico. If Don Ramon gave his word and Tazia is willing, of course we should go on with your plans."

"Good. The problem is that twice in the past two months efforts have been made on this *rancho* to steal one or both of these beauties."

"Who? Who would know, outside of your neighbors and friends? Who would stand to gain from it?"

"Señor Kirk. Someone who knew Tazia's father was dead. Someone who knew her brother would not be coming back. Someone who thought it was a possibility that he would be able to acquire Casa del Sol."

Kirk's eyes grew hard and cold. "Do you mean me, Don Federico?"

"*Santa María, no!*" exclaimed Don Federico. "If I gave that impression I am sorry. No, I do not believe you are involved in any way. But I do believe you know more than you think you do. For if what I think is so, someone who is either in your confidence or knows the situation well is responsible."

The answer suddenly burst upon Kirk's consciousness like a brilliant light. Of course he knew who was responsible. Who else but Garrett Flye had tried to get Tazia? Garrett Flye. Kirk rolled the name about in his mind. He had wanted Casa del Sol, the horses, and Tazia. Where was he now? If Kirk were right, Garrett would not be very far away, and he would certainly try again. Kirk was the only thing that stood between Garrett and everything he wanted.

For just a moment, he let the thought of Garrett and Tazia together slip into his mind. It filled him with the deepest sense of anger he had ever felt in his life toward any human being. While Kirk was alive, Garrett would never get to her.

"You *do* know something." said Don Federico softly, watching various emotions play across Kirk's face.

"Yes, you were right. I know more than I thought I did. I know exactly who is responsible. He wants this hacienda, the horses—and he wants my wife."

"Can we form a plan for plan for protecting them?" questioned Don Federico.

"Let us both give it some thought, Don Federico. By the night of the party, we should be able to put our thoughts together and form some type of plan."

"Excellent. Now I imagine we must be about our work. I will see you soon, Señor Kirk."

Kirk showed them out and watched them ride away. Don Federico's last words lingered in his mind.

"I do not know what is wrong between you and Tazia. I know that you love her very deeply and that there is a barrier you must break down to get to her. She is worth the effort, my boy. She is a lady of great pride, and she will make a wonderful wife and an excellent mother. She does not know that you stand between her and the world. You are her protection. Don't let anything happen to stop you from protecting her, not anything that *happens* or Tazia herself."

"Thank you, Don Federico. Believe me, there is no way I will ever leave Casa del Sol unless Tazia and the *rancho* are safe."

"I was not only thinking about safety, Kirk," he answered with a half-smile. "I was thinking that she loves you more than she knows. Don't ever leave the *rancho* at all. Stay here always and breed fine sons to hold the land when you are gone. Don't only protect her, protect yourself, as well."

31

For the next four days, Tazia managed to be wherever Kirk was not. She seemed to flit through the house like a ghost. He knew she was making preparations for the party, but he could not corner her anywhere to ask any questions, not that he thought she would answer him if he did. She was making her feelings perfectly clear. She considered Casa del Sol hers and him an intruder. She did not feel she had to ask his advice on anything. He knew that she rose early in the morning and often went riding, but he did not intrude on her.

Instead, he began a small campaign of his own. In every way possible, he worked with Juan and Marguerite, slowly winning their respect and affection. He complimented Marguerite on her cooking, her work around the house, and the responsibility she had shown in the way she had helped raise Tazia. Slowly, with gentle persuasion, he gleaned from her small details of Tazia's childhood.

Kirk took a completely different tack with Juan. He

asked questions about the running of the hacienda and listened with respectful attention to a man who knew a million times more about the breeding and raising of palominos than he did. At first Juan eyed him suspiciouly, but as he continued to show interest and did not try to take over, Juan began to unbend. They were not friends yet, and Juan still kept a close eye on him, but Kirk felt he was taking a giant step in the right direction.

He dressed in the early morning light that brightened his room. The house was still quiet. Closing the bedroom door behind him, he walked down the hall toward the stairway. As he passed Tazia's room, he could hear a slight movement inside. He stopped, contemplating the closed door for a moment. He wondered if she kept her door locked. He reached out and turned the knob gently. It opened almost soundlessly. He smiled to himself, not knowing whether she trusted him or believed she could wash him out of her life simply by ignoring him. The door swung slowly open. Tazia stood with her back to him. Obviously she had just begun to dress for the day. Her hair hung down her back in a thick mass, tangled from sleep. She was in her bare feet and had just put on her riding skirt. She was naked from the waist up, but her hair covered her skin. She was reaching out to pick up her blouse from a nearby chair when she heard the door click shut.

"Marguerite," she said without turning around, "get my brush from the dresser and help me." When she heard no reply, she turned around to face the door. The morning sun coming through the window behind her picked up the ivory gleam of her skin.

Tazia was so surprised to see Kirk there that she did not realize her state of undress until she saw how obviously his eyes were devouring her. Memories of their short time together flooded his mind. He could almost feel the satin softness of her skin and the warmth of her body against his.

"Good morning," Kirk said.

"Get out of my room! What right—"

"Tazia," he interrupted coolly. "You are my wife. I have every right."

She pulled herself up stiffly and quickly slipped the blouse on and began to button it. He watched her with obvious enjoyment.

"I shall remember to keep my door locked from this time on," she said frigidly. Turning her back on him again, she began to brush her tangled hair. She gave a small cry of surprise when he came behind her and grasped her arm in a tight grip. Against her every effort, he slowly drew her around to face him. Her face was set in an angry frown, and she held herself stiffly and as far away from contact as she could.

"Let go of me!" she snapped.

He pulled her even closer, his eyes burning into her.

"Do you think a locked door will stop me, Tazia? Don't push me or I might just show you how difficult it would be for you to keep me from taking what I want."

She glared at him, still trying to pull herself from his iron grip. "Murderer," she snarled.

The word struck him like a physical blow. He suddenly found himself losing his temper, which was something he rarely did and had been determined never to do with her. With a sudden jerk, he pulled her almost off her feet toward him. She began to fight, furiously striking him with her free hand. He felt the sting of one blow against his cheek. Another blow landed harmlessly on his shoulder before he captured both arms and twisted them behind her. She rattled off several words in Spanish that he thought he probably didn't want to understand. Slowly, methodically, he gained control of her. No matter how hard she tried, she could not twist free. Then he pinned her arms behind her with one hand and ran his other hand through the tangled silken mass of her hair. She glared at him and tried her best to break free, but it was impossible. He lowered his head and gently kissed the corner of her mouth, which trembled with fury. Very slowly, as though he had all the time in the world, he let his lips drift from one corner of her mouth to the other, then down the slender line of her neck to the throbbing pulse at the base of her throat.

Tazia was almost choking with anger — and another emotion she would never admit to him, or to herself. What he really wanted to do was to take her to the bed, pull the clothes from her, and make love to her until he melted the frozen core of her body. But finally he realized that he would not take her against her will. He wanted her, but he wanted her warm and willing, not fighting him every inch of the way. He kissed her again firmly, forcing her lips apart and invading her mouth until he was almost lost himself. He knew if he didn't leave the room quickly, he was going to take her by force and probably ruin everything he had planned.

Kirk looked into her rage-filled eyes. "You see, Tazia, no locked door or anything else could keep me from you if I wanted it that way. No matter what you may think right now, I did not murder your brother and I am not responsible for the death of your father. And most important of all, you are my wife, I love you, and I will never, *never* leave Casa del Sol."

He released her and turned to walk toward the

door. As he put his hand on the door knob, he heard her tightly controlled voice, "Kirk?"

He turned and looked at her. Amid the anger in her eyes were confusion and hurt. "Go away," she said softly. "Leave Casa del Sol. Leave me alone. There will never be anything more between us. Go and leave me in peace."

He contemplated her for several minutes while she stood and watched him, her eyes bright, her lips slightly parted. Her blouse rose and fell with every panting breath. As he opened the door, he looked back at her and said very firmly, "Never, Tazia, never."

Kirk might have stayed another minute or two to admire the beautiful picture she made, but Tazia flung the hairbrush at his head. It missed him by only an inch. Along with the brush came another violent stream of Spanish. While she searched about her for something else to throw, he beat a hasty retreat, pulling the door shut behind him just as something heavy struck it on the inside. He walked downstairs, savoring the tingling feeling of her mouth against his. He had felt—although Tazia would never admit it—a trembling response to his kiss. He smiled to himself. It was one small step in the right direction. One step only. But he planned many more in the days to come.

Kirk was about to enter the kitchen when a voice called to him.

"Señor Kirk."

He turned to see Juan standing inside the front door. "Yes, Juan? What is it?"

"Your brother is outside, Señor."

"Del," Kirk said happily as he moved with long strides toward the door. Juan stepped aside, and Kirk pulled the door open and stepped out into the bright sunlight. Del was just climbing out of a hired carriage. They both laughed as they shook hands.

"Del, what are you doing here?"

"Well," Del said with a wide grin, "I thought I was rescuing you from . . . heaven knows what. I hadn't heard from you in days and I began to worry. Jean and I thought maybe you'd been done away with, that your body was buried under a tree somewhere. So I just decided to beard the lion—or should I say lioness?—in her den."

"You can see that I'm well and happy," Kirk replied.

"Happy?"

"Well, maybe not exactly *happy*. But certainly making great strides in that direction. Come on inside. Let's get you something to eat and drink. Juan! Marguerite!"

Marguerite came running from the kitchen. "*Sí Señor* Kirk?"

"Will you get us something to eat? This is my brother, Del, Marguerite. Del, this is Marguerite, the greatest cook in the world." She smiled at Del, then disappeared into the kitchen.

"Now, how about telling me everything that's happened?" Del said. "How are things really going, Kirk?"

Kirk's smile faded as he motioned to his brother to follow him to the table. When they were both seated, he explained everything that had happened since he had arrived. Del listened in silence, watching his brother's face closely.

"Maybe you'd best forget the whole thing and come back home with us. She'll never change the way she felt about her brother, nor the way she feels about you."

"She's my wife, Del," Kirk said softly.

"Kirk, do you really think she'll ever be your wife

again? She thinks you're a murderer who's out to get Casa del Sol. How are you ever going to get over a mountain like that?"

"Not by backing away from it, that's certain. Del, marriage vows to me mean in sickness or in health . . . forever. This is just something we have to get through. Somehow, some way, the truth will come out, and she will know that I love her. Until then, this is one battle I cannot walk away from. I have too much to lose. I . . . I don't think I could ever survive the loss."

Del was a little surprised at Kirk, but he kept it to himself. Marguerite carried in a tray and set their breakfast before them. While they ate, Del told Kirk how they had waited for word from him and then become so worried about him that Jean had suggested they all ride out to discover what had happened. Del had to persuade them that it would be better for him to come alone, and he promised to return with all the news as soon as possible.

"Why don't you tell Jean and Louis to go on home? You could stay here with us for a while."

"What man in his right mind camps in the middle of a battleground? No, I think I'll go back with them. I just had to find out how it was with you."

"Well, we're throwing our first party next week. It should be interesting. Why don't you all come? Then you can start home afterward."

"A party! My God, that should be an interesting affair. I wouldn't miss it for the world—and I'm sure I speak for Louis and Jean, too. Louis misses Gabrielle very much and he can't wait to get back to her, so we will probably leave right after the party."

"Would you like to ride with me for a while? I'm going over to see a neighbor, Señor Reyes. I'd like you to meet him, Del. For some reason, I feel he could do

266

much to end this war, if I could just get him to tell me everything he knows."

Kirk went on to tell Del about the condition they had found Tazia's mother in. "I don't know what happened that day, Del, but whatever was said in that study killed Tazia's father and made a ghost out of her mother. I'm sure that only something about Manolo could have caused them that kind of grief. Only Don Federico knows for sure. He said something about riding our lands and talking together. I don't know if this is the right time to push him into remembering, but if that will bring Tazia out of this well of hatred, I'll try it."

Del agreed to go with him, and Kirk sent for Juan. He told him to put Del's carriage and horse in the stable and to saddle one of their palominos for him. While they were waiting for their horses—Tazia came downstairs. Although she did not show it, Del's presence brought back memories of her wedding. Thoughts of it burst unbidden into her mind, but she quickly brought them under control.

"Good morning, Tazia," Del said, smiling.

She merely nodded her head slightly, without smiling. 'Señor LaCroix," she said coolly.

"It used to be Del, Tazia," he said softly.

Again she did not answer his friendly overture. "Did you come for a visit? Or to help your brother take over Casa del Sol?"

"Just to see if everyone was well," he answered.

She gave a short harsh laugh and turned to face Kirk. "Do you need reinforcements . . . husband?" Her voice was soft, yet venomous.

"Tazia," Kirk replied slowly, "I need no help from anyone in taking or holding what is mine. I thought I proved that to you a short while ago."

Her body stiffened with suppressed anger, and her

purple eyes blazed with fury. She turned abruptly and left them watching her rigid back as she walked away.

Del gave a small whistle through teeth. "That is a very formidable woman," he said softly.

"*You*, my dear brother, have bitten off more than you can chew."

Kirk frowned as he watched Tazia's retreating form. "That is not Tazia, Del. Tazia is a gentle, affectionate, warm woman. What you saw is what her parents and her brother have created, and I intend to change that even if it takes the rest of my life."

As Kirk watched Tazia walk away, he noticed something different about her, but he could not put his finger on what it was. There was some new facet to her he did not know about. In the short time they had been together, he had known every inch of her, loved her beyond reason, and felt he had known her as well as a man could ever know a woman. Now there was something he should have known. He put it aside temporarily and led Del to the stable, where he stood in open-mouthed wonder at the beauty of the palomino he was to ride.

While Juan watched the two men ride away, he got the feeling, for the first time since Manolo's death, that all was going to work out well at Casa del Sol.

32

Del and Kirk rode slowly together across the land that Tazia loved so dearly. Del was open-mouthed at the beauty of this place Kirk now called home. He would have liked to stay here, but he did not want to make it any harder for Kirk than it already was. They rode in silence; Kirk let Del absorb the beauty around him.

"Want to change your mind about staying, Del?" Kirk asked.

"If anything could do it this almost has, but no, I think it would be easier for all concerned if I went home with Louis and Jean."

When they arrived at the Reyes home, Serafina greeted them.

"Good morning. Is Don Federico at home?"

"Don Federico is out riding now, Señor. He should be back within the hour. Señorita Cristina is here."

"May we come in and wait for his return?"

"Who *are* you, Señor?"

"I am Kirk LaCroix, and this is my brother, Del. I am Tazia de Montega's husband."

Serafina's eyes grew wide. Kirk realized that she must have heard a great deal about him. He wondered just which story she had heard.

"If you will wait one moment, Señor LaCroix, I will tell Señorita Cristina that you are here." She led the way to a study and closed the door softly behind her.

"This is a beautiful place," Del said. "These people own a small piece of heaven out here. I'm tempted, I'm really tempted to—"

His words came to an abrupt halt as the door opened and Cristina came into the room. She wore a plain, deep blue dress that matched the color of her eyes. Her golden hair was drawn back from her face and piled on her head in a cluster of curls. She looked fresh and lovely as she smiled brightly at her visitors.

"Good morning, gentlemen. I am Cristina Reyes. I'm sorry my father is not home at the moment, but if you would care to join me for my morning chocolate, I would be happy to entertain you until he arrives."

Kirk was the first to recover from the shock of this beautiful golden vision. "Good morning. I am Kirk LaCroix, Tazia de Montega's husband. This is my brother, Del. It is a pleasure to meet you, Señorita Reyes."

"And it is a pleasure to meet you, Señor LaCroix. Tazia has told me much about you." Her eyes held Kirk's without revealing any of the thoughts that dwelt behind them. She put out of her mind the things Tazia had told her about Kirk. She knew that Tazia had been badly hurt and was angry. No, she would find out for herself just what kind of man he was.

Cristina led the way to the dining room and told Serafina to bring her chocolate. "What would you gentlemen care for?"

"Nothing for me, thank you. I had breakfast early this morning before I left town," Del answered.

"I will take some chocolate, too," Kirk replied.

"Serafina, two chocolates, please."

"*Sí, Señorita*," Serafina said. Soundlessly she left the room.

"Señor Kirk, it is really a pleasure to have you here. Tazia and I have been very close since our childhood, and I would like to be a friend of yours also."

"Thank you, Señorita Reyes."

"Cristina, please," she said with a warm smile.

"Thank you. Cristina, I've come to ask a very great favor of you and your family."

"A favor? *Sí*, if there is anything you need at Casa del Sol, you need only ask. Our families are linked almost as one. Therefore, I feel as if you were already my brother, as Tazia is my sister."

She had been looking at Kirk as they conversed, and Del had sat silently admiring her fragile blond beauty. He had thought all Spanish women were dark, as Tazia was. Where in God's name did she get golden hair and blue eyes? They're like . . . like sapphires, he thought. He doubted that he had ever seen another woman, outside of Tazia, who was as beautiful, yet they were as unalike as day and night. Cristina was a small fragile-looking woman. Yet, somehow, he got the feeling this woman was not as fragile she looked.

"This is not a favor for Casa del Sol," Kirk began, "it is a personal favor."

A small frown crossed her face. "A personal favor?"

"Yes." Kirk leaned forward. "Cristina, will you tell me about Tazia's brother?"

Cristina's face paled a little, and her eyes registered her surprise for just a moment.

"Manolo?"

"Yes."

"But Señor Kirk, surely Tazia has told you all

about her family. What could I possibly add to what she has already said?"

Kirk then explained to Cristina all the things that had happened since the first time he had met Tazia. She did not interrupt him with foolish questions, but watched him intently as he talked. This was the other side of the coin, the parts of the story Tazia had left out. As Kirk spoke about his wife, Cristina became convinced that he loved her deeply. She also felt that Tazia was wrong in not telling him about the child she was carrying. Well, she thought, that is something that must be left to Tazia. It is surely not my place to tell him.

Kirk continued with the story of the killing of Manolo and watched with surprise the lack of shock to Cristina. It was as though she had expected something such as this to happen to him, he thought. Suddenly he realized that she hated Manolo as much as she loved Tazia.

He finished the story and leaned back in his chair to watch Cristina with expectant eyes. "Now you see why I have to know about him."

"*Sí, Señor* Kirk." Her eyes left his face and concentrated on her hands. "Manolo and I were never . . . close. There is not much I can tell you about him other than what you already know. He was beloved to his parents; Tazia adored him. He spent a great deal of time away from Casa del Sol. You see, he did not love it as Tazia does. To her, Casa del Sol is part of her blood. She feels very deeply for family ties and her roots. She gives herself completely to anything she loves. And she can be hurt very easily. She loved Manolo in spite of . . . I mean she loved him very much. Manolo's death was a deep shock to his parents. His parents had set their hearts on Manolo running Casa del Sol."

"And what of Tazia? What did they plan for her?"

"A marriage . . . to someone of their choice."

"Just like that, Manolo was to receive everything and Tazia was to be pushed into a marriage whether she wanted it or not?"

"*Sí, Señor* Kirk," she answered softly.

"Didn't her brother feel any compassion for her at all? Or did he just accept that she was to get nothing?" Kirk's eyes clouded with anger.

"Señor Kirk, try to understand. Our families are very old—and very proud. It has been this way since the beginning."

Del interrupted for the first time. "Did your father ever try to force you into a marriage you did not want?" he asked softly.

"No," she answered quietly. "There is a great difference between my father and Don Ramón. In the first place, my father has no sons. I will be his only heir, because it is impossible for my mother to bear any more children."

"But I thought you had a sister."

A faint tremble went through Cristina and her eyes dropped again to her hands. There was a sadness about her that could be felt like a tangible thing.

"There is a strong possibility that my sister will be entering an order of secluded nuns for the balance of her life. That leaves only me as heir to my family's possessions."

Something clicked in Kirk's mind and he glanced at his brother across the table. She was avoiding telling them about something, something they needed to know. They both had the same thought. There was a connection between their difficulties with Tazia and this family. Kirk leaned forward in his chair, his eyes searching hers. Somehow he had to learn what she knew. He was about to ask another question when a voice came from the doorway.

"Ah! Good morning, Señor Kirk. It is a beautiful morning, is it not?"

Both men rose from their seats and extended hands of friendship to Don Federico.

"Yes, it is a lovely day," Kirk answered. "I thought it would be a good time for the ride you suggested."

"Of course. If you would not mind waiting until I've had some breakfast. I am anxious to show you my lands. I would like you to see my beauties, especially El Furio."

They all sat down again as Don Federico joined them at the table. Serafina carried in his breakfast, and they conversed about horses for the remainder of the meal, much to Cristina's relief.

When breakfast was over, Don Federico rose and prepared to leave when Cristina asked, "Father, would you mind very much if I rode with you?"

"You would be most welcome, my dear. Would she not, gentlemen?"

Both Kirk and Del agreed. In fact, Kirk was amused at Del's enthusiasm.

The three men walked slowly to the stable while Cristina ran to her room to change.

When they arrived at the paddock they leaned against the high rail fence that circled it. Don Federico gave a sharp shrill whistle, which was answered by a horse's whinny. Through the doors of the large stable and out into the brilliant sun came the most beautiful piece of horseflesh Kirk or Del had ever seen.

"El Furio," Don Federico said softly, almost worshipfully.

The horse was magnificent as he trotted up to Don Federico's outstretched hand, tossing his mane proudly, as though he were allowing Don Federico a great honor. His mane was pale, almost white, while his coat was the color of molten gold. There was no fear in his eye for man. It was as though he knew he was king among his kind, and he would be subservient to no one.

Don Federico chuckled. "He is proud, is he not, gentlemen?"

"He's the most beautiful animal I've ever seen," Kirk replied enthusiastically. "You say Casa del Sol has a mare you would like to breed him with?"

"*Sí, Señor,*" Don Federico answered.

"I would like to see her. She must be an extraordinary animal to breed with one like this."

"Oh, she is, Señor. I assure you I would not let the blood of El Furio flow in the foal whose mother was not the equal of the sire."

They continued to watch El Furio prance about until Cristina came to join them. When all four of them were mounted, Don Federico guided them over his land enthusiastically. Although he talked a great deal with them, it was soon obvious to Kirk and Del that by some secret signal Don Federico and Cristina kept the conversation as far away from family matters as they could. At one point, Cristina and her father fell behind and carried on a short conversation in rapid, fluent Spanish. Kirk would have given anything to understand what they were saying, and he promised himself to learn the language as soon as he possibly could. Even, he thought with a dry laugh, to understand Tazia when she was angry with him.

Kirk also noticed that Del was maneuvering his horse to be next to Cristina and in a short while, Don Federico and Kirk were well ahead of them. He could hear them conversing quietly together, and he wondered just how long it was going to take Del to change his mind about leaving California.

When their ride concluded, Don Federico asked them to stay for lunch, but Kirk refused, and Del, although he was reluctant to leave, joined him to ride back to Casa del Sol.

They rode in silence most of the way. Then Del said softly, "You know Cristina has many of the answers to your questions, don't you?"

"Of course, but how do I get them out of her?"

"Well, I've been thinking," Del said very seriously. "If I were to stay here and get better acquainted with her . . . just to find out information, of course."

"Of course, what other reason could you possibly have?" Kirk replied seriously.

"Well, I might just be a very great help to you."

"*Very* great help."

"I'm a devoted brother."

"Oh, devoted."

"There's no sacrifice I wouldn't make," he said solemnly as he put his hand over his heart and cast his eyes heavenward.

"And the fact that the lady is very young, beautiful, and exciting has nothing to do with it?"

"Kirk, you wound me. You know I have only your interests at heart."

"Of course, how could I have been so coarse as to suggest any other motive?"

Del threw his head back and laughed. Kirk laughed with him, and they rode back to Casa del Sol prepared to face the future.

33

Louis had read the letter he had just received from Gabrielle over and over until he knew it by heart, but he unfolded and read it again, mostly because it made him feel closer to her. Jean was lying on the bed with his hands behind his head, watching him with half-closed eyes and a small flicker of amusement on his face.

Gabrielle had told Louis that his sister, Jeanette, had married and was very happy. She had visited them at Louis's old home, and they had become friends. Despite that, she missed him dreadfully and threatened that if he did not soon come back to her, she would come to him. Then she had told him how much she missed him and loved him.

Louis tapped the letter lightly against his fingertips and stared off into space. Jean was about to speak when the door opened and Del walked in.

"God, it's about time," Louis said. "We'd just about given up on both of you. How are things Del? Is Kirk all right?"

"He's fine, or at least he's working at it." Del laughed and sat down to explain everything that was happening at Casa del Sol.

"Well," Jean replied, "it looks like our old friend

no longer needs our help. I think I will be on my way back to Barataria soon."

"Yes, I guess it's about time for all of us to leave," Louis said. "But damn! I hate to go before I know everything. There's more mystery here than there was in New Orleans. What do you say we stay a little longer, Del?"

Del grinned. "Well Louis," he said slowly, "I'm seriously thinking of staying here permanently. Kirk's asked me to stay at Casa del Sol for a while, but I'm thinking of making the Pauma my home."

Both men looked at him in surprise. Del probably had a life in New Orleans that most men only dream of: position, money, women. They were very surprised that anything could draw him away from there. Jean smiled wickedly, his blue eyes glittering with undisguised deviltry.

"There wouldn't be another pretty señorita at Casa del Sol, would there?"

"Not at Casa del Sol," Del replied.

Louis was silent for a few moments, deep in thought. It would be nice to start a new life with Gabrielle in this beautiful place. But would she give up Five Points for him? Now that his sister was married, there was nothing to keep him in New Orleans, where he had never really been happy.

Del watched him. "It's a whole new life, Louis," he said gently.

Louis looked at Jean, and they both smiled.

"I suppose," Jean said gruffly, "you want me to carry your request back to Gabrielle and bring her back here if she decides to come?"

"Would you, Jean?"

Jean sighed, but his eyes glowed with humor.

"Write your letter. I think I'll be on my way tomorrow."

Louis went to his room and took up his pen, but when he sat down to write, he realized he didn't know exactly what to say to make her understand how badly he wanted her here. He had promised to get Five Points back for her. Now he was going to ask her to leave it behind and start all over again with him. He put these thoughts behind and wrote first to Jeanette, telling her he was well and describing how beautiful it was in California. He gave her sole ownership of their home and told her he was planning to stay where he was. When he was finished with his letter to Jeanette, he again found himself staring at the blank page upon which he wanted to put his feelings about Gabrielle and their future in a way she would understand and accept. Then, slowly, he began to write.

My Darling Wife;
A day has not passed, nor a night, since I left that I have not longed for your lovely presence. Gabrielle, I am going to ask you for a great sacrifice. I want you to come here to California and start a new life with me. I know it is much to ask, and if you refuse, I will understand. But this land is so new, new as our love, and I would like us to put all our past behind us and start over with no bad memories clinging to us.

I need you, Gabrielle. I thank God for the gift of you—not that I possess you, though I would like to. I cannot control your death or life, nor would it be proper to try. Your independence makes me wonder even more at the amazing fact that you seem to care for me when you need not. Without my love, you would still have excess; without your love, my life would be an empty shell resting on barren shores, reflecting false murmurs of non-existent seas.

I need you, Gabrielle. But more than that, I love you. I need a loving breast on which to rest, a funny little laugh to pierce my pretending, a soft embrace to take away my loneliness. I need to be silly with you, to play before you like a child. I need someone lovely to worry about, to show me how foolish are other worries. I need someone to live with, someone to die for.

I need you Gabrielle, but more, I love you. And I thank God for the delicate fragrance of your presence, for every day we can share together, for each day you toss and turn in my heart. Come to me, Gabrielle and let us begin our lives together anew. I love you.

Your devoted husband,

Louis

He read the letter over again. He knew that there was nothing more he could say so he put it into an envelope and sealed it. He then took both letters to Jean's room and gave them to him.

Del gave Jean written permission to sell his property in New Orleans, along with the permission he had already gotten from Kirk. Their money was to be transferred to the bank in Los Angeles.

Jean was moved to laughter. "Can you possibly imagine the three of you entrusting your entire fortunes to a pirate? There's enough money here for me to outfit a fleet of ships and retire in debauched luxury for the rest of my life."

"There's no one I'd trust with my fortune or my wife as much as I would you," Louis said, his eyes glittering with amusement.

"That is a dubious compliment, my friend. But," he sighed, "I shall do my best to bring them both to you intact."

"If you have to choose between them, Jean," Louis laughed, "bring Gabrielle. I need her far more than the money I left behind."

Del stood up and stretched. "Well, I guess I'd better start back. I'll inform Kirk that he has two temporary house guests until we can find some land for sale and get ourselves organized."

"Good idea. You go on ahead," Louis replied. "When Jean leaves in the morning, I'll ride out to join you." He chuckled. "Makes it a little easier if you let Tazia know I'm coming first. That way, you can handle the worst of her anger, and it won't be so hard for me."

"Coward."

"You're right."

Del closed the door on their laughter and went downstairs. His mind was on a certain beautiful blond señorita, so he did not notice that he was being followed when he mounted his horse and started back to Casa del Sol.

Del rode slowly, for he was in no hurry to reach the hacienda. He mulled over all the events of the past year. Fate, he thought, had the strangest way of interfering in one's life just when one thought it was all well-planned out. If someone had told him a year ago that he would leave New Orleans under the conditions he had and traveled three thousand miles to find the woman he had dreamed of all his life, he would never have believed it.

The man following Del cut away from the main road and rode up into the trees that paralleled Del's trail.

This is the *gringo* he had been told about, the man

thought. His build and coloring fit the description he had been given, and he was riding one of the great palominos from Casa del Sol. He had to be Kirk LaCroix.

The man grinned. He was small and slender, with olive skin and black hair and a full, black moustache. His narrow, gleaming eyes were those of a predatory animal. Spurring his horse forward to a rapid run, he quickly passed Del and rode on in the shelter of the line of trees that fringed the narrow road. He soon came to a spot he had marked out in advance where a tree had fallen at the outer edge of the trees. He dismounted his horse and tied it out of sight. Then he removed his rifle, pointed it toward the road . . . and waited.

After a few moments, the soft clopping sound of an approaching horse could be heard. Then Del came into view. The man waited motionless behind the tree until Del passed. Then very slowly and gently, he squeezed the trigger. Del's body jerked as the bullet struck, then slid sideways and fell to the ground with a solid thump and lay still. The man did not go down to see the result of his ambush. He had supreme confidence in his ability as a marksman. He quickly mounted his horse and rode back the way he had come.

Tazia had risen early. After a quick breakfast, she had questioned Marguerite on the whereabouts of the other members of the household. She learned that Kirk was working with Juan, trying to master the procedures for running a hacienda as large as Casa del Sol. Del had gone into town ostensibly to discuss his return trip to New Orleans with Louis and Jean. Tazia still found it impossible to forgive Jean for helping trick her into marrying Kirk. In the back of her mind lingered the words Garrett had said to her in the garden in New Orleans, "He does not love you . . . he does not love you." Tazia did not want to be with Kirk now, but she would have enjoyed discussing things with Juan and getting back to the running of the hacienda. She was annoyed that Kirk's presence kept her from this.

Tazia saddled her horse and was just riding away from the stables when Kirk came around the corner with Juan. Kirk watched her departure in silence, but his face spoke volumes that Juan recognized and understood. "Will she ever accept my being here?" he said. He spoke the words softly, but Juan heard him.

"Señor Kirk," he said, "in the raising of palominos, one breeds only the very best with the very best to acquire perfection. Sometimes the mare is skittish and proud, too proud to allow herself to be mated easily. One never, *never* tries to break this pride, Señor, but he enjoys the freedom and beauty of the female. If she is allowed to understand in her own good time that the stallion has the same pride and freedom as she, then eventually they mate. It is a beautiful thing, Señor, I have seen it often and it is always worth the time and patience one puts into it."

"Time and patience," Kirk laughed. "Don't worry, Juan. If there are two things I intend to spend an abundance of here, they are time and patience."

"Good. I think you will never regret it, Señor. The rewards will be well worth the effort."

"I know," Kirk murmured, almost to himself. "Believe me, I know."

They continued their work while Kirk listened and learned from Juan—not only about horses, but about the de Montega family as well. Slowly he gleaned small bits of information from Juan about the time when Manolo and Tazia were children. A clearer picture of Tazia's childhood began to form in his mind from what he heard now from Juan and from what he had already learned from Marguerite.

It was almost time for lunch when the two of them started toward the house.

"I'm surprised Del isn't back from town yet. He said he would be back for lunch."

"Maybe he was detained in town, Señor," Juan said helpfully.

"With Cristina and her father coming over for lunch, I doubt if anything town had to offer would tempt him, Juan."

"He is very attracted to Señorita Reyes?"

"That's an understatement. In fact, if Del does not decide to stay here, I'll be very surprised."

They were stopped suddenly by a shout coming from the direction of the road. Two riders leading a burdened horse were coming up the road. Kirk watched for a few minutes until he suddenly realized what he was seeing: it was Del's horse they were leading, and the burden across its back was—

"Del!" he shouted as he began to run. Cristina and her father were at the front gate of the house when they arrived.

"Del! My God. What happened?"

"He's been shot," Don Federico said grimly. "We found him lying on the road. I do not think it is a mortal wound, Kirk, but he will have a tremendous headache in the morning."

Kirk was so relieved, he found himself trembling. What if Del had been killed? He never would have forgiven himself for bringing him out here. Then another thought struck more fear into him than he had ever felt before in his life: where was Tazia?

34

Kirk watched silently while they put Del on his bed. The blood on his head had congealed, and the wound looked terrible to Kirk. He was assured by Marguerite that once she had washed and stitched the wound, Del would be all right.

Don Federico motioned to Kirk and led the way outside the room. "Your brother will be well, Kirk."

"Thank God."

"Kirk," Don Federico began, "who would want to kill you?"

"Me? But it's Del who's been shot."

Don Federico held up a hand, as if requesting patience to be heard. "Kirk, your brother has no claim on anything here. There is no reason for anyone to want his death. On the other hand, you have come here to be a new landowner. You have obviously made a serious enemy somewhere. Consider if I were to describe your brother to someone who didn't know him . . . "

"I don't follow you, Don Federico."

"If I were going to describe you to someone, someone I had hired to kill you, I would say you are a tall, blond, blue-eyed *norteamericano*."

Kirk was stunned for a moment. Then a torrent of

wild thoughts washed over him. His face paled, and his cheek twitched as he clenched his jaw. He tried to reject the first name that came into his mind, but it would not be rejected. Who else hated him enough to kill him, or to hire someone to kill him? Who else wanted him away from the hacienda, away from California? Who else but . . . Tazia? My God, he thought wildly, does she hate me that much after all we've been to each other? Does she really want me dead? He knew he had to find out the truth somehow, but at the moment, he didn't know just how he was going to do it.

At that moment the sound of someone running rapidly up the steps could be heard, and they both turned to face the stairs. Tazia, her face white as a sheet, came toward them. Suddenly she stopped, panting, her eyes widened in shock, and she said softly, "Kirk."

A deep pain struck him in the pit of his stomach. She was surprised to see him . . . to see him alive. She expected to find him dead. He did not know that Tazia had arrived home in a more solemn mood, determined to talk to him about their lives. When she had arrived at the gate, there was much confusion. She was told only that Señor LaCroix had been shot, and they didn't know whether he were alive or dead when Don Federico and his daughter brought him in. Panic flooded her, and she realized that no matter what had happened between them, she could not bear the thought of his death. She ran across the courtyard and up the steps as fast as she could. When she saw Don Federico and Kirk standing together, she was so relieved it made her dizzy. Then she stood in shock as she saw his eyes harden to blue ice.

"Surprised to see me, Tazia?" he asked coolly, although his mind was crying out other words.

She remained mute for a moment, unable to reestablish her equilibrium.

"Maybe you didn't expect to see me at all," he added.

"Kirk!" Don Federico said angrily. "What are you saying? Tazia would never do such a thing. That is a terrible thing to say to your wife."

"Maybe Tazia should tell you the whole story of our relationship, Don Federico," Kirk said brittlely. "Then you would understand why my loving wife would like nothing better than to see me dead."

"Kirk," Tazia gasped. "No, Kirk, you don't think . . . " Surely he didn't believe she would do a thing like this, she thought wildly. But he did.

"Tazia," he said through clenched teeth, "I told you once I would never leave you or Casa del Sol. Now you listen to me closely. Nothing you can do will drive me away, and if anything should happen to my brother, I will take that lovely neck of yours in my two hands and strangle you." His voice was so low that Don Federico could not hear what he said. He only saw Tazia waver on her feet as though he had struck her. She held out one hand toward him helplessly.

"Kirk . . . I didn't . . ."

Kirk gave her one last frozen look. Then he turned away abruptly, as though he could not bear to look at her any longer. He couldn't have hurt her more if he *had* struck her. He entered his brother's room and closed the door softly behind him.

Tazia moaned Kirk's name half-aloud, and her eyes filled with tears. Don Federico put his arm around her shoulders and said, "I think, my child, you have a story to tell me. I also think you need some help."

She nodded woodenly. Suddenly it seemed as though her world had exploded. Even Manolo's death had not left her with such an empty feeling.

Don Federico led her back downstairs and poured her a drink of brandy. When she had sipped a little and her cheeks had regained a small amount of color, he spoke softly to her. "Now, *querida,* suppose you tell me the whole story?"

She began haltingly as though her mind were incapable of grasping thoughts and putting them in order. Eventually, the entire story came out. Don Federico watched her with deep pity in his eyes. He was determined to find the proof necessary to convince Tazia of what her brother really was. Somehow he had to bring Kirk and Tazia back together again.

"Tazia, you know Kirk is a good man. Surely you must know there were things about your brother's death you did not understand. Why don't you both put all the past behind you and start all over? At least for the child's sake."

Tazia's eyes opened in surprise. "Cristina told you?"

"No, child. It was not necessary for me to be told, and if your husband were not so distracted, he also would see how you have changed."

Again her eyes filled with tears. She did not bother to wipe them away as they slipped down her cheeks.

"I am so confused," she cried softly. "Now it is too late. He thinks I tried to have him killed, that I'm responsible for what happened to Del. Oh, Don Federico," she cried as she buried her face in her hands and rocked back and forth in grief. "It is too late for any kind of happiness, too late."

"Tazia, it is never too late. When Del has recovered, go to Kirk. Tell him you love him—for you *do*, you know. Tell him! Don't let happiness slip through your fingers."

Tazia was reminded of what Molly had told her so long ago. She must have time to think, time to pull herself together.

They heard several people coming down the stairs, so both of them rose quickly and went to the door. It was Cristina, Marguerite, and Kirk.

"How is he?" Don Federico asked.

"He's going to be fine. He's conscious now," Kirk answered, his eyes on Tazia's tear-stained face. Confusion racked him. How could she plan such a thing and then act so upset about it? He tried to read her thoughts. Was she guilty? Did she want him dead? Or was someone else out to get him? He suddenly felt unbearably tired. He sat down in a chair and closed his eyes for a moment.

Don Federico motioned to Cristina, and the two of them left the room. Tazia sat down in the chair opposite Kirk and watched him. There were two fine lines between his brows that she had never noticed before. She studied him slowly. This man had loved her until her body sang for him. She could feel the touch of his lean, hard body against hers and the feel of his mouth against hers. She let her eyes drift up to his face, only to realize that his eyes were open and he was watching her. Their eyes held, and she could feel her body grow warm under his gaze.

"I had nothing to do with shooting your brother, Kirk. Please believe me. I would never be responsible for a thing as vile as that."

His eyes still held hers in silence. They penetrated her, bared her soul for him to study. What did he see? The truth, or what he wanted to see? He rose slowly from the chair and stood in front of her. Then he bent forward and put one hand on each chair arm. Very slowly he bent his head and brushed her lips with his.

"We've gotten everything so mixed up, haven't we, Tazia? I wish to God we could put all this bitterness

289

and doubt behind us and start all over."

"Is it ever really possible to forget the past when it has been filled with so much misery?" she replied.

"We could try. Make a small beginning now. Both of us. Don't fight me if I stay at Casa del Sol, Tazia, and I'll leave you in peace with yourself. I love you. I guess I always will, and nothing you can say or do will change that. I want to be near you. I'll not touch you unless you want me to, but I'll not leave."

"Then you don't believe I'm guilty?"

"I guess for a while I did, but I know you too well. What you do, you do in the open, not behind my back. And I doubt, knowing your temper, that you would hire someone to do it. You would do it yourself."

"Yes," she answered quietly, "I would do it myself."

"Is there a chance for a truce, Tazia? Or, at least, a cease-fire?"

"That will not cure our problems, Kirk. Do you plan now to stay here for good? What of your brother?"

"He told me that he was coming back to Casa del Sol to stay. So it looks like you've not only got me to put up with, you've got my brother, too."

"Kirk, would it not be best for you and your brother to go back to New Orleans? To the place where you were raised and were happy? There is nothing for either of you at Casa del Sol. Too much has happened between us; the gap is too wide for us to cross because now you no longer really trust me and I . . ."

"You?"

"I no longer trust *anyone*. Maybe if you were gone, I could try to pick up the pieces of my life and rebuild it."

"And what about me?" he asked, his face impassive. "Do I just drop everything I want and walk away? Did our months together mean nothing to you, Tazia?"

"They were a game you concocted to keep me from knowing you killed Manolo." She gave a bitter half-laugh. "Did the four of you toss a coin for me, Kirk? Or did you volunteer for the supreme sacrifice?"

Anger clouded his eyes in an unguarded moment. Then, suddenly, he reached down and gripped her by the shoulders, jerking her to her feet. His mouth came crashing down on hers, stifling the sound of protest she was about to make. His lips were hard and unyielding, and despite the angry sounds that emanated from her, his kiss was beginning to have an effect on her that she had not wanted, one that she was afraid of. She felt again the old physical hunger for him: it was a flame that seared her body and soul. Her mouth softened under his and she ceased to fight him. Slowly her arms encircled his neck as his hard arms drew her tightly against him. Their hearts beat together in a throbbing song of desire that washed over them and left them clinging weakly to each other. There was no way for either of them to deny the emotions that lifted and carried them along in a current they were unable to fight.

Slowly and reluctantly Kirk lifted his lips from hers, but he could not release her from his arms. He wanted to hold her forever. He felt that no matter how often he kissed her or held her, it would always be new and it would never be enough. They stood silent in the quiet room, holding onto each other as if they were the only people in the world.

"*Now* do you understand, Tazia, why I can never go back? After I have shared your love, after I have tasted your sweetness, do you think I could ever go back alone to that hollow world?"

"It's too late for us, Kirk."

"It's never too late. I will not give you up, Tazia," he said fiercely. He pulled her even tighter against him. "One day I will make you forget everything that has happened and realize that we have a million tomorrows ahead of us. One day I will teach you to trust again, to love again. Until that day comes, here I am, and here I will stay."

With these words, he gently kissed her again. Tazia, lost to passion, was on the brink of complete surrender when a soft knock sounded on the door. Kirk reluctantly released her. He could not read her emotions, but he wanted more desperately than ever to drag her to his room and keep her prisoner to his lovemaking until she surrendered to him.

"Tazia?" he said very quietly.

She raised a hand, palm outward, as though to protect herself from a blow she was not strong enough to withstand. Then she whirled and half-ran to the door, jerked it open and ran past a surprised Cristina up the stairs to her room, where she closed the door and bolted it. Then she threw herself across her bed and allowed her tears to fall. She had felt her body's response to his unspoken question. Another moment and she would have surrendered completely. She had to get Kirk out of Casa del Sol, and she had to do it soon. Somehow she had to make him angry enough at her to leave. Slowly a plan began to form in her mind. After a time, she rose from the bed, rearranged her hair, and unbolted the door and stepped outside.

35

Under Marguerite's excellent care and Cristina's beautiful presence, Del mended very rapidly. He and Kirk discussed the attempted murder, and both of them agreed with Don Federico: it had to have been aimed at Kirk.

"Kirk, no matter how I try, I can't see Garrett hiding in the trees to ambush me."

"He probably hired someone to shoot me. Then he would just appear at Casa del Sol some night when Tazia was alone. You know what happened to Gabrielle. I suspect he had that same plan for Tazia."

"Well, he must know we're both here now. Word has spread that it was I instead of you who was shot."

"I'm wondering what his next move will be," Kirk replied thoughtfully. "One thing is sure, he can't get to Tazia or Casa del Sol while either of us is alive."

"That puts us in a great position. We'll have to be on the alert for another attempt."

"Yes, and it's probably going to come when we least expect it, from a direction we'd never think of looking."

"How are things between you and Tazia now?"

"She wants me to leave."

"Why don't you tell her about Garrett and his

plans for her and the ranch?"

"She'd never believe me. She would think it's another ploy of mine to get . . . whatever it is she thinks I'm after. She just won't believe that I love her, that I'd live in a mud hut if she were with me."

"God, I wouldn't be in your position for the world. You're being fought on both sides. Maybe when Gabrielle gets here, she'll be able to convince Tazia of the truth about her brother. At least you'll be able to protect Tazia from Garrett. As for you two, maybe Gabrielle's story will help with that too."

"Maybe, but I won't pin my hopes on it. I have to convince Tazia myself that I love her. I have to break down that barrier of distrust she's built between us. She's an extremely proud and stubborn woman."

"Well, I can tell her she's up against an extremely proud and stubborn man," laughed Del.

They talked for a while about Don Federico and the horses they were going to breed. Del was amazed at the knowledge Kirk had acquired since his arrival here, and he watched with pleasure the bright enthusiasm that crowded his conversation when he spoke of his plans for the future of Casa del Sol. He could really be happy here, Del thought. Maybe things would work out after all. After all, all they had to do was find out where Garrett was and what his plans were and break through Tazia's stubbornness and pride. When he thought about it, he was amazed that Kirk did not just pack up and drag Tazia back to New Orleans with him. Their conversation stopped when Marguerite came in with a tray, accompanied by Cristina.

Cristina had ridden over to Casa del Sol almost every day to learn Del's progress. She had helped Marguerite prepare some of Del's meals and had often sat with him while he ate. She enjoyed his company very much, for he was witty and filled with good humor. She also enjoyed the way he watched her with admiration-filled eyes. She could feel his attraction for her and did not deny that she felt the same attraction to him.

"Good morning, Kirk, Del. How do you feel this morning?"

"Cristina," laughed Del, "a man could be dead, and one of your beautiful smiles would resurrect him."

You *are* recovering, she thought. "Marguerite tells me you can get up this morning. Perhaps you would like to come down and sit in the garden with me for a while."

"I can't think of anything I would enjoy more," Del answered. "I have to be on my feet in the next few days because I don't want to miss the party. It should prove to be . . . interesting."

"Everyone we know has been invited. There should be quite a few pretty young women for you to dance with. If you are able."

"I'll be able, but there's really only one pretty girl I'm looking forward to dancing with."

"Come," Marguerite said firmly as she set the tray across Del's lap. "eat your breakfast, Señor Del, if you want to regain your strength." Del obediently began to eat, but it was easy to eat with Marguerite's marvelous food and with Cristina here.

"Regain my strength! Marguerite, if you keep feeding me as you do and I don't soon get up, I'll be too fat to dance."

Cristina and Kirk both laughed. Then Kirk excused himself. There were things he had to attend to with Juan in the stables. After he left, Marguerite took the empty tray, and Cristina prepared to leave.

"I shall wait for you in the garden, Del."

"Good, I'll be right down."

Once out of bed, Del fought a wave of dizziness caused by lying down for so long. The scar across the side of his head was healing well, but it would always stay as a reminder of how close he had come to death. He dressed slowly and made his way downstairs. When he reached the garden, he dropped down onto the bench on which Cristina sat waiting for him. The shade of a huge tree was a cool oasis in the bright sunlit garden.

"It is very lovely here. It is obvious why Tazia loves this place so much. Spending one's life here would be very enjoyable," Del said.

"And you Del? Do you plan to stay here? I know your brother has no intention of leaving, but what about you?"

Del turned to face her and said very softly, "Do you want me to stay, Cristina?"

The soft rose of her cheeks deepened a little, but her eyes did not drop away from his.

"Yes," she said very quietly. "Yes, I would like very much for you to stay at Casa del Sol."

They sat very still, each of them aware of the deep emotion that drew them to one another.

"You're a very lovely woman, Cristina," Del said as he reached out and grasped her hand. He held it gently, turning over to trace the fine lines on her palm. A faint quiver was the only response she gave as they sat in silence.

"Cristina, you aren't . . . promised to anyone, are you?"

"No, Del, I'm not."

"Good, I want to consider making room in your life for me. I know this is too soon, and I won't rush you, but I want you to know how I feel. I want to be part of your life, an important part. And I want you to know you're a very important part of mine. I'm going to make California my home, and one day I hope to marry and raise my children here." He looked deeply into her eyes. "Do you understand what I'm saying?"

"Yes."

"Will you think about what I said? One day when all this trouble is settled, I shall remind you and ask for your answer."

"I shall remember every word. When the day of remembrance comes, I shall be prepared to give you my answer."

Del leaned forward and very gently kissed Cristina's lips. Then he smiled warmly at her.

"I want the first dance with you at the party. I think it is going to be a very memorable affair in more ways than one."

"Yes, I know what you mean. It's too bad that Tazia does not realize how Kirk feels about her."

"I think she does," Del replied thoughtfully. "I think she just finds it impossible to trust anyone again. She's afraid to give in and say she was wrong. She's afraid of being hurt again." Watching from the corner of his eye for Cristina's reaction, he added softly, "It's too bad someone she really trusts can't tell her the truth. It might make things a lot easier." His instinct was right! he thought. From her reaction, he could tell that she, and possibly her father, could say many things to ease the situation between Kirk and Tazia.

"I'm afraid," she replied softly, her eyes averted from his. "There is nothing anyone will . . . can say to change what has happened. There are some things that are better left to rest in peace. Your brother will have to find his own way to Tazia, as she will have to search her own heart and find the path to her own happiness."

Del knew it was no use to push the matter any further. For one thing, he did not want to say anything to upset Cristina or change her feelings for him in any way. What small seed of affection was growing in her heart for him he intended to nurture and cultivate until it blossomed into the love he sought. He changed the subject, and they discussed everything from houses to horses. He was reluctant to let her go when she finally did rise.

"I must be on my way. Papa will expect me home for dinner. I have enjoyed this morning very much, Del."

"Will you come again tomorrow?"

"Yes, if you'd like, we might even get Marguerite's permission for you to take a short ride."

Del chuckled. "I'll begin working on her today. Maybe I'll be able to get her to see how desperately I need to go riding tomorrow."

Cristina gave an answering laugh. "I will see you tomorrow afternoon. Good-by."

"Good-by."

He watched her walk away from him. The seductive sway of her hips intrigued him. A sudden warm desire for her washed over him, and he found himself almost rising to follow her. He leaned his back against the rough bark of the tree and closed his eyes for a moment, soaking up the peaceful warmth of the sun. After a few moments, he had the feeling he was being watched. He opened his eyes just a crack and searched the area. He could see no one, and yet the feeling persisted. Then he noticed that the curtains of one of the upstairs windows had been pulled aside and someone stood looking down at him. He could not make out who it was, but he continued to watch the window, and after a few minutes, the curtain dropped back into place and the person was gone. An eerie feeling of the unknown reached out and ran its icy fingers down his back. He didn't know why, but he had a feeling that whoever stood on the other side of that curtain was someone who had the key to the secrets of Cas del Sol.

Marguerite came into the garden looking for him.

"Señor Del, your brother would like to know if you would care to join him for lunch?"

"Yes. Yes, of course."

She turned to leave.

"Marguerite?"

"*Sí, señor?*"

"That window up there." He pointed to the window he had been watched from. "Whose room is that?"

"That corner window?"

"Yes."

"Why that is Señora de Montega's room, señor. Tazia's mother."

Del was stunned. "I thought Señora de Montega could not get out of bed."

"She cannot, señor. She does not walk or talk. She is completely bedridden."

"Oh."

"Why do you ask, señor?"

"Nothing, Marguerite. It's just my overactive imagination. Come, let's go in and have some lunch."

They walked inside together, but Del's mind was on the window. He wondered just how much of an invalid Tazia's mother really was.

36

The night of the party was clear and warm. A bright golden moon hung heavily on the horizon, as though it were too content to rise. The night sky was like black velvet, with a million glittering stars scattered against it. Tazia had arranged the party to be held in the garden. In one corner she had set up the table. Flickering candles were reflected in the gleaming silverware and crystal. The musicians were seated under the colonnaded porch, well away from the guests, so that it appeared that the music was part of the beautiful night.

Kirk, Del, Cristina, and Don Federico stood together, talking quietly. Don Federico had arrived early with Cristina, and Tazia had not come downstairs yet. In fact, Kirk had not seen her since early afternoon.

Marguerite came in to announce that some of the guests were beginning to arrive. When Marguerite had shown the guests to the garden, Don Federico introduced them to Kirk.

"Señor and Señora Alvarez, I would like you to meet Señor LaCroix. Kirk, Señor Alvarez and his wife are Tazia's godparents. Their hacienda is about forty miles from here."

"It is a great pleasure to meet you," Kirk replied. "Forty miles is a great distance. Surely you did not travel it tonight?"

"No," laughed Señor Alvarez. "We came into town last night. Theresa wanted to do a little shopping before we came. It seems we are going to regard this evening's festivities as a sort of wedding party. Theresa wished to purchase a small gift for the bride and groom."

"Where is our lovely goddaughter?"

"Tazia is still dressing. I'm sure she'll be down very soon."

"Not if I know Tazia. She will come down when all the guests are here—and not a moment sooner. She makes the most delightful entrances I've ever seen."

Don Alvarez chuckled as his wife clucked her tongue at him in mock anger.

"Our goddaughter is the loveliest creature in the world, and she does not need to make an *entrance* to prove the point. Do you agree, Kirk?"

"Wholeheartedly, Señora Alvarez."

"Of course, you're asking for an unbiased opinion," Del said, "and Kirk is the best person to ask that when it comes to Tazia."

They enjoyed the friendly laughter at Kirk's expense. More guests began to arrive, and Kirk had some difficulty trying to remember the names of everyone he was introduced to. There were at least twenty new arrivals in the past half hour, Kirk thought, and he wished fervently that Tazia would come down soon.

Del and Cristina were deep in conversation, slightly apart from the others. Kirk had seen to it that everyone was given something to drink, and he was now moving from group to group, getting to know the guests and making them welcome. It was obvious to Don Federico that Kirk was making an excellent impression on everyone. He was about to make his way to Kirk's side and tell him this when his eyes were drawn to the door, where some late guests were just coming in.

Dios mio, who invited him? he thought. He eyed the newcomers with deep misgivings. In the doorway stood a man and woman of about Don Federico's age. With them was an extremely handsome young man whose arrogant gaze roamed the crowd in search of one face. Don Federico knew for whom he searched. Kirk had not seen them arrive yet, so Don Federico moved quickly to greet them. He smiled at the older couple. "Doña María, Don Rafael, it is a pleasure to see you both. It has been a very long time."

"Ah, Don Federico, it is indeed a pleasure to see you again." Don Rafael smiled as he extended his hand to Don Federico, who clasped it firmly in both his hands. Then he turned and gently embraced Doña María, kissing both her cheeks.

He extended his hand to the young man. "Miguel," he said softly.

The young man's eyes glittered with amusement. "Don Federico."

"Doña María, you grow younger and lovelier with each passing year."

"You are so gallant, Don Federico. I have missed your beautiful lies very much," she replied with a teasing smile.

"Lies, Doña María? Never! You bring a ray of sunlight to the dark world."

Doña María laughed delightedly. "Then come and dance with me, Don Federico, and continue to brighten my evening with your lovely compliments."

"*Con permeso*, Don Rafael?"

"*Sí*, Don Federico."

Don Federico offered his arm to Doña María, and they moved away from the other two.

"I did not know that Miguel was home," Don Federico said when they were out of hearing of the others.

"It is funny you should mention it, Federico. I did not know that Tazia knew he was home either, but her invitation specifically stated she wanted Miguel to come. He seems quite anxious to see her again also. He has talked of nothing else all day."

"I hope," began Don Federico, "Miguel keeps in mind that Tazia is newly married. Her husband is not the type of man who would take Miguel's flirting lightly."

"But Federico, they are old childhood friends. I'm sure there is nothing more to it than that they are anxious to meet and talk over old times."

Don Federico smiled in agreement with Doña María, but his thoughts were otherwise. He knew definitely that Miguel did not think of Tazia as only an old childhood friend, and he was beginning to suspect why Tazia had made a point to invite him. He watched Kirk moving easily about the crowd of guests and wondered just how far he could be pushed before he would take action.

Kirk was just welcoming another couple when Tazia entered the room. He did not have to turn around to know that she had, for the man to whom he was speaking looked past him and his eyes brightened with pleasure. Kirk turned around and almost lost his breath at the sight of her. She was making her way slowly down the stairs at the side of the patio. The soft light picked up the ivory tone of her skin and made it glimmer like frosted pink pearl. She had pulled her hair severely back from her face and made a small knot at the back of her hair like an ebony rope, as thick as a man's wrist. The gown she wore was scarlet silk, and the full skirt swayed gently as she walked. The gown was draped off her shoulders and was cut so daringly low that Kirk half-expected her to tumble out of it. She wore no jewelry at all, and that only emphasized the loveliness of her skin and the brilliant gleam of her purple eyes. Without hesitation, she walked up to Kirk and smiled up into his darkening eyes.

"Good evening, husband," she said softly. The wicked glitter of her eyes made the skin prickle on the back of his neck. She was being sweet . . . too sweet. He had to remember to be careful not to believe this new Tazia.

"My darling," he whispered, and he bent his head and kissed her lightly. He could feel her muscles quiver as he took hold of her arm and drew her close to him. He was not going to believe; he would be careful; but he would also take advantage of any opportunities she gave him.

"I see you have met all our guests," she said calmly.

"Yes. At least I *think* I have. There are so many I'm afraid I've already forgotten some of the names."

"Do not worry about it." She smiled, but her eyes were cold. "You will not be at Casa del Sol long enough to ever meet most of them again."

"I thought we went through that all before. I'm not leaving, Tazia. You might as well accept the fact."

She shrugged and said softly, "Maybe, in time, you will change your mind. Sometimes things happen that one does not expect."

"I've also told you before, there is nothing you or anyone else can do to force me from here. First of all, I am beginning to enjoy working the horses with Juan, and I like the beauty and serenity of this place. And if I haven't mentioned it before, Tazia—or if you've forgotten—you're my wife, and I don't give up what belongs to me very easily."

Tazia's smile faded, and she snapped something quickly in Spanish, her quick temper flashing in her eyes. She got control of herself quickly and replaced the look with another bright smile.

The party continued to grow in gaiety as the food and wine were consumed. Tazia moved about from person to person like a brilliant scarlet butterfly, but she remained elusive to Kirk. It did not take him long to notice the flashing smiles she cast at the young man who drew her often to the dance floor. He searched out Don Federico and questioned him about the young man's identity.

"Ah, Miguel," Don Federico said, in what he hoped sounded more nonchalant than he felt. "They were childhood friends. They are probably laughing over some of the terrible pranks they were involved in around here."

Kirk was about to answer him when everyone's attention was drawn to the dance floor. There was a soft strum of a guitar, and the crowd began to move away. In the middle of the floor stood Tazia as Kirk remembered her the first time they had met: her eyes closed, her head thrown back, and her arms high above her head. Then came the soft gentle click of the castanets.

"Ah!" Said Don Federico softly. "Tazia is going to dance for us, Kirk. It is a miracle of beauty. Have you ever seen her dance?"

"Yes . . . once," Kirk answered, his eyes glued to the woman who stood like a brilliant flame in the middle of the candle-lit floor. The guitar strummed again and was answered by the rhythmic tap of her heels and the clicking castanets. It was then that Miguel stepped to the edge of the floor. He was a magnificent male animal. His black suit hugged his slender frame like a second skin, and his brilliant brown eyes glowed as they devoured Tazia's form. He clapped his hands together gently and was answered by the castanets. They began to sway to the beat of the music, Tazia, the flame, drawing to his doom the fluttering moth that desired her near.

Slowly they moved toward one another as their bodies began to pick up the now stirring beat of the music. Miguel circled her again and again, as though fate drew him irresistibly to her side. As the music became vibrant, Tazia moved faster and faster. Now they danced so closely they were almost touching. Again and again Miguel bent his head to touch her lips to his, only to find her elusive mouth just out of reach. The music began to build, and Miguel attempted again the touch that meant the death of the moth. Then, as the music reached its final note, he lifted Tazia into the air, whirled her about once, and claimed her lips with his.

"*Olé! Olé!*" someone shouted.

"Bravo!" Don Alvarez added. Everyone clapped furiously as Tazia withdrew slowly from Miguel's embrace. They both bowed deeply, accepting the applause with bright smiles on their flushed faces. Tazia watched the effect they had on everyone present —and she was satisfied. Her eyes searched the crowd until she found Kirk, who stood leaning against one of the columns. His eyes were intent on her, but his face showed none of the emotions he felt. If she had been closer, she might have seen the whiteness of his knuckles as he gripped his glass tightly or the muscle that throbbed in his cheek. Instead, she saw only an expressionless face, and her anger flamed. She turned, tucked her arm into Miguel's, and they walked off together into a dark corner of the garden.

At that moment, Kirk would happily have strangled her if he could have gotten his hands about her throat. *His* throat felt thick, and he could barely swallow. A wave of burning jealousy consumed him. He almost shook with the desire to rip the offending scarlet dress from the loveliness he knew so well and wanted so desperately. He knew this display had been planned by her, but still his whole being had responded. He was filled with hate and love and desire that made his blood pulse violently through him.

"Lovely, lovely," whispered Don Federico. "It has been a long time since I've seen Tazia dance. I'd almost forgotten how amazingly beautiful she is."

"Yes," Kirk agreed stonily. "She is lovely, there is no doubt. And who is that . . . gentleman she was dancing with?"

"I told you, Kirk, that they are old childhood friends. Miguel thinks of Tazia as his sister."

"Like hell he does. Miguel had better stay away from his 'sister,' unless he would like to find himself not so beautiful. It would give me great pleasure to beat in that face until Tazia has trouble recognizing it."

"Kirk, it is not necessary to be jealous. Tazia is a woman of honor. She would not betray you."

Kirk sighed heavily and raised a glass of wine to his lips as he said bitterly, "I wish that were true, Don Federico. I really wish that were true. But this was just another way for Tazia to tell me to leave, a threat of what she will make of our marriage if I stay."

"What are you going to do?" Don Federico asked, his eyes intent on Kirk.

Kirk was silent for so long that Don Federico thought he did not intend to reply. Then he drained his glass and reached for another. "Do?" he said quietly. Then he smiled, but Don Federico did not like this cold, merciless smile. "I intend to stay here and keep what is mine. One way or another," he added softly. Then he walked away from Don Federico and joined some of the other guests.

Don Federico continued to watch him the rest of the evening. Kirk consumed a great deal of wine, but he said nothing to Tazia. He watched her through narrowed eyes that looked like blue ice. Don Federico, along with Del and Cristina, would have liked to warn Tazia that she was pushing Kirk just a little too far, but she stayed away from them and continued to flirt openly and unashamedly with Miguel, until it was obvious she had him raging with desire.

When most of the guests were preparing to leave, it was obvious Miguel did not want to let Tazia go. But he had no choice, so he reluctantly accompanied his parents home. When Tazia had said good night to everyone, she returned to the patio, deserted now except for Don Federico, Cristina, and Del.

"I'm going to ride home with Cristina and Don Federico," Del said. It was obvious he did not want to be there when the explosion that had been building in Kirk all evening took place. Tazia smiled good night as she three of them left. Then she turned to the table and poured herself another glass of wine. She sipped it and smiled to herself. Kirk should be angry enough now to leave Casa del Sol, she thought. She was pleased that her plan had succeeded so well. She finished the glass of wine and turned toward the stairs. She would go to bed, and by morning Kirk and all her problems would be gone. She had just put her foot on the first step when she heard Kirk's voice coming from the shadows of the trees.

"Tazia," he said with deceptive softness.

She turned to face him, and he pushed himself away from the tree and walked slowly toward her.

37

Tazia watched Kirk walk toward her. He moved slowly, with the grace of a panther, but something about him struck her as very different. As he drew close to her, she realized with a sudden tingle of fear that he was drunk. Kirk was not only completely drunk, he was coldly furious. For the first time, Tazia realized her plan was not working in the way she thought it would. She felt a tug of real fright as she turned and tried to move up the stairs. It was too late for that. In a second he was beside her. He caught her wrist in a vise-like grip that made her cry out in pain. Then he jerked her around and pulled her into his arms. His arms circled her body like two iron bands. She could not escape him.

"Where are you going, my lovely wife? I thought you might dance for me again. That dance was for *me*, wasn't it, Tazia?"

She did not answer, and he tightened his arms until she gasped for breath.

"Wasn't it?" he snarled.

"Yes!" she flashed, her anger beginning to over-come her fear. "Yes, it was for you. So you would understand once and for all that you are not welcome here."

"And your pretty friend? Is he welcome in your home and in your bed, my lovely *puta*?"

She choked with anger at the insult.

"How dare you! How dare you call me names, you liar, you cheat! You mur—!"

"I know what you think of me, Tazia," he snapped. "But the difference between us is that you are wrong. I never lied about loving you, and you know deep in your heart that that is the truth. You remember our days and nights together as well as I do. You know that what we had together could never have been a lie."

"I won't listen to any more of your lies. I do not want to remember how you and all my friends used me to get what you wanted. I know the vile things you are responsible for. I just want you to go away, Kirk," she shouted. Tears were crowding her eyes, but she did not want to cry now. "I don't want to remember! I don't want to remember!"

"But you're going to," he muttered. "You're going to remember."

He kissed her then, a brutal demanding kiss. His lips were hard against hers, and she whimpered softly at the hurt he inflicted. His arms held her bound against him. She could barely breathe, and it was impossible to move. He continued to kiss her, but slowly it changed to a softer, seeking kiss that caused her to begin to tremble in his arms. Slowly the kiss brought back with a rush memories of all the kisses they had shared. She knew that if he continued to hold her and kiss her as he was, she would lose the battle.

Tazia let herself go limp against him, and for one surprised moment his hold loosened. She quickly brought her hands up against his chest and shoved with all her strength. If Kirk had not been drinking so heavily, the push would have been ineffectual, but he stumbled back against the wall. In that second, Tazia was gone and up the steps. She could hear him curse as he stumbled after her. If she could only reach her room, she could bolt the door and maybe Kirk would go away. She ran down the hallway, the sound of his footsteps pounding heavily behind her. She finally reached her room safely, and she bolted the door with relief. She closed her eyes and leaned against the wall, trying to get her breath, when she heard Kirk come up to the door. He tried the handle only once; then all was quiet. She listened for the sounds of his retreating footsteps, but all was silent. Then, suddenly, the door flew open with a loud crash. He had kicked the lock loose with one blow of his foot, and now he stood swaying and panting heavily in the doorway, her only avenue of escape.

"I told you before," he said, "no locked door would stop me if I really wanted to get in, didn't I, my love?"

Tazia was stunned for a moment. She started to back away from him, and slowly he stalked her. He watched her closely now for any attempt to escape. In a panic now, she realized what he intended to do. He was backing her toward the bed, the one place she had no intention of being forced into. She reached out to grasp any object she could find to defend herself. Her hand found a bottle on the table next to her bed. She picked it up and broke it against the edge of the table, leaving the sharp, ragged end protruding from her hand.

"Don't come any closer, Kirk, or I will kill you! You're drunk. Go to bed and leave me alone."

He uttered a low chuckle deep in his throat, but his eyes followed her hand as he continued to move slowly toward her. "Would you really kill me, Tazia? I wonder," he said as he lifted a hand and gently touched the side of her face. In a quick motion, she struck at his arm with the broken bottle. A thin stream of blood appeared on his sleeve. Both of them looked at it in shock. Tazia took another step backward and felt the bed behind her. She could go no further. She had to stand her ground now or surrender, and she had no intention of surrendering. They stood only a foot apart, the broken bottle reflecting the pale gleam of the candles burning in the room. Kirk disregarded the small cut on his arm, for it was a smaller wound than the one he carried deep within himself. They stared at each other, bothwondering whether she would kill him if he took another step toward her. Then, with the quickness of a striking snake, he feinted to one side. As she moved in that direction, he leaned low and threw himself at her, catching her around the waist as they both landed on the bed. The full weight of his body falling upon her tore the breath from her body momentarily, but it was long enough for him to disarm her and throw the broken glass across the room. She fought him furiously in complete silence. She kicked him and punched him with clenched fists several times before he managed to subdue her. If Kirk had not had so much to drink, the battle would have been shorter, but as it was, he finally subdued her with superior strength.

Tazia lay panting on the bed, glaring up at Kirk as he held a leg across hers and pinned her arms above her head. He bent his head to kiss her again, but she twisted her face away from him. Without a word, he transferred both her wrists to the left hand, and catching her chin in his right hand, he held her face still while he gently kissed the corners of her lips, her forehead and her cheeks. He paid no attention at all to the inarticulate sounds of rage that emanated from her. Then, very gently, he kissed her unwilling lips. As he slowly applied pressure, forcing her lips apart, she could feel a wave of languor begin to overpower her. Her senses reeled under this onslaught. Memories of their beautiful moments together washed over her. Her body began to grow warm with the sudden rush of passion that Kirk had always been able to stir in her. She did not want it to happen, but it *was* happening, and she was powerless to escape it.

Kirk continued to assault her senses relentlessly until he could feel her surrender. He released her wrists and let one hand run down over the soft texture of her arm to her shoulder. His lips released hers, only to move to her ears, then down her throat to the soft pulsing mounds of her breasts. She lowered her arms and caressed the back of his head and shoulders as she murmured his name over and over. Sliding his hands underneath her body, he maneuvered the opening to her gown and pulled it down and off her with several quick motions. Then he pulled her body against him and caressed the entire length of her with his gentle fingers. There was nothing between them now but his love.

Kirk lifted his head and looked into her eyes. "You know I love you, Tazia. Can you deny now that you feel the same for me, that we belong together? Don't let foolish pride stand between us. Let's bury the past. Let's start a whole new life now, tonight. Let's pretend nothing happened before, that this is our first night together." He watched her, praying that what he felt could be transferred to her, that she would feel that what he was saying was sincere and filled with love for her. She said nothing, but tears appeared in her eyes, and her body relaxed beneath him. She knew then that no matter what she felt, he was responsible. She could not deny the passion he roused in her; she never could belong to anyone else. Tomorrow she would face whatever problems needed to be faced. Tonight she wanted him desperately and completely.

Although Tazia had not answered his question, and he knew he still had many bridges to cross, still he felt he had won one big battle. He would face tomorrow when it came, but tonight Tazia was soft and willing in his arms, and that was all he could think of. She parted her moist lips and returned his kiss with the fire he remembered so vividly. He caressed her soft, velvety skin. God! How long it had been? he thought wildly as he sank into the sheer pleasure of loving her. With a few quick movements, he had undressed and discarded his clothes. Now they were blended together as one, breast to breast, thigh to thigh. He devoured her with hungry kisses, his hands drawing from her deep, violent responses. She gave a soft, passionate cry as he entered her violently and held himself throbbing deep within her. As they began to move together rhythmically, she clung to him, murmuring his name over and over. He knew that he would never ease this hunger for her, no matter how many times he possessed her, for each time only made the hunger deeper and stronger. She is mine! he thought, and nothing would ever take her away from him while he lived.

Afterward, Kirk held her against him as though he were afraid she would fade away into the blackness of the night. When he had gained control over his wildly pounding heart, he turned on his side and looked down into her wide purple eyes. He kissed her softly as a feather.

"I love you. No matter what has happened between us or what the future brings, I love you. You are my wife, and I shall never leave you."

"Oh, Kirk. What are we to do? There are so many things that are impossible for us to surmount. What is there between us but this physical thing when we are in bed and hatred when we are awake. What is the future for us?"

"The future is what we make it, and together we can make it perfect. But we each must come halfway. Oh, Tazia, can't you see? We are one. Don't fight me—belong to me, as I do to you."

"I cannot forget," she moaned softly. "How can I forget my brother? How can I just put aside what happened to my father?"

"Then do just one thing for me. Let's have a truce. Let's not battle one another until I can prove to you what really happened."

"Prove what, Kirk?"

"Give me time, Tazia. I'll give you the truth." He kissed her again. "In the meantime, I know one thing about which we'll never fight. Are we agreed? Do we have a truce?"

He waited while she considered what he proposed.

"Kirk, if you don't have this . . . proof, as you call it, within a reasonable time, would you then leave Casa del Sol? Go back to New Orleans?"

What she was asking hurt him more than he would admit to her, but he had no choice but to agree and stand behind what he proposed.

"All right, I agree. You'll be my wife in every way for, shall we say, six months. By then, I'll have all the proof you need."

"And no matter what the circumstances, do I have your word that if there's no proof, you will leave without argument?"

"You have my word of honor. No matter what the circumstances, if I don't have proof within six months, I'll leave without another word."

She was silent for some time. Kirk wished he could see her more clearly, but the candles had burnt low, and the light was almost gone.

"Tazia?"

"I have something to tell you, Kirk, and I want you to remember that I have your word of honor."

"What is it?"

"I'm expecting to bear your child in a few months." She felt the sudden jerk of his muscles from this new shock. Then he jumped from the bed and lit several more candles. He came back to the bed and sat on the edge, leaning over her, his face pale with the hurt and anger.

"Do you honestly think that was fair? Now you want me to leave not only you, but my child, as well."

"What's fair in this world, Kirk? Was what happened between us fair? You are convinced that you can prove you're right. Are you willing to stake everything on it?"

"Tazia, you're so—"

"What, Kirk? Untrusting? Frightened, disbelieving? Yes, I'm all those things now. I'm what you and your friends have made me."

"No, you're what your parents and that . . . that evil brother have made you, and somehow I'll break through and reach you. Someday you'll understand that our love was the only real thing in your whole mixed-up world." He sighed deeply. Unhappy frustration mixed with love for her warred across his face. "I hope it's not too late when it happens. I accept your terms, and you accept mine. Six months. Until then, you're my wife."

"Yes."

"Then show me," he murmured as he slid down beside her and took her in his arms, his mouth searching for hers.

She gave to Kirk, without restraint, all the fiery passion she felt for him. They made love, first violently, then tenderly. When they were both exhausted, she slept in his arms. He could not sleep because his thoughts whirled about in his mind. What could he do, where could he go for what he needed to find out? He knew Don Federico could tell him something—or Cristina—if either of them could be made to tell the truth. But how could he reach them? Many times he had tried to steer the conversation to Manolo, but each time he had been closed off.

My child, he thought desperately. Tazia. How could he ever give up either of them? He knew it was impossible to contemplate. He realized that she had never had any intention of telling him about the baby. He looked down at her sleeping quietly against him. If only things had been different, how happy they could have been here.

Kirk was not a man who gave up easily on anything he wanted, and he wanted Tazia and his unborn child more than anything in the world. If he couldn't find the proof he needed, then he had to make Tazia love him enough not to want him to leave. One way or another, he was not going to leave Tazia and Casa del Sol.

Bright streaks of a new dawn lit the sky before Kirk could fall asleep. After only a few hours, a gentle kiss on his ear followed by one on his cheek and then softly on his lips, brought him awake.

"Good morning," Tazia said.

"Good morning," he answered with a smile. "You know we're going to shock everyone in the house this morning?"

She laughed and curled up against him, running

her hand over his chest and around his neck.

"Shall we keep them guessing?" she whispered.

"Sounds like a good idea to me."

They were laughing together when a knock sounded on the door.

"Come in," Tazia called. She waited expectantly for Marguerite to come in. They were both rewarded by the shocked look on Marguerite's face when she saw Kirk in Tazia's bed. Del had told her only that morning about all that had happened at the party. She had expected an angry Tazia this morning and a cold and miserable Kirk. Instead, they both smiled happily at her.

"G . . . Good morning." She choked out the words helplessly.

"We'd like some breakfast, Marguerite." Kirk smiled innocently at her.

"Yes," Tazia agreed, "some breakfast, Marguerite, and"—she smiled wickedly at Kirk—"I think we'll have it here in bed."

Marguerite nodded and left the room in stunned silence, closing the door on the sound of muffled laughter.

38

Although Kirk and Tazia seemed to have come to an agreement, Marguerite and Juan, who knew her so well, still felt that they were sitting on a volcano, ready to erupt.

Louis arrived and was made welcome at Casa del Sol, but it did not take him long to sense the tension that existed there. He was anxious to find some land, but he had to wait for Gabrielle's arrival. The days seemed interminable to him. He and Kirk, along with Del and Juan, worked together daily. They had become very good friends and their respect for one another had grown.

Kirk and Tazia spent as much time together as he could manage. She was receptive to him, she laughed with him, and they spent quiet evenings together, but he still felt that part of her was kept in reserve. There were no words he could say to touch this hidden part of her, for he could not put his finger on exactly what it was that she held back. He was content to sit on cool evenings beside her on the patio. They were seated there one evening, enjoying the night air. Del and Louis had gone to Cristina's for dinner. Suddenly she uttered a soft, startled sound and turned to face Kirk, her eyes wide with surprise. He moved closer to her, alarm rising in him.

"What's the matter?"

She took his hand and placed it against her belly and watched his face. He sat very still, his hands pressed against her, his eyes filled with questions. Then he suddenly felt the gentle stirring of the child within. *His* child. A wave of tenderness overcame him. Without a word, he pulled her into his arms and gently held her against him. She lay still as he slowly caressed her long hair. In that moment, they both felt an irresistible oneness with this small, unnamed human they were creating. Kirk prayed that this was the key to that hidden room that would bring them together forever. He didn't want to say or do anything to break the spell of this moment.

Tazia slowly raised her head and looked at Kirk, who bent his head to kiss her warm, soft lips. The kiss began as one of tenderness, but it soon became questioning. Their lips parted, but he did not release her. Instead, he gathered her closer to him. For the first time in months, he felt in her the feeling of complete surrender.

Now, without a word, he stood up and pulled her up beside him. Slowly, Kirk, slowly, he reminded himself fiercely. Don't break the spell of this moment or it may be lost forever. He lifted her into his arms; she lay her head on his shoulder, her arms around his neck. Using the side steps, they moved slowly upstairs until they reached their bedroom. The room was cool and almost dark, but he could make out the whiteness of her face as he set her down. Then he gently began to remove her dress. She offered no resistance. It was as though she were as spellbound as he was at the beauty of this moment. She stood before him, and again he lay his hand on the roundness of her belly. This was his woman; this was his child; and nothing outside of death would separate them. As quickly as he could, he shrugged free of his clothes and sat on the edge of the bed, pulling her down on his lap. He caressed the smooth mounds of her breasts and touched them with gentle kisses until he felt her stir and move against him with more pressure. Kirk found her willing mouth with his and began to kiss her with more passion. Slowly her mouth parted, and he could feel the fire in her begin to build. Her arms circled his neck now to bring him closer. He kissed her throat at the spot where he could feel the beat of her heart and then let his kisses follow his hands down the length of her body. He kissed each breast, each curve with gentle abandon as he felt her body move against his hands in search of more. He kissed the curve of her waist, the roundness where his child lay cradled, and the softness of the inner flesh of her thighs, until he heard her soft whispers of passion. Then his seeking lips found the center of her need and touched her again and again until her writhing and murmuring gasps of pleasure told him she was ready for him.

Kirk raised himself up on his arms, not wanting to hurt her, and then he slowly eased himself deeply into her. Then all thought was driven from them except this searing need for one another. As he began to move, her body demanded more, and she wrapped herself about him and drew him as close as she could, whispering words of love in his ear. He forgot his own restraint and took her fully and deeply. It was like finding an oasis in the middle of a burning desert. As they moved together, he felt again and again the magical fire only she created in him. Their bodies became one flame, one need, until they were blinded by the glow. They reached the peak of passion together and exploded into the blinding star-filled night, clinging to one another.

It was some time later before they slowly came back to reality. "Tazia, I didn't hurt you, did I? I'm afraid when I have you in my arms I can't think rationally, let alone keep myself under control."

"No, *mi amore*, you did not hurt me. It was a wonderful thing. I have never felt like this in my life before. Even when we were first together, it was never like this."

Mi amore . . . my love, he thought. It had been a very long time since she had used such endearments with him. He turned on his side and looked down into her wide purple eyes. He kissed each eyelid, her cheeks, and then, slowly, her lips.

"It will always be this way for us. We belong together like the sun and the sky. I love you, Tazia." She did not answer him, but she took his face in her hands and drew his lips to hers. He held her tightly, and soon his hands began to explore her soft, willing body again. They made love once more and then slept, wrapped in each other's arms.

It was several hours later when Kirk awoke in the first gray light of dawn. He did not even try to go back to sleep, for he wanted to savor the night and the sweet closeness of her body at his side. It was then that he realized that although he had told her how much he loved her, never once did she say she loved him, too. Even though their bodies cried out to each other, she had never made that final, irrevocable commitment by saying, "I love you," words he so desperately wanted to hear from her again.

Too soon to suit him, Kirk heard the sounds of an awakening household. He reached down and pulled the covers over them and waited for the inevitable knock on their door by Marguerite. When it did, he beckoned her in. He put his finger to his lips and pointed at the still-sleeping Tazia. She nodded silently and left the room, pulling the door shut very gently. Her heart was light, for she thought that all was well now between her little child and this tall American who obviously loved her so deeply. She went downstairs and found Del and Louis seated at the table, waiting expectantly for Tazia and Kirk to come for breakfast.

"Well, Marguerite, how long do we have to wait for breakfast? I'm famished, and I promised Juan I'd help him move that group of horses to the lower pasture." Del grinned at her.

"I'm afraid you two gentlemen will have to eat alone. The *patron* and *patrona* are still in bed," she answered with a bright smile.

"Again," Louis laughed. "Del, I think things are looking up around here. This is the second time this week we've had to eat breakfast alone."

Del rubbed his hands together and chuckled with delight. "Bring on breakfast, Marguerite, and some hot coffee. We can toast the lovebirds, wish them the best, and get on with our day."

Marguerite smiled and went to get their breakfast. She liked Kirk's brother and his friend very much. She could see that they were all working toward the same end: to make Casa del Sol the happy home it had been a long time ago.

After breakfast, both men prepared to go to the stables to meet Juan. They were walking across the garden when Louis stopped short.

"Del, wait a few minutes for me. I'll be right back. I've forgotten something."

Del waited while Louis went back into the house. He was looking around the beautiful garden when his attention was drawn again to the window of the corner bedroom. The curtains were pulled aside again, and someone stood in the window looking out. He knew it wasn't Marguerite, for she was in the kitchen when they left the house. He doubted that it was one of the maids. What reason would they have to watch from a window when they had direct contact with everything that went on in the house?

No, he knew who it was. But why should Tazia's mother play the invalid? Why would she remain unmoving and unspeaking in that lonely room when she could join the family? And why, when Tazia needed her more than at any other time in her life, did she leave her to face her problems alone?

Louis returned and was about to speak when he noticed Del's attention to the window.

"What are you looking at so intently?"

Del shrugged, for upon Louis's arrival, the curtain had dropped back into place. He knew that if they went to the room they would find her in bed and uncommunicative. He promised himself to bring the subject up to Kirk at the first opportunity. They went on to the stables, where they met Juan, saddled their horses, and went about their daily business.

Kirk and Tazia rose later and had breakfast together. Then Kirk went to join the other men for the day's work. Don Federico was bringing El Furio over, and they were going to put El Furio with the mare they had chosen. It would probably take some time, so they had invited Don Federico and his family for dinner. They planned to make it a small dinner party, so Marguerite and Tazia spent the day making preparations for the evening's festivities.

The men spent the day working hard and then gathered at Don Federico's ranch to help bring El Furio to Casa del Sol. He was led out of his stall stomping and resisting all the way.

"God, but he's a beautiful animal!" Louis said.

"He's not just an animal," Don Federico admonished. "He is almost part of my family. When we breed him with the mare you've chosen, they should drop some beautiful foals," Kirk replied.

"It should make the horses of our ranchos more valuable than they are already are."

"*Sí*, if the next few years see more of El Furio's offspring, we should do quite well."

"I hope El Furio has a long happy life," Louis said, "for I intend to start my own *rancho*, and one of his foals would be an excellent beginning."

"Señor, you may consider one of his foals my personal gift when you are ready to begin."

"Oh, Don Federico, that is most generous of you," Louis replied. "Gabrielle and I will be most grateful."

Kirk and Del moved closer to examine El Furio, and Don Federico turned to speak privately to Louis.

"When does your lovely lady arrive, Louis? That should give us a great excuse for another fiesta."

"She should be in Escondido any day now. I'll probably be going to pick her up the day after tomorrow. I don't know how long I will have to wait."

"I'm quite anxious to meet her."

"Not as anxious as I am to have her here," Louis replied. "Outside of the fact that I can hardly wait to see her, I'm hoping the things she can tell Tazia will help her understand Kirk. Although they seem to be getting along better, still there is something missing, and I'm hoping Gabrielle can change that."

"Yes, that would be excellent," Don Federico replied softly, his eyes seemingly intent on the horse. "If Gabrielle can answer Tazia's questions, then maybe . . ."

"Maybe what, Don Federico?" Louis asked.

Don Federico hesitated only for a moment. Then he smiled. "Maybe all will be well, and we can then build our *ranchos* into the greatest horse-breeding *ranchos* in the state of California."

Louis smiled in reply, but he did not really believe that that was what Don Federico had intended to say.

Don Federico rode El Furio to Casa del Sol. They made a magnificent entourage: Cristina, lovely in a deep-green riding habit, all of them mounted on beautiful palominos. They finally arrived at Casa del Sol, where Tazia made them welcome. Then, when El Furio had been taken care of to Don Federico's satisfaction, the men joined the ladies in predinner drinks. Cristina exchanged her riding habit for a dress of deep, burnished gold and Tazia wore a blue gown that complemented her eyes. It was obvious that the LaCroix brothers were completely enamored of the two women, which was remarked upon often and with much happy laughter by the others. The dinner was a credit to Marguerite's excellent cooking. Tazia made sure that the best wine of Casa del Sol flowed freely, so that everyone was in a warm, mellow mood. Kirk leaned back in his chair and smiled at Tazia, who sat at the opposite end of the table. He had never seen her look lovelier. Her eyes seemed to glow with the reflected light of the candles, and her skin seemed to have softened since she became pregnant.

It was only a month since Kirk had arrived; he had five more months to prove to Tazia that she was wrong about him and that he loved her beyond anything else in the world. Five months, he thought, but the child would be born in a little over three. No matter what he had promised her or how she felt toward him, he had no intention of leaving her or his child. There was no way he could live in peace anywhere else.

Kirk rose slowly to his feet and lifted his glass of wine. If he were going to make his position clear, now was as good a time as any to do it. "Ladies," he said with a broad smile and a slight bow, "and gentlemen, I should like to propose a toast."

The men rose to their feet and lifted their glasses.

"To my wife, Tazia de Montega LaCroix: the most beautiful woman in California—no, in the world," he added with a laugh. Tazia rose and accepted their toasts gracefully. "And," he added softly, "I also give you our future son—or daughter."

"Wonderful," Don Federico said.

"Marvelous," added Louis.

"I'm so very happy for you both, Kirk. I hope you and your family will live many years in happiness here at Casa del Sol," Cristina said.

Tazia's face had paled slightly, but she raised her glass as her eyes caught and held Kirk's across the table.

"To honor," she said softly. "To promises kept and not kept: may they be rewarded as they deserve."

There was absolute silence, for the current between the two could be felt like a living thing.

"Well!" Don Federico said. "I'm afraid Cristina and I must be on our way. I must rise early in the morning. Tomorrow we shall see about bringing together the future of our *ranchos*."

Everyone stirred, and the atmosphere became a little less strained.

"Don Federico," Tazia said, "Can you not spend the night here? You and Cristina are most welcome. Please."

Cristina smiled, and Don Federico shrugged. "Why not, *querida*? I would very much enjoy a game of cards, and I'm sure you women have much to discuss. You always do, don't you?"

Tazia and Cristina climbed the stairs as Kirk watched. Tazia had made it very clear that she intended to hold him to his word, and he had made it clear that he intended to stay. It would remain a stand-off for a while. But not forever, Tazia, my love, he thought. Not forever.

39

Jared Stone cursed and threw the bottle he had been drinking from across the room and watched it smash against the wall. He was damn sick of hanging around this town, waiting for Garrett to get back from wherever he was. It had been over three months now, and Garrett kept saying the time wasn't right yet. How the hell long was he going to take to get around to getting rid of that LaCroix fellow? The first time hadn't worked out too well, getting Kirk's brother instead of him, and Garrett had really been mad.

Then one day, he had come in with a half-smile on his face. He had found out that the mistress of Casa del Sol was expecting a child.

"It'll be soon, Stone. I promise you. The time is almost ripe for us to get what we want. They are breeding the horses now." Garrett chuckled, but there was no humor in it. The laugh bubbled with suppressed hatred and jealousy. "Let them breed their horses. Let them have their child. Let them think that all is well. Then, when they least expect it, we will strike. Casa del Sol and the beautiful palominos will be ours, all of them, and Kirk LaCroix and his brother will be very, very dead."

Two weeks ago, Garrett had gone off somewhere, having told Stone to wait for him. Well, he was getting tired of waiting. If Garrett wasn't back in a few more days, he intended to take matters into his own hands.

He stumbled to his feet and went to the window, drawing the curtain aside to look down on the too-familiar street. When this was all over, he intended to take Tazia and the money Garrett had promised him and put as much distance between them and this town as he could. He licked his dry lips as he thought again of Tazia. He had seen her often in town, although she had not seen him. It gave him a great deal of pleasure to watch her and think of them together. He would teach her how a real man was to be treated, and when he was done and was tired of her . . . well, she could earn a lot of money for him. He was still standing there when the door opened and Garrett walked in.

"Stone. You look like hell," Garrett said icily.

"Well, how do you expect me to look, cooped up in this damn room all the time. I've got to get out of here. When are we going to do something?"

"It won't be long now. Have patience."

"Patience? You've been traveling around. You ain't been closed up here like I have. Don't talk to me about patience."

"Stone, our lady at Casa del Sol is due to have her baby anytime now. After she does, it's one more club to use over LaCroix's head. Don't be a fool. Calm down. We'll have everything we've ever wanted."

"I still don't know what your plans are," Stone grumbled.

"You'll know soon enough. There's no sense in mulling them over and over. When the time comes, it will all be done swiftly and very effectively."

"Okay, okay. I'll stay out of sight a while longer, but we'd better get something done quick. I don't intend to spend the rest of my life in this dump. I'm going to take my money and the pretty lady and have me a time."

Garrett's eyes, cold as the eyes of a snake, narrowed as he gazed at Stone.

You pig, he thought. Do you really think I would ever let you put your filthy hands on one hair of her beautiful head? Aloud, he said softly, "Of course. I hope you get what you deserve, Stone."

Stone turned to look at him. "I need another bottle. Send one up when you go, and send me over a girl from Myrna's place. I need a little pleasure, too."

Garrett nodded and turned to leave the room. He hated Stone for his animal nature, but right now he needed him to carry out his plans. When he had what he wanted, well . . . Stone would meet with a very unpleasant accident. Garrett was about to walk out the front door of the hotel when he stopped abruptly. Across the street, where the incoming coaches stopped, were Del LaCroix and Louis Plummer. They were standing together, talking, as though they were waiting for something or someone. He stood just inside the door and continued to watch them, wondering what these two could possibly be waiting for. After about half an hour, a huge coach rolled to a stop. This was the reason they were waiting, but for whom? He kept his eyes glued to the scene before him and was rewarded when the doors opened and Gabrielle Saint-Albin stepped out.

He had always wondered where she had disappeared to when she escaped from him and Manolo that night at Five Points. He had to admit that Manolo had been a little rough on the girl, but that was the way Manolo was. There had been streaks of viciousness in Manolo that had occasionally frightened even him. It was one reason he had set things up to get Manolo killed. Getting rid of him had been a relief. He watched as Gabrielle threw herself into Louis Plummer's arms.

Well, well, well, another weapon to use on the LaCroixs. He didn't know how Louis and Gabrielle had gotten together, but Louis probably knew more about Garrett and Manolo than he had thought. Garrett watched as Raf climbed out of the coach, which answered his question. He knew now how Gabrielle must have gotten away from them at Five Points. Only to fall into my hands again, lovely Gabrielle, he thought with a silent laugh. Oh yes, he had definite plans for the two beautiful ladies of Casa del Sol.

Across the street, Louis was holding Gabrielle in his arms as tight as he could. She was laughing and crying at the same time.

"Oh, Gabrielle," he whispered against her hair, "you have no idea how much I've missed you. It seems forever since I've held you in my arms."

"Louis. Oh, Louis," she murmured. She clung tightly to him while Del and Raf looked on with wide grins of enjoyment. When Gabrielle could get free from Louis's arms, she smiled at Del. "It is good to see you again, too, Monsieur LaCroix."

"I'm practically family," Del laughed. "You call me Del, and"—he reached out to Gabrielle—"I never got to kiss the bride."

Gabrielle laughed and obediently kissed Del. Then she turned and motioned to Raf. "This is Raf, my bodyguard and one of the dearest friends I have."

Del extended his hand to Raf. "Welcome to the family, Raf."

"Thank you, sir," Raf said with a grin.

"I can't wait to get you to Casa del Sol," Louis said.

"Why?"

"I'd like to see which of you is bigger, you or Juan."

"Ummm, I think Juan's got him beat by about an inch," Del offered.

"Oh, really?" Louis said, eyeing Raf critically.

"Yes, Juan's as big as that mountain over there, and Raf is as big as the mountain minus one of the trees."

They laughed together as Louis led Gabrielle to their carriage and they started for Casa del Sol.

After they had settled themselves for the long ride home, Louis began to tell Gabrielle how the situation was at Casa del Sol. He explained in detail what had happened. He felt her tremble at the mention of Manolo de Montega's name, but he held her hand tightly in his. He was rewarded with her warm smile. The past was a dead thing now to Gabrielle, thanks to Louis, and she did not intend to let it reach out and mar the happiness they had found in each other.

When they arrived at the hacienda, Gabrielle was delighted with its beauty. "I can see why you want to make this our home," she said to Louis. "It is truly one of the loveliest places I have ever seen."

"Can you be reconciled to giving up Five Points to start over here?" Louis watched her reaction closely.

"Louis," she said softly as she stood close to him, her hand on his arm. "Wherever you are is home, and I shall be happy as long as you are there."

Del opened the front door, and Louis took Gabrielle's hand and tucked it under his arm. Once inside, Gabrielle exclaimed again over Tazia's beautiful home.

"Oh, Louis, Tazia must be so very happy here. She has everything a woman could ever want."

"No, Gabrielle, I don't believe Tazia knows how to be happy. She has never had any happiness before, so

I don't think she recognizes it for what it is."

Gabrielle looked at Louis questioningly, but a foot-fall on the stairs kept Louis silent.

"I'll explain everything to you when we're alone. Kirk needs your help, Gabrielle, but if it is too hard for you, then we'll find another way."

Tazia came down the stairs slowly. She was heavy with the child she carried, but the remainder of her body was still slender. Her skin glowed with good health.

She's one of the most beautiful women I've ever seen, thought Gabrielle.

Tazia's hair was parted in the center and drawn back to a chignon at the nape of her neck. She wore a deep-blue gown that picked up the violet color of her eyes and made them look large and innocent.

"Welcome to Casa del Sol, Mrs. Plummer," she said with a slow, gentle smile. "You have no idea how impatiently we have all awaited your arrival, especially Louis. I hope you enjoy your stay here."

"Please call me Gabrielle. I would so like us to be friends."

"Gabrielle," Tazia said quietly. "I'm sure we will be. Louis tells us that you are planning to make your home here. Let me be the first to welcome you to California and to tell you how happy we are to have you here."

"Thank you." Gabrielle looked closely at Tazia. She seemed to have a deep serenity about her, but a shadow in her eyes lurked. There is something terribly wrong, and that is making Tazia unhappy, she thought. Well, maybe when she and Louis could talk together, he would explain it to her. If there was any way she could help, she would.

Tazia called one of the servants and he carried Gabrielle's luggage upstairs to Louis's room. When they were inside the room, they waited impatiently for the servant to set her baggage down. When he had finally left the room, Louis pulled a laughing Gabrielle into his arms and kissed her long and thoroughly, something he had been aching to do since she stepped off the coach. Finally she put both hands against his chest and pushed him a little away from her, gasping for breath. "Louis, you'll smother me!"

Louis grinned, took his arms from about her waist, and gently caressed the curve of her breast under her restricting garments. She could see the warmth flood his eyes, and her body weakened and became pliant in response.

"Oh, Louis, I have missed you so very much. Our bed is very large and very lonely when you are not there."

"Gabrielle," he murmured as his lips found hers again. There was no resistance now as she molded her body against his. They were lost to time and place, caught up with the flow of love. They made love with a depth they had never reached before, and Louis knew with renewed conviction that this woman made him a whole man, gave him the strength he needed to face anything. With her by his side, he thought, there was nothing they could not accomplish. He told her of his plans to start a small *rancho* on the order of Casa del Sol, only certainly not as large. He also told her of the foal that Don Federico had promised him as a start. There were a few moments of relaxed silence between them, and then Gabrielle said very quietly, "Louis?"

"Yes?"

"Tell me what's really going on here at Casa del Sol, and why you think I can help."

He turned to face her and very gently caressed her

face with his fingertips. She continued to watch him intently.

"Gabrielle, you know I would never ask you to recall any of the terrible things from the past if I didn't think it was a matter of great importance."

She smiled. "Louis, the past can never hurt me again, as long as I have you. Tell me what you want me to do."

"Well," he began, "you know Tazia and Manolo were brother and sister?"

Gabrielle nodded, waiting for Louis to continue. He began with Kirk and Tazia's meeting and marriage and the subsequent battle. He told her about how Tazia had left Kirk and returned to California, only to have Kirk follow her and tell her about his ownership of Casa del Sol. He went on to explain what the situation was between them now.

"For a while, we thought everything between them was going to resolve itself, especially when Kirk found out about the baby. Now it seems that they are both suspended, waiting for something to happen, but I don't know what it is. It's got everyone on edge, especially Kirk and Tazia. When they're in a room together, you can feel it."

"What do you want me to do, Louis?"

"Talk to her. Tell her what happened at Five Points between you and her brother. Somehow she's got to be made to understand what kind of person her brother really was and why Kirk was right in doing what he did."

"Do you think she will believe me? After all, I am your wife, and we are both Kirk's friends. She might think it's a trick of ours to get her and Kirk back together again."

"At this point, Gabrielle, anything is worth a try."

"Very well. I shall do my best to convince her that

what I'm telling her is the truth."

Louis smiled at her, grateful for her understanding. "Well," he said softly, "why don't you try to convince me that you love me and you've missed me?"

"I thought I already had done that."

"Oh, I'm a very difficult man to convince." He laughed as he gathered her to him. "It takes repeated efforts to convince me of anything."

Gabrielle sighed. "Then I imagine I shall just have to keep trying."

"Excellent idea," he replied. "If you start now and work diligently at it for the next sixty or seventy years, well, who knows, you might succeed."

She laughed with delight as his lips took hers again. All their concentration was again centered on the renewal of their love for each other.

After Louis had gone upstairs with Gabrielle, Del winked at Raf and led him out to meet Kirk and Juan. Tazia went to the kitchen to tell Marguerite to prepare for another dinner guest and for their indefinite stay.

Kirk asked where Gabrielle was. Del replied with a broad grin. "Gabrielle is unpacking, and Louis is . . . helping her. I imagine we won't see either of them until dinner."

Kirk hid his amusement and offered to show Raf around Casa del Sol. As they toured the *rancho*, Raf warmed to the friendly attitude Kirk and Del extended to him. He was amazed when it was made obvious that he was expected to join them at their table for dinner. He felt good about Louis's friends. He felt, for the first time, that they all had a happy future.

40

Dinner that night was a pleasant affair. Tazia had put forth every effort to make the evening enjoyable. There seemed to be no strain at all between her and Kirk, but everyone except Gabrielle knew that it took very little to set off that sensitive temperament. After dinner, they sat on the patio, enjoying their brandy. Tazia had sent Juan to Don Federico's hacienda to invite them to meet Louis's wife. Don Federico was unable to come, but Cristina accepted and planned, to Del's delight, to spend the night at Casa del Sol.

The evening ended on a contented note. It was amusingly obvious to everyone that Louis desired to get Gabrielle alone again. Then, when they had retired, Raf stretched, yawned, and announced his plan to retire early. This left Kirk and Tazia with Cristina and Del.

Kirk sat close to Tazia on a small couch. He lifted her hand and gently brushed his hand across it, then slowly turned to face her. "It was a beautiful dinner and a lovely evening, Tazia."

"Thank you, Kirk." Tazia stirred uncomfortably.

Kirk immediately realized that Tazia had been quietly pushing herself all evening. "I think it's time for you to get some rest," he said firmly. He stood up and drew Tazia slowly to her feet despite her desire to be the gracious hostess.

Tazia had to admit she felt extremely tired. She turned to Cristina and Del.

"Cristina, you know where your room is. I hope you will excuse me."

"Of course, Tazia. You should not push yourself so, not when it's so close to your time."

Kirk watched Tazia with worried eyes. She would never admit anything was too much for her.

"Well, I'll see you in the morning. Good night, Cristina."

"Good night, Kirk."

Kirk slipped his arm around Tazia's waist, and they walked together to the bottom of the steps. Tazia looked up the length of the stairs and uttered a small sigh. She lifted the skirt of her gown, but before she could take the first step, Kirk bent down and lifted her up in his arms. He chuckled.

"What's so amusing?" Tazia asked softly as she lay her head against his shoulder.

"You're a little heavier since the last time I carried you!"

"You're a beast to bring up such a thing to a lady, especially to a lady who's carrying your child."

He took her to her bedroom and began to remove her clothes.

"Kirk, this is not necessary. I can call Marguerite to help me."

"Do you want to get Marguerite out of her warm bed? I'm quite capable, you know, madam." He laughed, but then his eyes became serious as he looked down at her tired face. "Let me help you, Tazia," he said softly. She offered no more resistance, for she felt more weary than she had ever felt before. Slowly, gently, he removed her clothes. Then he took

339

a nightgown from the dresser drawer and slipped it over her head. With tender hands, Kirk removed the pins from her hair. Then, to her astonishment, he drew her hair behind her head and braided it. He turned back the covers of the bed and lifted her into it. After he had drawn the covers over her, he stood looking down at her for a few minutes. He did not like the way she looked: her face was very pale, and her eyes seemed clouded. Finally Kirk removed his clothes, slid into bed beside her, and drew her to him.

"Kirk."

"Shhh, just rest, Tazia," he said quietly. "Let me hold you." She relaxed a little as his hands gently rubbed the soreness from her back. She sighed deeply, and within a few minutes, she was asleep. Kirk slid a hand over her body. He thought the child had shifted its position. It was still three weeks before the baby was due, and he was beginning to worry that it might come too soon. He couldn't bring himself to face the possibility that anything could happen to either of the people he loved. He held her close, and after a while, he drifted off to sleep himself.

Del and Cristina had watched Kirk carry Tazia up the stairs. "I'm worried about Tazia," Cristina said. "It's too soon for the child, but Tazia looks so . . . ill."

"Don't worry. Kirk won't let anything happen to her. In case you've forgotten, he happens to love her very much."

"How are things between them now, Del?"

"Well, it's hard to tell. They seem to be fine for a while, and yet . . . sometimes I still feel that some huge, dark thing hovers between them, keeping them from reaching out and touching one another. We're hoping that somehow Gabrielle can help dispel some of Tazia's ogres—if she'll just listen to Gabrielle and accept what she says as the truth."

"Do you think she will?"

"I hope so, because I don't know anyone else who can," he said. Then he turned to her and added softly, "Do you?"

She averted her eyes and walked a few steps away from him.

"Why do you ask me? There is nothing I can tell her that would change anything."

"Why can't you trust me, Cristina?"

"Please, Del . . . I—"

"I know that you have some secret, one that might be the key to setting Tazia free. Don't you think that you could trust me not to reveal anything you tell me?"

"It's not that I don't trust you, Del. I do, but . . ."

"But what?"

"I have others to consider."

"Your father?"

"Yes."

"Your sister?"

She looked at him in surprise, and he smiled. "I've been figuring things out a little at a time."

"Del, I've been hoping that things between Tazia and Kirk would resolve themselves. I promise you, Del, if they don't, and if Tazia will not listen to Gabrielle, then I will speak. Does that satisfy you?"

"Cristina, I don't want to cause you or your family any grief. You know how I feel about you. Do you honestly think I would do anything to hurt you?"

She looked up into his intent, honest face and accepted what she saw written clearly there.

"No," she murmured as his arms slowly drew her close to him. She lifted her willing lips to his and surrendered to an emotion she was no longer capable of fighting. Once Del had sensed her surrender, he found he could not stop. Of all the women Del had been with, none had ever affected him as the gentle little creature he now held. He wanted her, all of her, now and for all the days to come. He held her tightly, enjoying the soft curves of her body as she pressed unrestrainedly against him. Before he lost complete control, he moved away from her. This was not the time or place, nor was she the kind of woman he could have for an evening.

"Cristina, do you love me as much as I love you?"

"Oh yes, Del, I do," she whispered softly.

"Then trust me. Tell me what it is that makes you so unhappy and so afraid to speak."

Cristina could no longer see the emotions on his face, yet she felt his strength, and she knew with every womanly instinct that this was her man. "Del, will you swear not to repeat what I tell you unless we have my father's permission?"

"But what of Kirk and Tazia? This could mean their whole lives to them. Surely it cannot be so bad that we cannot use it for their benefit?"

He felt her tremble, but she held his hand tightly as she repeated in a low, strained voice.

"If you cannot swear to this, Del, I cannot tell you, no matter how much I love you or what it means to Tazia and Kirk."

He could feel the determination in her. Maybe he could find a way to get her to say something to Tazia. In the meantime, it was best that at least *he* knew, he thought. "I agree. I will say nothing to either of them unless you or your father agrees, or one of you decides to tell them. Is that agreeable?"

"Yes," she answered quickly. Then, still holding his hand, she led him to the bench beneath the great tree in the center of the patio. The moon, large and yellow, had just risen, and in its pale light, the garden seemed to glow softly. Del could just make out Cristina's pale face and large shining eyes.

"Come, sit with me," Cristina said, "and I will tell you a story. It's not a very pretty story. But when you've heard it, I think you will understand Manolo de Montega better — and probably hate him as much as I do."

He sat down beside her, and in a quiet voice, Cristina began. "Manolo was five years older than Tazia and I and seven years older than my sister Juanita. For some reason I still do not understand, Tazia's parents absolutely adored him. They made all their plans around him. He was heir to Casa del Sol, and I think they were even contemplating a marriage between our two families to unite our *ranchos*, although I would have killed myself before I would let Manolo de Montega touch me."

Del was a little startled at her cold pronouncement. Manolo must have been very bad for his gentle Cristina to feel this way. He said nothing, however. He just sat in silence and waited for her to continue.

"There are so many incidents from our childhood that I could tell you to show you what Manolo was, but I cannot remember them all. Manolo was a cruel, vicious child who grew into an even more vicious man. Needless to say, around his parents and Tazia, he was sly enough to keep them believing in him, but it used to make me so angry when Tazia would defend him or take the blame and the punishment for something he did. From the time she was born, it was pounded into her that Manolo was more than her older brother, he was almost a god. When I was about fifteen and Manolo was twenty, he made his first attempt to add me to his conquests. He suggested that since, in all probability, our parents would want us to marry, we should—oh, how shall I put it?—try to see if we were *physically compatible*. I believe those were the words he used."

Del's hand shook a little as he tightly reined in his anger.

"That was the first time, but it was far from the last," she went on. "It became a sort of contest between us. I avoided him for some time. Just before he left for New Orleans, he seemed to lose interest in me. I didn't know why, and I really didn't care. It was the day after he left that we discovered the reason. He had seduced Juanita instead," she said softly. For several minutes she did not speak, and he could feel the pain the memories brought back to her. "We had thought," she continued, "that Juanita was spending the night with a friend. It was not until the next day that we found her note. It said that she loved Manolo and was going with him to New Orleans to be married.

"I told father what had happened between Manolo and me. He was enraged, and we prepared to follow them. We did, as far as the coast. It was not necessary to find a ship to follow Juanita to New Orleans, because she had not boarded one. We found her in a brothel, where Manolo had . . . sold her services. She had been amusement to him on the journey. You see," she said bitterly, "Manolo tired very easily of his . . . amusements. Oh, God! Gentle, sweet Juanita, forced to . . . with animals! Animals! She completely lost her reason. By the time we found her, there was little left of the sweet, loving girl she had been. Mother took her away to see if we could find a doctor to help her. My father was so angry that he went to Manolo's parents. He told them the truth about Manolo's past. At first, they did not believe him, but when father told them about Juanita, they were so shocked and hurt—I think that was the blow that caused Don Ramón's heart attack. To think his son was such a depraved beast that he would do this to a sweet child like Juanita. It was simply too much for him. His heart attack on top of everything else caused Tazia's mother's condition. We felt that Tazia had suffered enough. We swore to each other that it would never be mentioned to her. Can you see, Del, why it would be better for Kirk and Tazia to work out their problems themselves? I do not think I would have the courage to tell her the truth."

Del sighed and put his arm around her shoulder. She lay her head on his shoulder, and he held her in silence while she regained her equilibrium. Then he gently kissed the top of her head.

"You're right, Cristina, it would be a murderous thing to do to her. God, this whole thing is a mess. I have to agree with you: if Gabrielle can't do something to help, then we will have to let them work out the problems by themselves."

"I knew you would understand, *querida*," she said as she nestled closer to him.

Del was quick to take advantage of the situation. He pulled her into his arms and kissed her. It started as a gentle kiss, but as her lips warmed under his, he felt his world stir and then begin to slip rapidly away from him. Before he realized exactly where they were and what they were doing, he found himself holding her tightly against him and devouring her lips with a hungry kiss. His mind told him to stop before he compromised her completely. What if someone found them? It would make things very embarrassing and difficult for Cristina—not to mention Don Federico's anger. These were the things his mind told him. But the language of his senses and the closeness of her warm, willing body put everything else out of his mind. She murmured softly in Spanish as his hands began to explore the treasure he had found. He knew he had no intention of stopping now unless she did, and she gave no signs of wanting him to stop.

It was a good thing that Del looked up at that moment. The moonlight caught the windows at the corner of the house and illuminated them. It also revealed the form of the woman who stood looking down at them.

"God damn!" he muttered.

"What?" exclaimed Cristina, surprised as much at his language as at his reaction.

"Cristina, turn your head slightly until you can catch sight of the corner of the house." She turned and gasped in shock as she realized not only that they were being watched, but who was doing the watching.

"But that's Tazia's mother's room. It can't be her. She's not capable of moving. She's an invalid."

"No, she's not an invalid," he muttered angrily. "And I, for one, would like to know why she's playing the invalid and why she's spying on us. This is not the first time I've seen her at that window."

"It's not?"

"No. I've seen her several times, but I've not said anything to anyone. Like you, I felt that Kirk and Tazia had enough trouble."

"Are you going to say anything this time?"

"No, not to Kirk or Tazia, but tomorrow I intend to go to that room and have a talk with the lady. There are a lot of questions to be answered, and I think she has many of the answers. How in God's name could a normal woman allow her daughter to go through the life Tazia has led? And why doesn't she speak up now that Manolo is dead?"

"Perhaps she doesn't know the situation between

Kirk and Tazia now. Maybe she thinks they are happy together, so she is staying in that room to nurse her grief for her lost son."

"I'll be willing to wager that she knows everything that goes on in this house."

"If that's true, Del . . ."

"Yes, if that's true, I'd say she's more of a sadistic monster than her son ever was."

"I would hate to believe that was so."

"Well, I'm going to find out tomorrow," he said. Then he turned back to her and grinned. "But she has very effectively spoiled my entire night."

Cristina smiled in return. "Maybe it was best for me," she said. "I think I was getting a little carried away."

"Just a little?" he questioned softly as his lips found her earlobe and then drifted down to her throat.

"Well," she said softly, "maybe more than a little."

He chuckled in delight and kissed her very thoroughly. Then, with a supreme effort, he moved a little away from her. "Cristina! Leave me now and go to your room. Maybe you'd better lock the door, too, because if you stay here one more minute, you're going to end up in my room. I'll make you mine and you'll never get away."

She rose slowly to her feet and stood beside him as he looked up at her. She smiled and whispered, "Thank you." Then she turned and walked away. He watched her leave him with sincere regret. When he looked up at the window again, as he expected, it was vacated.

"Until tomorrow, lady," Del said quietly to himself. He went upstairs to seek his own cold, lonely bed. He thought for some time about Cristina. He decided then to ask her to marry him as soon as possible. He had no intention of spending many more nights like this without her.

41

Although Kirk was asleep, he felt every movement Tazia made. In the wee hours of the morning, he felt her stir restlessly and murmur softly in her sleep. He quietly rose from the bed and lit a candle, but when he went back to her bedside, her eyes were open, looking up at him.

"The baby?" he questioned.

She nodded her head, and her eyes filled with tears. "It's too soon, Kirk," she choked. "Am I going to lose my baby?" Her voice was filled with a pathetic need for his reassurance. Even Kirk had no idea how much this child meant to her. It was to be the one person she could love without restraint or fear. He sat beside her and held her hand. He wanted to say something to help her, to make her a little less afraid.

"Tazia, three or four weeks is not too early. I'm sure the baby will be fine and healthy. Everything will be all right. You just be patient for a moment. I'm going to get Marguerite."

She nodded her head, but the fear did not leave her face, nor did she release his hand for a few moments. Finally Kirk withdrew his hand and reached for his clothes, pulling them on as quickly as he could without seeming to rush. The last thing he wanted was for her to know just how scared he was. He bent down and kissed her lightly.

"I'll be right back. I'll get Marguerite and send Juan for the doctor."

He closed the door and moved rapidly down the stairs. He went first to Juan's room and knocked several times before a sleepy-eyed Juan open the door.

"Señor Kirk, what is the matter?"

"I want you to go for the doctor right away, Juan. The baby is coming. Hurry, get dressed and go as quickly as you can. There's no time to waste."

"*Sí, señor.*" Juan was already moving to put on his clothes.

Then Kirk went to Marguerite's door, but before he could knock, the door was open and Marguerite came out of her room, fully dressed.

"Marguerite—"

"I know, Señor Kirk. I could not sleep. Since last night, I have been worried about her. I heard your footsteps above me, and I knew immediately what was wrong. You have sent Juan for the doctor?"

"Yes."

"Good. In the meantime, I will go to her. Since it is so soon, she is probably very frightened. This baby is her whole life to her."

"Marguerite."

"*Sí, señor?*"

"*She* is *my* whole life," he said softly. "Don't let anything happen to her. If it comes to a choice . . . you understand me, Marguerite? If it comes to a choice, don't let anything happen to Tazia."

"*Sí, señor.* I understand. But you must not talk like that. Nothing is going to happen to either of them. We will bring you a fine healthy son, and Tazia will be a wonderful mother."

He smiled, but his eyes still held hers intently. "Just remember what I said, Marguerite. No matter what the doctor says, I want Tazia safe."

"*Sí*," she repeated in a soft whisper. She pulled her door shut, and they went back upstairs to Tazia's room.

Marguerite took over and made Tazia as comfortable as she could. First she washed her face and hands and changed her nightgown. Then she changed the bed and gathered together several clean sheets. Tazia seemed to be relieved of some of her tension by Marguerite's calm presence. Marguerite had suggested several times that Kirk find himself something to occupy his time, preferably somewhere else, but Kirk ignored her suggestions and went to Tazia's side. He sat on the edge of the bed and held her hand. Whenever a pain would grip her, he would hold her hand even tighter. It was obvious to Marguerite that he was suffering every pain with her.

Soon the whole household was astir. Cristina came as soon as she was told Tazia had gone into labor. Marguerite took her aside and suggested that she find some way to get Kirk out of the room.

"I know he wants to be with her, but don't you think he will be in the doctor's way?"

Cristina turned and looked toward the bed. Kirk was bending over Tazia, one hand holding her and the other brushing the hair from her forehead. There was such a look of tender love on his face that Cristina shook her head no.

"Marguerite, look at him. He obviously loves her very much. If Tazia has ever needed anything in her life, it is this kind of love. Leave him alone. Maybe this is what he needs to prove to her that he loves her more than anything. Maybe the ghost of her brother can now be buried, and she can turn to Kirk as she should have long ago."

"I hope Juan hurries with the doctor. I'm afraid that I can not handle anything that becomes complicated. The baby is coming too soon, and I am not sure of anything."

Cristina smiled and patted Marguerite's shoulder.

"You will be fine, Marguerite. You underestimate yourself. I'm sure you have handled many bad situations and have helped deliver healthy babies."

"But . . . this is Tazia. She is like my own. What if something should go wrong?" she whispered.

"Don't talk like that. Don't even think like that. The doctor will be here soon. In the meantime, I shall help you, and we will stay with her until the doctor arrives. And Marguerite . . ."

"*Sí?*"

"Say nothing more to Kirk. Let him stay with her. Maybe he can give her some of his strength."

Marguerite nodded, and they both went back to Tazia's bedside.

The hours passed slowly. Each time the pain struck her, Tazia would cling more tightly to Kirk's hand. He spoke to her softly and soothingly. After a while, he became the center of her universe. She felt as though her body were being torn apart. Wave after wave of blinding pain left her whimpering and clinging desperately to Kirk. Although she refused to cry out, she said Kirk's name over and over. Each time he would reply.

Marguerite began to worry about the doctor's arrival, when a light knock came at the door. She went to the door and spoke to someone outside. Then she came back and put her hand on Kirk's shoulder. When he looked up questioningly, she motioned for him to accompany her. His face went white, and pinched lines appeared at the corners of his mouth. Outside the door, Marguerite whispered, "The doctor is not in town, and Juan cannot find him anywhere. There is no one else we can call."

"Are you sure he tried everywhere?" Kirk asked sharply.

"Señor Kirk," Marguerite replied in a gentle voice, "Juan has loved Tazia since she was a child. Do you not think he has tried his best?"

"Of course he has," Kirk replied. He ran his hand through his hair in an absentminded gesture of desperation. "Marguerite, you will have to do this alone. There is nothing else we can do."

Marguerite hesitated slightly, but enough for Kirk to realize there was more wrong than just the doctor's absence.

"What is it, Marguerite?"

"Señor Kirk. The baby is lying the wrong way. If he is not turned, he will be born in the wrong position. That could cost Tazia her life—and maybe the baby's, too."

"Well, *do* something. Can't you turn him around?"

"No, I . . . I just don't know how," she said, her eyes filling with tears.

"Oh God!" Kirk groaned. He leaned heavily against the wall for a moment. Then he straightened up and spoke grimly to Marguerite. "Get everyone together. We'll send them out to the neighbors. Surely there's a midwife somewhere who can do this."

She nodded and went swiftly to follow his order.

Kirk went back inside.

"Cristina, go to Marguerite. She needs some help."

Cristina was a little surprised, but she said nothing. After she had closed the door behind her, Kirk went to Tazia's side.

Her hair was wet with perspiration, and her face

abnormally flushed with exertion. She was panting a little from the pain and gathering her strength for the next wave. For the moment, her eyes seemed calm. She held his hand tightly. "Kirk?" she whispered.

"I'm here, darling," he murmured as he kissed her fingers gently.

"Am I going to die?"

"No!" he said angrily. "Don't talk like that. You're going to be fine."

"Kirk, I want to tell you something."

"Save your strength, Tazia. You can tell me after the baby is born."

"No, I must tell you now. I want you to know in case . . . well, I want you to know."

"What is it?"

"No matter what has come between us, or what my anger and pride have caused me to do, I have never stopped loving you, Kirk. Even when I shouted my hatred the loudest, I never stopped loving you."

"Oh, Tazia," he said as he pressed his lips to her fingers. "When this is over, the three of us will begin again. We'll make up for all the time we've lost." He felt a lump in his throat, and his eyes were shiny with unshed tears. She murmured something to him in Spanish.

"Damn!" he choked. "I've really got to learn your language."

A slight smile lit her face for a moment, but it was soon replaced by a look of agony as more pain struck. She gripped his hand until her nails cut through his skin. He said nothing. He simply held her hand tightly until it passed and she lay back against the pillows.

God, I wish Marguerite would hurry, he thought as he watched Tazia's eyes glaze over with pain.

Marguerite was downstairs talking to everyone in

the household. She had called them all together to explain the gravity of the situation. When she had finished explaining, she asked, "Can anyone help? Does anyone know what needs to be done?"

There was silence for several moments, and Marguerite's heart sank like lead. There was no one to help, and she felt that it was going to cost a life, maybe two lives.

Then a quiet voice broke the silence.

"If Kirk will let me, maybe I can help her."

Marguerite's eyes lifted and met Raf's across the room. "You can help?"

"Yes, if you ask Kirk first," he replied.

"I don't think Kirk will care who helps, as long as someone does. Why should you think otherwise?"

Raf grinned. "Marguerite, where I come from, there's a law against a black man even *touching* a white woman. Kirk may not like the idea."

Marguerite smiled. "I don't think you know Kirk very well. But come, we will ask him."

Raf accompanied her back up the stairs. Kirk was relieved to see Marguerite return, but he was surprised to see her accompanied by Raf. Marguerite explained as quickly as possible, for the inarticulate moans coming from Tazia told her there was no time to be wasted. Kirk said nothing until she was finished. Then he looked at Raf. "You can help?"

"Yes, sir."

"You've done this before?"

"A couple times in the slave cabins at Five Points."

"Raf, if you can help her, please try. I would be very grateful for anything you can do. It's been hours, and she's growing weaker. I . . . I don't want to lose her, Raf," he added softly. Raf nodded his understanding and then turned to Marguerite. He rattled off a list of things he wanted her to find. Some of them made her eyes widen in surprise, but she said nothing. She merely nodded her head when he was finished and went to gather them. Raf went immediately to the girl and examined her. Kirk was surprised at the huge man's gentleness.

Raf worked over her for a few minutes, all the while talking to her in a gentle singsong voice, which helped soothe even Kirk's jangled nerves. Marguerite returned with a tray loaded with the things Raf had asked for. Quickly he took a container and mixed some things together. Both Kirk and Marguerite watched him in silent fascination. He went back to the bed with the container in his hands. He lifted Tazia very gently by the shoulders.

"Drink this, little lady," he said softly. "It'll make things easier for you. Easy now," he cautioned as he put the container to her lips. She drank obediently. Then he lay her gently against the pillow.

"It'll take just a couple of minutes for that to start working." He began to roll up his sleeves.

"Then what?" Kirk questioned.

Raf grinned. "Then we're goin' to turn your baby around and help him into the world."

Tazia had ceased moaning, and her eyes seemed more alert. Raf turned to her and smiled again. "You have to help me, you understand? It'll take me, you, and God to get this baby started. Are you ready?"

She nodded her head and reached over her to grasp the posts of the bed. Raf bent over her.

"Bear down," he said crisply. She obeyed with a ragged, gasping moan. "Again!" he commanded. "Again!"

Tazia's sobs rocked the quiet room, but she did her best to obey him. She moaned again and cried out Kirk's name. He moved quickly to her side and took one of her hands. He was amazed at her strength as her whole body pulled against him.

"One more time," Raff said. "He's almost turned." Tazia caught her lip between her teeth and put all her strength into pushing into the world the child she wanted so desperately. A heart-stopping moan came from her as her body concentrated every ounce of strength it had.

"Ha!" Raf cried. "We've got it. We've done it, little lady."

He lifted the small bloody object and handed it to Marguerite, who wrapped the baby and carried it to the other side of the room to wash it. Raf bent over Tazia again. "You're quite a lady, Mrs. LaCroix, and you've got a nice healthy baby."

Tazia smiled. Slowly her eyes closed in exhaustion.

Kirk turned to Raf and extended his hand. "I owe you more than I'll ever be able to repay. Will you accept my gratitude for now?"

Raf took his hand with a smile.

"I owe you Tazia's life—and my son's."

"No, sir."

"What?"

"You might owe me Tazia's life, but not your son's."

"What do you mean?"

"You never asked me what the baby was."

Kirk looked at him in surprise. Then he laughed. "What is it?"

"A baby girl. And she's going to be a pretty little thing, too, with a mama like she's got."

Both Kirk and Raf grinned broadly as Marguerite began to laugh. She carried the child to Kirk, and he took her in his arms gently.

"My daughter," he whispered softly as he looked down at the tiny face of the little girl in his arms.

"What are you going to name her?" Marguerite

asked.

"We'll wait until Tazia's awake. I would like to name her Mercedes. Then we can call her Mercy. For that's what she was: God's mercy."

Marguerite went back to the bed and covered Tazia.

"Let her sleep as long as she can," Raf said. "The drug I gave her will keep her asleep for quite a few hours. After what she's been through, she needs it."

Kirk agreed and handed the baby to Marguerite. "Come downstairs and have a drink with me, Raf. I might even get drunk. It isn't every day a man has a daughter, you know." Raf laughed along with Kirk. The rest of the household was waiting in fearful suspense. When they came down, all eyes turned to them expectantly. Kirk walked to the table and poured a drink for each of them without saying a word.

"Kirk, I'm going to strangle you if you don't tell us what's happened," Del said.

Kirk handed each of them a glass, and Cristina and Gabrielle smiled brightly.

"Do we toast a daughter or a son?" Gabrielle asked.

Kirk raised his glass. "My friends, I give you a toast to Tazia de Montega LaCroix, who has given me the most beautiful daughter in the world." They raised their glasses in silence and drank.

Kirk's mind was not altogether on his daughter, for he recalled with a feeling of supreme happiness the words he and Tazia had exchanged. "I never stopped loving you, Kirk," she had said. Well, today began a whole new life together, he thought as he drank the wine that saluted the birth of his daughter. He hoped she would be the final tie to bind them together forever.

42

Raf was right; Tazia slept for hours. Several times Kirk went in to check on her. When she finally did wake up, she found Kirk hovering near her. He went to the bed and smiled down at her.

"How do you feel?"

"Fine, now that I've seen our daughter . . . and her father." Kirk grinned proudly. "She is beautiful, isn't she?" He leaned forward and kissed her lightly. "Thank you."

She looked up at him in a way he had never expected to see again. "I thank *you*, Kirk. If it weren't for your strength—yours and Raf's—I'm sure I would never have come through it."

"Tazia, I warned you that you couldn't get away from me easily, didn't I?"

She smiled. "I want to thank Raf for all he's done for me."

"He'll be back soon. He's gone to town with Gabrielle."

He leaned forward and caressed her face with his hand. "Has Marguerite told you what I'd like to name the baby?"

She nodded, her eyes holding his.

"Is it all right with you?"

"It sounds like a lovely name. Oh, Kirk," she added softly.

"Tazia, there's no need to say anything now. Let's just enjoy our daughter. When you're well, we'll make our plans. We *are* going to make plans for our future, aren't we?"

She nodded again.

He bent close to her. "We have everything in the world ahead of us, darling. Hurry and get well." He was just about to tell Marguerite to bring the child to them when a knock sounded on the door. Louis and Del came in.

"Tazia." Del smiled. "It's good to see you looking so well. You had us all pretty scared."

"Are all mothers as beautiful as you are?" Louis asked.

Tazia laughed. "Only if they're as happy as I am."

"Where's my godchild?" Del said.

"*Your* godchild!" Louis replied quickly. "*My* godchild."

"Well, if you insist, we'll share her." Del laughed.

"I can see that this baby is going to very spoiled," Tazia remarked as all three men clustered about Marguerite and the baby.

"She's lovely," Louis said as he gently tickled her palm. Her tiny fingers immediately closed about his finger. It was very obvious that they also closed about his heart at the same time.

"Well, I'm relieved," Del said very seriously.

"Relieved? Why?" Tazia asked.

Del grinned wickedly. "She doesn't look a bit like her father, thank God. She's the image of her mother. For a while, I was worried she might come out looking like Kirk."

Kirk chuckled. Then he took the child from Marguerite, walked to the bed, and put her in Tazia's arms. He sat close to her to watch the tiny face. "She's so beautiful," he whispered. "Del's right, she does look exactly like you. Pity the poor hearts when she gets older."

"Well, has Doctor Raf told you when you'll be able to get up?" Del asked Tazia.

"In a few days," she said. "Why, is something special going on?"

"Oh," Del said, shrugging nonchalantly, "not unless you consider planning a wedding as something special."

All eyes turned to him in surprise while he laughed. "Cristina and I would like to get married here at Casa del Sol, if it's all right with you and Kirk, Tazia."

"Oh, Del! I think that's marvelous." Tazia's eyes shone with happiness. Both Louis and Kirk congratulated him.

"I'll be up soon and we'll make plans. It's the most wonderful thing in the world. Cristina and I will really be sisters now."

"Don't you rush getting out of bed," Kirk said firmly. "Del will just have to practice a little patience." He turned to face Del, his eyes gleaming wickedly. "That should be something to see," he added.

Del grinned back at him. "Kirk, I'll bet it would amaze you if you knew just how much patience I've been practicing."

They all laughed. Kirk, who had one eye on Tazia all the time, reached over and picked up his daughter. Then he said to Tazia firmly, "You need as much rest as you can get. I'm kicking these two out, and I want you to get some sleep. Marguerite and I will take care of Mercy."

Tazia obeyed, for she wanted to get out of bed as soon as possible, and following orders seemed to be the quickest way to accomplish that.

Del and Louis left the room together and started down the hall. Then Del stopped. "You go on, Louis. There's something I have to do."

Louis left Del there. He stood in the hall for a few minutes, silently contemplating the closed door of the bedroom at the end of the hall. Then he slowly moved toward the door. He made no noise as he walked and he opened the door without knocking. Caught completely unaware, Tazia's mother was startled. Within seconds, her eyes recovered their blank look.

"It's a little too late, Señora de Montega. I think we both know that." He closed the door and leaned against it. "I think it's time for us to have a little talk," he added softly.

She sat very still, propped up against the pillow, but her eyes acquired a look of curiosity.

"Good morning, Señor LaCroix," she said. Her soft voice had a strong accent, as though English were very difficult for her.

"Well," he said, "I was right. You're *not* an invalid. Why are you pretending? And why have you been spying on me?"

She motioned to a chair. "Please, sit down, Señor LaCroix."

Del watched the woman with curiosity as he sat down. She was not as he pictured her in his mind. He had been prepared for a cold, arrogant woman, hard and demanding. This was the only kind of woman he could picture after learning about Tazia's childhood, not to mention the things that had happened since he had arrived at Casa del Sol. What he had imagined and what he saw were in conflict.

There was a soft gentleness about her face that failed to match his picture of her. Her hair was dark, almost as dark as Tazia's. It was braided and hung

361

over her shoulder. From what he could tell, she was about Tazia's height, maybe a little shorter. Any resemblance between her and her daughter ended there. Her eyes were large and deep brown; her skin was the deep olive color of the true Spaniard. There were lines etched at the corners of her eyes and her full, wide mouth that told of deep suffering. She gave the impression of being a lady of gentle birth. Del hid his surprise and waited for her to speak. She watched him with a half-smile on her lips, her eyes shining with a trace of humor.

"I see you are quite prepared to dislike me, Señor LaCroix. Do you always form your opinions without knowing all the facts?" He flushed a little at her accurate accusation. He suddenly felt very apologetic, like a little boy caught in mischief.

"No, I do not, usually. I'm beginning to be sorry that I did this time." Now she smiled, and it changed her face completely. It became illuminated, as though someone had lit a bright light behind her eyes.

"I knew you were a very intelligent young man the first time I watched you. You have proven me right."

"Thank you," he replied. Suddenly everything seemed to be turned about. It was *he* who felt he should be explaining to her. He didn't like the way things were going, but he could not stop himself. "I'm sorry to have intruded on you this way. I know you've been watching from that window. What I'd really like to know is why you feel the need for this type of secrecy. Casa del Sol is your home. Why should you remain a prisoner here, albeit a self-imposed prison? It makes no sense to me."

"No, I imagine it doesn't make sense to you. I don't know if it's possible to make you understand at all. There are some emotions that are difficult to put into words, Señor LaCroix. One of them is hatred . . . and another is fear."

"I guess," he began hesitantly, "what I really want to know is why Tazia has had to pay the price for whatever it was. Why couldn't your daughter reach out to you, as she should have been able to do, in her time of need? Most of the pain she has been through is directly caused by that one thing: lack of love from you, her own mother, and from her father. It is a shame she has found it so difficult up until now to respond to love from my brother. She does not understand the emotion. She has never shared it before." He looked at her, his blue eyes steady and questioning. "Can you just answer that question? Maybe that would be enough?"

She sighed deeply. "I shall try my best, Señor LaCroix," she said, her voice deep and mellow with sadness. "It began so very long ago." Her eyes flickered with remembrances. "I must take you back to my youth. I was fifteen when I met Ramón de Montega. I met him, Señor, on our wedding day."

He looked at her in surprise.

"Yes, on our wedding day. Don Ramón was twenty years my senior. I was a frightened child. Frightened first by my domineering father, then by Don Ramón himself. Our marriage was arranged by my parents and Don Ramón. My parents wanted me to marry a wealthy man, and Don Ramón wanted a son . . . a son. That was all he ever really wanted. We were married only a year when Manolo was born." There was a faint mist of tears in her eyes as she drifted back over the years. "By the time Manolo was five," she said in a soft, pain-filled voice, "I already knew what he was. Don Ramón was a cold, unfeeling man; his son was worse. Slowly, very slowly, I began to hate them both."

Del looked at her with genuine shock. "But I thought—"

"That I loved him more than Tazia? No, Señor, you are wrong. If I had known at his birth what a monster he would become, I would have killed him before he drew his second breath," she said vehemently.

She was silent for a moment while she got her emotions back under control. Del said nothing. He was too surprised to speak.

"This house had been my prison for five years. I existed under Don Ramón's watchful eye. The care of my son was in his hands alone. He taught him to be arrogant and brutal. There were no choices given to me. I was expected to live in complete obedience to Don Ramón, and I did . . . until the summer Manolo was five. We took a vacation to Madrid to visit some friends. There I met Rodrigo Martinez. He was a wonderful man, gentle, kind and considerate. We fell in love. There was nothing we could do to stop it; it was beyond our control. We were together as often as we could be, stealing every opportunity to be with each other. Then we became reckless. I wonder today just how long Don Ramón knew of our liaison, how he planned to catch us together. How he . . . oh, Rodrigo," she whispered softly, her eyes filled with tears. Del felt a sudden, deep compassion for her.

"Rodrigo is Tazia's father, isn't he?" he asked her in almost a whisper. She nodded her head yes.

After a while, she continued her story. "We were together, Rodrigo and I, at his home in the country. We felt safe and secure for the few hours we had. Then Don Ramón burst in on us. It was no match. Don Ramón was an excellent swordsman. He was considered by everyone to be quite a gentleman, for he had killed his wife's lover and was not punishing his wife at all. Punishment! They did not know the meaning of the word. If my life was cold and empty before, it became a million times worse. Don Ramón made it clear that he would raise Tazia as he wished. If I interfered in any way, we would be separated, and I would never see her again. The only love I could show her was through Marguerite, who was my only source of help. By the time Tazia and Manolo were grown, I knew it was too late. Then Don Federico came to us with the news of Manolo's activities and his terrible, terrible treatment of his daughter. At first Don Ramón would not believe him, but Don Federico offered proof that could not be denied. Don Ramón became so angry it was unbelievable. The terrible thing is, I think his anger was not directed at Manolo, as it should have been, but at Don Federico for bringing him the truth. The fight was a terrible thing to witness. Don Ramón thundered with rage. Then suddenly he clutched his chest and collapsed, dead of a heart attack.

"I . . . I don't know what happened to me, Señor LaCroix. I must have collapsed then. I had a complete breakdown and remained so until long after Tazia came home. When I did regain my mind, Marguerite told me of the situation between my daughter and her husband. She told me all about Kirk and you. If I had spoken then, Tazia would have used me as a shield, and Kirk would have been forced away from Casa del Sol. Marguerite and I decided to remain silent for just a little longer. She believed that Kirk and Tazia would resolve the problems between them, and then I could speak. Do you understand?" She added the last words in a soft, pleading voice.

"Yes, yes, I do. Now I can tell *you* something that will bring you some of the happiness you deserve." He went on to explain about Tazia's baby and how Kirk

365

had helped her through its birth. "I think it helped to exorcise some of her ghosts and bring the two of them together. Now, getting to know you will help Tazia make her life whole again." Del added with a gentle smile, "You have the loveliest granddaughter in the world."

Her tears fell unheeded now as she smiled a tremulous smile. "Thank you, Señor LaCroix. That means a great deal to me."

"I thought it might, Señora de Montega. I want to apologize very deeply for the things that were in my mind when I entered this room. As you said, I formed my opinions before I knew all the facts. We have all been very unjust to you. You deserve some happiness after what you have been through."

"Thank you again for your kindness."

Suddenly an idea occurred to him, his ever-present sense of humor rearing its head. "Could I ask you for a great favor?"

"But of course."

"Cristina Reyes and I are to be married here as Casa del Sol soon. Wouldn't it be a wonderful surprise for Tazia if you were to appear at the wedding?"

"You are a romantic, Señor LaCroix." She laughed.

"Incurably," he chuckled.

"Will the wedding be soon? I would love to see my granddaughter."

"Believe me, it cannot be soon enough for me. I would be happy if it were tomorrow, but we have to wait a short while until Tazia is well. Do we have a bargain?"

"Yes. I'm sure after all this time I can keep my silence for a few weeks longer."

"Good. Now I'm going to find Marguerite. Maybe one night soon, she can smuggle the baby into your room."

"That would be wonderful. Now that everything is settled to your satisfaction, Señor LaCroix," she said, "will you tell me about yourself and your brother? Also about that very handsome young friend of yours and his wife — and especially about my daughter's stay in New Orleans and her marriage. I have missed so much."

"First," he began, "we start with you calling me by my first name, which is Del." He relaxed in his chair with a broad smile. First he told her about Tazia's arrival in New Orleans and how they had first seen her dancing.

"She always danced so beautifully," she whispered.

"Yes, I agree." Del told her then about Louis being smuggled out of New Orleans and his subsequent meeting with Gabrielle Saint-Albin. Finally he related the details about Tazia and Kirk's marriage and how Garrett had spoiled everything.

She sat very still, absorbing every detail of his story, occasionally asking a question or two, but for the most part listening intently. Del went on to tell her about Tazia's flight, how Kirk had followed her, and the continued battle between them until the birth of their daughter helped heal many of the wounds.

"My poor child. All the suffering she has been through because of one man who was not worth the lifting of her finger."

"She still does not know about her brother. If there were some way the truth could come out, it would be wonderful for both of them," he said hopefully.

"Are you suggesting I tell her?" She smiled.

"If you wish. I don't want to cause *you* any more grief either."

"Why don't we just watch how things go between Kirk and Tazia. Rest assured, if I see that it is necessary for my daughter's happiness to speak, speak I will."

"Thank you. That is a very great relief. Now I'd best be going before someone wonders where I am. It has been a great pleasure meeting you Señora de Montega, and again I want to apologize for my evil thoughts. You are one of the most beautiful ladies I have ever met, and I consider it an honor to know you."

"After meeting you and learning what kind of man your brother is, I am looking forward to the happiness that will soon exist here. Here, in a place that has known so little happiness. Make your wedding soon, Del. I want to join my family again."

"It will be soon, I promise," he said as he rose and walked to the door. He opened it just a crack and looked around. No one was in the hall. He smiled over his shoulder.

"Good-by for now."

"Good-by, Del."

He closed the door softly behind him and went downstairs. Leaving the house, he found Louis still waiting at the stable for him.

"Where have you been?"

Del laughed happily. "Preparing the greatest wedding present in existence." Louis looked at him questioningly.

"Not now, Louis, but you'll find out soon. Very, very soon."

To Louis's annoyance, Del was still grinning to himself as they rode out through the gates of Casa del Sol.

43

Mercy was the catalyst that drew Tazia and Kirk to one another and closed the link to make them one. No matter what else Kirk was involved in, when the child was brought to Tazia, he seemed to be there, enjoying his tiny daughter. Tazia found herself waiting expectantly for him and enjoying the quiet moments the three of them spent together. Within a week she was well enough to rise for a few hours a day, but this time Kirk supervised her strictly. He would not let her tire herself. With this kind of treatment and the affectionate care of everyone else in the house, it was not long before Raf claimed that she was completely well. Upon this pronouncement, Tazia, Gabrielle, and Cristina began plans for the wedding with Marguerite. No one but Del knew how difficult it was for him to keep the secret about Tazia's mother, when everyone was bubbling over with contentment. Several times he and Marguerite, who had been pleased to join forces with him, had smuggled Mercy out of the nursery and into Tazia's mother's room. It had helped her wait out the long hours left until the day of the wedding.

Del was having an extremely difficult time for another reason. Watching Louis and Gabrielle in their love for one another had been hard, but now Kirk and Tazia seemed to find each other again. Del spent many miserable hours in their presence until he thought he could stand it no longer.

A week before the wedding, Del found Cristina on the patio with Tazia and Marguerite, deep in discussion about some last-minute wedding plans. He had not seen her alone for almost a month. They had not even shared a quick kiss for days, and he had decided that enough was enough.

"Good afternoon," he said with a bright smile, his eyes intent on Cristina. "What are you lovely ladies discussing so seriously this afternoon?"

"Flowers," Tazia answered quickly. She subdued her amusement at the warmth of the gaze that passed between Del and Cristina. "But I really think," she said innocently, "that it's a decision the two of you should make." She let her eyes rest on Del with an unspoken message deep within them. "Why don't you take Cristina for a ride? Marguerite could pack you a small lunch, and you could discuss . . . flowers or anything else about your wedding you care to discuss."

"Wonderful idea," he said enthusiastically, and before Cristina could say a word, he took her hand and pulled her to her feet. He smiled down at Tazia, then bent to kiss her cheek. As he did, he whispered softly, "Thanks, Tazia, I'll repay this act of kindness sooner than you think."

Her bubbling laughter followed them as they left.

Tazia was still smiling to herself when Kirk came to the doorway. He watched her for a while, enjoying her beauty. Then he walked toward her. It made his heart leap when he saw the look of pleasure that came over her face as she saw him approaching. She stretched out her hand, and he took it in his. Slowly he pulled her to her feet and into his arms. His head bent to claim her lips. She offered no resistance. Her arms came up around his neck, and he could feel the long lines of her body pressed against him without restraint. Since the birth of their daughter, Kirk had occupied another bedroom. As yet, Tazia had not invited him back to hers, and he had hesitated to try for fear she was not well enough or, worse, that she would not accept him. Now, as his lips reluctantly left hers, she murmured in Spanish.

"Oh damn, Tazia, we've really got to start some kind of language lessons. That sounded like something I've been dying to hear, and I can't stand the idea of missing an invitation just because I don't speak Spanish."

She laughed and tightened her arms about his neck and again said to him in Spanish, *"Mi amore, te amo. Mi precioso, ahora y siempre."*

"If you keep doing that, I'll just have to use my imagination and take advantage of our lack of communication."

Her eyes widened and softened a little. Her face grew serious as she reached up and slowly pulled his face down to meet her parted lips, soft and seeking.

"Ummm, that did it lady," he said softly, and he put his arm about her waist and walked slowly toward the patio steps that led to their room.

Del and Cristina rode out through the gates of Casa del Sol. The day shone with brilliant sunlight. As they rode along together, Del searched for a place he knew, away from the main trail about a half mile, where there stood a grove of trees on the banks of a small tributary to the San Luis Rey River. It was a cool, shady spot, perfect for a secluded picnic. When they arrived, Del helped Cristina down from her

371

horse, taking the opportunity to kiss her several times in the process. Her eyes shone with bright laughter as she spread their blanket and opened the basket Marguerite had packed for them. As they ate, they shared their laughter and their plans for the future. After the meal, Del lay back on the blanket, his hands behind his head, and watched as she packed the remains of their lunch back in the basket. Then she knelt by his side and smiled down at him.

"Are you happy?"

He smiled in response and raised his hand to brush some breeze-blown strands of hair from her face. She tipped her head a little to the side, questioning his silence.

"You know the greatest thing in my life was when I decided to stay out here. Cristina, I'll do everything I can to make you happy."

"Oh, Del," she murmured, "I *am* happy. When we get married next week, I'll be the happiest woman in the Pauma Valley."

"Do me a favor?"

"What?"

"Unpin your hair. I want to see you with it down."

Without a word, she lifted her arms and slowly began to remove the pins in her hair. It fell about her in a burnished-gold cascade. She shook her head and let it flow across her shoulders. Del took the strands of her hair in his hands and drew her closer to him. He brushed her lips with a gentle kiss and pulled her into his arms. He knew without asking that no matter how much she wanted to wait until after their wedding, she would surrender to him now if he wanted her to. The knowledge of this was the only thing that stopped him from taking her. He began to chuckle softly.

"What are you laughing about?"

"Did you do that deliberately?"

"Do what?"

"You know what," he laughed. "What if I called your bluff and tried to make love to you anyway? What would you do then?"

"What do you think?"

"I don't really know." He looked at her with real surprise. "Damn, I don't really know."

"Why, Mr. LaCroix. I'll bet this is the first time you've not gotten what you want. I think you're a little spoiled."

"Oh, you wait until we're married, lady. You'll not be so sassy. There'll be nothing to protect you then."

"What's protecting me now?" Her eyes gleamed and crinkled at the corners with laughter.

"I don't believe this, but I guess I am spoiled. Cristina, I want everything perfect between us. I'll wait, but not very patiently. Cristina?"

"Yes?"

"Don't give me too many opportunities like this one. If you do . . . well, I'm not Sir Galahad. I'll take advantage of them."

"Thank you, Del. We'll be married in a week, and it will be perfect, Del, simply because, in my eyes, *you* are perfect, and whether you believe it or not, I don't think you would take advantage. Before we leave here, I want to say one more thing."

"And what's that?"

She kissed him and rose quickly to her feet. "You wouldn't have been taking advantage; I would have given you anything you wanted if you had continued."

He sat up and watched her walk back to her horse, swinging her hips and laughing back over her shoulder. Then he rose quickly to his feet and followed her. They rode slowly back to Casa del Sol, happy and expectant of the future.

The seven days before the wedding were the longest days Del had ever spent. The day before the wedding, guests and gifts began to arrive, and the hacienda was thrown into an uproar. Del slipped away for an hour to Anna de Montega's room to make some plans with her. Then, suddenly, it was the night before the wedding. Del and Cristina walked together in the garden for a few minutes before going to bed. Both of them were silent, but they were content just to be together.

"Del?"

"Yes."

"Can you tell me yet?"

"Tell you? Tell you what?"

"Whatever it is you and Marguerite have up your sleeves."

He stopped and put his arms about her waist and drew her against him. "Do you know *every* thought in my head? I thought I was being very clever."

"You *are* very clever," she said brightly, "and yes, I know every thought in your head, since they're usually directed at me. That's my job, isn't it?"

"I have a big surprise for tomorrow. Let me keep it until then, all right? I promise it's the last secret I will ever keep from you."

"Very good. Until tomorrow. Then we'll be one person. Oh, Del, I want you to know I love you so very much."

"I know," he whispered as his lips found hers. He was just beginning to get involved in the kiss when an amused voice from the doorway interrupted.

"Practicing?" Louis stood smiling at them as they reluctantly drew apart. "Cristina, your father is preparing to leave. He asked me to see if you were ready."

"Yes, I am." She turned to Del. "Until tomorrow," she said softly.

374

"Until tomorrow," he answered. He watched her as she passed Louis and went inside.

"She's a lovely lady, Del. You're a very lucky man."

"I know."

"I've just been up to see our goddaughter. She grows prettier every day."

"I'm grateful for what she's done for Kirk and Tazia. I have never seen them as in love, even after they were first married in New Orleans."

"Well, I think Tazia has just discovered what kind of a person Kirk really is. The way he reacted when she needed him showed her just how much he loved her. I think that is when she fully realized she loved him, too."

The two men strolled through the garden for a few minutes in silence. Louis noticed that there were deep frown lines between Del's eyes.

"What's wrong, Del? You should be a very happy man tonight."

Del shrugged his shoulders. "I don't know. I just have this feeling. . . ."

"What kind of feeling?"

"You'll think I'm crazy, but I have this feeling that Cristina and I shouldn't leave right away on our honeymoon. I think something's about to happen, and I don't know what it is." He laughed uneasily. "I told you you'd think I was crazy."

"No, I don't think you're crazy. Knowing all the things that have happened to us in the past year, I wouldn't be surprised at anything. Just what do you think could happen?"

"That's just it. I can't put my finger on any particular thing. It's just this feeling I've got. Louis, keep a close eye on things until we get back. Kirk and Tazia are so involved with Mercy and Casa del Sol they could be taken by surprise very easily."

"Surprise? By what or whom?"

"Garrett Flye."

"Del! It's been months. Garrett has probably given up. There have been too many of us here for him to do any harm. He's probably back in New Orleans, involved in another card game, and he's completely forgotten about us."

Del turned to face Louis; his eyes showed no sign of humor.

"You and I both know that's not Garrett's way. No, he's still around, and sure as hell he's got some kind of plan that involves my brother and Tazia. He hates too strongly to give up easily. I don't know what he could do, but knowing him, he'll do something to get Kirk or . . . to get Tazia. And I don't know which would be worse. If anything happened to either Tazia or the baby, it would be very effective revenge on Kirk, don't you think?"

"God, Del. What man in his right mind would harm a child like Mercy?"

"Who," he said softly, "ever said we were dealing with a man in his right mind?"

Louis gave serious thought to what Del had said. He thought back and realized that Del was probably right. Garrett had always been a cold, hard man.

"What can we do?"

"Unless we know when the danger is coming, there's nothing we can do but wait. I just hope nothing happens until I get back." Del added in a low voice, "But mark my word, it's going to happen. There's a lot at stake for Garrett, and he always was a big gambler. Look at what he has to gain: Casa del Sol, the palominos, Tazia, and probably Kirk's death."

"After Gabrielle's story, I believe he's capable of anything. Rest assured I'll keep my eyes and ears open while you and Cristina are gone. When you get back, we'll form a barrier Garrett will never get through. Remember, we have Juan and Raf, too. Raf has no love for Garrett, because of what happened to Gabrielle at Five Points. I'll alert them both. Don't worry, enjoy your honeymoon. We'll watch over Casa del Sol until you get back."

Del nodded agreement, but his mind could not shake off the idea that something dreadful was about to happen to the people he cared most deeply about, and he was helpless to do anything to stop it.

Night settled on Casa del Sol, but it found many of the inhabitants unable to sleep. Kirk lay very still and listened to Tazia's steady breathing as she slept next to him. He felt confident of the future now. He pulled Tazia a little closer and smiled to himself. Tomorrow, Del and Cristina would be married. It would be a happy affair, and they would find land close by and build their new lives. He felt good about the situation between him and Tazia, and he absolutely adored his daughter. All would be well, he thought.

In another room, Anna de Montega lay sleepless. Tomorrow, she would be reunited with the daughter she had loved from a distance for so many years. Her mind drifted back over old memories of times when she had so desperately wanted to be close to her beautiful daughter. She prayed that after the wedding all their lives would be joined in happiness.

Louis and Gabrielle talked in quiet whispers of things Del feared, and Gabrielle agreed that the possibility of something happening was great.

It was Del who remained awake long after every one else slept. He could not shake the feeling that something dark hovered over them and was about to cause some problem. He wanted his wedding to

Cristina to be perfect for her sake, and he wanted them to enjoy the honeymoon they had planned for weeks, but he still felt the urgent desire to ask her to stay at Casa del Sol for a while until this feeling was dispelled, or until they could find where Garrett was. If he was still in New Orleans, that would be another matter, but when Jean's ship had delivered Gabrielle and Raf, Raf had told him that Jean had searched for Garrett in New Orleans, but he had been gone for weeks. That meant one thing to Del. Garrett was somewhere here in California, and if he was, that meant only trouble for Kirk and Tazia. He thought of Mercy, too, who owned the hearts of everyone in the house. He wondered if even Garrett's dark heart could harm a child like her. It was almost dawn when he finally drifted off to sleep.

Several miles away, in a small hotel room, another man lay sleepless. His face was shadowed as he lay deep in thought. His plans for the residents of Casa del Sol were almost complete. Soon, he thought, very soon, Kirk LaCroix, you will regret crossing me. You will regret taking the woman I want. I shall take from you everything you have gotten. Casa del Sol will be mine, along with the palominos, Tazia, and, my friend, your daughter. Soon, Kirk . . . very, very soon.

44

The chapel at Casa del Sol had been chosen for the wedding ceremony. Its dark wood beams and white ceiling were lovely. Candlelight was reflected from the dark oak altar and the rows of pews. The top of the altar had been covered with a white lace cloth, and the gold chalice reflected the glow of the candles. White flowers were piled in abundance on the two steps that led to the altar. The aisle down which Cristina would walk had been covered with a deep-red carpet.

Del was standing before his mirror, putting the finishing touches on his clothing, when he heard the chapel bells begin to ring with a soft, mellow tone. He wondered whether Cristina could hear them, too. His hand shook a little as he realized that the bells were calling both to him and to Cristina. In two hours, she would be his wife. He turned from the mirror just as the door opened and Kirk and Louis walked in.

"We've come to escort you." Louis grinned and said, "Just in case you lose your nerve, we're here to see that you get to the chapel on time."

"Lose my nerve!" Del laughed. "Have you two been

blind all this time, or don't you remember what Cristina looks like? No man in his right mind would lose his nerve with a prize like that waiting for him."

"Well, it's time," Kirk replied. "Are you ready?"

"As ready as I'll ever be, but you two will have to go on alone," Del said calmly.

"Alone?" Louis asked.

"Alone?" Kirk echoed, mystified.

"Alone," Del said firmly. "I'm coming down by myself. I have something to do before the ceremony, and it's to stay a secret until the last second. So, Louis, I want you and Gabrielle seated along with Kirk and Tazia and the rest of the family. My surprise is going to shock you all so much you'll have to be sitting down at the time."

"What is it?" Kirk asked. "Come on, Del, you can tell us. We won't breathe a word to anyone."

"Nope. I want you both beside your wives when I spring it. It's going to make the day even happier. So just get going, you two. The longer you wait, the longer it will be before you know what it is."

Kirk sighed. "Come on, Louis. I know my stubborn brother too well. We might as well do as he says. It's the only way we'll ever learn what it is."

Del stood in the open doorway and watched his brother and Louis disappear down the stairs. Then he turned and walked down the hall to Anna de Montega's room. He knocked on her door, keeping one eye on the hall so no one would see him. It was the first time he had seen her out of her bed. He could see immediately that she was frightened, although she stood very erect and smiled at him. He stepped inside and closed the door. He wanted to reassure her if he could.

"Are you ready, Señora de Montega?"

"Del, are you sure we're doing the right thing?"

"What are you afraid of?"

"What if . . . what if Tazia rejects me? After all these years and all the times that I was forced to reject *her*."

He smiled reassuringly and put his hands on her shoulders. "There is only one way to discover what will happen, and that is to go down and find out. But I have enough faith for both of us that not only will she not reject you, she will be tremendously happy to have you back again."

"Do you really think so?" she asked hopefully.

"I know so," he replied. Then he laughed. "And I don't want to hold up my wedding one minute longer. So, madam . . ." He bent his elbow and gestured toward the door with his other hand. "Shall we go?"

She tilted her chin in a way that reminded him of her daughter and tucked her hand under his arm.

"I'm ready." She smiled up at him as they left the room together and started down the stairs to the chapel. As they approached the chapel, Del could feel her hesitate for a moment. The soft sound of music could be heard as she turned to look at him. He gave her a smile and squeezed her hand reassuringly. Then he reached out and pushed open the double doors that led to the chapel.

All the guests had been seated, with the exception of Kirk, who stood, as Del's best man, at the altar. Tazia sat beside Louis and Gabrielle. Next to them sat Don Manuel. In the seats behind them sat Marguerite, Raf, and Juan. And behind them sat the rest of the guests. All eyes turned toward the open door in surprise, for the bride was not expected until after the groom had arrived.

There was a gasp of shock as Del, smiling, came down the aisle with Anna de Montega, whose eyes sought out Tazia's in the crowd. Slowly Tazia rose to her feet. Her eyes were wide with surprise, and she was too stunned to move. Anna had almost reached her side before Tazia fully realized what was happening. She stepped out into the aisle to face the mother she had never known, her face a mirror of the dozens of questions she wanted to ask. They looked at each other in silence. Then Anna held out her arms to her daughter.

"My child," she said softly. Her eyes sought an answer in Tazia's face. She was rewarded by the tears that fell down Tazia's cheeks as she threw herself into her mother's arms. Sobs of happiness were mixed with soft Spanish words as Tazia received the love she had sought in vain so many years. This was one time Kirk felt he did not have to understand the language. What he saw spoke with an eloquence that needed no translation.

Del grinned broadly, very pleased with the results of his surprise. "Ladies," he said laughingly, "I hate to interrupt something I've taken so much care to accomplish, but I would like to get on with my wedding. Afterward, we can all celebrate together."

Still clinging to one another, Tazia and her mother returned to the pew. Kirk's eyes caught Tazia's as she turned to face the altar, and he could see there the final happiness that would make their lives complete. He smiled, and the warm smile she gave in return made him exuberantly happy.

Del joined Kirk at the altar, and Kirk whispered softly to him, "I won't ask you how you accomplished this. Just know that you have my eternal thanks."

"I know," Del grinned, "and I've already made plans for the reward I'm going to receive."

"Reward?"

"Uh-huh. Just wait until after the honeymoon,

brother. You're going to repay me very well for my contribution to your happiness."

Kirk chuckled. "I'd give you just about anything you ask for, but I think your greatest reward is coming now." Del turned slightly to face the chapel doors. His soft intake of breath elicited a smothered laugh from Kirk.

Cristina, her arm tucked under Don Federico's arm, walked slowly down the aisle. She had chosen a simple gown. Its neckline was high, and the sleeves were long and tightly fitted about her slender arms. The bodice was also tightly fitted, revealing her exquisite figure. The dress was made of ivory-colored silk. From her shoulder to her waist, it was completely unadorned, except for a small cross on a fine chain, which her father had given her as a wedding present. From the waist downward, the dress flowed out in a wide, full skirt that was covered with tiny seed pearls. Her golden hair had been brushed until it shone, then piled on her head in a cluster of curls. Soft wisps of curls framed her face. Cristina wore a lace mantilla that gently framed her radiant face and fell to the floor. In her hand she carried a small bouquet of white flowers. She was so lovely that Del found himself holding his breath as she walked toward him.

Surely he would waken, and this beautiful dream would disappear, he thought. She stopped when they reached the altar, and Don Federico took her hand and placed it in Del's. They stood for a moment, lost in each other. Then they turned and knelt for the blessing of God on their happiness.

Great care had been taken by Tazia and Marguerite to make Del's and Cristina's wedding a happy one. They had been cooking and baking for days and had almost worn out Juan and Raf with the decorating and preparations for the reception. There was much laughter and many toasts to the bride and groom, some serious and some amusingly suggestive. Cristina was swung from partner to partner, but Del did not let her stay away from him too long before his arms were about her again and they danced away from her admirers.

Del and Kirk stood together sipping their drinks. Del's eyes followed his new bride around the floor. As she danced by, she threw him a kiss over her father's shoulder. Kirk spoke, but Del's mind was so intent on Cristina that he did not realize for a moment he was being spoken to.

"Sorry, what did you say?"

"I said, 'Cristina is a lovely bride.' You're a lucky man, Del. I guess we're both lucky."

"I agree. Everything seems almost too good to be true."

Kirk looked intently at his brother. "You, too?"

"What do you mean, *me, too?*"

"I've had the feeling for a while now that something's about to happen that I won't like. It's like a ghost of a memory. You know it's there, but you can't put your finger on it."

"Kirk," Del began, as a frown drew his brows together, "Cristina and I can wait to go on our honeymoon. If you think it would be better, we could stay here at Casa del Sol. I mean . . . just for a while, until everything . . . well, at least until we try to find out just where Garrett is and what's going on."

"No." Kirk laughed shortly. "I appreciate the thought, Del, I really do, but I think we'll be all right. Raf and Juan are here with me. We'll keep our eyes open for any signs. You'll only be gone two weeks. It's been months since we've seen any sign of him. We'll probably be all right for a while longer.

Go and enjoy yourselves. I'm grateful for the thought, though."

Del, grinned again. Then he pulled a watch from his vest pocket and looked at it. "Bet you've been doing that every fifteen minutes," his brother laughed.

"I have, and not very patiently, I assure you, but it's finally time to leave. If I can capture my bride away from this crowd, Juan has the carriage waiting, and we'll be on our way."

Kirk clapped him on the shoulder as he moved toward Cristina. She was laughing at a remark someone had made, and as Del came up beside her and placed his arm about her waist, she looked up at him. Her eyes were glowing with laughter and happiness as she leaned against him and held his arm.

"It's time to leave, my love," he whispered. She nodded and slipped her hand in his, and they walked toward her father to say good-by. Amid the happy laughter, they made their way to the waiting carriage. Within a few minutes they were out of sight.

Del pulled Cristina against him, and she lay her head on his shoulder. They rode along in silence for some time, each content just to be alone together. Then a barely suppressed giggle from Cristina drew Del's amused attention.

"What's so funny?" he asked.

"Do you know, husband of mine," she whispered, "I don't even know where we are bound. You never told me what arrangements you had made."

"I thought," he grinned, "we might just stop in the middle of nowhere and pitch a tent. Would you mind?"

She tilted her head to look up at him. Her eyes were twin mirrors that reflected the love she saw clearly in his eyes. "I would not care where I was, as long as we were together," she answered softly.

Very gently he touched her lips with his, until she stirred in his arms and lifted her hands to his face and pulled his mouth against hers. He could feel the hunger that answered his own, and he tightened his arms about her and took her mouth in a fiery kiss that left her breathless and clinging weakly to him. She would never know the restraint it required for him not to respond to her then and there.

"I've reserved a suite at the hotel for three days; then we leave for Los Angeles. We'll spend a week there and start back."

"Marvelous. I can buy some beautiful clothes and gifts in Los Angeles."

They spent the balance of the ride quietly enjoying the freedom to hold one another and the silence of comfortable closeness.

When their luggage had been carried up to their room and Del had finally closed and locked the door, he turned to Cristina. For a moment, she was frightened, which Del realized in an instant. He slipped out of his jacket and loosened his tie. Then he went to the table that had been set up for them at his order. He poured each of them a drink of champagne and turned back to her with the glasses.

"Let's drink a toast to the luckiest man in the world—me—and to the most beautiful woman—you!" He smiled and lifted his glass to touch hers. "To us."

She sipped obediently.

"No! You have to drink it all for good luck," he said. Again she obeyed. Then he took the glass from her hand and refilled it. She did not seem to notice that he did not refill his own. He began to talk nonchalantly, as though they had spent many nights together.

"You know, Cristina, we've never really told each

other all about ourselves." He smiled as he sat on the couch. "Come, sit with me and tell me all the things I'd like to know." She smiled her gratitude and went to sit beside him.

"Cristina," he said softly as their eyes met. "We have all the time in the world. There's just you and me in the world tonight."

She leaned forward and touched his face gently, and he turned his face until his lips touched the palm of her hand.

"I love you Del. I want to be a good wife to you. Have patience with my silliness."

Del took her in his arms and held her against him. "Cristina, to me you're perfect. It certainly doesn't require any patience to love you. I want you to be as happy as I am." He tilted her chin up with his fingers. "Do you understand, Cristina? There's no hurry. Tonight I'll be content just to have you here, just to know you belong to me."

The words he spoke renewed her faith and love for him. "I'll be right back," she said softly as she rose and turned toward the door that led to the bedroom. Del sat very still for a few minutes. Then he went to the table and poured himself a drink, which he swallowed rapidly. He poured another drink and carried it to the window, where he stood and watched the activities on the street below. His mind drifted over the past year, and he felt a deep sense of contentment at what it had given him. The bright thoughts of his future were marred only by the small, nagging worry in the back of his mind about his brother and the others at Casa del Sol. He loved Cristina too much to do anything to upset her now, but he had a strong desire to pick up their things and head for home as raidly as they could.

Suddenly he became aware that he was looking not

through the window glass, but *at* it. Reflected in the glass, he could see Cristina standing in the doorway of the bedroom. He was unaware that she had been watching him and reading very accurately his unguarded face.

Cristina had brushed her hair, and it hung about her face and shoulders in golden profusion. The gown she wore was emerald-green, and its sheerness hid nothing of the loveliness beneath.

Without saying a word, he walked slowly toward her, until they stood with their bodies almost touching. He gently put his hand through her silken hair. Then he drew her closer to him and touched the corners of her mouth with his lips. A small smile formed on her lips as she took the one last step that brought them together and slid her arms around him. There were no doubts or fears left now. Del murmured her name as his mouth sought hers again and his arms bound her tightly to him.

45

Holding her close, Del felt Cristina's body tremble in his arms. A sudden wave of tenderness overtook him, so he loosened his hold a little but he did not release her. Instead, he began to caress her gently. His lips captured hers again and again in soft, feathery kisses until he felt her lips begin to seek his in longer, more passionate kisses.

Del lifted her gently in his arms and held her close against him. He felt her lips trace a line down the side of his neck as he carried her to the bed. The room was nearly dark, but he could still see her as he laid her against the pillows. Then he quickly removed his clothes and eased down on the bed beside her. He was delighted when she sought him and pulled him closer to her, answering his hungry kisses with a deep fire that surprised him. He murmured her name while his hands moved over her, pushing aside the thin gown that covered her. He kissed her throat and then the soft roundness of her breasts. He heard her gasp and felt her body respond passionately to his touch. His hands and mouth found the places that sent shivers of delight through her. This passion, this deep, burning fire that engulfed her was new to Cristina, and Del could feel her unsureness. He touched his lips against her again.

"I love you, Cristina," he whispered.

Slowly he slid his hands down her body and touched the soft inner flesh of her thighs. He let his hands explore slowly and gently until he found the soft, moist center of her need. Then he pulled her body under him, and catching her mouth against his, he entered her. He could feel her stiffen; he heard the muffled cry she made against his mouth. He lay still within her, waiting for the pain to pass. After a moment, her trembling ceased, and her hands began to caress his back. Then he began to move, slowly at first, feeling her body respond to him. Then, suddenly, it was as though she had turned to liquid fire and he was caught in the flow. Unable to control it any longer, they merged as one and moved together. She clung to him and whispered in his ear as they reached the bright pinnacle together and tumbled over the edge, clinging breathlessly to one another.

It was a long time before Del could get himself to move. As many women as Del had been with, none had affected him like the small, soft creature he now held. He felt a peace and oneness with her like nothing he had ever felt with another. He rolled over on his back and pulled her with him. Her head lay against his chest, and he gently stroked the soft, silky strands of her hair. Her hands crept across his chest, and she pulled herself tighter against him. She lifted her head slowly and kissed his face several times before she spoke.

"You were not disappointed in me, Del? Do you still love me as much?"

"No," he said softly. He chuckled at the startled look in her eyes. "I love you *more*—more than I ever thought I'd love anyone in my life. You are perfect,

390

my darling, and I adore you." To prove his words, he pulled her tight against him and kissed her thoroughly. She sighed contentedly and nestled closer.

"I am so happy you came to Casa del Sol. It would have been terrible if I had missed you in my life. I can't imagine feeling this way with any other."

"Me, too. Coming to California was the best move I've made in a long, long time. You know, it's funny how fate works. Two people, three thousand miles away from each other, yet destined to be together. After having found someone as wonderful as you, it makes me a firm believer in fate."

"No matter what ever happens in our future, I'm content to have known and loved you. Even if we had no more time together."

He tightened his arm about her and kissed her quickly. "We have all the rest of our lives together, and I intend to live to be a hundred and love you every day."

Cristina shivered, as though she were cold, and clung tightly to him. "I love you, Del. More than my own life." Del pulled her under him and kissed her until she warmed and her mouth sought his in a renewal of their passion.

The three days they spent in Escondido were happy for both of them. They looked forward to their trip to Los Angeles. Still Del could not shake the feeling of approaching trouble. Often, after Cristina was asleep, he would remain awake, worrying about what could happen.

The night before they were to leave, he could not shake off the feeling any longer. He was so nervous that he rose quietly from their bed and stood by the window, looking out on the deserted town. He looked, but he did not see. Instead, his thoughts turned inward to touch again on that strange feeling of impending disaster. He was so engrossed in his thoughts that he did not hear Cristina rise from the bed and cross the room. She stood behind him and slid her arms around him, resting her cheek against the center of his back.

"What's wrong, my darling? Can you tell me?"

For a moment he was silent. There was no way to put his thoughts into words.

"I don't mean to interfere," she said softly, "but I cannot bear to see you as troubled as you have been since we left Casa del Sol. I want to do something to help, if I can. Won't you tell me what is bothering you, my love?"

He turned and took her into his arms. "I wish I knew, Cristina. I just wish I knew." He went on to explain his uncertain feelings. She listened without interrupting.

When he had finished, she said, "Then we'll go back to Casa del Sol instead of on to Los Angeles."

"But—"

"No, it's simple. We will return and stay there until you are sure in your mind that everything is well. We have a whole lifetime together, my dear. We can take many trips. I want you happy, and I want your undivided attention."

He chuckled. "You really don't mind going back now?"

"Not one bit."

"You're wonderful . . . and very understanding," he replied.

"You're easy to understand."

"Oh?" he said, lifting an eyebrow in question.

"Certainly. You love completely, both your brother and me. You can't bear for either of us to have any problems. I wouldn't want you any other way. As I said, we'll go back, and when your mind is at ease about Kirk, then you can give me your undivided attention."

He laughed and rocked her tightly in his arms.

"We'll go back in the morning," he said as his mouth captured hers, "because tonight, lady, you have my undivided attention."

He heard the muffled sound of her laughter against his shoulder as he lifted her and carried her back to the bed.

The next morning, Del made arrangements to leave, and within two hours, they were on their way back to Casa del Sol.

They arrived just before it was time to retire for the night. Both Kirk and Tazia were surprised to hear the approaching carriage. They were even more surprised to find out who its occupants were.

Kirk did not have to question Del about the reason for their return. He knew. He smiled at his brother who grinned rather sheepishly in return.

"Still taking care of me, big brother?" Kirk asked in amusement.

"Not really, Kirk. I just . . . ." He shrugged.

"No need to explain. I know how you feel, and I appreciate it."

He turned to Cristina. "I appreciate the sacrifice you've made, too."

Cristina smiled and held Del's arm as she looked up at him. "It is no sacrifice to see your husband contented."

"Are you hungry?" Tazia asked.

"I could eat a horse," Del replied with a laugh.

"Come, we won't wake Marguerite. We can all go to the kitchen, and I'll prepare something for you to eat."

As they turned to go to the kitchen, Louis and Gabrielle came to the top of the stairs. "I thought I heard a carriage." He smiled brightly at Cristina. "I was afraid you might change your mind about staying married to him, Cristina, but I didn't think it would be so soon."

They all laughed together as they made their way toward the kitchen. Tazia placed bread, cheese, and some meat left from dinner on the table. She brought out six glasses and poured each of them a glass of wine. The conversation was warm and filled with laughter while they all sat and ate at the table.

"Well, as you can see, Del," Kirk said, "everything is fine here. There have been no problems. I think we've all been alarmed for nothing. We've been waiting around afraid of someone who, in all probability, has forgotten we're alive."

"Well, Cristina and I have decided to postpone our trip until sometime in November. The work here will then be finished for the year, and we can be back before Christmas."

"Good. You two can help us get our new home started. I have to ride out tomorrow and look at a piece of land I'm thinking of buying. If it's as good as I think it is, Gabrielle and I are going to start building soon. We should have the house up and be able to throw a party before you leave," Louis said. "With the colt Don Federico has promised us, we're going to start our own *rancho.*"

"Come to think of it, brother," Del said with a grin, "I believe you still owe me a small debt, which I'm about to collect."

"Name it. If it's in my power, it's yours." Kirk smiled.

"Well," Del said as he reached over and took Cristina's hand, "between Don Federico's land and yours, is there a piece of land neither of you wants to use? If so, I'd like to build there. That way, Cristina can be close to her family."

Kirk threw a questioning look at Tazia, who smiled and nodded her head.

"It's yours."

"Great! When Christmas is over and Cristina and I are back, we'll look into building."

"Why wait?" Kirk asked happily. "Why not build now? When your come back, it could be to your own home. We'll fill up the valley with LaCroixs, big and little."

They all laughed with enthusiasm about the adventure of beginning a new home.

Del reached out and took Tazia's hand. "We owe you a great deal. Your coming to New Orleans was the best thing that ever happened in the lives of the LaCroix men. Now, thanks to you, Cristina and I will have a new home. I'm grateful to you, sister."

"You've given me a great deal in return." She smiled. "Casa del Sol has never been as happy as it is now. You've given me back the mother I never had, and now I have Mercy to love, also. Now that we're all together, we can put all memories where they belong. From tonight on, we'll make this the happy home it should have been from the first."

The meal then became a laughing celebration, and it was several hours before they sought their beds.

When Kirk had closed the door to their bedroom, he and Tazia didn't begin to undress immediately. Kirk watched her as she moved about the room, slowly removing her clothes and brushing out her hair.

When Tazia was ready for bed, she looked at Kirk and discovered with surprise that he had been watching her quietly. "What is it, my love?" she questioned.

He walked across the room and took her in his arms. He kissed her long and lingeringly until her senses began to swim. When he finally released her lips, he held her against him and spoke softly into her scented hair.

"Tazia, do you know what day this is?"

"Day? No, what day is it?"

"Well, if my calculations are correct, it's been six months today since we made our agreement."

"Oh, Kirk."

"I don't ever want to leave you, Tazia. I love you more than my own life, but it is *you* who must say to *me*, 'Stay, Kirk, for I love you, too.'"

As she looked up into his eyes, she knew with finality that she *did* love him more than anything in the world. She placed one hand on the side of his face. There were tears in her eyes. Not tears of pain, but of happiness. There was no room in her heart for both hatred and love. Love had won the battle, and hatred was banished forever. Slowly she moved her hand up until her fingers were woven in his thick hair. Then she drew his head down until their lips met again.

"Stay, Kirk, for it is *you* I love. Now and forever," she whispered.

With a sound of deepest pleasure, he lifted her in his arms and held her.

Happiness found the inhabitants of Casa del

Sol. This was the beginning of what they thought was a peaceful, loving future. But the hand of fate was not being taken into consideration. It was about to strike again, and this time it would almost devastate the lives at Casa del Sol. It would strike at the one person no one would expect and leave broken hearts in its wake.

46

Louis and Del built houses similar to Casa del Sol. Don Federico gave Louis the colt he had promised. Mercy learned to sit up and then to creep. She was just beginning to attempt her first steps, with the hearty encouragement of her father and her two god-fathers, who thought nothing of sitting on the floor in front of the fireplace after dinner, passing the delighted child between them. She had possession of the hearts of the three men and took complete advantage of them.

It was the evening before Del and Louis were to begin moving, the last night they would all spend together at Casa del Sol. They were seated comfortably, sipping wine. Mercy had fallen asleep in her father's lap, and he was not ready to release her and let her be carried up to bed. He caressed her hair as she slept. There was a silence in the room that was utterly peaceful.

Cristina sat on the floor in front of the fireplace with her head against Del's knee. Louis and Gabrielle sat together on the couch, while Tazia sat on a small stool in front of the fireplace, strumming a guitar. She began to sing, almost in a whisper, the words to a love song she remembered from her childhood:

My love is like the night wind,
Touching, with the warmth of his caress,
The strings of my heart.
It makes them sing.

My love is like the morning sky,
Touching, with the warmth of his kiss,
The depths of my soul.
It makes it sing.

My love is like the brilliant sun,
Touching, with the light of his desire,
The center of my being.
It makes it sing.

Together our song will reach the heights,
and we will sing.

The emotions of the song touched all three of the men. Tazia put the guitar aside and rose to walk to Kirk's side.

"Shall we put her to bed, *querido?*" she asked softly.

He nodded. Holding Mercy close, so as not to disturb her sleep, he rose slowly from the chair and carried her upstairs.

Louis and Gabrielle also rose and said a quiet good night.

Del and Cristina sat in silence. She soon drifted into a light sleep. Del did not disturb her, for he was content to sit and look at the fire, imagining how good it would be the following night, when they were in their own home. He had enjoyed every moment of the past few weeks—the building of the house, helping Cristina pick and arrange the furniture, and most of all, their times together, when he had made love to her or had just found a quiet moment to hold her close and tell her how much he loved her. He let his hand drift over her hair to her soft cheek, and with gentle fingers, he caressed the side of her face.

God, how much I love her, he thought. She had become the center around which his whole world revolved. He did not know how long they had been sitting when Cristina suddenly sat bolt upright with a cry that sounded as though she were terrified.

"Cristina! What's wrong?"

She looked at him with wide, frightened eyes. Then she threw herself into his arms. "Oh, Del. Hold me! Don't ever let me go."

He held her against him and caressed her hair.

"Did you have a bad dream?"

"Yes. Oh, it was horrible."

He kissed her and held her tightly. He was amazed at the way she clung to him. She was really terrified. "Cristina, tell me about it. We'll chase away the goblins by laughing together. Tell me what you dreamed."

She was kneeling between his legs, and she looked up into his eyes for a long moment. Then she put both arms about his neck. "It's all right, Del. It's gone, and I don't really remember much of it."

She smiled, and he kissed her again gently. He hugged her, and as he did so, he realized that she was trembling violently. She was still afraid. He held her tight, confident that he could make any bad dreams disappear.

Cristina closed her eyes and lay her head against his chest. She wanted to hear the strong beat of his heart, to feel the strength of his love, for she had dreamed of death. Violent death. The fear that held her was that she had always had a dream before something tragic happened to her family or to someone she loved—and it had always come true. No matter how she tried, she could not erase the fact of the past dreams; nor could she remember who had died in her dreams.

Slowly she lifted her head and drew his lips to hers. She let herself be immersed in his kiss so she could push the evil to the back of her mind. Finally, as Del lifted her and carried her to their room, she let it fade away completely.

Evening faded into dark night. Casa del Sol was bathed in white moonlight, creating many shadows along its walls. It was from these shadows that four forms moved slowly and stealthily toward the house. They found their way to the window they sought. Without speaking, one of the men made a cup of his hands, and another used it as a foothold to be hoisted to his shoulders. From there, he was able to reach the low-hanging roof. In seconds, he was up on the roof. Then he took a large coil of rope from his shoulder. He dropped one end over the edge and made the other end fast by looping it about his waist. He braced himself to let the second man climb up. Soon all four men were on the roof. They moved soundlessly to the window and very gently pushed it open. The room was dark. They did not speak. One of the men went to the cradle in which Mercy lay asleep. Another went to the door that joined a second room. He made a small sound against the door several times until he heard movement inside.

Marguerite slept in the room next to Mercy. She was a light sleeper, and her ear was always tuned to sound from Mercy's room. The small tapping sound from Mercy's room puzzled her, and she wondered with a smile just what the child was up to. Mercy seemed to have inherited Del's delightful sense of humor, and she looked for deviltry to get into.

Marguerite rose, slipped on her robe and slippers, and went to the door. She went inside Mercy's room and looked toward the cradle. She was surprised to see no movement there. She was puzzled. Where had the noise come from? She took another step. Suddenly a rough hand was clamped over her mouth, and a strong arm about her waist lifted her from the floor. She struggled furiously, afraid more for Mercy than for herself. It did no good. She was not strong enough to fight off the man who held her. He was joined by another, who quickly gagged her and tied her hands behind her. Then he tossed her over his shoulder, as though she weighed nothing, and carried her out the window and over to the edge of the roof. One of the other men went rapidly down the rope ahead of her captor, who pulled the rope back up, tied it about her waist, and lowered her. The others followed. Marguerite was terrified to see that one of the men carried Mercy as he came down the rope. They made their way to the wall surrounding the hacienda, then over the top to the other side, where the horses were tied. Marguerite was relieved when she was put atop a horse and Mercy was thrust into her arms. She held the child close to her while one of the men mounted behind her. They were soon riding rapidly away from Casa del Sol.

Marguerite did not know how long they rode, but the sky was beginning to streak with the first gray light of dawn when they stopped to rest the horses. It was a very short stop, giving Marguerite only a few minutes to tend to Mercy, before they were forced up on the horses again and they resumed their flight. She asked questions but none of the men would answer her. She tried showing her anger by demanding that they return to Casa del Sol, but this was answered with a blow that nearly knocked her off the horse. She said no more, but she held Mercy close to her, afraid of what they might do to the child. They traveled until noon, when they stopped again for a short, silent meal. Marguerite was given food for Mercy, who, after she ate, curled up against Marguerite's breast and went peacefully to sleep, secure in the familiar arms of her nurse.

It was just turning dusk when they stopped again. They spread blankets on the ground around a fire and prepared food. It was obvious to Marguerite that they intended to spend the night here. After she fed Mercy, she held her close and sang to her until she slept. She placed the baby on the blanket and covered her. Then she moved toward the fire, knelt beside it, and pulled a blanket close about her shoulders. She contemplated the position they were in and the man she knew was behind it. She wondered how long it would be before Garrett Flye made his presence known.

She watched the fire burn low. One of the men silently exchanged places with another to keep guard over them. She would protect Mercy with her life, if necessary. She knew it was no use trying to communicate with her captors. She would wait patiently and watch. If any means of escape presented itself, she would seize it. It pained her to think what Tazia and Kirk were going through at this moment.

They started out at dawn and rode for the entire day. It was well past dark when they arrived at a small cluster of houses, which were all dark with one exception. In front of this house, they dismounted and took Marguerite and the baby inside. Marguerite, clutching Mercy to her, stood facing a man with his back to her. She knew who it was, who

403

it *had* to be. Slowly he turned around and looked at her. It was he, she thought, as his hard, cold gaze fell upon her. From Tazia's description of Garrett Flye, it could be no one else. She squared her shoulders and returned his gaze without showing the fear she felt.

"Release us, Señor Flye, or Kirk LaCroix will surely kill you for taking his child."

"Well," he said, chuckling, "I see you know who I am."

"But, of course," she replied. "Tazia has described you to me."

"Ah, Tazia. And how is she?"

"I'm sure at the moment she is frightened and furious. She will know without doubt who is responsible for this evil thing. Return the child to her parents, I beg you, Señor. She has done you no harm. Attack those who are able to defend themselves, not an innocent baby."

His eyes turned so cold and evil that she took a step backward and clutched Mercy tightly, causing her to cry out. She began to wriggle in Marguerite's arms and cry in confusion as Marguerite struggled to hold her.

"I do not care about this child. Keep her quiet and out of my way. She is merely a tool to get at LaCroix —and a very effective tool, I should think, if he cares as much for her as you say."

"Oh, he cares for her a great deal, Señor. I should imagine there are search parties out looking for her at this moment. If you let us go free now, we will go back to Casa del Sol and maybe Kirk LaCroix will spare your life."

He threw back his head and roared with laughter. In the depths of her heart, she realized that this man was insane. For the first time, real terror struck her. He would stop at nothing to get at Kirk . . . nothing

. . . not even the death of his child.

Garrett moved close to Marguerite. His piercing, cold eyes mesmerized her.

"Spare my life! Kirk LaCroix will be groveling in a few days. Kirk, his brother, and Louis Plummer—I have plans for all of them. Spare my life! They will be begging me to spare theirs, but I shall not. No. The men shall die. As for the women, Cristina Reyes and Gabrielle Saint-Albin, I have other plans for them. They will be taken to the vilest, filthiest brothel along the border. In time, they will wish they were dead. As for Tazia . . . she will warm my bed for as long as I desire her. Then . . . who knows? If she begs hard enough, I might return her daughter to her. Or maybe I'll have her raised by some friends who train young girls in . . . shall I say . . . erotic entertainment?"

Marguerite's face had gone pasty white, and she trembled with fear. She had to find some way to get Mercy away from this monster. If she could not, and he succeeded in his plans, she would kill both of them, for Mercy would be better dead than in the power of this beast. She said nothing more; she did not want to rouse him any further. Garrett seemed to be waiting for someone. Marguerite moved to the only chair in the room that stood beside the cold fireplace. She sat in silence, holding a reluctant Mercy on her lap. Garrett seemed to be lost in thought, and he paid no more attention to either of them.

Marguerite knew that Juan was capable of tracking the horses over just about any kind of terrain, and she prayed that he would be able to catch up with them before they left this place. Garrett gave quick, harsh orders in Spanish, to Marguerite's surprise, and food was brought to her and Mercy. After being fed,

Mercy was content to be rocked to sleep. Marguerite lay her gently on the bed in a small room that adjoined the main one. She could still hear Garrett moving about in the other room. The next day, she would do everything in her power to slow them down. For now, she knelt beside the bed, crossed herself, and prayed fervently that Juan and the LaCroixs would find them soon. After her prayers, she rose and slid very gently into the bed beside Mercy, pulling her into her arms. After a while, she drifted off into sleep.

Marguerite did not know how long she had slept when a strange sound penetrated her sleep. For a few confused moments, she couldn't place it. Then, with a groan of desperation, she realized what had wakened her. She rose from the bed and went to the window. Pushing open the heavy wooden shutters, she looked out with tear-filled eyes at the steadily falling rain.

47

Tazia woke early, which was usual for her, but she lay curled against Kirk's back, her knees bent to follow the curve of his body. She threw one arm about his waist and pressed her check against his back. She was reluctant to move, content with the warmth of his body. She closed her eyes again and pressed even closer to him. She must have dozed off again, for the window was filled with bright sunlight when she opened her eyes. Kirk had turned and now held her against him. He must have been awake for some time.

"You know, you're beautiful when you're asleep, as innocent as a baby." He smiled at her.

"Um," she said suspiciously, eyeing him, "speaking of babies, I'd best be up looking after our daughter. And you'd better get up, too. You know how much she looks forward to having breakfast with her papa."

She tried to move, but Kirk's arms held her tight, and he laughed at her not-too-strenuous resistance. "I haven't heard a sound, and you know Marguerite will call us as soon as she's up. She probably knows I'd like to have you alone for a while, and being her papa's darling, she's sleeping soundly."

Tazia lay her head against him and ran her fingers

lightly over his chest.

"Believe me, darling," he whispered, "that's guaranteed to keep you in bed an hour longer."

Kirk turned on his side. With his free hand, he gently caressed her hair. Then he let his hand drift slowly down over her cheek to her shoulders, down the soft warmth of her body until it rested on her hip.

"Tazia, I think I'm probably the happiest man in the world at this moment. I have everything that is possible for a man to want. Casa del Sol, Mercy, and the love of the most beautiful woman in the world."

It was almost an hour later when they went downstairs together. When they walked into the dining room, they were surprised not to see Mercy there with her godparents and Marguerite, bustling over breakfast. Del and Louis showed surprise that Mercy was not with *them*.

"Where's my goddaughter?" Louis laughed. "I'll bet the sleepyhead's still abed."

"I think I'll go get her," Del said. "It's always a pleasure getting that warm morning kiss." He left the room, but he was only gone a few minutes when he came back.

"Kirk . . ." he began. His face was very pale. Kirk felt his heart begin to thud painfully against his side. Then he suddenly stood up and ran past Del up the steps.

"She's not there!" Del shouted after him.

Kirk stopped in the middle of the steps to look at him again. Over Del's shoulder, he could see Tazia's white face and large, fearful eyes. He came back to her side and took her hand.

"She's not there," Del repeated softly. "The window is open, and both she and Marguerite are gone."

"Kirk," Tazia moaned softly as she sagged against

him, all strength gone from her body. "Oh, my God! Not my baby!"

Kirk's face became grim. "Go get Juan and Raf. Have the horses saddled. We've got to track them down." He held Tazia by the shoulders and looked down into her tear-stained face. "I'll find her, darling. Don't worry, I'll find her." He kissed her and then went to gather his things. Cristina and Gabrielle moved to Tazia's side, and they watched the men leave the room. Soon the fading sound of hoofbeats was all that could be heard on the still morning air.

It had taken Juan only a few minutes to find where the intruders had come over the wall and where they had tied their horses. From there, they tracked slowly. Occasionally Juan would dismount and kneel on the ground to trace the faint trail. They did not talk much, each of them wrapped in his own anger and disbelief at what had happened. There was no question of stopping to eat. They traveled on grimly until Juan, no matter how he tried, could not follow the tracks any longer. Reluctantly they stopped and made camp for the night. They sat around the fire, wrapped in blankets, for sleep was impossible. Kirk's mind could barely control his desire to kill the man responsible for his daughter's abduction. He thought of Mercy's bright eyes and soft hair, her faith and trust in him, and her quick smile. He thought, too, of Tazia's fear-filled eyes as they left Casa del Sol.

The next morning, before the sun had even reached the horizon, they mounted their horses and were on their way again. Kirk noticed that Juan kept looking back over his shoulder and then up to the sun-filled sky.

"What's the matter, Juan? Have you lost the trail?" Kirk asked fearfully.

"No, Señor Kirk," Juan answered grimly, "I have

not lost the trail. But I pray we find them soon."

"What is it, Juan?" Del asked quietly.

"Rain, Señor Del," Juan replied very softly. His eyes told Del how much he feared this. He pointed over their shoulders to the mountains beyond Casa del Sol. Low, black clouds hung ominously in the sky, moving slowly but steadily in their direction.

"Rain! Juan, if it rains . . ." Kirk could not finish the sentence. They all knew that if it rained, it would wash away every print and Juan would have nothing to follow.

The longer they traveled, the darker the sky became. Kirk urged them on to as much speed as they could muster without losing the trail completely. But it was obvious to all of them that the rain was overtaking them. At dusk, they felt the first small drops, and within minutes, it developed into a steady downpour. Juan stopped and drew them all around him. He quickly described their location and where Casa del Sol was. Then he pointed out other landmarks in the area to use as references.

"We must separate. Raf, you and Del and Louis go in this direction." He pointed and made a circular motion with his hand. "If you follow my landmarks, you will make a large circle and be back here by tomorrow night. Kirk and I will go in the other direction. We will meet you here. I hope . . . I hope one of us is successful. *Vaya con Dios,*" he added softly.

Without another word, they separated and began the long, arduous search against the overwhelming odds of time and nature.

Tazia tried to control her rising panic as the hours dragged by. She wanted to scream, to run from the house to find her child herself, but she knew this was impossible. Cristina and Gabrielle watched her as she

410

became quieter and quieter, pacing the floor and clutching her hands to keep them from trembling.

"Tazia," Cristina said softly, "Kirk will find her. Come, we will go to the chapel together."

She took Tazia's hand, and Tazia smiled weakly, but she went with them to the chapel. They knelt in the peaceful candlelit chapel, and Tazia closed her eyes and prayed for the safe return of her daughter.

The hours dragged by slowly. Tazia would jump at every sound, her nerves stretched almost to the breaking point. She refused to eat, and as the daylight hours stretched into night, she began again to pace like a caged animal. They did not try to get her to go to bed, for they knew she would not be able to sleep until she knew where Mercy had been taken and if she was safe.

It was almost unbearable for Gabrielle and Cristina to watch Tazia's agony. She was in a state of complete nervous exhaustion and had finally fallen asleep on the couch. Covering her gently, they let her sleep for a short time while they each curled up in chairs near her and slept fitfully themselves.

Tazia came awake suddenly, memory flooding in on her. She rose stiffly from the couch. She felt disoriented and extremely weary. Something drummed into her sluggish mind . . . what was it . . . what was . . . oh, God! She cried and ran to the window. She gave a low moan, and for the first time since her daughter had been kidnapped, she began to cry. Cristina came up behind her, and Tazia threw herself into her arms and sobbed uncontrollably. Cristina looked over her shoulder at the softly falling rain. Tazia continued to cry until they became worried that she would become ill.

"Tazia, you must get yourself under control," Cristina said sternly. "Listen to me. They will not

411

harm the child. Tazia are you listening?" She shook Tazia gently by the shoulders. "If they were intending to harm the child, they would not have taken her nurse along. They want you and Kirk. You will hear from them. They will keep her safe. It is something they want from you and Kirk. That is the reason behind this. Tazia, get hold of yourself and listen to me."

Tazia focused her eyes on Cristina and slowly dragged her pain-filled mind to what she was saying. "Cristina?"

"Yes, I'm sure. It's not the child they want, it's—"

"You are so very clever, my dear, to have figured that all out so quickly."

All three women turned to face the group of men who stood in the doorway.

Garrett, Stone, and six men they had hired stood in the doorway. None of the three had heard them enter. Both Tazia and Gabrielle turned white with fear. They knew Garrett, and they knew why he was here.

Only Cristina greeted them with white-hot fury. "How dare you come in here like this. Leave this house at once!"

Garrett chuckled and winked at Stone.

"She'll fetch a nice price over the border, Stone. I imagine they will take a great deal of pleasure with this one before they break her."

Cristina gasped, her face now red with anger.

"Señor Flye," Tazia said softly, "leave my friends be. Return my daughter, and I will do anything you want. I will go anywhere you want, only bring Mercy back and let Cristina and Gabrielle go."

"It is much too late for you to bargain with me, Tazia. I will have you, willing or not, and your friends will turn us a nice profit. But more than that,

Kirk and his brother will be paid for interfering in my affairs. *No!* It is too late for bargains. As for your daughter, I've not decided yet how she will pay for being her father's daughter, but I've plenty of time for that, don't I? She's still a child yet."

Tazia cried out in pain at his words. She knew there were no way out for them. Three women against eight men were impossible odds.

"My father will track you down and kill you for this night," Cristina said.

"No, I think not. You see, I know your father is in Los Angeles. He went there yesterday to pick up your mother and your sister. He will not be back for two weeks. By that time, there will be no trail to follow. You will have completely vanished."

Garrett ordered Stone to tie them up. "We have to be gone before they realize they've been on a wild-goose chase and come back here. Hurry up, Stone."

Stone moved toward Tazia with a grin on his face. As she started to back away from him, quick as a panther he reached out and grabbed her. She fought him like a tigress, but it was impossible to escape him. Within a few minutes, he had her hands tied behind her. Two of the other men had gone after Gabrielle and, despite her screams and fighting, soon had her tied securely.

Cristina backed away from her pursuers and then suddenly disappeared through the library door. The sound of their footsteps at her heels lent wings to her feet. There was a gun in the desk in the library. I must get to it, she thought desperately. She reached the desk and pulled the gun from the drawer as the two men reached the library door. She turned and fired quickly, too quickly. The bullet ricocheted off the door frame. Both men were taken by surprise and reacted like the animals they were. One of them pulled out his gun and fired at her.

Gabrielle moaned and Tazia screamed Cristina's name when they heard the two shots. For several moments nothing happened. Then the two men reappeared.

"She is dead, Señor Flye," one of them said quite calmly.

"You damn fool. Couldn't you have taken her alive?"

"She shot at us first, Señor. She might have killed one of us. We have two; why worry about the other one? She is not worth dying for."

Tazia began to cry softly. "Cristina, dear Cristina." She looked at Garrett, crying and filled with hatred.

"Del will track you down and kill you for this. There will not be a place far enough for you to run to nor deep enough for you to hide in."

Garrett stared at her, and for the first time felt a slight touch of apprehension. He shrugged it off and ordered them to bring the women along. Tazia was put up on Stone's horse in front of him. He chuckled as her body stiffened at the feel of his arm about her waist.

"Get used to it. You belong to me now, and this time you don't have anyone to help you."

"Pig!" she said. "Kirk will find me, and your life will be worth nothing when he does."

"No. Where we're taking you, no one will ever find you again."

They all rode along in silence. Both women thought only of Cristina. Both were praying that she was not dead, that Del would find her in time, yet both knew deep in their hearts that it was almost impossible.

48

When the men had completed the circle and met again, Kirk was dismayed to find that none of them had seen any sign of the abductors. They made a fire and ate a light meal. They were all so exhausted they could barely think.

"It's as if the ground opened up and swallowed them," Kirk muttered.

"Señor Kirk?"

"Yes, Juan."

"It has occurred to me that there is something odd about all this."

"Odd?" Del questioned. His mind was numb, and he could not seem to think clearly. "In what way?"

"I think, Señor Del," Juan said slowly, "we have been drawn away from the hacienda on purpose. I think . . . I think it is the women they really want. They took Mercy's nurse. Why? To care for her, I think. To keep her well, to use as a weapon against you. No, I do not think we will find Mercy out here. I think she is closer to Casa del Sol than we realized."

Louis groaned. "Of course! It's Tazia and Gabrielle they're after, probably Cristina, too. We'd better move fast. If they get away again, we'll never find them."

The fire was put out hastily, and the men remounted their tired horses. They rode as rapidly as they could without killing the horses. When they rode through the gates of Casa del Sol, absolute silence greeted them. They reined in their horses in front of the house. The front door stood half-open. They dismounted and ran to the door, pushing it open to find . . . silence. Heart-stopping silence. Del, Kirk, and Louis stood and looked at the large empty room and knew with sinking hearts that they were already too late.

Juan went quickly to the other rooms, then returned white-faced to their side. "Señor Del," he said gently, "come with me. Please hurry."

Del stared at him as his heart began to thud painfully against his side.

"Hurry, señor."

Del followed him with feet that felt weighted with lead. Juan led him to the library and stepped aside to let him enter. His eyes were filled with pity and his face was pale and grim. Del looked across the room. There, curled against the wall, lay Cristina in a pool of blood. The low, strangled sound that came from him was an agonized cry of pure pain. He ran to her side and knelt beside her. Gently he turned her over and lifted her against him, disregarding the blood that stained his hands and clothes.

"Cristina . . . Cristina," he moaned as he rocked her body against himself. His world crumbled about him, and he could feel nothing but a blinding white-hot pain that seared his being and left dead his heart and mind. In their place came a fierce desire to kill. As Del knelt with Cristina's body across his lap and rocked her gently back and forth, his tears fell unheeded.

Kirk and Louis came to the library door.

"Damn them," Kirk whispered as he watched his brother's grief.

"My God! This was so unnecessary. We would have done anything they wanted. Why did they have to kill her?"

Kirk pointed to the gun that lay on the floor beside Cristina's body. "She was trying to defend herself."

"For this they shot her? They're animals! They should be hunted down and *killed* like animals."

Del had risen from the floor with Cristina's body in his arms. With unseeing eyes, he passed the two men and carried her upstairs to the room they had shared. He lowered her gently to the bed. With tender care, and in complete silence, he removed the blood-soaked dress and threw it aside. He washed the blood from her and turned to the closet. He took out the dress he liked to see her in most. Slowly, with infinite care and love, he dressed her and folded her hands across her body. Then, with a last, gentle kiss, he brushed his hand across her cheek.

"They'll pay, Cristina. Believe me, they'll pay." Then he turned and left the room.

He walked back down the stairs like a man in a deep trance. The rest of the men had awaited him in silence. Fresh horses were saddled, and without speaking a word, they set out to track down the men who had killed Cristina and carried away Tazia and Gabrielle.

Marguerite fed Mercy her lunch and put her to bed for a nap. She wanted a few more minutes alone to study the area, for she felt she knew the way to get home from this place, if she could only get herself and Mercy to a horse. She had saved some of the food they had given her and tied it in a small bundle, which she hid under the bed. Garrett and the other men had left the house the night it had rained. They had not yet returned. She was guarded by only one man, but to her distress, he seemed to watch every move.

She was still standing on the porch of the small house when she saw the riders approaching. It took her only a few moments to realize who they were.

The men pulled their horses to a stop and dismounted, pulling the two exhausted women with them. Both women were pale, their clothes dirty. They were pulled along roughly and shoved toward the porch. Marguerite saw that Stone took every opportunity to manhandle Tazia as he took her down from the horse. If Garrett saw Stone's actions, he paid no attention to them.

When Gabrielle and Tazia saw Marguerite standing on the porch, they gave cries of happiness and ran to her. She comforted each of them as gently as she could.

"Mercy," Tazia pleaded. "Marguerite, is she—?"

"She is well, *muchacha*. She is asleep. I have guarded her well, but I think there was no intent to harm her."

Tazia ran inside and lifted her sleeping child into her arms and held her close while she cried with relief. "Marguerite," Gabrielle said quietly, "Cristina is dead."

"Oh, *Madre de Dios*," she moaned. "Del will go out of his mind. They were so happy, just beginning their lives together. Poor Del."

"Marguerite," Gabrielle continued, "listen to me. If they do not take you along with us, and if Louis should find you . . . I overheard them. They're taking me across the border to Ensenada. You know why. Garrett is taking Tazia to Five Points. He does not believe they will ever find him there. You must tell them."

"Do not worry. I will tell them," she whispered.

The women were allowed to rest for only the few minutes it took until fresh horses were saddled and the men had eaten. Then they were on their way again.

Marguerite watched them leave. After a while, she realized that the man left to guard her was a different one. She prayed that he was less alert and conscientious than his predecessor.

Tazia, who was sitting in front of Stone, was becoming angrier and angrier at his constant fondling of her. Her nerves finally reached the breaking point when his hand roamed freely over her body.

"Garrett! Garrett Flye!" she shouted at the top of her voice. Her shout surprised everyone, and they all pulled their horses to a stop.

Garrett looked from Stone's surprised face to Tazia's, flushed and angry.

"Again, Stone?" Garrett asked, his voice deceptively soft. "I thought I warned you once."

His cold eyes sent a shiver of warning down Stone's spine, and he began to sweat. "I didn't do anything. She's trying to start trouble."

"If you want to drag me, you can," Tazia snapped, her chin held up proudly, "But I will not ride another inch with him."

"Put her down, Stone."

For a minute, Stone glared at Garrett, but again, as always, when face to face with a real threat, Stone's courage faded, and he roughly dropped Tazia to the ground. At the same moment her feet hit the ground, the sound of a shot echoed across the valley. A surprised look crossed Stone's face as blood stained the front of his shirt. Then he slowly slid sideways and fell to the ground with a solid thump. He was quite dead.

Both Tazia and Gabrielle stared in shock at Garrett's undisturbed face. He showed no sign of any feelings at all. The fact that he had just killed a man in cold blood did not seem to faze him. Tazia lifted her eyes from Stone's body to meet Garrett's cold and amused gaze. She felt a shiver of fear course through her. This man had no feelings, no emotion whatsoever, except for his own desires. She knew it would be impossible to reason with him. He did not care who he destroyed to achieve what he wanted. She also knew that what he wanted was not just her, but a way to destroy her husband. She was simply a tool for him to use at the moment. She had thought that maybe he fancied himself in love with her, and she hoped that she might use that fact to reach him and reason with him. Now she knew that was not the case. He would keep her as long as he felt it was necessary. Then he would get rid of her as though she were nothing.

Their gazes locked together. He could see that she had recognized the truth. He admired her control and felt a sudden surge of desire for her sweep through him. He slid back in his saddle and reached out his hand to her. His eyes never left hers.

"Come here," he said with deceptive softness. She would not give him the pleasure of forcing her to do his will. Without a word, she went to his side, took his hand, and placing her foot in the stirrup, she was pulled up in front of him. She heard him chuckle as his arm encircled her, and she stiffened against the contact.

I must have patience, she thought. Wait and watch. If he thought she was not resisting, maybe he would lower his guard. If he did, even for a moment, she wanted to be prepared.

"Are you just going to leave him there?" she asked.

"He is carrion. He got what he deserved. I warned him more than once."

They rode on in silence. Garrett made no move to touch her, except to support her in the saddle. There was no conversation. It seemed to Tazia that they rode forever. Her body was exhausted. Her back ached from holding herself so stiffly. Cramps pulled at the muscles of her legs, and her head ached unbearably with worry about Mercy and Cristina. She was also terribly hungry. They had not stopped to eat until the sun was beginning to set. Tazia was in despair at the number of miles they had put between them and Casa del Sol. Now another thought invaded her mind: what did they have planned for her and Gabrielle when they did stop for the night? Her question was soon answered.

Garrett ordered them to stop, and the men began preparations to eat. There was no fire, for they didn't want to take a chance of it being seen by anyone. A piece of dried beef and a crust of bread were thrust into the women's hands. They both ate in silence. A blanket was given to each of them, and they were ordered to get some sleep, a feat neither of them thought possible. They clung to each other in quiet, desperate fear.

The long night passed slowly. Before the first gray light of dawn, they were mounted again and on their way. Tazia knew it was still many miles to the border. She also knew Ensenada, a small, dirty little place that she was sure no one would think of, especially Kirk, who did not know the area well. She wondered if even Juan would think of Ensenada.

When they finally reached the town, both women were in a state of complete exhaustion. They were pushed unceremoniously into a one-room shack and left alone. They could hear the bar on the outside of the door being dropped into place. They were too tired to even talk. They merely waited for whatever fate Garrett had in store for them. It was several hours later when they heard the grating sound of the bar being lifted. Garrett came inside and, ignoring Gabrielle completely, he said to Tazia, "Come with me. We're leaving."

The women exchanged glances.

"What about Gabrielle? What will happen to her?"

"That is not your concern. You'd best forget her. You'll never see each other again. My men have plans for little Gabrielle," he said coldly.

Gabrielle was in a state of absolute terror when Garrett grabbed Tazia by the arm and dragged her from the room, barring the door after him.

Slowly Gabrielle sank down on the chair, too frightened even to cry. Long, silent minutes stretched into hours.

Then, after several hours of devastating silence, the bar was again lifted from the door. Gabrielle rose and faced the door. It swung open, and two of the men entered, the same two who had shot Cristina. Gabrielle knew there would be no mercy here.

She began to back away from them, but they followed her until she had backed against the wall. One of the men reached out, grabbed her arm, and pulled her toward him. She began to fight, but it was useless.

"Please," she cried, "where are you taking me?"

One of the men laughed. "We have a buyer who has paid quite a bit of gold for you. I think he wants to sample what he's bought." Gabrielle uttered a little cry as they dragged her from the house. She saw the saddled horses and realized that she would never be found by anyone once she was across the border. She would vanish completely. Despite her struggles, the two men pulled her toward the horse. They were about to lift her up on it when a calm, cool voice froze them in their tracks. "Take your hands off her."

They both whirled about, shock registering on their faces as they saw four men watching them. Three of the faces bore signs of furious anger. But it was the fourth that made them begin to sweat.

The eyes of the fourth man were cold, blue pools of death. They knew without a doubt that this was the husband of the woman they had killed. And they knew there was not one drop of mercy in the heart of this man.

49

Marguerite sat patiently watching her captor as he finished the last of the food she had prepared. She had eaten a little for the sake of appearances, then deftly hidden some of the food. He was careless, she thought. He often became lazy and would tip his chair back against the wall and close his eyes for a little catnap. Marguerite made no moves during these naps, for she realized he was testing her. Time after time she let the opportunities pass by, until she could see him begin to lose interest in her. She would move slowly about the room, tending to Mercy or doing something to get him used to her activity.

She had just put Mercy to bed and come into the room, where he sat in front of the warm fire. He sat with his side toward her, and she could see that his mind was elsewhere. She began to putter about the room, and after giving her one cursory glance, he went back to his thoughts.

Slowly she began to search for something to use as a weapon. Her hand closed on a pan, which she discarded. It was not strong enough. He had to be knocked unconscious with the first blow, because she would not get another chance. In the corner of the room were the logs that had been brought in for the fire. One of these would be perfect, but could she get close enough to him to use it? She moved very slowly toward the pile of logs, her heart pounding furiously and her throat dry. If he knew what she intended to do, he would probably kill them both. Mercy's life was in her hands. She hesitated. Then, determined to get them both free, she began again to edge toward the logs. She reached them just as the man stirred in his chair and shifted his position. She almost fainted from the fear that he would turn toward her and sense what she was trying to do. Her hand hovered over the log. Slowly she lifted it from the pile. The distance between them was almost six feet. She held the log down at her side and began to inch her way toward him. After what seemed an interminable time, she finally came up behind him, lifted the log high over her head, and brought it down with a satisfying thump. The man seemed to fold in two; he sagged forward and collapsed on the floor.

Now she moved very rapidly. She wrapped her robe tighter about her, and then she tore her nightgown into strips. She knelt beside the unconscious man, pulled his arms behind him, and tied them together as tightly as she could. Then she tied his feet together. She knew that eventually he could be able to get away, for he was a large, strong man, but she hoped for enough time to make good her escape with Mercy, to get far enough ahead that he would not catch up with her.

She moved quickly and efficiently, gathering up the food she had stored away. She ran outside and saddled the man's horse and brought it around to the front of the house. She tied the food in a bundle and attached it to the horn of the saddle. Then she went back into the house and gathered Mercy up into her arms. Aroused from sleep, Mercy began to protest.

Marguerite comforted her as best she could as she ran back outside, mounted the horse, and with a sharp kick of her heels, urged him into rapid flight.

She felt sure she knew the direction in which Casa del Sol lay, and she headed the horse in that direction. Mercy began to whimper at the rapid gait of the horse, but Marguerite only held her more tightly and urged the horse to greater speed. It was important that she put as much distance as possible between them and their captor before he got free. They rode like this until Mercy began to scream in violent protest, so she slowed the horse to a walk until she could calm the angry, frustrated child. The sun was beginning to set, and now Marguerite was struck by another fear. She could find her way well enough in the daylight, but what about at night? She didn't know what to do. She was afraid to go on and afraid not to.

She watched the last rays of the setting sun and let her horse slow to a walk. She knew she must stop soon to care for Mercy's needs. It was beginning to get cold. The robe she wore was little protection against the elements, but she was more worried about Mercy than about herself.

She pulled the horse to a stop and dismounted. Holding the child in one arm, she led the horse off the main track into the depths of the surrounding trees. Still holding the reins, she let Mercy slide to the ground. Then she tied the horse firmly to a bush. If it should manage to get away they would be completely lost. There was no way to have the longed-for warmth of a fire, for even if she dared, there was no way for her to start one. She managed to soothe Mercy's ruffled feelings and crooned gently to her as she fed her a little of the food she carried. She did not know how long they would have to travel before they were either found or made their way home, so she did not eat herself. Then she bundled up the remaining food and tied it firmly to the saddle. Lifting Mercy against her, she remounted, and holding the child across her lap and letting her head rest against her breast, she let the horse move slowly ahead. They would not be able to travel fast now because the darkness obliterated any trail she might have followed. Mercy was now completely secure and content, so she closed her eyes and fell into a sound, relaxed sleep.

As they moved slowly down the trail, Marguerite let her mind drift back to all that had happened. She prayed that Kirk and the others would be able to track down Tazia and Gabrielle before they were dragged across the border. She thought of Cristina, and her heart wept—not only for Cristina, but for Del, as well.

A large silver moon had risen and cast a pale light over the landscape. Marguerite was pleased, because now she could see clearly for a great distance. She urged the horse to a faster gait. They traveled for another hour, when she began to realize that the horse was tiring. They had only given it a few minutes rest earlier, while they ate. She would have to stop for a while or the animal would collapse and leave them completely stranded.

Marguerite reined in the horse and, with the sleeping child still in her arms, dismounted as gently as she could. Mercy was wrapped securely in the one blanket they possessed. She lay the baby down at the base of a tree. Then she unsaddled the horse and hobbled him so that he could not drift away. With one or two hours sleep, both she and the horse would be able to travel better. She lay the saddle on the ground, put the saddle blanket around her, and lay down with her head against the saddle. Within a few minutes, she was asleep.

She did not know how long she had slept or exactly what it was that had awakened her. It couldn't have been long, for the moon was high in the black sky. She lay very still, trying to listen for the noise that had stirred her awake. It came again. Someone was in the shadows of the trees, moving as quietly as possible in her direction.

Oh, Blessed Mother, she thought in panic. The guard had gotten loose sooner than she thought and caught up with them. She reached for Mercy. She would jump up quickly and run for the surrounding trees, she thought. Her arms never reached the child. Strong arms grabbed her roughly and pulled her upward. She gave a sharp cry as she began to fight with all the strength she had left. The man gave a muffled gasp as her blows connected several times.

"Santa María, Marguerite! Must you kill me before we get a chance to rescue you?" The sound of the familiar voice made her weak with relief.

"Juan! Oh, Juan!" she sobbed as she fell against him, not only because of her joy at seeing him, but because her legs would no longer hold her. He patted her shoulder gently with one hand while the other arm supported her trembling body.

"Señor Kirk! Señor Del!" he shouted. She heard the horses' hooves approaching from several different directions. Soon she was surrounded by the anxious questioning faces of the search party.

"Marguerite," Kirk began. "My daughter . . . Mercy. Where is she? They haven't harmed her, have they?" As if to answer his question herself, Mercy stirred from her sleep and began to cry. In a few steps, Kirk was at her side, lifting her into his arms, comforting her with gentle words and the security of his touch. She wrapped her tiny arms about her father's neck and clung to him, still whimpering, but eased by the familiarity and warmth of the arms that now held her.

"Marguerite, where are Gabrielle and Tazia?" Louis questioned.

"They've taken them across the border."

"Across . . ." Juan began. Then he hesitated as he realized the full impact of what she was saying. "Where? Where do they plan on crossing the border, and when?"

"They are headed for Ensenada. They left this morning."

"This morning! Then they won't be there until late tomorrow."

"Do you think we can get there in time, Juan?" Louis asked, his voice thick with worry.

"They don't expect us, so they'll camp tonight. We will cut across the hills and travel all night. If luck is with us, we should be at Ensenada at almost the same time."

"Good," Kirk said. "Raf, you take Marguerite and Mercy back to the *casa*."

Raf nodded. He would like to have gone on with them, but he realized the situation. Juan was needed for tracking and to guide them. Louis and Kirk had to find their wives, and Del . . . Del was, at this moment, walking death for the men who were responsible for the tragedy in their lives.

Kirk turned toward Marguerite, his voice very gentle. "Thank you, Marguerite, for caring for Mercy. I will never forget it."

"She is like my own, señor."

"Marguerite?"

"*Sí*, Señor Kirk?"

"Tazia . . . was she all right when you last saw her?" His eyes searched hers for the answer he so desperately wanted to hear.

"*Sí*. She was not only well, but spitting fire at the

man responsible for this, threatening him with your vengeance when you caught up with him." Kirk looked past her and motioned toward his brother, who stood quietly a little away from the rest of the party, looking in the direction of the hills. His eyes were cold and his face a frozen mask.

"I don't think it's *my* vengeance he'll have to worry about," Kirk said quietly.

Marguerite nodded.

"You know about Cristina?" he asked.

"*Sí*, Tazia told me. They were not sure she was . . ."

"Yes, Marguerite. She's dead."

"Oh, poor Del," Marguerite whispered.

"He hasn't spoken a word to anyone since he found her, Marguerite. I pity those men when we catch up with them."

She nodded. Her eyes filled with pity for the pain she knew dwelt in Del's heart.

Marguerite, Raf, and Mercy left the group and headed back to Casa del Sol. The others mounted their horses and, with no further conversation, followed Juan as he led the way over the hills toward Ensenada.

They traveled in absolute silence. Each man was lost in the depths of his own fear and grief and anger. Kirk wanted only to find Tazia, to hold her again and keep her from any further harm.

Louis's thoughts were on whether they would find Gabrielle in time and the gnawing guilt that he had drawn her away from a place she could have been happy in to a place where she faced danger, even death, because of her love for him.

Del's thoughts were a murky place, filled with hate and the deep desire to kill the men who had taken his beloved Cristina's life so mercilessly. There was no future for him. His only thought, his only motive for being alive, now that Cristina was gone, was to get his hands on the men who had killed her. He did not want to think beyond that point.

They moved steadily through the rest of the long night. It was just after daybreak when they crested the hill that led down to the small border town of Ensenada. They sat on their horses and surveyed the town. It consisted of only a small cluster of adobe houses with a small square in the center. On the quiet morning air, the sharp bark of a dog could be heard. This seemed to be answered almost instantly by the crow of a rooster. There was no movement anywhere. Obviously the quiet little town slept later than usual.

"Well, Juan?" Kirk said softly.

Juan pointed, and their eyes followed. At the far end of the town, about sixty feet from the last house, was an adobe shack that sat isolated from the rest. In front of it were tied three horses, already saddled.

They touched their horses with their heels and circled the town, coming up to the back of the building. They had almost reached it when the door was thrown open and two men came out, laughing and dragging a frightened Gabrielle with them. Her clothes were dirty and torn. Her face was tear-stained and wide-eyed with fear. She was pleading and trying her best to fight free. Both men were enjoying the play and laughing at her helplessness.

Louis's eyes blazed with rage. His whole body trembled with the violence of his hatred. A hand reached out and touched his arm, calming him temporarily. Louis nodded and pulled himself rigidly under control. Del smiled. The smile was deadly.

"Take your hands off her," he said softly.

Both men whirled about, amazed at their presence. One made a hesitant move toward his gun.

431

"Oh, yes," Del said softly, "reach for it. It would give me a great deal of pleasure to kill you where you stand."

At the sound of his voice, the man's hand stopped, and small beads of perspiration broke out on his forehead. Louis dismounted, and with a sobbing cry, Gabrielle threw herself into his arms.

"Where is Tazia?" Kirk asked.

"She . . . she is not here, señor," one of the men answered.

Kirk's heart beat painfully against his ribs.

"Where is she?"

"Señor Flye took her with him."

"Where?"

"Señor,"—the man was shaking so badly he could barely speak—"he spoke of a plantation; but I do not know where. I swear to God, I—"

"God," laughed Del bitterly, "what do you know of God?"

"Five Points," Gabrielle said softly to Kirk. "He's taking her to Five Points."

"Good," Del said. "Kirk, you, Juan, and Louis can take Gabrielle. Head for Five Points. Maybe you can catch up to them before they get there."

"And you?" Kirk asked.

"I'll catch up with you by tonight," he answered quietly. "I've some business here to take care of first."

"Señor!" one of the men cried. "You are not going to let him kill us?"

Kirk looked from the men to his brother. Then, without another word, he turned his horse away. Gabrielle, Louis, and Juan followed. The two men stared at the gun in Del's hand as he stepped down from his horse. Death looked them squarely in the eye as he motioned them back into the house. He followed them inside and closed the door softly behind him.

50

Kirk watched Gabrielle and Louis as they moved away. Despite her disheveled state, her weariness, and all the misery she'd been through, Gabrielle insisted that she wanted to go on with them to find Tazia. But Kirk realized it was exhaustion speaking. Louis tried to argue with her. He wanted to send her home, but she adamantly refused. Now Kirk reined in his horse and looked at Gabrielle. His eyes were gentle and kind, but his voice was very decisive, "Gabrielle, you're going home with Louis. Now!"

"Kirk, I've got to know Tazia's all right. I've got—"

"You've got to take care of yourself, too, Gabrielle, and," he added with a small laugh, "you're worrying Louis to death." He came to her side and put his hand on her arm. He could feel the muscles tremble.

"We'll find her, Gabrielle. Don't worry. We'll find her and bring her back safely. In the meantime, make it easier on all of us. Go back with Louis. It will make us all feel better, and we'll be able to travel faster." He said the truthful words as gently as he could. Although she didn't want to accept the truth, she realized she would only slow them down. Reluctantly she nodded her head. Louis exchanged a quick look of relief with Kirk. They left the party when they stopped for dinner and to rest the horses. They ate a small amount of food standing up, without bothering to light a fire.

They traveled slowly, Juan watching for the trail Garrett and Tazia had taken. It was just nearing dusk when Juan informed Kirk that Del would soon be catching up to them. Kirk looked back, but he could not see his brother anywhere.

"How do you know, Juan? I don't see any sign of him."

Juan shrugged and smiled. "I just know. Should we wait for him?"

Kirk nodded. They pulled their horses to a stop. Both of them dismounted and loosened the horses' cinches to let them breathe.

"Kirk, you know what he did back there?" Juan said softly. He squinted slightly against the sun as he watched Kirk's face.

"Yes, I know."

"You didn't try to stop him."

Kirk didn't speak for a moment, but let his eyes search the area behind them for signs of his brother. Then he turned to face Juan again.

"No, I didn't try to stop him. If it had been Tazia they killed so brutally, I would have done the same thing. Do you really think I or anyone else could have stopped him? Why didn't you try if you thought it was wrong?"

"I didn't say I thought it was wrong, and I probably would have done the same thing, had it been my woman. It's just that your brother is not the kind of a man who can kill without it having an effect on him. That is what worries me. Since we found Cristina, he has not spoken of her or her death. In fact, he has not spoken much at all. I think he is driving himself until Garrett Flye is dead, but . . . what

434

then? What will happen to him? I am afraid for him. For what will happen when this is all over. He will be in many small pieces, Kirk, and he may not be able to put them all together again."

"I don't know what we can do to help him, Juan. When he found Cristina like that . . . well . . . it's as though part of him died. When this is over, we'll have to try to help him pick up the pieces and start his life over again."

"That's just the point, Kirk. It's what I'm trying to tell you. I don't think he wants to pick up the pieces and start over again. I think he's dying inside, and I'm afraid there won't be anything left."

"What can we do? We can't stop him from coming with us to catch Flye."

"We could try."

"He'll never listen to me."

"If and when we catch up with them, and if Tazia is all right, what do you intend to do, walk away with Tazia and let Del handle Flye?"

Kirk's face flushed with anger.

"This is between me and Flye. It's my wife he's kidnapped and me he wants to kill."

"Then are you going to tell that to your brother?" Juan persisted.

"Yes, if necessary."

"Do you think that will stop him?"

Kirk thought this over. He didn't want to have to stand between his brother and the man responsible for Cristina's death, but he began to understand Juan's point. It might come to just that. He wondered, in Del's present mental condition, just what he would do. As if in answer to his thoughts, the sound of an approaching horse could be heard. In another few minutes, horse and rider could be seen cresting the nearest hill, headed in their direction.

Both men remained silent until Del joined them. The brothers looked at one another, and Kirk realized Juan was right. Del's eyes were clouded blue, completely unfathomable and devoid of life. He moved as though he were in a dream.

"Del?"

"Let's go on, Kirk. They're getting too far ahead of us."

"Del, wait a minute. I want to talk to you."

"What?" Del asked impatiently. His voice was sharp, as though his thoughts had been suddenly interrupted by an unwelcome intruder.

"Juan and I are going on alone," Kirk said.

"Like hell, you are. I want Garrett Flye. I'm going to kill him just like he had Cristina killed."

"Just like you killed those two back there?" Kirk asked quietly.

Del looked at his brother's face for a moment.

"Yes. Just like I killed those two. Not as quickly as they did Cristina. In fact, as painfully as I could. Do you want me to tell you what I did, Kirk? First I shot one in the leg, then the other, then each arm, until they cried as Cristina must have cried. Then the shoulders. They begged, and I reminded them of what they had done to deserve what they were getting. Then—"

"Stop it, Del."

"Why? Garrett deserves the same and I'm going to see he gets it."

Kirk and Juan exchanged looks. Neither of them could believe this was Del—happy-go-lucky Del, who had always laughed at everything the world had to offer. They knew Del's love for Cristina had been a miracle in his life and that her death had hurt him badly. But they were touched now with deep fear. If Del were allowed to go on like he was, the life that

436

paid the price would be his own. Kirk felt that when Del did come to his senses, he would not be able to live with himself in the black void of his life.

"Del, you can't go on like this. I know how you feel, but don't you see what's happening to you? You're going to become just like they are. Killing for the love of killing. Cristina wouldn't have wanted it this way."

Del gave a short, harsh laugh. "You expect me to just walk away from all this without making him pay? Damn it, Kirk!" It was almost a sob. "He had Cristina killed. What do you want me to do? I just can't let him get away with it! I can't!"

"Del . . . all right, I can't stop you from going along, but I'll tell you this: I will stop you from killing again. For your own sake."

Del stared at them both for a few minutes. His eyes were angry, and Kirk knew he was not accepting what he had said the way it was meant. "Do you think you can stop me, little brother?" he asked Kirk with deceptive softness.

"If I have to, Del, I will. Both Juan and I care too much about what happens to you. You'll be killing yourself as much as him, and we can't let that happen."

Del snarled. "How can you sit there and tell me you don't plan to kill the man who stole Mercy and Tazia, who almost had Gabrielle worse than dead? The man who had Cristina killed?"

"I didn't say I'd let him go, Del," Kirk replied. "I just said I'm not going to let you become, like him, a cold-blooded killer. Juan and I will take care of Garrett. It would be best if you would go back."

There was silence for a few minutes while Del considered what his brother had said. His mind was in a turmoil. He could not think rationally. The emotional experience of what he had just done to the two men in the cabin had shaken him to the core. He could not believe it himself, the way he had felt when he had killed them. He had thought it would give him some release from the anguish of losing Cristina, but it had not. He had attributed that to the fact that Garrett was still alive, and his hurt and anger was now centered on Garrett. He felt that once Garrett was dead he would be able to have peace. He did not know in his pain-filled mind that peace would not come in that manner, that he would have to live with the pain for a long time. He had to find Garrett. He could not let Juan or Kirk stop him. His mind became devious. He smiled at Kirk, hoping he could be convincing.

"All right, brother. Garrett's all yours. But I am still going along."

Kirk watched him closely. Del did not fool him for one minute; he knew his brother too well.

"You won't go back?"

"No," Del said softly, "I won't go back. If you don't want me to go with you, I'll go alone. But I *will* go."

Kirk sighed in defeat. He promised himself to watch Del closely when they caught up with Garrett. He could not let his brother kill again. His eyes met Juan's, and he could see they both had the same thoughts.

"All right, Del," he said quietly, "you win . . . for now." He turned his horse, and the other two followed in silence.

They traveled for hours in complete silence, each of them caught up in his own dark thoughts. Kirk's mind was filled with thoughts of Tazia, and he prayed they would catch up to them before Garrett could do her any harm. He hoped Garrett thought they did not know where he was headed. It would let him travel slowly and more confidently and give them time to catch up.

438

Del's mind was also on Garrett, and his black thoughts were filled with revenge and death.

Juan rode in silence, for he had made up his mind to protect both men from themselves. He made his own plans and waited and watched for the opportunity to fulfill them.

Tazia was so exhausted she could barely keep from falling from her horse, but she did not look forward to the time they would stop. She wondered if Kirk and Juan would be able to find her. She knew they had no idea where they were headed. She watched Garrett's back as they rode along. He held the reins of her horse in his hand, and her hands were tied to the pommel of the saddle. She knew, with a sinking heart, that they would stop soon. Her mind turned to Cristina and Gabrielle. If they had not found Gabrielle by now, she was lost. Her heart twisted in pain as she thought of Cristina. She bent her head and let her eyes close for a moment, swaying tiredly in the saddle.

It was a few seconds before Tazia realized that her horse had come to a stop. They were in the center of a thick crop of trees. Garrett had chosen this place to stop for the cover it provided. He had already dismounted and was removing the saddle from his horse to let it rest. He hobbled it and let it begin to crop grass. She had a brilliant flash of anger. He would care for his horse before he even thought of her. He came to her side and untied her hands. She almost cried out with pain as the blood rushed back. When he pulled her down from the horse, she almost collapsed against him, but her pride and anger would not give him that much satisfaction. Instead, she staggered to a tree and sagged to her knees. He took some dried meat and the water canteen from his saddle, walked to her side, and eased himself down beside her, offering both to her. Tired as she was, her eyes snapped with fury, and she slapped weakly at his hands. He chuckled and began to eat himself.

"You'll get over your stubbornness when you're hungry enough, my dear," he said laughingly.

"I'd rather die than eat your food!"

"Oh, I'll not let you die." He laughed again. "I've got plans for you. Your husband should be looking frantically for you by now. He has no idea where you are or where we're going. By the time he finds you again, he won't even want you."

"I don't care what you do to me. Just tell me where my daughter is. Is she safe? What are you going to do with her?"

"Your daughter will be taken to a place where she'll never be found. As she grows older, she will be trained for . . . entertainment. Then Kirk will be informed of her whereabouts. By then, it will be too late—for her and for you. I should like to see him suffer, but I will have to be satisfied with just knowing he will."

She stared at him in horror.

"You're insane," she gasped. "Why hurt my child? It's Kirk and I you want. Let Mercy go. Please, let her go." Tazia was chilled again by the look in his eyes. "I'll do anything you want, Garrett," she pleaded, "anything—only let my daughter go."

"I don't need your willingness, Tazia. You will eventually do anything I want anyway. But my revenge on the LaCroixs will be complete."

"Garrett!"

He rose to his feet and drew her up beside him.

She began to shake as she realized that nothing she said or did would reach this man. There was no conscience to touch. She realized that it was deeply satisfying to him to see her suffer so. She stiffened as his hands moved over her and he drew her against him. She closed her eyes. She must not let him reach her mind. She thought of Kirk . . . of Del . . . Gabrielle . . . Cristina. In desperation, she tried to imagine he was Kirk, but that did not work. Garrett's revenge was beginning. He began to unbutton her blouse. He removed it and dropped it in a heap beside them. Then he loosened the pins in her hair. She caught her lower lip between her teeth, biting it hard, refusing to cry as his hands fondled her breasts. Then he worked loose the riding skirt. Slowly the balance of her clothes followed.

"Why don't you fight me?" he whispered against her ear as his hands drew her against him. "Fight me, little tigress."

That's what he wants, she thought, the satisfaction of beating her down, of taking her against her will. She refused to let him see her fear or to give him the satisfaction of subduing her. Instead, she made her body go limp and gave no response at all. His anger flashed as he pushed her to the ground and took her as brutally and violently as he could. When he was finished, he rolled over on his side and glared at her. Somewhere inside, a deep feeling of satisfaction began to rise in her.

He rose and stood above her. "Get up and dress," he snarled. He turned away to saddle the horses.

She smiled to herself. If she could continue as she was, if her mind and body could stand it, maybe she could make him angry enough to make a mistake. When he did, she would take advantage of it. Her mind held one thought only. I must find a way to kill Garrett Flye.

51

Kirk, Juan, and Del traveled at a steady pace as rapidly as they could without losing the trail. By early evening, they came to the place where Garrett and Tazia had stopped. They pushed on, traveling until all light was gone and they were forced to stop. Juan did not light a fire. They ate the cold food he had packed and sat in silence, not even making a pretense of trying to sleep. If Kirk and Del had known that Tazia and Garrett were less than twenty miles ahead of them, that they could have caught them if they had ridden only two or three more hours, things might have come to a violent conclusion then. Juan sensed just how far ahead they were, and after Kirk and Del had fallen into a light sleep, he rose silently, saddled his horse, and rode slowly until he was some distance from their camp. Then he urged his horse ahead and resolutely covered the distance between himself and the couple he searched for.

By the time they stopped for the night, Tazia was more than exhausted. She had completely lost all trace of time. She held on to her senses only by sheer force of will, hers against Garrett.

She had realized his true character: he wanted reaction from her. He wanted her to cry, to beg, to fight him. He wanted to assert his power over her, and she would not let him succeed. When he pulled her down from her horse this time, she did not resist. Instead, she stood quietly with her head bowed so he would not see the hatred that flashed uncontrolled in her eyes. He handed her food, which she ate docilely. Then he spread a blanket on the ground and turned to face her.

"Come here," he commanded harshly.

She did not lift her head, but she walked slowly toward him. When she reached his side, he grasped her with one hand behind her head and pulled her to him. Catching her jaw with his fingers, he jerked her head up so he could see her face. Their eyes locked, and she fought every desire she had to let him see how much she hated him. She focused her eyes on the top of his head, keeping her thoughts away from him. He pulled her into his arms and kissed her violently, his mouth attacking hers ruthlessly. She did not respond. It took every effort she had not to bite him or spit at him. He released her lips finally. They felt bruised and sore. His eyes burned with uncontrollable anger. Then suddenly he reached up and slapped her as hard as he could. Tazia knew that rousing her fury and making her fight back was the only way Garrett had of becoming aroused himself. Tears sprang to her eyes, but she held herself still. He slapped her again and again until her knees trembled and she almost fell.

"Damn you! Fight back!"

She stood frozen.

"What will it take to make you fight?" he asked. "I had Cristina killed," he said angrily. "I've sold your husband's best friend's wife into prostitution."

Still no reaction from her.

"I will make your daughter's life a living hell."

She remained silent.

"I arranged your brother's death!" he shouted. He was suddenly rewarded by a fleeting shadow that crossed her face.

"Ah, your brother. Your dear, sweet, wonderful brother," he laughed. "Shall I tell you the truth about your brother?"

She could not help herself. "What do you know of Manolo? He was not the kind of animal you are," she snapped.

He threw back his head and laughed heartily. Then he reached for her again and began to caress her. As he did, he began to talk. He told her everything about Manolo. He could feel her body begin to tremble in fury, and it excited him. He continued to talk, pouring out all the wicked, vile things for which Manolo was responsible, including the story of Juanita Reyes. He dwelt on Juanita a long time, telling in great detail all she had suffered at Manolo's hands. Amid the painful knowledge that what he said was the truth came the uncontrollable fury at what had been done to her life and to the lives of those she loved, that all of it was for nothing . . . nothing.

The fury rose up in her, and she began to fight him, lashing out with her fists and her feet. He enjoyed the battle and fought her to the ground, tearing away the rest of her clothes.

When he had finished with her, Garrett rolled away and got to his feet, grunting with satisfaction. Tazia curled in a ball on her side and began to cry. This, more than anything else, satisfied him completely. He felt an exuberant sense of complete revenge as he looked down on her.

"This is the beginning, Tazia, my love," he said with a chilling laugh. "By the time I am through with you, Kirk will not even be able to look at you without revulsion. I will bend you to my will, and when I am finished, I will send you back to him." He laughed wildly and turned away from her—to come face-to-face with Juan. At that moment, Garrett Flye looked deeply into the eyes of death.

"You will never hurt this family again, señor," Juan said softly. He reached up with one huge hand and clutched Garrett's throat. Garrett fought, but it was as though Juan were oblivious to all feeling. The blows fell on him unheeded. His eyes never left Garrett's body. When he was sure he was dead, he released him and let his body crumble to the ground. Then he went to Tazia's side, wrapped her in the blanket, and lifted her as gently as a baby. She recognized who held her, and with a choking sob of relief, she lay her head against his chest.

Only a few streaks of light touched the black sky when Kirk wakened. He lay still and let his thoughts gather themselves to meet the coming day. Since they knew Garrett did not know they were so close on his trail, he was sure they could catch up to him sometime during the day. But what was he to do about Del when they did? To save his brother's sanity, he would kill Garrett as soon as they found him and hope the explosion they were watching for in Del would not happen. He turned over to look at his sleeping brother. He was surprised to see Del sitting up, wide awake. Following Del's gaze, he looked at the place where Juan should have been sleeping. It was empty.

"Del?"

"Juan's gone."

"Gone where?"

"Where do you think?"

It took Kirk's still sluggish mind several moments to grasp what had happened. "He knew," he said in amazement.

"Yes, he knew," Del answered, his voice low and angry. "I imagine Garrett and Tazia were very close to us last night, and he let us just go to sleep. He planned to go on himself."

"The question is, Del," Kirk said slowly, "who was he protecting, you or me?"

Neither spoke for several minutes. Then Del said very quietly, "I imagine he was protecting both of us."

"You are right, señor," came a soft voice from the trees.

They both turned around to see Juan carrying the still form of Tazia in his arms. Kirk rose slowly, fear squeezing his heart into a tight knot.

"She is only asleep, señor." Juan smiled. "She has been through much, and we have come a long way tonight."

Kirk reached out and gently took Tazia from Juan. She stirred, murmured Kirk's name, and then relaxed again in a deep sleep. He held her against him as relief flooded through him so fiercely he almost cried out. To have the whole nightmare over, to have both Tazia and his daughter safe almost overwhelmed him. Then he caught a glimpse of his brother's grief-filled eyes and realized how Del must feel seeing Tazia safe, knowing he would never see Cristina again. He lay Tazia on his blanket and covered her.

"We'll let her sleep for a while. Then we'll start for home."

"Kirk," Del said hesitantly, "I'm not going back to Casa del Sol with you."

"Del . . ."

"I can't," he said softly, his eyes looking inward at the emptiness he would find if he returned home. "I just can't. Not now, maybe not for a long time."

Kirk looked at his brother in silence. He realized the truth of what he said, but it hurt him that Del was so unhappy and that no one had the power to ease his suffering. "Where will you go, Del?"

"I don't even know that yet." He laughed rather shakily. "I only know I'm not strong enough to go back to that house and face it without her."

"What can we do to help you?"

"Nothing, Kirk. I guess I just have to work this out myself. I'll be back one day. When I can."

"If there's anything you need . . . anything at all. Money . . . anything," Kirk said helplessly.

"I've plenty of money, more than I'll ever need. What I *do* need no one can give me. I have to find my way out of this myself. I'm going to leave before Tazia wakens. I don't want to hear everything that happened."

Del held out his hand to Juan. "Thank you, Juan."

"*Vaya con Dios, amigo*," Juan replied as he shook his hand firmly.

Del turned back to his brother, and they looked at one another in silence. Then they embraced. Del turned abruptly away and saddled and mounted his horse. In a matter of minutes, only the sound of receding hoofbeats could be heard in the early morning air. Kirk watched his brother until he was out of sight.

"He'll be all right, señor," Juan said quickly. "He is stronger than he thinks. In time, he will return."

"I hope so, Juan. I feel so helpless. There ought to be something we could do."

"There is, señor."

"What?"

"Don't worry about him; let him go in peace. Have faith in him. He will go away and lick his wounds and find out that what he is searching for is still here, where he left it. He will return."

"I hope so, Juan."

They began to gather together their things and pack up. Then they waited quietly until Tazia awoke.

She stirred, opened her eyes, and sat up abruptly. Her eyes widened in pleasure as she looked into her husband's face. He reached down and pulled her to her feet.

"Oh, Kirk," she whispered. They touched, kissed, and held one another for several minutes as though they were each afraid the other might suddenly disappear.

"Kirk . . . Mercy—"

"She's home. Marguerite took excellent care of her. They're both safe, waiting for us at Casa del Sol."

"Gabrielle. Kirk, they took Gabrielle to—"

"Shh, Tazia, Gabrielle's safe, too, with Louis." Then her eyes darkened with remembered pain. "They . . . they shot Cristina. Kirk is she . . . ?"

"Yes, Tazia, I'm sorry. She's dead."

"Oh," she moaned, "poor Del. Is he all right, Kirk?"

Kirk explained to her how Del felt and how he had gone away before she wakened. She said nothing, but her eyes filled with tears of pity for Del, and she clung even closer to Kirk.

"Kirk, there is one thing more I must say to you, and then we will put the past behind us."

He raised a questioning eyebrow, but he remained silent as she began to speak.

"Garrett . . . he told me all about Manolo. All the things that I should have known years ago. I know now how you and all my friends tried to protect me. I'm only sorry that such a man has brought so much suffering into your life."

"Tazia, if it hadn't been for Manolo, I would never have found you. I guess I can forget him and be grateful for the one good thing his life accomplished."

She smiled gratefully up at him, and he returned the

smile. Kirk bent to kiss her lips one more time before he lifted her to his horse and they started for home.

It took them several days and nights to get home. Kirk took complete advantage of the time to hold Tazia and nurture a warm togetherness they had never quite had before, when all the secret past lay between them.

When they arrived at Casa del Sol, they were greeted warmly and with much laughter and kisses. Tazia could not get enough of holding Mercy and was reluctant to even release her for bed that night.

Kirk learned that Cristina's parents and Juanita had arrived home the day after the search party had left. They were heartbroken about Cristina's death. They had taken her body for burial in the family cemetery. Tazia and Kirk went the next day with Louis and Gabrielle to put flowers on the grave.

"Oh, Kirk, she was so young. They were so much in love. Why did it have to happen like this? They had so much to look forward to."

"I don't know, Tazia. There's no logical reason for some of the things that happen in our lives and the lives of the people we care for. We just have to have faith that everything will come out all right, without understanding why."

"Yes, I guess we do. But I don't think I will ever understand why this kind of thing happens. I hope Del's hurts can heal a little and he will find it in his heart to come back to us soon."

"I hope so, too," Kirk replied softly. "Shall we go home?" They walked hand in hand back to Don Federico's house.

Kirk had not met Cristina's mother, Catherine, nor her sister, Juanita, so they were invited for dinner. They entered the house and were greeted by Don Federico and his wife. Kirk smiled and looked into blue eyes so like Cristina's.

"I have been so looking forward to meeting Tazia's husband, Señor LaCroix." She smiled warmly.

"Kirk," he said with a smile.

"Kirk," she replied, "I want you to meet my youngest daughter, Juanita. Juanita?" she called softly.

A quiet voice answered from the doorway of the dining room, and Kirk turned to meet her. The shock when his eyes met hers was so sudden and so strong that he was left speechless for a moment. Except for the fact that she was a little taller and her hair a few shades deeper gold, he was looking into the warm, blue eyes of Cristina Reyes.

52

Juanita Reyes rose slowly from her knees in front of the altar. There was a small smile of inner contentment on her face. She turned from the altar and walked very slowly down the aisle of the small convent chapel. Outside, her father and mother waited for her. For the first time in over a year, she would see her home. Juanita was young, but the last years had not been kind to her. Sheltered and pampered by her family, Juanita was unprepared for the tragedy that struck her. Under this strain, her mind had cracked. She could remember with calmness now the things that had driven her to the brink of insanity—the events and the person. She could only vaguely remember when her mother had brought her here. She had been in such an overwrought state that no one but her mother could even come near her. She would cry for hours on end and could not tolerate food. The sisters and her mother had worked with patience and kindness until, slowly, she began to heal.

In gratitude, she remembered with a smile, she had informed the Reverend Mother that she wanted to become a novice and remain at the convent. She could still see the kind eyes of Mother Louisa as she spoke to her.

"Go home first, my child."

"But Reverend Mother, what is the use of going home only to return? Is it not best that I stay and take my vows now?"

"*Mi niña*," she said with a smile. She had taken to calling her "my little one" while she was recuperating, and it had become a part of her.

"Go home with your parents. They have missed you so very much. After a year, if you still want to join us . . . well, we are here, and we shall always be here. You are very young, and you have time to make your decision."

Juanita had agreed reluctantly. She did not realize that the Reverend Mother knew of her fear to rejoin the outside world again. It was a world she had been protected from for the past year. She was afraid, but she straightened her shoulders and opened the heavy wooden doors of the chapel. The Reverend Mother and Sister Anna were waiting for her. Sister Anna had become Juanita's dearest friend during the stay.

"We will say good-by to you here, my child. Your parents are waiting in the carriage outside."

She drew Juanita to her and kissed her cheek. "We will miss you, *mi niña*. You must come and visit us one day."

"Thank you, Reverend Mother. I would love to, if I may."

She patted her arm gently, then turned and walked away.

"*Niña*, will you return to take your vows here?" Sister Anna asked hopefully.

"I hope to, Sister. I will go home for a year, as mother suggested, but I really believe I shall return to join you when the year is over."

"I'm glad. Well, good-by for now, *niña*." She smiled. Then she turned away and reentered the chapel, closing the door softly behind her.

Juanita looked at the large double doors that led to the outside world. She was afraid, afraid to meet people, afraid of men. She swallowed the lump that had formed in her throat, gripped her trembling hands together for a moment, and then reached out, opened the door, and stepped out into the bright California sunshine.

Her parents were standing by their carriage, close together in conversation. They both turned toward her when they heard the sound of the closing door. Her mother smiled and walked to her side. Drawing her arm through Juanita's, she led her toward her father. Juanita's eyes misted with tears. It had been over a year since she had seen her father. The last time they had been together was when her father had carried her from the brothel in which Manolo had left her. She had been near death then and completely out of her mind. Father and daughter now exchanged loving looks. Don Federico could not control the tears in his own eyes.

"My child," he said softly as he extended his arms to her.

"Father!" she cried. She threw herself against her father's chest, relieved to feel the warm welcome of his arms closing about her.

When he released her, he took her by the shoulders and looked into her eyes. "Welcome home, my daughter. We have missed you very much. A part of us has been missing for a long time. Now we are overjoyed to have it back again."

"You . . . you don't hate me, Father?" she asked.

"Hate you! My child, how could I hate you? You are part of my body, part of my heart. I could never, never hate you."

She was speechless with joy.

Her father motioned toward the carriage. "Come,

we must go home. You will be delighted with all the news we have to tell you on the way home. Come, come."

He seated both mother and daughter comfortably before he took the seat opposite them, where he could enjoy looking at them as they talked on the way home.

She listened with delight as they told her all the news from home: Tazia's marriage, the birth of Mercy, the coming of Louis and Del, and, finally, the marriage of Del and her sister, Cristina.

"Cristina is married? Oh, how wonderful! Tell me all about my new brother."

They described Del and the wedding and how completely happy they both were. They also told her of the house they had built not far from their own. Juanita was delighted. "We can be together often, like we were before . . . before . . ." She was unable to continue. Her smile faded and her eyes clouded over with suddenly remembered pain.

"Juanita," her father said firmly, "you must put the past behind you. Forget all that has happened. We will begin a whole new life."

The balance of the journey was spent talking of old times and a bright new future. They arrived home, and as the carriage pulled to a stop and Don Federico stepped from it, he was met by his brother, whose face looked anything but happy. He welcomed Juanita, but as soon as he possibly could, he pulled his brother aside.

"Federico, I have some tragic news, and I do not want to upset Juanita and her mother until I tell you first."

"Tragic news? What has happened?"

Speaking slowly, he told Federico all that had happened in his absence. When he came to Cristina's death, his face paled as he watched his brother's painful reaction.

"Oh, God, I have regained a daughter — only to lose another. I must tell her mother."

He took both women inside the house and ordered drinks of brandy to be brought to them. There was no other way. He broke the terrible news to them as gently as he could. Nevertheless, Juanita's mother grew pale, and with a small, inarticulate sound, she crumpled in a heap at her husband's feet.

Don Federico carried his wife to their room, while Juanita stood alone in front of the huge fireplace. Was the world filled with nothing but pain and tragedy? she thought. Was there no escape from the terrible things that happened? Juanita resolved that she would return as soon as possible to the convent and the only peace of mind she had ever known.

The next few days were days of silent mourning until they buried Cristina in the family cemetery. They had come home and were all sipping wine, immersed in their own thoughts, when they heard the arrival of Kirk and Juan with Tazia. They rose to meet them. Juanita was never to forget the look of amazement in Kirk's eyes when he turned to look at her. As time went on, she could not help but observe that his eyes continued to stray in her direction. It was two hours later when, by chance, they were alone for a few minutes.

"Señor LaCroix?"

"Yes, Señorita Reyes?"

"You must call me Niña. All my friends do."

"It is my pleasure. And you must call me Kirk."

"Good!" She smiled. "It is a good beginning, no?"

"Yes," he laughed, "it is a good beginning."

"Now that we are friends, can you tell me about Cristina and your brother? Everyone seems determined to protect me."

"They loved each other very much. Del has gone away. I don't know whether he's ever coming back. I hope someday he does, but," he sighed, "I imagine the house they built together would have too many bad memories now."

"The house, it is empty, *sí*?"

"Yes, it is. I imagine it will stay that way until Del returns."

"Kirk, would it be too much to ask if I could go there occasionally and care for Cristina's things? Just until your brother's return?" she added hastily. "I could see that the gardens were tended, and I could care for the house. He would want to find it so when he came back, would he not?"

"You are a very compassionate woman, Niña. I'm sure he would be grateful for the care you could give the house, but I don't really believe he will come back for a long time. I hate to see you spending all your time on an empty house."

"A house should never be left empty, Kirk. It mourns, just as people mourn. We must see that it remains a place that knows happiness and light. Your brother will need these things if he returns, and I would really like to do it."

"Well, if you really want to, and with your parents' permission, it would be a great favor to me. I really did not know what I was going to do with it. I can't spare the men to care for it. If you can get by with one or two servants, then I would be grateful if you would oversee its care."

"Marvelous. I thank you, Kirk. It will give me something on which to spend my time."

"A beautiful girl like you should never have to worry about a way to spend her time. I'm sure the young *caballeros* in the area will be beating down your door as soon as they hear of your return."

The smile he expected never appeared. Instead, her eyes clouded over, and she averted her head.

"I think not, Kirk," she said softly. "I think I will have all the time in the world."

Kirk didn't know what he had said to hurt Juanita, but it was obvious that he had. He was about to apologize when she again looked directly into his eyes. He was shocked again at the amazing resemblance between her and her sister. Before he could speak, she asked in a subdued voice, "What is it about me that surprises you so, Kirk? I saw the look in your eyes when we first met."

"Do you know that you look remarkably like your sister? I'm afraid it shocked me for a moment. But there is something deeper and quieter about you. You're the same, and yet you're different."

"Yes, we always looked quite a bit alike, but Cristina was much prettier than I." She said the words without any trace of jealousy.

She really means it, he thought.

Before the conversation could go on, they were joined by the rest of the family and talk turned to other things.

True to her word, Niña spent most of her days at Del's and Cristina's home. The neglected garden was put in order, and the house began to glow under her care. She seemed to be content with the hours she spent alone there. Occasionally Tazia or Gabrielle would ride over with her. Both of them were amazed at what she had done with the house. Sometimes she would even spend the night there, curled up in the large chair in front of the fireplace. She would read until the hour was late, and then she would go to bed in the large fourposter in the master bedroom.

Days rolled into weeks, then into months. There was no word from Del, and Kirk began to believe that he would never return. This day had started out bright and sunny. Niña had decided to ride over to the house early because there were some new plants she wanted to put in the garden. She dressed in a flowing peasant skirt and a white blouse. On her feet she put a pair of old, worn sandals. She braided her hair carelessly and let them swing freely down her back. Gathering her things, she slipped from the house before anyone could see her go and demand that she take them along. To-day she wanted to be alone to dig in the rich earth, to plant her flowers, and to begin to think seriously about her future.

When she reached the house, she put her horse in the stable, rubbed him down, and fed him. Then, taking her gardening tools and plants, she walked through the quiet house to the garden.

She hummed a little to herself as she put the plants into the black soil. Working with her fingers in the earth gave her a feeling of oneness with the house. She stopped working for a moment and sat back on her heels. The realization struck her that for the first time in a very long while she was happy.

When she had finished with her gardening, she stood up stiffly and brushed the dirt from her skirt. It was the first time she had noticed the darkening sky. The air was filled with a heavy stillness. There would be no going home tonight, she thought. It was about to rain.

She went inside and spent a long time taking a bath. Her clothes were very dirty from gardening, so she took one of Cristina's old dresses from her closet and put it on. She washed her hair and let it hang loose to dry. Then she went downstairs and prepared some dinner. It was just beginning to rain when she rose from the table. She washed the dishes and put them away. Then she went in and lit the fireplace. There was a brilliant flash of lightning accompanied by a crack of thunder. It began to storm in earnest now, with a ferocious wind and a violent pounding of rain.

She was not afraid of the elements. Instead, she felt a deep security here in this house. She sat on a low bench in front of the fire and studied the flames, allowing her thoughts to drift.

Suddenly the front door opened and the shape of a large man appeared in the doorway. He pushed the door shut behind him and turned to face the girl in front of the fireplace. Niña could see his blue eyes widen in surprise. His face seemed to suddenly drain of all color.

"Cristina," he whispered.

Niña rose slowly to face him. She knew, her heart now wildly fluttering, that this man must have been Cristina's husband, Del LaCroix.

53

Del headed his horse away from Kirk and Juan. He didn't know where he was going, but he knew he could not bear to go home and face the house that would be so empty without Cristina. He traveled alone for almost two weeks before he was forced to stop in a town to get supplies. That night he drank himself almost senseless and then took a blond whore to bed. She heard him whisper Cristina's name in his sleep, and she felt pity for this big man who was in so much pain. When she awoke the next morning he was gone. He had left some money on the dresser and left before dawn.

He traveled on, knowing he was running away from ghosts, but without the courage yet to face them and find the release he needed.

Three months later, he was back in New Orleans. He wanted to go to Barataria to see Jean and Molly and tell them what had happened, but he still could not bring himself to talk about Cristina yet.

It was Jean who found *him*. He was told everything that happened in New Orleans, including that his friend Del was back, drinking very heavily.

Del sat alone at a table. It was obvious he was already very drunk. He had brushed aside overtures from several women and now sat quietly nursing his drink. Jean came into the saloon and, after questioning the bartender, slowly made his way to Del's table. He could not believe this was the same man he had last seen laughing and happy at Casa del Sol. His clothes were dirty, and his eyes were reddened by drink.

"Del," he said quietly.

His head came up, and blue eyes stared dumbly at him.

"Go away. I don't need any company."

"Del, it's me, your old friend Jean."

Del's eyes tried again to focus on his face, but they failed.

"Go away, just go away," he mumbled.

God, Jean thought, what has happened to him to hurt him so badly? He motioned to two men, and they came immediately to his side.

"Leave him alone until he passes out. When he does, bring him to me. See that no harm comes to him, for he is a very dear friend of mine. You understand, *mes amis*?"

They nodded.

The two men waited and watched while Del continued to methodically drink himself into insensibility. It seemed to be the only way to fight the pain that consumed him. After a while, when the liquor had numbed his body and mind, the two men appeared at his side. . . .

Early the next morning, Del blinked open his eyes and, with a groan, shut them again. He turned over on his stomach and buried his head in the pillow. The room was spinning nauseatingly, and he didn't know which was worse, keeping his eyes open or tightly closed.

The door was gently opened, and a head appeared around the corner, acknowledged the fact that Del was

461

awake, and immediately departed. Before long, Jean appeared. He walked across the room, dragged a chair up close to the bed, and sat down. As he put his feet up, he said firmly, "Good morning, my friend. How do you feel this morning?"

A groan of complete misery was the only reply, and Jean chuckled. Before he could speak again, the door opened and a servant came in with a tray. Jean took the tray and dismissed him. He set the tray on the table beside the bed. Then he sat down heavily on the edge of the bed which brought another groan from Del.

"Come, my friend," laughed Juan, "drink this and you will feel better."

"I would have to die to feel better," Del replied miserably. Despite his resistance, he was forced to drink from the glass Jean offered. Then he collapsed back against the pillows and closed his eyes. He lay very still until he could feel his heaving stomach begin to settle down and the pain behind his eyes lessen. He cracked them open slightly and with a noble effort, smiled.

"Good morning."

"Ah! You're back among the living."

"God protect me from friends who won't even let a man die in peace," grumbled Del.

Jean grinned. "If one is going to dispose of himself, my friend, there are much easier ways of doing it."

Del grinned, too, but he could not reply. He closed his eyes again. He did not want to answer questions. There was no way of explaining, even to a friend like Jean, exactly how he felt.

"Jean?"

"Don't worry, *mon ami*. There are no questions. If you feel like talking one day, I am here. If you do not, feel free to come and go from here as you please. Just take care of yourself, and remember . . . you have friends here."

Del was grateful for Jean's understanding, which he needed so desperately. Maybe the time would come when he could talk to him, but for now, the wounds were too fresh and deep for him to probe.

"Thank you, Jean," he said quietly.

Jean smiled and gave a little shrug of his shoulders. "If you feel up to it, you could come down and share some breakfast with me."

Del nodded, and Jean left the room. Del rose shakily from the bed, and after he had bathed and dressed, he had to admit that he felt much better. He went slowly down the stairs and joined Jean at the breakfast table.

For the next few days, Del followed the same routine. He rose early, bathed, ate breakfast, and then went on solitary excursions around the city. He renewed some old friendships and wandered the streets of the city of his birth. No matter how he tried, the long days always finished the same way. He would be carried home completely intoxicated and put to bed.

Jean began to worry about his health. It was obvious to him that he carried some terrible burden that was becoming too heavy to bear. After several weeks, he decided to reach out and try to help Del, whether he wanted help or not. It was early evening, and Del was preparing to leave the house when Jean appeared at his study door.

"Del, before you leave, come and have a drink with me. I would like to talk to you." He could see hesitancy in Del's eyes, along with a quick flash of fear.

Del joined Jean in the study. Jean poured two drinks, handed one to him, and sat down in the large chair in front of the fireplace. Del sat down on the edge of another chair with his elbows on his knees, holding the glass of brandy with both hands. As he looked into the golden-brown liquid, he could feel Jean's eyes on him.

"I have watched you for some time, *mon ami*, and I would not presume to interfere, but I begin to realize that you are trying to stop living, aren't you?"

"Jean—"

"Del, first let me say I know you don't want my help, but you need it desperately. I have an aversion to my friends being harmed, even by themselves. If you could talk, take the pain out of that dark corner where you keep it and bring it out into the sunshine, maybe you would find it would go away."

"No, Jean," Del replied. "I don't believe this will ever go away."

"Why not try? What do you have to lose?"

Del sat silently contemplating the glass of brandy. Jean could see the tension in him. His hands were white with pressure around the brandy glass, and there were beads of perspiration on his forehead. He sat in silence for so long that Jean thought he had better leave him alone. Maybe he was right; maybe he was too late. Then, very quietly, Del began to talk. It was as though someone had opened floodgates. The whole story came pouring out. When he came to Cristina's death, his voice became cracked and strained, as though remembering was too painful to be borne. Then he was suddenly silent.

"And so you ran away," Jean said softly.

"I ran," Del agreed. "I ran because I could not stand and face that dark emptiness alone. I could not live in the house we had built together with such love. I could not live with her memory in my mind day after day."

"And have you not carried the pain and the memories with you wherever you went?" Jean could see the uncertainty and misery in Del's eyes. "Do you think you can put grief in its proper place when you run from it, my friend? I will tell you that you cannot. It lives in your heart; it travels with you no matter where you go.

There is only one way. That is to face the thing squarely. To exorcise the ghosts. To put grief where it belongs. There is no way to bring your wife back to you, but do you think her soul would rest if she knew what you were doing? The living must go on living, and that is often the hardest thing to do." ·

"That is sometimes impossible," Del added softly.

"No, not impossible, but very, very difficult. You know that you are welcome here as long as you choose to stay. But you must listen to me. You will never be whole again, never be free of your ghosts if you do not go back and face them. The choice is yours, *mon ami*," he said gently. "You can live out the balance of your life running away, or you can stand up like a man and face things squarely."

Deep in his heart, Del knew Jean was right. He felt he had always known the truth. Being able to talk had given him the ability to look at the problem, to put it into words, and maybe to really face it for the first time.

"I will tell you a story, my friend," Jean said. "I was a very young man at the time and had suffered what I considered a great loss. I was visiting friends in Spain, and they took me to a bullfight. It was a magnificent thing to watch the courage of the matador as he allowed the bull's horns to come within a hair of his body. Before the final kill, he had fought the bull so brilliantly that the animal stood completely still, and as one final gesture of courage, the matador put out his hand and rested it between the bull's horns. The animal was completely mastered. He stood motionless as the matador turned and walked away from him. Afterwards, we joined the matador and his friends at their table for a drink. I asked him then if he was not afraid at the final moment. I shall never forget what he said—and I think it applies to you. He said, 'Señor, I am not afraid of anything that I can face and master; it is what I cannot face or touch that frightens me.' I believe that is true of all of us. Once we face a problem, we realize we can master it. Maybe we cannot eliminate it completely, but we can put it where it belongs and not let it ruin our lives."

"Perhaps you are right, Jean. Give me some time, let me think. Maybe I can still drum up enough courage, or whatever it takes."

"You are not a weak man, my friend." Jean smiled. "Maybe you're just a little foolish and a little frightened. Given enough time, I'm sure you will make the right decision."

Jean rose from his chair and set his glass on the table beside him. "Now I must leave. I am joining a very lovely lady for dinner, and I don't want to be late." He laughed, but his eyes became serious again as he walked over and put his hand on Del's shoulder. "Think over what I have said, Del. Think about how you want to spend the rest of your life. You are a young man, and there are many years ahead of you. Don't waste them looking backward. Look ahead. As I said, you are welcome here for as long as you choose to stay, but I for one do not think you will. Good night, my friend."

Del sat in silent contemplation for a long time after Jean had gone. Del knew he was right. Slowly he rose from his seat, went upstairs, and packed his few belongings.

Within two hours, Del was on his way back to California, back to face the specter of the past. He didn't know if he could really do it or not. He only knew he had to try. The journey was slow because he took the time to sort out his feelings and plan what he would do. He decided to go straight to his own home before Casa del Sol. He wanted to try to face his problem without anyone's help, and he knew if he went to Casa del Sol first, he would be smothered by well-intentioned friends, trying to make everything easier for him. That was the last thing he needed.

The sky was black as he crested the hill that led to his home. He was surprised at first to see a glimmer of light in the windows. The wind began to blow, accompanied by driving rain, as he rode his horse through the front gate. The sound of the storm drowned out the sound of his horse. He stabled the animal and looked with surprise at the other horse in the adjoining stall. Kirk has probably sent someone to look out for the place, he thought. He slung his saddlebags over his shoulder and left the barn. He had to run across the yard to the door. The rain was beating down furiously, and the wind tore at him, almost knocking him off his feet. He slammed up against the door, threw it open, and then turned to push against the wind to close it.

The room was warm, lit only by the fire in the fireplace. As he turned back, he could see someone seated on a low bench by the fire. She rose and turned to face him. The firelight behind her kept her face in semidarkness. Then she took a step backward, and the glow of the fire touched the burnished gold of her hair.

Del was stunned. He felt himself begin to shake. It was impossible! Ghosts were not as real as this. He stared with disbelief as her face appeared in the glow of the fire. All the past pain and longing bubbled to the surface. In his mind, Cristina was suddenly resurrected from the dead. She wore the same pale-blue dress he had seen her in so many times. Her hair fell about her shoulders in golden splendor. With an anguished cry, he called out her name. In a few steps, he was beside her, his arms about her, lifting her slender body against his and capturing her soft, warm lips in a blazing kiss.

54

The gasping cry and her struggle brought him to his senses. He released her, and she staggered back from him, her face white and her eyes wide with fear.

"My God," he mumbled in shock, "I'm sorry, I'm very sorry. Who . . . who are you?"

Juanita tried to catch her breath and control the violent trembling of her body. After a few minutes, she regained some semblance of control, and she looked up into his unbelieving eyes.

"You are Del LaCroix?"

He nodded his head, waiting for her to say who she was.

"I'm Juanita Reyes, Cristina's sister," she said.

"I thought"—he laughed shakingly—"I thought you were a ghost. Forgive me for my violence. It's just . . . I . . ."

"You needn't explain, Señor LaCroix," she replied softly. "I understand."

Watching her face, he realized with wonder that she really did understand. He sagged onto the bench and put his face in his hands for a moment. Then he looked up at her.

"You . . . you look so much like her . . . it's amazing."

"I'm sorry, Señor LaCroix. If I had known you would be coming tonight, I would not have been here. I know this must be difficult for you, seeing me here like this."

Del looked about him for the first time. He could see that someone had taken a great deal of care with the house. Firelight reflected off the polished wood floor, and the furniture had been cleaned and polished until it, too, reflected warm light.

"You've been here, caring for the house?"

"Yes. I hope you're not angry with me. I'm sorry for having intruded. It's just that I couldn't bear to see this lovely house so lonely and uncared for."

"No, I'm not angry. I'm grateful to you. I realize now I never should have left without seeing to everything. My only excuse is that I could not face my loss. Of course, in my selfishness, I did not realize that others were suffering the same loss. Her parents, you. Are they well? Your parents, I mean. Can they forgive me, do you think, for the heartless way I left them to face everything alone?"

"I'm sure they both understand your grief, Señor LaCroix. And there is no need for forgiveness among family. We all have to understand and tolerate each other's weaknesses."

Del looked into her eyes, so much like Cristina's, yet so very different. Suddenly a deep weariness of soul and body overtook him.

"Are you hungry, Señor LaCroix?" She watched him intently, reading the emotions on his face.

"Yes," he said, "I guess I am. I haven't eaten for hours."

"Then relax by the fire for a while, and I will get you something to eat."

She left the room very quietly. He sat and looked into the fire, half hearing the thundering roar of the storm outside. It was a small thing compared to the storm that brewed within him. As he had looked into her blue eyes, a sudden urgent desire for her swept through him. He felt ashamed and weak. Christ! This was his dead wife's sister. He remembered the story Cristina had told him of what had happened to Juanita. She had known her share of pain, more even than he, and she had not let it break her as it had done him.

She returned and set a plate of cold meat and cheese and bread on a small table. She had also brought a bottle of wine. She sat opposite him and contemplated the flickering firelight across his face. It picked up the blond streaks in his hair and beard and made his eyes glitter like blue fire. His features looked like they had been carved from granite. He is a strong man, she thought, much stronger than he thinks he is.

"You will be staying here now?" she asked.

"Yes, I guess it's time I took over my responsibilities," he answered with a smile.

"Then I shall return home first thing in the morning."

"Señorita Reyes?"

"Juanita."

"Juanita," he replied. "I want you to know how grateful I am to you, and I want you to feel free to come here whenever you choose. I think you belong here, maybe even more than I do."

"Thank you, Señor LaCroix."

"If I can call you Juanita, surely you can call me Del."

"Well, I thank you, Del, but . . . I do not think it wise that I come here again," she added in a soft, almost whispering voice. She has read the look in my eyes accurately, he thought, and his face flushed a little. Again she read the emotions he felt.

"No," she said with a smile, "I am not afraid of you. You are not the kind of man to take a woman by force. I am only afraid *for* you. It is not necessary for me to make it any more difficult for you than it already is. You have your own battle to fight."

He looked closely at her again. For one so young —she could barely be twenty—she was a woman of deep understanding. Again he felt the desire to reach out and touch her.

"I will leave you now," she said. "Your room is empty. I have been sleeping in the guest room. Good night, Del."

"Good night," he said. "And Juanita—"

"Yes?"

"Lock your door. I'm not really the strong man you think I am."

She looked at him closely, then nodded her head and left the room. He sat for a long time, sipping the wine. After a while, he realized the fire had burnt down to embers and the bottle of wine was empty. He could not face going upstairs to the huge, lonely bed he would have shared with Cristina. He removed his boots and lay down on the couch, covering himself with his coat. In a few minutes, he was asleep.

He drifted up from sleep slowly, not wanting to awake. The smell of food cooking and the absence of the storm were the first sensations he felt. Then Juanita walked through the doorway from the kitchen. The shock of seeing her again was even worse than the night before. At least at night it had been vague and shadowed. In the bright sunlight, her resemblance to Cristina brought a thick lump to his throat and a reawakening of the deep ache within him.

"Breakfast is ready."

She had twisted her hair into a chignon at the nape

of her neck, and she was wearing a rose-colored dress. It made her look bright and very young. Del washed and changed his clothes and went to the breakfast table. He didn't realize how ravenously hungry he was. He did justice to the meal, washing it down with several cups of hot, black coffee. Then, sliding his chair back from the table, he laughed. "My horse is going to hate you."

"Your horse?" she asked.

"Yes, when he has to carry my overloaded carcass from here to Casa del Sol."

He liked the sound of her laughter. It was throaty and warm like bubbling sunshine.

"I think your brother will be very surprised to see you. They had hoped for a long time for your return, and we all prayed for your safety. You had many people deeply worried about you."

"Even you?"

"*Sí*. After hearing so much about you, I felt as though you were really my brother. I prayed also for your safe return."

"Thank you. Well, I guess I'd better be going."

"I also should return home before my parents begin to worry."

"Juanita?"

"*Sí*? she said expectantly.

"Would . . . would you mind if I came to see you occasionally. I . . . I like talking to you."

"Do you think it's wise, Del?"

"Maybe not, but I'd still like to," he answered with a grin.

"Then do come. I'm sure my parents would be delighted to see you again."

"Thank you."

They walked to the stable together, and she watched as he saddled their horses. Then he turned to her.

Before she could move, he took her by the waist and lifted her into the saddle. She felt a tingle through her body as his hands circled her waist and lifted her up effortlessly.

"I'll see you again . . . soon," he said.

Juanita nodded, and kicking her heels against her horse's side, nudged him into a fast trot. Suddenly she wanted to get away. Away from this man whose blue eyes spoke dangerously to her. She did not want to learn to care for any man. She didn't believe that deep trust existed in her. Since Manolo and the horror that had followed him, she had felt unclean, felt that she had nothing to offer any man. She had given Manolo every ounce of blind, trusting love she possessed, and he had broken and disregarded her and that love. It was better if she stayed away from Del LaCroix, for she could only be hurt by him. He had loved her sister too deeply, and she looked enough like her for her to realize how easy it would be for him to transfer that love to her. But that love would never be for her, only for the woman who looked like his dead wife.

Juanita slowed her horse so that she could regain her composure. She thought she had herself completely under control by the time she arrived at home. Her father was the first person she saw. He was about to ride out.

"I was just coming to check on you, Niña. We thought you were safe from the storm at Del's house, but I decided to ride over, just to be sure."

"I'm fine, father," she laughed. Don Federico's eyes narrowed slightly as he gazed at his young daughter. Something was different about her, and he didn't know what it was.

"Are you really all right, child?" he asked gently.

"Of course," she said. "Why do you ask? Don't I look well?" she said with a small laugh.

"Yes, you look well," he answered. But, he thought, you look different, and he was curious about what had caused the difference.

Her mother came out onto the porch. "Niña, we were worried about you. I'm glad you're home, *cara*."

She stepped down from her horse and handed the reins to a small, wide-eyed boy, who ran to help her. She walked up on the porch and kissed her mother.

"I'm going to change, mother. I'll be down in just a few moments." She walked to the door and turned to look at her parents. Very softly and as gently as she could, she said, "Oh! By the way, Del LaCroix came home last night." She did not stay to see the surprised looks on their faces. She closed the door behind her and climbed the stairs to her room.

"Madre de Dios," her father exclaimed softly, as the words she said registered with him.

"Oh, Federico," his wife said. "How it must have hurt him to see Juanita there. The poor man has suffered enough."

"I shall ride over to see him, my dear," he replied. "Don't worry. I'm sure he's fine." I'm sure he's fine, he thought, but I'm not so sure about my daughter. I cannot let her be hurt again by anyone. No matter how much I like Del, I must not let him hurt Juanita.

He kissed his wife and mounted his horse, heading it in the direction of Del's house. When he arrived, there was no one there. He reasoned that Del must have gone to Casa del Sol to see his brother, so he dismounted and prepared to wait for his return.

Del was at that moment arriving at Casa del Sol. He didn't even have time to get down from his horse when the door was thrown open and Tazia ran out to meet him with a warm smile of welcome.

She threw herself into his arms and he kissed her soundly. Then he held her at arms' length.

474

"You look magnificent, as usual, Tazia," he grinned. "And where is my goddaughter?"

"She's inside. Oh, Del! You do look well. I'm so glad you're back. We've missed you terribly."

He slid his arm around her waist, and they walked together into the house. Kirk, attracted by the sound of Tazia's animated voice, was coming down the stairs. Del smiled up at him. "Kirk."

"Del!" Kirk almost shouted. He ignored Del's proferred hand and grabbed him in a bear hug.

Del grinned. "This life must agree with you. "You're strong as an ox. Let go of me before you break my ribs."

They all laughed together.

"You're home to stay, Del?" Kirk asked hopefully.

"Yes, I've been home since last night. I didn't want to brave the storm, so I stayed home and rode over this morning."

"Have you eaten?" Tazia asked.

"Everyone keeps trying to feed me. Do I look undernourished?" Both of them looked at him in surprise.

"Everyone?" questioned his brother.

"I didn't have a chance to tell you, I had a welcoming committee when I got home, in the very lovely presence of Juanita Reyes."

55

Del wiped his sweaty, dirt-stained hands across his shirt and smiled at Juan. They were repairing the fences around Del's ranch. Del had thrown himself into work after his arrival. Rising at dawn and working until the sun set, he fell into bed too exhausted to do anything but sleep. Slowly the ranch began to grow under his hands, and with Juan's help. His face had turned brown and his hair had lightened under the hot sun, until he looked like a blue-eyed Indian.

He was contented, he thought, or almost so. He still fought the dreams of Cristina that haunted him at night. Often he slept out under the stars with Juan for company. On these nights, it was not dreams of Cristina that haunted him, but other, more forbidden ones, for Niña's face kept drifting into the mists of his dreams. He had seen her very few times in the eight months he had been home, and it had not taken him long to realize she was avoiding him. The day he had come back from Casa del Sol to find her father waiting for him had made him realize how afraid they all were for Juanita. Don Federico had made it clear that Juanita was to be protected from any further hurt.

When they had met after that, it had been mostly by accident. Del saw signs of her presence about the house—fresh flowers on the table, new blossoms in the beautiful garden. But he knew she waited for him to leave before she came. This irritated him, for he had to be honest with himself, he wanted to see her again, to talk with her and hear her laugh again. And deeper down, he wanted her physically.

Now, he and Juan were both quitting work early. Tazia and Kirk were going to have a party, and he had not seen Louis and Gabrielle for weeks. He told himself this was the reason, but he also knew Juanita would be there, and he wanted, just once, to dance with her. He wanted to put his arms about her and look into her soft, understanding eyes. He felt a sudden pang of disloyalty to Cristina, but he pushed it to the back of his mind. He had to forget; he had to live again.

"Well, Juan, I guess we're done for today. It's time to go home and shine ourselves up. The party tonight should be exciting. I haven't been to a party in a long, long time."

"Yes," Juan grunted as he rose from the ground.

"And I think you are looking forward to an especially good evening, no?"

Del turned to look at Juan. He could see no sign of resistance.

"You think it's wrong, Juan?" he asked, "I just want to *be* with her, to talk to her. There's nothing more to it than that."

"Del," Juan began slowly, "I don't think it is wrong. In fact I think it is a very good thing. You both have much to offer each other. No matter what anyone else thinks. Listen to your own heart and mind. But . . "

"But what?"

Juan looked at him intently. "Don't lie, either to yourself or to Niña. She is a very intelligent, sensitive girl, and it is perfectly normal for you to want her as a man wants a woman, only don't tell yourself it's for any

477

other, noble reason. You are a man. She is very much a woman. I have known her all her life. Despite what has happened to her, she has a great deal of love to give. Don't either of you sacrifice your life to a memory or to whatever anyone else thinks is right or wrong."

"Thanks, Juan. I imagine you're the only one who would see things that way. I loved Cristina. You know I loved her, and no one could ever take her place. But I've got the rest of my life to live, too. Niña's been through a lot, and I know she thinks I see Cristina when I look at her. I guess it will take a lot of time to convince her that isn't so."

Juan nodded in agreement and smiled, "She's done a pretty good job of staying away from you so far."

"You've noticed," Del said wryly, and Juan gave a small laugh. "There is not too much that happens in this family that I don't notice. They are very important to me."

"Well, at least Niña might talk to me tonight. There's no way out of it." Del grinned. "If nothing else, I'll let her know how I feel. For now, I guess that will be enough."

Juan nodded again, and they began to gather their equipment together. They traveled back to Del's house, where they separated and Juan continued on to Casa del Sol. Del knew as soon as he went inside that Niña had been there. The house had a freshness about it, and flowers were on the tables. The windows to the garden stood open and the smell of blooming flowers pervaded the air. It annoyed him, as it always did, that she had made a point of being gone before he arrived. Damn it! he thought. Couldn't she even talk to him? Was she that afraid? Then another idea occurred to him, which brought a smile to his face. It wasn't *him* she was afraid of, it was herself.

He took his time getting ready for the party, and

when he finally left the house he was magnificent to behold. His sun-streaked hair and beard gleamed with freshly washed brightness against his tanned face. It made the blue of his eyes rather startling by contrast. He had dressed in royal blue, with white lace at his shirt front and sleeves. When he arrived at Casa del Sol, he found that Louis and Gabrielle had already gotten there ahead of him. Tazia and Kirk welcomed him, and soon they were sipping drinks and talking.

Soon another carriage could be heard approaching. Del turned expectantly toward the door and could barely hide his disappointment when Don Federico, Don Manuel, and Catherine came into the room. There was no sign of Niña.

It was some time before Del could get either of the Reyeses alone. Finally he managed a few words with Catherine. "Señora Reyes, may I speak to you alone for a few minutes?"

She hesitated, but there was really no graceful way she could refuse. With a small nod of her head, she put her hand in the crook of his arm, and they walked out into the warm moonlit garden.

"It's such a lovely evening," she said, trying to make small talk, in the hope of not touching on the subject she knew was uppermost in his mind.

Catherine had realized months ago that Del was drawn to Juanita, but, like everyone else, she was sure that it was because of her resemblance to Cristina. She and Juanita had talked about the subject only once, and she was surprised at this new self-composed Juanita. They had circled the question for a while before Juanita had smiled and said, "Mother, why don't you say what's on your mind?"

Catherine had done so. "Niña, how do you feel about Del LaCroix? I know he's very attracted to you, but how do *you* feel?"

479

Juanita had contemplated the question for quite some time before she spoke. "He needs time, Mother," she said quietly. "When he looks at me, he sees Cristina. I could love him. It would not be a difficult thing to do. I am just as attracted to him as he is to me, but it has to be *me*, not my sister's ghost. If it is meant to be, it will be. I will leave everything in God's hands. For the time being, for my own peace of mind and until he is sure of himself, I will stay away from him."

"You're very wise for your age, child," Her mother smiled. "He is a good man, and we care for him, but *you* are most important to us now. If you feel the need, you could go visit the Rodriguezes for a while. I'm sure they would be happy to see you."

"Mother, it does no good to run away from problems. I tried that once. I shall never do it again."

Catherine thought of those words as she prepared herself mentally for what Del was about to say.

"Yes," he agreed, "it's a lovely evening. Too beautiful to be spent alone. Why didn't Juanita come with you?"

"She wasn't really feeling too well," Catherine said. "She decided to stay home and rest. You know Juanita has been through a very bad year. It is best that she stay away from . . ."

"From me?" he asked gently, his eyes probing hers.

She did not speak for a time. They walked to a bench and sat together. "Del," she said as gently as she could, "I know this is hard for you, but just imagine how hard it is for Juanita. She knows how much you loved Cristina. Can you blame her for feeling as she does? That she is taking her sister's place? That you see Cristina in her?"

Del sat forward on the bench, his elbows on his knees. It was quiet in the garden, and the soft strains of music drifted out on the warm night air.

"Señora Reyes, I want you to understand. I loved

Cristina very deeply, and for a while after she died, I felt my life was over, that there was no use in anything again. I even ran away like a coward, because I couldn't face coming back here and not finding her."

She nodded her head, but said nothing.

"I left California and traveled for some time alone, drifting, lost. I tried more than once to find a woman to replace Cristina. It didn't work. Then I realized the truth. You can't replace anyone or any emotion. What Cristina and I had was beautiful, but it was gone, and I had to face that fact. With the help of a friend, I did, and I even found enough courage to come back here. I've faced all my memories and recognized them for what they are: beautiful memories. But one can't live the rest of his life on memories. I have to look ahead, not back, and I really believe that Cristina would have been the first person to understand that. If . . . if it had been me instead of Cristina, Señora Reyes, would you have wanted her to live out the rest of her life in dedication to my memory? Wouldn't you have encouraged her to look ahead, to find a new life?"

Catherine realized the truth in what he said.

"But do you think Niña will ever fully believe that you don't see Cristina in her?"

"I don't know. It's a chance I have to take. With time, maybe I can convince her. I know I have to try, if you'll let me."

She sighed. "Losing Cristina was a great blow to all of us. Her father has grieved deeply. What happened to Niña was almost more than he could bear. He wants her to be happy and I guess he is afraid you will hurt her."

"None of us can be protected from hurt in our lives. But we can't allow ourselves to be defeated by it. I think Niña is very strong, stronger even than you and Don Federico think." Del's eyes were filled with compassion and pleading. "Let me have the chance, Señora Reyes. Let me try to prove to Niña that I've put the past behind me." He said the words quietly, but she could sense the tension in him. He waited for her answer.

"I shall speak to my husband, Del, and tell him how you feel. If he thinks it is wise, we will step aside, but you would still have to convince Niña. I will say and do nothing to affect her decision."

"That's enough for me." He smiled in relief.

"I'm going to do my best, if Don Federico agrees, to convince her. When will you speak to him?"

"When we are alone tonight. I will send you a message."

"I appreciate your understanding, Señora Reyes. I'll never forget it."

"I want my child's happiness, Del." She smiled again, a warm friendly smile. "I agree, Niña is much stronger then people think. I also believe you are going to have a harder time than you think. Once given to an idea, Niña seldom gives up on it, and she is convinced you're still living with Cristina's memory."

"You have no idea how tenacious *I* can be," Del said.

She was about to speak again when another voice interrupted.

"Ah, there you are, my dear. I've been searching all over for you."

Don Federico stood in the doorway, a warm smile on his face. Tazia stood beside him.

"I would like to dance with you, Catherine—if you would care to."

Catherine rose and went to her husband's side. With a word to Tazia, she took her husband's arm, and they went inside.

Tazia sat down beside Del. "How are you, Del?" She turned her head a little as she leaned back against a tree. Her eyes searched his face.

"I'm all right, I guess, Tazia. At least, I'm better tonight than I've been in a long time. A little disappointed maybe," he added.

"Because Niña didn't come?"

"Yes, I'd hoped . . . well, I thought . . ."

"I know," she said sympathetically. "I've known for months. Kirk and I have been both hoping things would work out between you. It's easy to see the attraction. What is the reason Don Federico and Catherine don't want you two together?"

"Niña is sure that I see her only as Cristina's reflection."

"Is that so?"

"No, I don't know how to convince everyone, but it is not."

He went on to tell her of the agreement he had made with Catherine and his hopes that her intervention with Don Federico would prove fruitful. Tazia encouraged his hope by showing her confidence in the wisdom and fairness of Don Federico and Catherine.

"Come in and dance with me," she said. "Have some fun tonight. It should give you some peace of mind to know that you have a lot of friends on your side."

He smiled and stood up. Tazia tucked her hand under his arm, and they walked back into the house.

He did enjoy the evening very much, thanks to Tazia and Gabrielle's close attention to him. Kirk and Louis laughingly informed him they were just a little jealous of the attention he was getting.

After the party, he said good night to everyone. He refused the offer from Kirk and Tazia to spend the night and a similar offer from Louis and Gabrielle to go home with them. He wanted time alone on the ride home to put his plans in order.

He rode slowly, enjoying the bright moonlit night.

Soft night sounds were the only things that broke the stillness. He thought of Niña and ways he could prove to her how he felt. What words could he say to make her understand, to make her realize that he had put the past behind him. For one quick moment, he allowed Cristina to enter his mind, and with the thoughts of her came a sense of peace, as though she had reached out from beyond the grave to console him, to tell him that everything would be well.

After he arrived home, he left his horse in the care of his stable boy and walked to the house. When he opened the door, he was struck again with the sense that this house spoke more of Niña than anyone. Traces of her presence were in every room.

He walked across the room and out through the open doors into the garden, Niña's garden. She had had several comfortable benches placed strategically throughout the garden so that a person could relax and enjoy the beauty of the flowers. He sat on one of them and rested. He closed his eyes and probed his mind and his heart until he was finally satisfied that life with Niña was what he really wanted.

It was very late before he sought his bed, but he slept the sleep of a man who knows where he is going and what he wants. He awoke the next morning refreshed and ready with a million arguments to use in case Don Federico decided against him. They were unnecessary. A timid knock on his door brought him a message from Catherine. For a moment, he hesitated to open it. Then he ripped open the envelope. His eyes lit up with happiness when he read the few words on the paper: "We wish you the very best. You have her father's blessings, and mine. Catherine Reyes.

56

Catherine and her husband had discussed Niña and Del on the ride home from Casa del Sol. Don Federico was a wise man, who realized the truth of his wife's feelings. He agreed only to let Del try to convince Niña. "The final decision," he said, "must be Niña's. She alone can tell Del to stay." Catherine went to Niña's room when she arrived home, to find that Niña was still up.

"Niña, are you tired? Or may I come in and talk with you for a while?"

"Come in, Mother," she replied with a quick smile. "I would like to talk to you also. I've . . . I've made a decision about my life, my future."

Catherine felt a sudden premonition that she was not going to like what Niña was about to say, but she held the smile on her face as she went in and closed the door behind her.

"Decision? What kind of decision?"

"Now, don't be distressed, Mother, but I've decided to return to the convent as a novice and to eventually take my vows there."

Catherine's heart sank. She knew this was the wrong thing for Niña to do, and she frantically searched her mind for the words to reach her daughter.

"Niña, are you sure you've given this enough thought? It's a very serious, very final step."

"I've been thinking about it since we left the convent. Maybe I should never have come home. It's only made everything more difficult."

"What about Del, Niña? What about the way he feels about you? He has a great deal to offer — his love, a beautiful, comfortable home you already care about."

"Mother," she began. She hesitated while she sought the right words. "I can't be in my sister's shadow. How can I care for a man when I shall always wonder when he looks at me if he really sees me or . . . someone else? I would rather go away and give him some peace of mind, too."

"But you *do* care, don't you, Niña?" Catherine asked quietly.

Niña turned to face her mother. She wanted to lie, to say no, she didn't care, but lying was not a thing that Niña could do. "Yes, Mother, I care. I think I have since the first night we met. That is why I have to go, don't you see?"

"No, I can't believe you would run away from everything that could make your life happy."

"Or very *un*happy," she answered, almost to herself.

"Are you too afraid to take the chance to see? Why not give the relationship a chance to grow? Niña, give it a few months before you make your final decision. Then, if you still feel the same way, there will be no argument from your father or me."

"Mother, this is useless. Why make it worse for Del and for me? Isn't it better to break it off right now?"

"I'm only asking you to give it a few months. Is that so much to give, Niña. We . . . we don't want to lose you, too," she added, her eyes misted with tears. Niña ran to her mother's side and put her arms around her.

"I'm sorry, Mother. I didn't realize how it would be for you and father. I've been so busy thinking about myself that I didn't take into consideration what Cristina's death has done to you. Of course I will stay a while longer."

Catherine held her daughter close to her, thanking God she wasn't going to lose her child. She promised herself to send a note to Del as soon as possible. She hoped desperately he would be able to reach her before she was lost to them all.

The next morning, she sent a note to Del. Then she waited, nervous with suppressed tension, to see what would happen next. She had grave misgivings.

It will take an act of God to bring those two together, she thought. She had no idea that at that moment the forces of nature were gathering to do just that.

Del visited often after he received the note, but several weeks passed and Catherine could see no change in Niña's attitude. She was kind and treated Del well when he came to call. They rode together, picnicked together, and spent evenings of laughing enjoyment with her parents, Kirk and Tazia, and Gabrielle and Louis. Still, much to his distress, Del could see the searching look in her eyes, and he was at a loss as to how to reach her.

They had shared a late supper one night with her parents, who had discreetly gone to bed early so that they could be alone. Niña smiled at this, but said nothing. Now they sat together in the garden. They were silent, but it was the easy silence of people who were close and did not need to speak.

"Niña."

"Yes, Del?"

"I have to talk to you about us. Will you listen?"

"I always listen to you, Del."

"Oh, you *listen*," he said with a grin, "but you don't *hear*."

She turned to him and he took her hands in his and looked fondly into her eyes as he spoke, "I love you, Niña. That's as plain and simple as I can make it: I love you."

"Del, don't—"

"You said you were going to listen. Don't I deserve the chance to finish?"

She sighed and relaxed.

"All right, I'm listening."

"I know what you think, but you're wrong. When I look at you I see only Niña Reyes, a beautiful woman whom I love very much. I'm not a weak man, Niña. I've put my past and all its ghosts to rest. I don't think you've done the same."

She tried to withdraw her hands from his, but he held them tighter.

"I don't think it's me and Cristina that's bothering you. I think it's you and Manolo. You're using Cristina and your resemblance to her as an excuse, but you're afraid to love again. You're afraid you'll get hurt."

She gave a startled, pain-filled cry and pulled her hands from his and stood up. He rose to his feet, and as she tried to turn away, he grabbed her by the waist and pulled her into his arms. She struggled for a moment, but it was obvious to both of them she hadn't the strength to escape him.

"Let me go, Del. Please, let me go," she said. He could feel her tremble against him, but he held her tight.

"So you can run away and hide? No, I tried that, Niña. It doesn't work. You have to face things. What Manolo did to you was terrible, but he's dead. Cristina meant everything to me, but *she's* dead. *We're* alive . . . alive, Niña. And we belong together. We

488

can make each other happy, if you'll just let go of the past. Reach out to me, Niña like I'm reaching out to you. There's a whole world of happiness ahead of us."

"I can't," she sobbed, "I can't. Leave me alone, Del. Go away and leave me alone."

He watched her face as it crumpled into tears, and bitter defeat washed over him. He had tried his best and lost. He felt drained. He couldn't bear to hear her cry as she did. Gently he tipped her chin up. Her cheeks, wet with tears, and her moist, red lips only defeated him more. Slowly he bent his head and touched the softness of her mouth with his.

"Niña, I'm going to leave. You think about what I said. If I don't hear from you in two days, I'm leaving California forever. I'll go back to New Orleans. I'll leave you in peace with your memories. Keep one thing in mind, however, I love you . . . only you."

He kissed her again and then turned away. He could still hear her crying softly as he left the garden.

When Del reached the stable, he had to wait until his horse was saddled. Then he mounted and left the stable and headed toward home. He thought it was just his mood, but his horse seemed skittish. Even though Del was a good rider, it was difficult to keep the animal under control. It pranced from side to side, rolled its eyes, snorted and tossed its mane as though it were afraid. Del spoke soothingly to the horse and patted its neck, but it did no good. Then Del noticed that the night was absolutely silent. There were none of the usual sounds of night animals. He pulled the horse to a stop. He could feel the beast tremble in fear.

"What is the matter?" he asked in as gentle a voice as possible. The animal's ears twitched, but still it showed definite signs of terror. Del looked back over his shoulder, and his eyes widened. A low rumbling began to build, and it seemed to him that the ground was rippling like waves of water. Trees began to shake, and the roaring grew louder and louder until it was like thunder. The ground shook violently under them, and Del cursed as the horse gave an anguished whinny and began to stomp the ground in terror. Now the crackling roar surrounded him, and the ground heaved and rolled like violent ocean waves. He heard the sounds of trees falling nearby. Then a crack at the edge of the trees along the road, and suddenly about sixty feet of ground seemed to disappear. A huge black hole stood in its place.

Del was so astounded that he could not think. Then suddenly he realized what was happening. When they had first arrived in California, Del and Kirk had been told about earthquakes, but neither of them had taken seriously what they heard. Now it was obvious to him that the stories were not exaggerated. The horse was in a state of wild fear, so Del released his tight hold on the reins and let him run back toward the Reyes hacienda.

Del prayed silently that they were all safe. He didn't know if he could stand the loss of Niña too. All his ideas of leaving California were gone. He knew he could never leave her. If she was all right, he would stay and fight for her as long as necessary. "Please, God," he begged, "let her be safe. Let her be safe!"

Niña had listened to Del's retreating footsteps. She stood frozen, while her mind fought the implications of what Del had said. Was it Manolo? Was it what he had done to her? Was she afraid to love? She could still feel the pressure of his mouth against hers, still feel the strength of his arms about her. "I'm not a weak man," he had said. "I've put my ghosts behind me. Why can't you?" Niña faced the truth for the first time since Manolo. She rocked on her feet as she realized that she had just sent away the only man she had ever really loved. She would not wait until tomorrow, she thought. She would go to him tonight. She turned and was about to take a step when the shifting earth and a horrible rumbling sound knocked her off her feet. Getting up hastily, she could barely keep her balance as the ground rocked and swayed under her feet. She screamed her mothers' name as half of the house seemed to fold into itself. The cloud of dust and debris that flew about her frightened her, but she still ran toward her parents' room. Inside, she stared in open-mouthed amazement. The stairway had been ripped from the wall and hung in midair. Her mother and father stood at the top.

"Mother!" she screamed. "Father!" The rumbling ceased, and everything was still again.

"Juanita!" her father shouted. "Get out of the house, go outside!"

"No! No! Not until I get you out safely."

"We will go out the window of our bedroom and climb down on the lower roof. Now get out!"

The words had barely left his lips when the rumbling began again. The remainder of the house seemed to shiver. Then the door she had come in collapsed with half of the wall. She looked up. Her parents were already running down the hall toward their bedroom and freedom. She turned to run, when the stairway collapsed completely. It fell directly between her and the exit. She was trapped in a space that was barely enough to move in. She could hear the thundering roar and the violent trembling beneath her feet. Very slowly and calmly she knelt, crossed herself and began to pray. "Hail Mary . . ."

Del crested the hill, barely able to keep his frantic horse under control. He was just in time to see half of the house collapse.

"Niña!" He put his heels to the horse and flew down the hill at breakneck speed.

He arrived in front of the house and leapt down from the horse, allowing it to run free. There was no doorway. In fact, there was no front wall at all. The pile of debris was higher than his head. He could hardly keep his footing as the ground throbbed beneath his feet like a live thing.

"Niña!" he shouted over the roar. "Catherine! Don Federico!"

"Del!" came a strong voice from behind him. He spun around and faced Don Federico and Catherine.

"We're all right. We got out safely. But Niña . . ."

"Where is she?" he demanded.

Don Federico pointed to the collapsed half of the house and said softly, "She's in there. She was standing under the stairway when it collapsed."

"Help me!" Del said wildly as he began to dig at the debris. Both Don Federico and Catherine began to pull at the fallen beams while the rumbling slowly ceased and everything became quiet again. Only the sound of their desperate searching could be heard. Del kept shouting Niña's name but hope for her began to fade. They worked their way in until they could see the curve of the collapsed stairway.

"She might be behind it!" he shouted. Together they pulled and heaved until they moved a small portion and he could see behind it. "She's there!"

"Del," Niña sobbed as he reached in and pulled her from the wreckage. "Oh, Del! Oh, my darling."

His heart sang as he pulled her into his arms and held her, grateful for the way she clung to him and whispered his name over and over. The three of them sat outside the house, tired and dirty, but grateful to be alive.

Niña clung to Del's hand and occasionally lay her

head against his shoulder.

"I hope everyone at Casa del Sol is all right," Don Federico said. The words were barely out of his mouth when they heard a shout. It was Juan riding toward them with a wide grin on his face.

"Juan, how is everyone?" Del asked.

"Now that I have found you all right, Señor Del, everyone is accounted for."

Del breathed a sigh of relief. "Well, it's all over, thank God. Now we only have one big event to look forward to."

Everyone looked at him questioningly. He smiled down at Niña. "Our wedding of course," he said softly. Niña smiled and nodded her head. The sound of soft laughter could be heard, and they all looked in surprise at Catherine, who was holding her husband's arm and laughing delightedly.

"What's so funny?" Don Federico asked.

"Tonight, I was thinking that only an act of God would bring these two children together. I didn't realize how closely He was listening!"

They joined her in laughter, clinging to one another in the sheer joy of being alive—and being together.

Epilogue

They stood together and spoke the vows softly to one another. It was a small, quiet wedding, as Niña had wanted. There was to be a small family dinner afterward. They had found after they had all gathered that the earthquake had totally destroyed Del's house and had done considerable damage to Louis's.

Niña had stood beside Del as they looked over the remains of his house.

"Oh, Del, I'm so sorry. Your beautiful home."

"*I'm* not."

"You're not?"

"No. We're going to be married next week. Then we'll build a house of our own. *Ours*, Niña. We'll start out new. The last link to the past is gone. There's nothing but a bright new future ahead of us."

She had smiled, feeling warm contentment inside as he took her in his arms and kissed her as she had never been kissed before—with tenderness and love.

Now he turned to her as the priest spoke the words that made them man and wife. The smile on his lips and the warmth of his blue eyes made her feel happier than she had ever been. They went from the chapel to Casa del Sol for dinner. It was a joyful dinner, and Del and Niña were the victims of some happy jokes, which brought the old familiar glint of laughter to Del's eyes and a blush of confusion to Niña's face.

Then Del rose and lifted his glass. He looked from one happy face to another: Kirk and Tazia, happiness obvious in their faces and in their home; Louis and Gabrielle, who were expecting their first child in the spring, and Catherine and Don Federico with Don Manuel.

"I give you all a toast," he said, "to the happiness of all my friends who live in the valley. Let us hope the bad times are gone and the bright future is here to stay. To Casa del Sol." He raised his glass higher. "To my lovely wife, Niña, and our house in the sun." They drank in silence, each one too filled with happiness to speak, but content in the drawing together of their family. Remembering their pain and their losses, but hopeful for the brightness of their future together.

YOU CAN NOW
CHOOSE FROM AMONG JANELLE TAYLOR'S
BESTSELLING TITLES!